PROJECT 137

By
Seth Augenstein

pandamoon
publishing

This book is a work of creative fiction that uses actual publicly known events, situations, and locations as background for the storyline with fictional embellishments as creative license allows. Although the publisher has made every effort to ensure the grammatical integrity of this book was correct at press time, the publisher does not assume and hereby disclaims any liability to any party for any loss, damage, or disruption caused by errors or omissions, whether such errors or omissions result from negligence, accident, or any other cause. At Pandamoon, we take great pride in producing quality works that accurately reflect the voice of the author. All the words are the author's alone.

www.pandamoonpublishing.com

Jacket design and illustrations © Pandamoon Publishing
Art Direction by Don Kramer: Pandamoon Publishing
Editing by Zara Kramer, Rachel Schoenbauer, and Heather Stewart, Pandamoon Publishing

Pandamoon Publishing and the portrayal of a panda and a moon are registered trademarks of Pandamoon Publishing.

Library of Congress Cataloging-in-Publication Data is on file at the Library of Congress, Washington, DC

Edition: 1, version 1.01
ISBN 13: 978-1-945502-99-6

Reviews

"Augenstein skillfully weaves throughout his narrative the spirit of Ishii as an impetus for the latter-day fictional project. The story ultimately reveals the horrors of a run-away biological and chemical weapons program. Augenstein's engrossing descriptions prompt the reader to wince in sadness and empathy for the victims. His vivid imagery is testimony to superb writing skills." — *Dr. Leonard A. Cole, author of Clouds of Secrecy.*

"A dystopian thriller so supremely paranoid it actually brings reality into focus." — **Ben Loory, author of** *Tales of Falling and Flying*

"Fans of Michael Crichton rejoice! Here is a fast-paced techno-thriller, made all the more chilling by the fact that the story's inspired by secret experiments that took place during World War II." — **Susan Breen, author of** *The Fiction Class*

In 2087, it's not unusual for folks to live well into their hundreds. Medical miracles, like saving folks who should die in a car accident, are commonplace, thanks to machines that scan, pinpoint and repair wounds quickly. In 2087, smart phones have been replaced by Atmans, and everyone has one embedded in their arms. Folks keep themselves alert by sniffing energy sticks. The most popular TV show is "How Low Can You Go" where people do the indescribable to win money. And yet, oddly enough, for the average person, transportation is still by car, some of which are very old models. What a strange future world! For Dr. Joe Barnes, other than his newly pregnant wife, his patients are his primary concern. When inexplicably not only his patients, but even doctors start dying from what looks like bubonic plague, Dr. Barnes, with the help of his century-old mentor is hell-bent on finding the cause. What he uncovers, too late for hundreds of people, has its roots in World War 2. What he also uncovers is how many of his colleagues are not who he thought and that both he and his wife could very soon join the pyre of bodies piling up in the hospital's basement.

Project 137 by Seth Augenstein is a complex and captivating read…even for those not really into future worlds. After finishing the book and thinking about the horrific circumstances and bloody scenes depicted in this novel, I found myself compelled to research the topic of human experimentation. Could governments, and specifically in this story the US government, truly sacrifice large populations for medical science? What happens in Project 137 set in 2087 isn't all that improbable. Project 137 doesn't strain incredulity the way many futuristic books do. In fact, what happens in this novel is alarmingly possible. Seth Augenstein has done his homework researching medical experimentation in our history and has cleverly plotted this story around compelling characters, some believable and others bordering on monstrosities. But what would a riveting medical thriller be without a human monster or two? If you're hankering after a good read that will leave you thinking long after you set the book aside, pick up Project 137. — **Reviewed by Viga Boland for Readers' Favorite, Five Stars**

The historical basis for the tale's medical horrors lends them an appalling credence, underscored by glimpses of a debased, cruel popular culture as seen in a reality show that's slightly reminiscent of Terry Southern's *The Magic Christian* (1969). ...an involving, tense, and visceral near-future thriller. — ***Kirkus Reviews***

University of Pennsylvania School of Dental Medicine, which in 2008 awarded him its Alumni Award of Merit.

Cole is a Fellow of the Phi Beta Kappa Society and has been a recipient of grants and fellowships from the Andrew Mellon Foundation, the National Endowment for the Humanities, and the Rockefeller Foundation. He is on the Board of Directors of the World Association for Disaster and Emergency Medicine, the Advisory Board of the International Institute for Counter-Terrorism, a trustee of the Washington Institute for Near East Policy, and a former board member of the Columbia University Graduate School of Arts and Sciences Alumni Association.

He has written numerous articles for professional journals as well as general publications including *The New York Times*, *The Washington Post*, *Los Angeles Times*, *Foreign Policy*, *Scientific American*, and *The Sciences*. He has testified before congressional committees and made invited presentations to several government agencies including the U.S. Department of Energy, the Department of Defense, the Centers for Disease Control and Prevention, and the Office of Technology Assessment.

He has appeared frequently on network and public television and his 10 books include *The Anthrax Letters* (National Academies Press/Skyhorse, revised 2009), named an HONOR BOOK by the NJ Council for the Humanities. He is also co-author of *Local Planning for Terror and Disaster: From Bioterrorism to Earthquakes* (Wiley, 2012). A member of the Aspen Institute's WMD Working Group on Homeland Security, he is co-author/editor of *WMD Terrorism* (an Aspen Institute report, 2012). Reference: http://www.leonardcole.com/

Foreword

By Dr. Leonard A. Cole

Seth Augenstein's *Project 137* is a fictional thriller stemming from a scarcely believable though real part of history. The book's title is a numerical inversion of a 1930s-1940s secret Japanese program based in China, called *Unit 731*. The program involved gruesome biological and chemical warfare experiments including vivisections of screaming strapped-down infected victims. After World War II, the head of the program, General Shiro Ishii, escaped punishment by American authorities in exchange for tissue samples and other information about the experiments. U.S. post-war programs also included exposing unwitting populations to simulant biological and chemical agents. While posing ethical questions, the tests were devoid of the sadistic character of the Japanese effort.

Augenstein's creative tale is set in a futuristic 2087 America. In this fictive scenario medical treatment in general by then has advanced. At the same time the country's governance had become increasingly authoritarian. The Orwellian-titled Bureau of Wellness is in charge of the secret *Project 137*. The project massively expands upon the early Japanese and American programs. Large populations of unknowing victims are deliberately exposed to infective and other debilitating agents. Augenstein skillfully weaves throughout his narrative the spirit of Ishii as an impetus for the latter-day fictional project.

The story ultimately reveals the horrors of a run-away biological and chemical weapons program. Augenstein's engrossing descriptions prompt the reader to wince in sadness and empathy for the victims. His vivid imagery is testimony to superb writing skills.

* * *

Dr. Leonard A. Cole is an expert on bioterrorism and on terror medicine. He is an adjunct professor at Rutgers New Jersey Medical School (Emergency Medicine) and at Rutgers University-Newark (Political Science). At the medical school he is director of the Program on Terror Medicine and Security.

He received a B.A. with highest honors from the University of California at Berkeley. Trained in the health sciences and public policy, he holds an M.A. and Ph.D. in political science from Columbia University, and a doctorate from the

Dedication

To my father, who showed me America.

PROJECT 137

"There's a possibility this could happen again," the old man said, smiling genially. *"Because in a war, you have to win."*
—A cheerful old farmer, <u>The New York Times</u>, August 17, 1995

"Clinging to the fence like a monkey, mad Norberto laughed and said, 'The Second World War is returning to the Earth! All that talk about the Third World War was wrong! It's the Second returning, returning, returning!'"
—Roberto Bolano, <u>Distant Star</u>

A LUMBER MILL

They watched the east. Under the black brims of their caps, the guards atop the high smokestacks stared unblinking at the jagged horizon. Stiff they stood, watching for any sign of the invasion to start the final actions. They followed orders perfectly, the commander noted, as he watched everything unfold, his life's work unravelling utterly.

Again and again, the lookouts glanced down at the ground within the brick wall of the complex. The workers below stared stupidly back up at them. The guards screamed down, and the workers would go back to frantically digging, connecting wires to the dynamite, piling the papers deep in the hollow drums. But after a few minutes the laborers would again stare up with mouths agape at the men in their perches.

"Are they coming?" one hollered, holding the shovel up high to block the sun.

"Dig faster, idiot!" a guard shouted back.

The commander, Shiro Ishii, watched as the hands moved faster, as the panic grew. He had thick glasses, a moustache and sideburns. The ribbons of a general dangled on his olive coat, which was dark with sweat. The cap in his hand, with the red band and gold star, was covered by the dust that whipped around him on the summer wind. He stood in the same spot, watching everything he had worked so hard for come apart. Every plan, and every hope, were buried within the growing mounds of rubble—and still it wasn't going fast enough. The Russians would come over the hills…at any moment.

The holes were filled and covered. The explosive primers were set. Matches were struck and put to the papers in the cans. Shouts rang out across the complex, and explosions cracked the sky.

Building after building blew in deafening shockwaves: barracks, cafeteria, laboratory, animal pen, the administrative offices. Slides of rubble spread across the brick wall perimeter. Shards of stone and wood and brick were the only remains of a complex that had taken years to build. The Emperor's favorite pet project had cost millions of precious yen, and the lives of some good men. But the tide of war had ebbed back to the Home Islands, and this facility needed to be relegated to history. Only the buildings with the high smokestacks remained. Two detonations had not taken them down—nothing could fell them, it seemed. They had been built to last beyond this lost war.

The general twisted the end of his moustache with thumb and forefinger. He watched the smoking rubble. An orderly—one of Kitano's men—ran up, stopped short, saluted. His oversized sleeves dangled off his skinny arms, and he blinked rapidly. A terrified sweat beaded his brow.

"G-General Ishii, s-sir," the young private stammered. "The Lieutenant says we're ready to begin detonation of…l-l-lumber mills one and two at your c-c-command. Sir."

The general looked at the young soldier, who squirmed a bit, hand rigid at the sagging hat atop his head. Ishii turned to the smokestacks, still billowing wisps of black ash.

"You know, Private," he said. "I built this entire place up from a dream I had. I willed it into existence. I made it happen. It was my special service to the Emperor."

The private's hand trembled, he bit his sweaty lip. But he stood at attention. Ishii walked around him, still twisting his moustache.

"This was a place of science, and of learning. It was truly one of the wonders of the world," said Ishii. "Things we accomplished here could have changed the world. But now we are destroying it, and running away, as if we were ashamed. Ashamed of all these miracles we made happen."

The private coughed. Ishii stopped behind him and stared at his thin, pale neck.

"General, sir. The Lieutenant and some other officers said the Russians—"

"Yes, the Russians are coming," said the general, walking quickly around to face the private. "Of course they're coming. But we must be calm. We all need to remember some things—but forget everything else. Do you understand, Private?"

The private's eyebrows rose. It was clear he did not truly understand. Ishii watched the smokestacks. The guards climbed down the ladders from their perches, back to the earth. The signal had been given. As if a trance was broken, Ishii banged the dust off his cap, put it on his head, and brushed off his jacket.

"Private, you may relay the destruction orders for the two lumber mills," he said. "Tell Kitano I'm heading to my plane now."

The young man whimpered. The general stared.

"But General Ishii, sir," he said. "The men await orders about the...logs."

The general looked at him, and a smile twisted his lips.

"Private, you should know our operation is sanitary. Utterly clean," Ishii said. "If we burn the lumber mills, it follows that we'd destroy the logs, too."

The young eyes reached his superior's face, then flicked away again.

"Y-yes, sir," he said. "It's just, sir..."

"Yes, private?"

"W-well, it's just that, we've been burning incense in the northern lumberyard outside the walls where we put the rest of the...l-l-logs, sir. Some of the enlisted men are saying they're scared of what will happen if we don't have time to say the p-p-prayers. They worry there could be...r-r-retribution, sir."

A woman's scream echoed in the distance. The crack of a single rifle echoed down the valley, like a tiny joke ending the global holocaust that had burnt the world down to so many embers.

Ishii snickered, and clasped his hands behind his back.

"Tell the enlisted men to do their jobs, and do it quick," said the general. "Otherwise, they will have to fear me, and not some stupid ghosts."

The general nodded, the private saluted, and then took off running back the way he came. Ishii didn't move, still glaring out over the small figures—Japanese in uniforms and Chinese in prisoners' rags—amid the sprawling destruction. He took one step toward the wall, where a car waited. But he spun on his heel and cupped his hands around his mouth.

"And, Private—make sure nothing is left!" Ishii yelled. "We don't want the Russians finding any of our hard work! Or the Americans!"

The young private stumbled in the dust, spinning around, saluting, running onward. Ishii saluted the driver of his car, got in, and gestured toward the airfield. He didn't look back as more explosions rang out across the valley, bricks tumbling to still more pieces in the pile.

ANNUS MIRABILIS

U.S.A., 2087

    I squinted at my terminal, sitting in my office, another workday. I reviewed the charts, cross-referenced the vitals and fluids against the Bureau of Wellness data on the screen. All were standard observations, but I triple-checked them for my own peace of mind. Everything told me one thing.

"The kid's lucky to be alive," I said, to the empty office around me.

    James Cruzen, the shattered teenager down the hallway, was in dire condition. I scanned each traumatic wound, each deadly break and slice. The teen's legs and ribcage were shattered, his spinal cord severed. Burns scorched his right side, his skull was fractured, and his brain was leaking fluids. The horrific car crash would have killed this boy outright in the early part of the 21st century, in the days of cancer and people dying in their 80s. Back in those days, he would have died within minutes of the impact. Not so in 2087, our year of wonders, this Annus Mirabilis.

    I yawned. Hours of staring at the charts and the 3-D anatomical scan of the boy on my screen had made my eyes heavy. My own reflection blinked back at me: the thin face in its late 30s, a steadily receding hairline, glasses that grew thicker with each year I put off surgery. I tilted the monitor and the reflection thankfully vanished. I got up from my desk, stretched my hands high to the ceiling, and yawned again.

    Cruzen was alive, due to the care administered by good, modern hands. A medevac drone had airlifted him to the nearest hospital: here, Saint Almachius the Vulnerable Regional Medical Center and Wellness Waystation. The doctors had him in the operating room fourteen minutes after the anonymous emergency call. The O'Neill-Kane machine's eight arachnid arms scanned his body, pinpointed the trauma, and cauterized the wounds. The burns were cryogenically cooled. Stem cells patched the gaps in his spine, and the surgeons mended the fractured bones within an hour of the paramedics pulling his smoking, broken body out of the burning car. They plied him with artificial cells grown in a lab in Japan. And in just a few hours,

Cruzen was unhooked from most of the electronic monitors, and moved up to a quiet room in the Saint Almachius Intensive Care Unit. His bed faced a big bay window with a panorama of the streaming ultrahighway between his stirruped feet. The latest chemicals—drugs built from the atom up, designed to catalyze the healing process, to effect miracles—soon had him well on his way to recovery. The very next day some friends visited, slapping him on the shoulder and joking about the near-miss he'd had. Cruzen really was a lucky young man, though the little jerk would never know, or appreciate, it.

I strolled slowly to the doorway, toward this least favorite patient of mine, who had grown fond of making demands of me and my staff.

There was a reason for my grudge. On the third day of his stay, Cruzen started talking about a girl. It made no sense. The girl was from his Digital Philosophy class, the one who had the crush on him, he said, seeming to ramble. He couldn't remember the name. The nurses thought he was delirious. But then he started hitting the red buzzer button next to his bed. I had rushed to his bedside. When I arrived, Cruzen was barking at the old nurse about someone named Esmeralda, whether she had been hurt, whether she was in the same hospital. The nurse just stared at him.

"Honey, you were alone in that car," the nurse said. "You're lucky they got you out before the natural gas exploded. It ended up taking out most of the state forest, sugar."

"I was with a girl, you idiot," he said. "I'm not hallucinating. Get me a doctor. Now."

He hadn't yet seen me, for the bandages covering his left eye. The nurse rolled her eyes at me, shook her head, then left. I turned and followed her. I double checked the brain scan for any brain trauma in young Cruzen—and whether the O.N.K. had missed something. It never overlooked anything, but if there's one thing medical school had taught me, it's to cover yourself. I always had to check. I could never leave the hospital in the evening without knowing I had tied up every last loose end.

But sure enough, the machine was right all along. There were no problems, I told him on this fourth day, as I arrived with the latest stem-cell booster injections. These were the very treatments that were keeping him alive and on the road to recovery.

"Dr. Barnes," said the teenaged patient, staring with his one eye at his Atman screen, where he watched a rerun of *How Low Can You Go.*

I reviewed the electronic charts over my FocalSpecs. The teen pointed to the small test tube dangling from my neck.

"What is that?" the teen said, pointing.

"A memento from when I was your age," I said. "It's not important, James. My question is, how are you feeling?"

"Not good," said the patient. "The stupid nurses keep bothering me. Why is this taking so long?"

"You know, you should be thankful," I said. "Your recovery wouldn't have been possible a hundred years ago. You would have died within an hour of the crash."

No reply came from the bed—only more tapping into the device on the teenager's thin wrist. I went to the cabinet and pulled out some supplies: two syringes, two cottonballs, and a bottle of rubbing alcohol. With the familiar clap of the closed cabinet, Cruzen glanced up. They always did—something about that snap of that cabinet door put them all on notice.

"No more shots, Doc," he said. "Can't we just skip them this time?"

"No, these are booster shots for the stem cells. If you don't get them, you die," I said, crossing my arms to emphasize my point.

"But I don't want to."

"I took an oath to heal my patients. I take that oath seriously, James. So you can take the treatments willingly, or I can call in the nurses to hold you down while we tap your spine."

The teenager stared. With a snort, he leaned forward off the pillow. He winced when I jabbed the point into the nape of his neck.

"Dr. Barnes, don't you think there should be some kind of home regimen for this? Is that too much to ask?"

"The Bureau of Wellness hasn't approved them yet for home use," I said, dabbing the spot of blood, affixing a bandage. "These things take time. And each of these shots is a half-million dollars. You should just be thankful your parents can afford them. Not all my patients are so lucky."

I tossed the cotton balls and syringe in the hatch leading down to the basement incinerator. I sat in the bedside chair, setting aside my own Atman, this one handheld. I smiled.

"I've got to ask a few things," I said. "You have no serious brain injuries—just a minor concussion, as far as the O'Neill-Kane can tell."

The teenager rolled his eyes.

"But what I want to know," I said, "is what you're saying about a passenger in your car."

"I've told all the nurses and the police a thousand times," the teen said. "Esmeralda and I were driving back in time to catch the semifinals of *How Low Can You Go*, and we saw part of the forest on fire, these bugs started falling on the car and attacking us, and we crashed through the guard rail. That's the last thing I remember."

I nodded. Somehow, I kept a straight face. It was one of my best bedside-manner skills.

"James, have you ingested any hallucinogens in the last month?"

The teen brandished his middle finger at me. I smiled and shook my head.

"Just had to ask, James. It's just a very—interesting—story," I said. "And just who is this Esmeralda—your girlfriend?"

"No—just some fat girl who wanted to have some fun," Cruzen said. "I barely knew her. We went to the diner, and she was going to come back to my house to watch the show, spend the night with me. She was sitting right there, in my passenger seat, when we crashed. After the bugs fell on the car."

"Bugs. Okay," I said, ignoring this brat's vile comments about the girl. "Tell me about these bugs."

"There were millions of them. They dropped from the sky," the kid said. "They had pincers or something. Hurt like hell. Esmeralda was freaking out."

"I'll ask around if we have a patient by that name," I said, patting his leg. "But a lot of what you're telling me just doesn't sound possible. Teenaged girls don't just vanish out of car wrecks, James. Bugs don't just fall out of the sky."

"Believe what you want, Doc," the teen said. "But that girl is still missing, isn't she?"

I tapped his elbow, picked up my device, stood, and walked out the door, not even glancing back at that bratty child on the mend whose survival depended on me. A camera in the hallway audibly tracked and zoomed in on me as I left. I felt its electronic eye on the hairs on the back of my neck. I cringed away from the voyeuristic lens, as I always did.

As I walked the hallway back to my office, I recorded some notes into the case history for the overnight staff. I was convinced there was no patient named Esmeralda. There couldn't be, since I'd been the doctor on call the night of the accident. The kid had suffered brain trauma, and he was probably still delusional. Hell, the toxicology screens hadn't come back yet—any of the new synthetic ergolines or cannabinoids the kids took nowadays could explain the delusions. I tapped a button, requesting further scans from the O.N.K., something to explain why the kid was asking deliriously after a girl who didn't exist. But I also made a note to triple-check the hospital census for anyone named Esmeralda. Just in case—and for my peace of mind. Always that peace of mind, that complete attention to detail that made me good at what I do.

That day, a Wednesday, seemed neverending. My sidekick, Nurse Betty Bathory, had come down with a summer cold, and I walked my rounds without her. But I was not totally alone. As I walked to each patient's room I'd call her, and between great whooping hacks of phlegm, she updated me on vital signs, blood levels, dietary patterns. She had all the medical information at her fingertips on her own device, and she briefed me before each patient, preparing to give the news, good and bad. In truth, she was as much a part of any success as I was. Sometimes I even told her how important she was.

"What's the prognosis, Betty?" I asked.

"Joe, it's not good. Be gentle," the nurse said, sneezing.

It went like that. After what seemed like days, the afternoon was almost over. I checked my Atman. The screen flashed—I was due for a five-minute break before briefing the night-shift nurses. So I turned right, walked down the hallway, and entered the doctors' lounge. I sat down and pulled out one of my energy sticks. I cracked it, shoved it up my nose, snorted, then sat back in the plush chair under the TV. Last night's episode of *How Low Can You Go* was on. My brain whirled, but with clarity, like it always did with the energy sticks. It kept me going.

I tried changing the channel, but the show was on five different stations. On the screen, a woman applied a red-hot poker to her sister's arm in exchange for five-thousand dollars. The live audience roared with applause, which drowned out the screams of agony. The broadcast cut to a woman with surgically-plump lips, weeping with joy, reaching into darkness, whispering inaudibly into the camera, then kissing her wrist. It was very dramatic—an advertisement for the new Atman Gen Four, the implant that had already sold out weeks before the widely-anticipated release date.

"You know you want it," cooed the breathless voice.

I groaned at the sheer stupidity of it. But I startled someone or something behind me, which jerked. My heart leapt up in my throat. The sound came from the couch in the dark corner nearest the locked drug cabinet. I squinted into the darkness. It was a man in the shadows—a man in navy-blue nurse's scrubs. I had never seen him before. Our eyes met, and I approached with my hand extended in greeting.

"Joe Barnes," I said. "And who are you?"

The nurse had a lopsided haircut over a misshapen head. He glanced in the direction of the door, and his shoulders slumped when he saw I had cut off his escape route. Only then did he reach out and shake my hand, with one limp pump. His fingers were cold and damp.

"Charles Culling," said the man, pulling away quickly, as if I had bitten him. "I'm the new night-shift nurse."

"I heard the Bureau was considering giving us more funding," I said. "I just thought it would have covered fixes to the O'Neill-Kane. So where are you from?"

"Pennsylvania," Culling said. "Spent a few years on a night shift over at Wessex Medical Center. Before that I was at Clara Maass."

"Ah, Clara Maass. That's our sister hospital. I know lots of people over there," I said. "Do you know Dr. Danish or Dr. Michaelson? They pretty much run the geriatrics wing over there. We used to play in a weekly poker game."

"I've heard the names," Culling said, fidgeting in his pocket. "But they wouldn't have heard mine. I've always been on the graveyard shift. I don't really know anybody."

The nurse's jaw clenched in those sallow cheeks. His eyes were focused on the door. I smiled and stepped aside to make room to pass. The nurse shot past me, out into the hallway.

"Nice meeting you, Charles," I called out. But the door clicked shut, without a response. They were hiring more and more weirdos around the hospital every day, it seemed.

I jammed twenty dollars in the machine, snorted another energy stick, and walked back through the lounge to my office. After the end of the long day of tending to the sick and agonized, it was time for my nightly routine. I hung the stethoscope on the brass statue of the wise man on my desk, dictated my notes, and sent the master file into the hospital database. Then I hung my white coat on the big worn hook on the door, next to the shelf with my stacked diplomas which I'd never gotten around to hanging. As I walked out to the parking lot I called my wife Mary to tell her I'd be a little late for dinner, but that she should still set out a NutriFast bag to defrost for me.

The hospital's security cameras followed my car as it left the parking lot, then turned for the ultrahighway and disappeared behind the strip malls in the dusk.

Mary and I had a quiet dinner, talked a bit about the small things, and went to bed early. Just another end to another day, one among hundreds, and thousands.

* * *

I returned to the hospital at the break of dawn, as usual. Charging into the office, apple clenched in my teeth, I swept the coat off the door hook and onto my shoulders. I grabbed the stethoscope off the wise-man statue, checked the terminal, and started my rounds. The first three patients were sleeping, but the machines showed normal vitals, blipping along. I whistled as I marked them off on my Atman. I reached the fourth room down—the room of the bratty teenager with the snapped spine. I took a deep breath and went inside.

The wall monitors were all blank. No signs of life. The teen's face and skin had turned gray. But no alarm had been activated. I rushed over, felt for a pulse, found none, and punched the emergency button. No other indications—no wounds, no swelling, no secretions. Within seconds a team of nurses and specialists appeared, pushing me out of the way, defibrillating the kid's heart, infusing him with chemicals, then slamming with fists directly on his chest. Nothing worked. I hovered at the edge of the huddle. Minutes later, Cruzen was pronounced and hauled off to the basement morgue. The electronic filing of the teen's death began as the O'Neill-Kane performed the autopsy.

After the commotion, the doctors and nurses scattered. I could not catch my breath, and my heart raced wildly. I was left with the empty bed, still imprinted with the impression of the body that had laid there. I walked over to the lounge. I stuck another twenty bucks in the machine, and got my morning energy stick, two hours ahead of schedule. I hadn't lost a patient in three years. And this one was young, just a child. Even with a catastrophic injury, the speed of his death was baffling. There had been no alarm, no warning. As I snorted the last bit of the stick, my head light and airy, I found my feet taking me back to my dead patient's room, step by step, down the hallway, snapping my fingers like I always did. I swiped my Atman and entered.

The room was lit brightly by the morning sun. The orderlies had removed most of the sheets, but the ghostly shape of the corpse remained imprinted in the fabrics.

The boy had meant nothing personally to me. But he had been under my care, and an unexplained death would haunt me forever. I needed some kind of an answer. I scanned the walls, the pastel landscapes in dark frames, the computer terminal, the wires leading to the monitors and oxygen hookups in the bedboard, the medicine cabinet. Something about it was all wrong. The standardized layout—everything square, in its right place—was off. These hospital rooms were so familiar to me, I could always pick out the slightest thing amiss. I rounded the other side of the bed. The sun streamed warm through the spotless window.

"Joe," said a voice.

Betty was at the door. She was wearing her nurse's scrubs, which hung loose around her petite body. Her dark hair was pulled back taut in her ponytail. The normal rouge of her lipstick wasn't there that morning. Her nose looked raw, like a gin blossom, from her lingering cold. But she smiled at me. She held out her wrist, pointing at the blinking screen there.

"Top of the morning," she said, hacking up a bit of phlegm. She cocked her head down the hallway. "Let's go. Other patients to keep alive. No time to dwell on one dead brat now."

"Go ahead. I'll catch up with you. I have to check one more thing."

She shrugged at me and turned. The door clicked shut behind her. I glanced at the computer monitors on the wall, like an enormous scoreboard, and shook my head. I was imagining things. There was nothing strange about the room, the location of death. I was just rattled because there was no explanation. But I had to keep reminding myself—there had to be some reason. They'd drummed that into us in medical school. The answers really had always been there—if not from the O.N.K., then from the other scanners, monitors, and sensors. Even through the Blackout, we'd managed to keep a technological grip on Death, and make her behave in our antiseptic walls.

And yet, this was different, somehow. I turned to the door, carefully stepping around the wires splayed out over the floor.

Something bright and white at my feet caught my eye. It was halfway under the bed. I stooped to pick it up. A piece of crinkled paper. I shook my head. I hadn't seen a loose piece of paper since the Blackout. It was much lighter than I remembered, almost as light as air. But adhesive coated one side—it was a sticker of some kind. I flipped it over, unfolded it carefully, trying not to rip it. It was a label with a lengthy serial number. Staring at it for a moment, I stuffed it in my pocket, and headed off after Betty. I had other patients to keep alive, and the dead would just have to wait.

ONCE, A PHILOSOPHER...
TWICE, A PERVERT

U.S.A., 2087

I watched the boiling pot on the stove. The deep heat roiled the tormented bubbles up to the surface, again and again. Mesmerized, I thought back on the long day behind me, and that shape of a dead teenager pressed into the empty hospital bed, and the unexplained death. I cycled through the same half-dozen diagnoses, without finding any satisfactory answer.

"Honey, these things happen," Mary said, pulling a pair of NutriFast protein sacks from the freezer. "People die, no matter how good you get at saving them. You aren't gods, you know."

"I know that," I said, stirring the water. "But it doesn't change the fact that we have no idea why this happened. And it happened on my watch."

Braids swinging, she set the bags on the table and pulled out knives and forks from a drawer. She sliced open one bag, then the other. She brought them both over to the boiling pot and poured them in, the protein powder from the freezer bag, and gluten-free wheat, the sugar-free legumes and other sodium-free bits sliding from the other bag into the tumultuous water. She clicked the timer on her new Atman. I stirred.

"I wish you would stop dwelling on it," she said. "You can't be there every moment of the day, watching over every patient."

"No," I said, wiping the sweat from my brow. "But this one—I don't understand it. It makes no sense."

"What did the O.N.K. show? Was it drugs or something?"

I placed the spoon on the stove.

"That's exactly why I'm baffled," I said. "The O.N.K. found nothing wrong with him. It's like the kid died of old age. His heart was healthy, but it just stopped beating. There were no traces of drugs other than the stem-cell boosters—and that couldn't have killed him. Everything just...shut down."

She smiled. She pulled me close and kissed my forehead. Then she turned back to the fridge. I watched and admired her: the black hair in the tense braids, her lean limbs tanned and taut and rippling with strength even in the years after two tours in the Middle Eastern wars with the Marines, and her soft face with those big gray eyes. That was her feature that made my heart stop. Whenever I returned home from work, she always seemed to glow—like she was something incandescent to pursue at the finale of each day. She was my daily prize, and her love was a need for me as basic as food or drink.

"You'll figure it out, honey," she was saying. "It's always the simplest explanation, isn't it? That's what you learn in the Marines. Breaking it down, Barney-style. I don't know what that means. But that's what we called it."

"In medical school we called it Occam's Razor," I said. "Because if you cut to the most direct solution, it's usually the right one."

I left the kitchen, heading down the corridor nearest the stairs, over the Iranian rug in the dining room, to the front window looking out to the street. Down the yard and along the driveway, far off, solar streetlights cast dim halos in the dark heat of summer. Against the night I could see the shapes of the other new houses in the neighborhood—all doctors and lawyers, married, starting families in brand-new houses in a suburb just far enough outside the radius of a demilitarized Newark to feel safe. Thirty miles. It was close enough to be reachable, and far enough away from…someone, something, anything, everything. You could never be sure of anything anymore, the world had gone crazy, and the times had never been more dangerous—that was what everyone seemed to say, every damned day.

A steady line of cars rolled down the road, with flashing lights. The funeral procession, coming from the kid's house. They rolled slowly past and I peered into each tinted window without seeing anyone inside.

Cruzen, according to the hospital intake forms, lived a few streets over. His jetsetting parents owned one of the biggest estates in the neighborhood. The father was a federal judge; that's where I had recognized the name. The kid had a perfect upbringing in an affluent suburb, the best of everything, a bright future. Now he lay cold in a coffin, cause unknown. His parents were mourning a few blocks over—they'd returned from summering in the Alps to plan their teenager's funeral. I sighed.

I had failed that boy. I had failed that boy the same way the doctors had failed me the night I was orphaned, the night they couldn't save my loving parents from something so simple it was laughable. I had sworn never to fail that way—to leave a child jettisoned alone out in the world like I had been. But I had, and here I was watching a funeral procession pass my very door. The cars continued rolling down the road through the darkness.

I shut the curtain and walked back to the kitchen, to the boiling pot. Mary stared down at her Atman with a strange smile on her face, but as soon as she heard my footsteps, she stepped to the fridge and rooted through a collection of bottles. I stirred the protein and carbs in the pot, scowling at its thickening pastiness. I hate NutriFast, but Mary insisted we needed our supplements.

"Honey, snap out of it," she said, shaking a container of tofu sprinkling and vitamin spice powder vigorously, with two hands. She came over and kissed me, looking purposefully into my eyes. "You are a good doctor. You did everything you could. And you'll figure out what happened."

The timer on her Atman beeped, and she pinched her wrist and silenced it. I turned off the burner and strained the boiled food in the sink. Setting the table, with the plates and the chopsticks, I headed over to the wine rack, pressed a button, and Merlot streamed into a pair of glasses. Mary punched away at her Atman with a weird intensity, a look of fire in her eyes. She came over, hesitating mid-stride at the sight of the wineglasses on the table. Another strange indication of whatever was going on with her, but again, I ignored it. I ladled out dinner and whistled up at the ceiling. The lights dimmed a bit, and the stereo came on. The soft strains of violins, something from before the Blackout, hummed overhead.

We ate in silence. I didn't notice for a few minutes, but I realized suddenly that all I could hear was my own chewing. She wasn't eating. Mary was always the one to start the conversation over dinner—about our days or her parents, or about our next vacation. We'd been married for seven years, and we'd never run out of things to talk about. I set my chopsticks down and scrutinized her over my Merlot. She was engrossed in her Atman, completely lost in its glow. Was this a new milestone, a terrible descent to the silence of a middle-aged marriage? My stomach upended. Had we reached a sort of dead end to our intimacy? Our passion?

Her Atman beeped again. A smile spread across her face. I set my wineglass down.

"Do you have to use that when you're at the dinner table?" I said. "I knew you never should have gotten that damned thing implanted."

"I don't know why you never got yours installed," she said, not glancing up. "I couldn't get anything done without it. I'm going to get the Four once they work out all the bugs."

I scoffed.

"I respect the natural beauty of the human form," I said, the same way I chided all my colleagues and friends who'd gotten the implants. Out of the corner of my eye I saw her mouthing the exact same words as I said them, but I continued.

"Those things work off the natural electrical currents in your body, Mary. Who knows what they could be doing to your brain? Your heart?"

She laughed.

"Joe, you're paranoid," she said. "The Bureau of Wellness approved them. They're safe. Safer than that wine you're drinking."

I gulped down the dregs of my wineglass, stood and went to the wall. I placed the glass under the spout of the dispenser, and it shot out a stream of perfectly-aerated, room-temperature Merlot. I returned to the table with an intransigent look on my face.

A smirk crossed her face, her hands hung down at her sides. Something was amiss—she was acting strangely. Her plate and her glass were untouched. I pretended not to notice—I just dug into my dinner. But after a few more moments, I felt her stare. I glanced up.

"Why aren't you eating?" I asked. "And you've barely touched your wine. It's Thursday night. We drink wine. It's wine night, Mary."

Her smile widened to a grin.

"I don't think I'll be drinking wine for a while," she said.

I stared at her blankly. I had no idea what she was talking about—she wasn't a drunk. She'd been fine with her drinking since she had gotten the right medications from the Veterans Affairs psychiatrist.

But she beamed her electric smile at me, as her eyes searched my face. This was strange.

"I can't drink wine," she said. "No alcohol for me. For nine months."

Her words hung there for a second.

And my heart leapt up.

"Oh—oh my God," I said. I tried to rise, but she was already around the table, grabbing me, squeezing me tight. We laughed and kissed like we'd won the lottery. In a way, we had beaten the toughest odds of all, considering all the exposures she'd suffered during the tours in the Middle East. After years of trying to have a child, medicine had again come through for me—for both of us, for our family-to-be. It was a time to celebrate.

Hours later, after a joyful call to her sister in Nebraska, we went up to our big pastel bedroom. She kissed me and turned out the light. She attached the big mask of the Dormus over her face, set its oxygen tubes out straight, folded her hands under the pillow, and fell asleep. The machine gusted softly with her breathing. It was always so easy for her, that drift off to the blank abyss so graceful and effortless. But not so for me. For a while I just sat there and tried to picture the face of my unborn child: the girl a miniature version of Mary, and the boy a shrunken vision of me. The thoughts whirled in my head, nearly making me dizzy, and finally I sat up in bed. Propping a pillow behind me, I scoured files on my Atman over and over again. I could not help myself—when these particular mental itches started nagging me, I had to scratch them. Otherwise I would just lay there and brood all night long—without that crucial peace of mind.

The night of his death, James Cruzen's vitals had all been normal—even better than normal, according to the data. The teenager's recovery had been perfect. Death was clinically impossible. I cross-referenced case histories and stem-cell booster injections. After twenty minutes of research, I discovered it. A single study in the annals documenting sudden patient deaths as a side-effect of stem-cell boosters, published by researchers at some Ivy League school six months earlier. It concluded the pluripotent cells' effects had not yet been fully cataloged, and that work under controlled environments had to be conducted in the future. I highlighted the name of the lead researcher, someone named Yoshiro Fujimi, and sent it to my work computer. My mind was at ease, finally. I yawned and stretched out in the soft sheets.

But as I did one final nightly check of the patient census, I noticed something more. One name popped out at me from the lengthy list. I did a double-take and sat up in bed. The name Esmeralda Foyle was there, entered in the night before last.

The girl was in Saint Almachius somewhere, after all.

Foyle, Esmeralda—age seventeen, admitted for traumatic injuries, no date or time of admission. There was a strange serial number attached, beginning with the old alphanumeric BOW-137. The picture showed a pretty girl with green eyes and baby-chubby cheeks. A tattoo of a neon yellow rose with bristling thorns grew up the side of her neck. A vacant stare, no smile.

Esmeralda. She couldn't be the same one Cruzen had been talking about. How could a patient go missing, with all the mandatory checks at the hospital? I rubbed my eyes, set the device aside. I'd make it a priority tomorrow, after a good night of sleep, I told myself. I took off my FocalSpecs and set them on the nightstand. My mind continued to cycle the possibilities. But I needed sleep. All the checks had to wait for the morning rounds at the hospital. I affixed the Dormus over my nose and flicked the switch. But nothing happened. I flicked it on and off again—nothing. Cursing, I tossed the mask over the side of the bed and curled up with the pillow. Mary slept on, without stirring, her own Dormus gusting slowly with rich oxygen.

Sleep eluded me for hours, as thoughts of Cruzen and Esmeralda and the hospital database raced through my mind. How could patients just die of treatments proven to be safe? Could the girl possibly be at the hospital, in some unknown room, some unknown bed? Could the boy have been telling the truth about a vanished patient in our midst? I turned again and again on sweaty sheets, my mind reeling. Eventually I drifted off—and without the anesthetizing effect of the Dormus, I dreamt for the first time in years.

Something about a river, the water cool and dark. Sinking deeper and deeper into it, without ever reaching bottom.

* * *

Buzzing jolted me off the pillow. It was still before dawn, and I felt sick from sleeplessness, but it was time to rise. Mary stirred, the mask still affixed over her face, the Atman buzzing in her wrist. I silenced both alarms and pushed myself up from the damp sheets. A shave and a shower, then a shirt and pants and tie. When I reached the kitchen, the coffee maker turned on at the sound of my footsteps. I snorted an energy stick. I whistled, and the TV wall flicked on; the situation in Korea was still the lead story. That idiot on *How Low Can You Go*— Steeling or whatever that idiot's name was—was biting poisonous snakes, and winning thousands of dollars every night at nine eastern, eight central time. I sipped my coffee, and silently cursed the tastes of the American public.

Mary padded down the stairs, her robe open to reveal only her camouflage nightie, her braids undone, like the ends of rope fraying off her head. She skipped the coffee and poured herself a glass of water, walked in front of the sink and stared out the window at the dawn. I admired her form, and at that moment she seemed to glow in the sunlight from the window. She had never been so beautiful to me.

"Good morning, hon," she said. "Feeling better?"

"Damned Dormus broke last night," I said, tearing my gaze from her bare legs. "I actually dreamt a bit. Something about a river, and an island. First dream since I was a kid."

"That's terrible. We'll get it fixed," she said, smiling broadly at me, gently shoving me out the door. "But get moving, so you're not late, Dr. Barnes. Have a good day."

Outside, the day was already hot and humid, and that rotten-egg scent hung over the neighborhood and its cloverleaf of cul-de-sacs. The hundred-home development had been built atop a wetland during the pre-Purge real estate boom. Something was always a bit off in the air on warm summer days, or when it rained, or the first spring days when everything was in bloom. The Bureau of Wellness water-treatment plant they built down the street a year earlier seemed to improve things a bit. But overall, it was a good neighborhood, with professionals like us and the Cruzens a couple streets over. Crime and property values were not a problem.

But when we paid off the mortgages, we would move west. As far west as we could go, to find a better place for the child. Moving west had always been a pipe dream, a remote option. Now it was a necessity. The baby would change everything. I needed to pull this child away from the ultrahighways, the Atman ads, and the headlong rush of the East. Out West things were slower, and safer. Especially since the Blackout, and the loss of the grid out there. There was more oxygen and elbow room out there to let a family grow and thrive. My child would not be pushed headlong into adulthood like I was, or sent half a world away to fight in wars like Mary had been. The child would have better than we did.

A mile later, I reached the ultrahighway. The traffic had already piled up. It crawled along all eight lanes. Some people in the jam around me laid on their horns; others laughed at game shows on their heads-up displays; some checked their Atmans for news. The holographic billboards flickered ads for personal lubricants and TV shows into the brilliant sky, between the strip malls and exits, disappearing into the morning light. I flipped on the radio and turned to the national news station. Only five miles until the hospital, but that could take an hour or more if any lanes were closed. The road construction was neverending, as the state continued to widen the ultrahighway to a ninth and tenth lane for the millions who streamed east to offices each morning, then reversed course and chased the sunset back home.

I turned the radio up to a minor roar to drown out the horn of a raving woman in the car next to me. The broadcaster's dignified voice explained the state of the world. Her name was Saxas, an intelligent software program relaying the events of the day across the United States. The stations had decided to computer-synthesize the voice, half British and half American, to appeal across all demographics after the Blackout. The result was a flat transatlantic tone that didn't sound quite human and didn't really belong anywhere. Saxas was international and tireless—the faceless voice of everyone and nobody, everywhere and nowhere. But she had announced all the great upheavals of the last few years, ever since the Blackout. Nothing phased her—that wasn't in her programming.

"…from the annual Pyongyang Summit, the East Asian Federation has announced that all remaining tariffs and trade barriers will be lifted between Japan, China, and Unified Korea over the next five years," Saxas intoned. "A unilateral alliance for regional security will be created, they announced.

"On the domestic front," Saxas continued, "a group of medical experts have lashed out against the Surgeon General's declaration of victory in the War on Cancer last month."

I turned it louder.

"Some say the long-term side effects of stem cells and genetic therapies have not been fully cataloged. Others claim there could be dire consequences for survivors.

"In other national news, the missing persons' database continues to grow, with at least 250,000 people of all ages reported missing in the last decade. Interest groups say it's a growing epidemic that threatens stability in some U.S. cities, especially those with active Intifada insurgency. Authorities have yet to comment on the estimates.

"And locally, a tractor-trailer crash in the right lane on the New Jersey stretch of the ultrahighway is causing a twenty-minute delay," Saxas said, dully. I turned the radio down and banged my head on the steering wheel.

I arrived forty minutes late at the hospital after passing the wreckage of a small school bus and a jackknifed tractor-trailer. I thought of stopping to assist the response but figured the six ambulances and fourteen paramedics would be better equipped to deal with the gaggle of crying schoolkids abandoned along the chaotic roadside.

My first patient of the day was already gowned and waiting for me in an examination room. George MacGruder sat on the examination table, his craggy face contorted with premonitions of doom. In truth, he was my favorite patient.

"How long this time, doc?" MacGruder said, his feet up on the examination table as I walked in. I lifted his feet and placed them back on the ground, careful to not catch a glimpse underneath the gown.

"Sorry I'm late. Just a fenderbender. Rubberneckers for miles," I said.

"I wasn't asking why you were late. You're always late. I expect this," the patient said. "I was talking about my prognosis. How long do I have?"

I shook my head, a slight smile on my face. I scanned MacGruder's retinas, then used my Atman so that the wall monitors cycled through the latest test results from the O'Neill-Kane.

"George MacGruder, eighty-eight years old, Blood Type AB-positive, blood sugar normal, cholesterol satisfactory, heart rate and body-mass index average, carcinogen scans show no abnormal cell growth," I said, pulling a stool underneath me. "There's no doubt about it—you're a perfectly healthy senior citizen."

MacGruder pounded his fist into his open palm. He shook his head.

"There has to be something, doc. My grandfather. My father. My mother. My aunt," he said, counting on his fingers. "They all died before their eighty-ninth birthday. They were all fit as a fiddle when they turned eighty-eight, and then—boom. Dead."

"What did they die from?"

"Bathroom fall," MacGruder said, counting on his fingers. "Two car accidents. One suicide."

I smiled and shook my head.

"No, George," I said. "If you can avoid slipping in the shower or jumping off a cliff, you're doomed to live into your nineties, at least. You know, people are living into their one-thirties now. You might make it fifty more years. You could outlive me."

"Christ, I hope not," the patient said. "I'm bored at eighty-eight. How the hell will I kill fifty years? I'm retired. I don't golf. No real books left, since the Blackout. My clothes will only last another few years, and I promised myself I'd never have to go shopping again. There has to be something wrong. Do me a favor—look over those results again."

I stood, patting MacGruder's veiny wrist.

"I'm sure you'll figure out your existential dilemma," I said. "These are good problems to have. Just think—you could be dead from that brain tumor we caught ten years ago."

I tapped my Atman twice to power it down. I stuck my hand out, and my old patient and friend shook it.

"You're good for another six months, George. Guaranteed—or your money back," I said.

"A thousand bucks says you're wrong," MacGruder said, shaking his head, a sheepish but relieved grin spreading along his face.

We stepped to the doorway.

"You're on," I said, grinning. I leaned in close. "And actually, George, I've got some good news. I'm going to be a father."

MacGruder hooted. He grabbed my hand and pumped it vigorously.

"Congratulations, my good man! I knew you'd make it happen, eventually. You can't ever give up hope! Great news—the best of news."

"Thanks, George. It's a medical miracle, truly."

"Miracles visit those who faithfully open the door," MacGruder said, scratching his chin philosophically.

I visited three more patients: Mrs. Goldfarb, Mr. Mastrangelo and Mrs. Jefferson. All three were long-time patients of mine, too. Each of them heard my news. Mrs. Goldfarb pinched my cheeks; Mr. Mastrangelo, grinning, socked me in the arm; and Mrs. Jefferson left lipstick kisses on my face and rumpled my white coat with a scandalous hug. Afterward, I staggered down the hallway. Something about the news of a coming birth could drives even normal people to madness, hysteria—I had seen this over my years in the hospital.

My office was quiet, calm. I scanned the data from my rounds into the terminal, then poured myself a glass of distilled water from the cooler next to my desk. As I drank I looked up at the digital monitors on the wall, which flashed pictures and thank-you notes from patients, all of whom were still alive. MacGruder appeared there, along with Goldfarb and Jefferson and Mastrangelo. All of them had survived malignant brain tumors. All of them were still alive, because of the appropriate medical treatment. I always smiled when I saw MacGruder appear on the screen, holding an enormous fish on a boat off the Pacific coast, his shit-eating grin as wide as the horizon behind him. These pictures kept me going, no matter how tough a day I was having.

I pulled up the patient census on the terminal. I searched again for the name Esmeralda, and the same entry popped up. Esmeralda Foyle, age seventeen, admitted at an undisclosed time, the same strange old alphanumeric serial number prefix: BOW-137. But there was one small difference. The reason for admission had been altered. It wasn't traumatic injuries now—instead it was for cosmetic surgery. All the other fields for notes and further information were blank. The picture of the cherub-faced girl had vanished, replaced by the holographic seal of the Bureau of Wellness: a staff with two snakes coiled around it, with a quiver of arrows fanned out at the top, an eagle screaming silent above it all. The symbol had always given me a queasy feeling, for some reason—like it was a veiled threat or had some hidden meaning that eluded me. But I could never precisely place my uneasiness about it until that moment. Here it seemed to be hiding something from me, from any and all prying eyes.

The Atman rang, and I jumped. I rubbed my face. I picked it up on the second ring.

"Hello," I said.

"Joe, it's Betty."

"Betty. How you doing? Where are you?"

"Dandy. I guess you saw George MacGruder. I hope you said hello for me."

"I did. He asked about you and your sweet derriere. I think those were his exact words. The man's like a hormone-addled teenager."

She chuckled, somehow amused by the creepy, but non-threatening, worship of an old man.

"Quite a character, that George. If he was only twice my age, he'd have a shot at this sweet derriere. Anyway…I won't be there for another hour. I pulled late shift yet again."

"You never told me that."

"Yes, I did. Yesterday. I told you I drew the short straw because of that new hire. You were too busy staring at that chart from that little brat who dropped dead."

"James Cruzen."

"Yeah, the twerp," she said. "You know, he actually groped me when he woke up from surgery? I had half a mind to report him, but he dropped dead before I got the chance."

"Did he say anything to you about a girl with him in the car?"

"No—but I heard he was delirious. Possible brain trauma," she said. "Or the crafty little jerk made up some crazy story about a girl and bugs falling from the sky so he wouldn't get arrested for burning down half the state forest in that car crash."

I shifted in my chair.

"So, what about this new hire?" I said. "What's his name, Culling? Hiring him doesn't mean you're going back to nights, does it?"

She sighed.

"Just for a few days," she said. "They're seeing if he can be trusted with overseeing the wing on the undead shift. But boy am I glad I don't have to work with him regularly. Dude gives me the creeps, Joe. Just being in the same room is too much. The guy looks like he just crawled out of some dive bar."

"I met the guy briefly. Pretty strange person."

"Know what I mean?" she said. Some beeping came from her end, behind her voice. "Oh, Joe—I've got to go take care of something. Catch you later."

"Alright."

We hung up. I tapped my desk, then leaned back to my refrigerator, took out an energy stick, and snorted it.

But even with the clarity from the stimulant, my thoughts returned to the limp body of James Cruzen—the image of that corpse, that blank face. That visage of death I'd never gotten accustomed to, whether old or young, diseased or healthy. The juiceless husk, the soulless meat. I took another sip of water and glanced at the wall monitor, at MacGruder's stupid grin over that huge dead tropical fish in his tiny clawlike hands. But it was no good. No happy pictures of the teenager, no thank-you note, no happy story of Cruzen's recovery would ever appear there. Five minutes of my lunch break remained, but I couldn't purge the vision of the boy's gaping mouth out of my mind.

There was one thing I could do. I picked up my Atman and tapped the screen. Within seconds I found it. A picture, a curriculum vitae, and a number for the researcher at the Ivy League school who led the stem-cell research program I had been reading about. Yoshiro Fujimi: a dapper-looking man, mixed-race, with traces of Japanese heritage around his eyes and cheekbones, and graying hair rebelling around his ears. An impressive track record of stints at major academic institutions, and some work for the Bureau of Wellness—all places for the brightest and best-connected in the country. I picked up the Atman and dialed.

It rang. Nothing—it just kept going, for minutes. My thoughts wandered as it rang on and on: the fleeting image of Cruzen's dead face—the blackness of the open maw, the dead unseeing eyes, that abyss.

"Hello?" a woman suddenly answered.

"Oh—hello?" I said, startled. "Hello?"

"Yes, can I help you?" the woman snapped back at me.

Her voice—I couldn't place that voice. But it was so familiar. I composed myself, quickly collecting my thoughts.

"Hi, my name is Joe Barnes, I'm a doctor here at Saint Almachius the Vulnerable in New Jersey. I was looking to speak with Dr. Yoshiro Fujimi."

"If you're looking for the Doctor, he's on sabbatical in Guatemala. An important project. He won't be back until December, at the earliest."

"It's important I reach him."

"In that case, you can call back in December," she said.

There was a click. She had hung up. I put the Atman down. What was a researcher with that kind of pedigree doing down in Guatemala, especially after the Cartel Wars? But most of all, that voice haunted me. I knew that voice. I tried calling the number again, but this time it was disconnected.

With a strange feeling of dread, I returned to my afternoon rounds. The hours dragged. But with each new room, new pulse and new terminal, I couldn't keep focused. My mind wandered into places from the past that horrified me. Occasionally, the terrifying future of a baby and a family unmoored my stomach.

So I focused on the Cruzen death. I searched on my pocket Atman for more stem cell research as I walked the halls. As I wound through the scant medical literature, I remembered how quickly it had all progressed—how science had leapfrogged over the Hippocratic Oath in a few short years. The few pre-Blackout entries were huge, voluminous, boring studies. But after the Purge and the Blackout, the studies became mere summaries of a whirlwind of questionable work. I reached my office and sat at my desk. I proceeded to read nineteen of the thirty-nine publications I'd found, when Betty Bathory walked in.

"Hey, slacker. Getting in some reading?" she said, falling back into the patients' chair.

I blinked. "What time is it?"

"Time to call it a day. I can take care of the last few fogeys. Go home, Joe."

"I'm just finishing up here. Checking if the stem cells could have killed the kid," I said. "I don't know whether that's possible. Apparently no one does."

She waved me off.

"People die. It happens everyday, for good reasons and bad." She shook her head. "Joe, you care a lot—sometimes too much."

She paused.

"So anyway, I was talking with Mary just now."

Her thin, plucked eyebrows arched over her eyes. Betty and Mary had been friends for years. It was as if I had two wives—one at home, one at work. One a retired warrior who shared my bed, one a crack nurse saving lives by my side. Betty stared me down. She knew.

"Yes, Betty, she's…" I began to say, a smile breaking across my face.

"Oh my God," she said, clapping her hands, lunging around the desk and hugging me. "I knew it! It finally happened! You guys are going to have a bayyyy-beeeee!"

She kissed me on the cheek, leaving lipstick smudges she quickly wiped off with her thumb. She waved her arms in the air, as she raved around the office.

"…and we should get a follow-up test just to be sure and we could run the DNA Tapestry Test and start Mary on the Bureau's vitamin infusions…"

I barely understood her, in her whirlwind of excitement. I pinched my nose with thumb and forefinger, waiting for a quiet moment. She was like that—she would get carried away in fits of passion every so often. It made her a good nurse, how deeply she cared. She raved for a minute more, then the room was quiet. Detecting the silence, feeling her gaze, I looked up from my terminal.

"Joe, what's the matter with you? Can't you be excited that your wife is going to have your first child? For once, can't you just be happy?" she asked.

"I'm incredibly happy, it's just that…" I started to say.

"It's just that you're still thinking about the dead kid," she said, completing my thought for me. Her mouth twisted, her hands went to her hips. "You're unbelievable, you know that? I'm going to get started on my rounds." She went to the door. But she stopped at the threshold.

"You know, when you get like this, you sound like Old Man Wetherspoon, Joe." Then she left, the door shutting behind her.

* * *

Old Man Wetherspoon. The man had an answer for anything and everything. I hadn't thought of that. I hadn't been down to the basement in days, maybe weeks. I stood from my seat, and walked out the door, down the hallway to the central hospital elevator. I could already hear the grizzled old voice as I walked down the stairs toward the Old Man's darkened lair.

Cornelius Wetherspoon was a man out of time—a gambler who had bet his life savings on an American millennium…and lost. He owned ten houses within a short drive of the hospital, but they were all empty and dilapidated and cost so much in taxes he still couldn't retire, even at the age of 105. He had come of age during the Bush administration, and had been an enthusiastic, charismatic supporter of the Grand Old Party as a young doctor, even going so far as to run for state office once in the 2010s against an impossible-to-beat liberal incumbent. Despite his defeat, Cornelius Wetherspoon emerged as a wunderkind. Heading into the 2020s, there was no stopping him. Except for Nixon II. First he had been primed for a key position in the new administration—probably in the Bureau of Wellness—because he had made such a good showing against the liberal, in spite of the odds. But like his disgraced ancestor, President Richard Malthus Nixon owed too many people. So instead of the qualified Cornelius Wetherspoon, the new president picked a pair of knucklehead New England doctors who had delivered New Hampshire in the primary using any means necessary. Wetherspoon, then in his 40s, had seethed. But still he bided his time. Within the Committee to Re-Elect the President the second time around, Wetherspoon tried even harder, made himself indispensable in delivering New Jersey's precious electoral votes. But almost every state in the nation went to Nixon II anyway. And this time the President hired no one for any of the open positions, claiming the need for budget cuts. Wetherspoon suffered in silence, although he told his story to anyone who would listen for the next half-century.

The longer he lived, the deeper the wrinkles etched into his face, and the more people turned out to be sonsofbitches who inevitably betrayed him. His wife ran off with a colleague, his teenagers had bastard children and became drug addicts, the hospital administrators all tried to cut corners and killed patients by degrees, as he tirelessly recounted. Residents came and went, his second wife died the night Pakistan nuked Kashmir, his children died in the 2040s, and he started drinking a fifth of Scotch every night. Rebounding, he attended Alcoholics Anonymous, decided after five meetings they were just a bunch of sniveling weaklings, and quit the booze through sheer willpower. He tried to phase himself out toward retirement at the hospital, but every time another retirement date loomed he quietly withdrew his notice of resignation as the taxes encroached closer to fiscal disaster. The hospital didn't know what to do with him—a doctor who had trained as a student to treat the cured epidemics of HIV and cancer, but who had lasted through the Great Purge to the incredible gains of genetic modification and stem cells. He was a walking museum, a fount of institutional knowledge. The administrators wanted him out. They coaxed him to quit with severance packages, promises of bonuses, implied threats.

But he ignored them. The bitter widower remained in his tiny office, surrounded by the ramparts of old paper books, reading. Occasionally he emerged to give the nurses and young doctors terse nuggets of advice, passing by and barking that a bandage was too tight or that a second opinion was needed, or even criticizing patients for not trying hard enough to heal. He hated the O'Neill-Kane machine with a passionate rage and had even been seen once punching its arachnid arms out of anger. (He was promptly reprimanded, but they still couldn't fire him). Students were terrified of him. No error slid by him as he made his silent circumlocutions of the hospital, like an assassin.

I was never frightened of him, though. I had come one day into the office to ask a routine question about laxatives and care of the elderly. I had figured he was the seniormost doctor, and he could help me out with a quick answer. But Old Man Wetherspoon—then just ninety-five—would not make it easy.

"Someone tell you to ask the bitter old man in the basement for advice?" Wetherspoon had croaked.

"No, I saw you're the most senior physician in the hospital directory," I had said, standing by the doorway. "I've heard you're the expert. I have a patient who has irritable bowel syndrome and a norovirus, but still isn't defecating."

The Old Man put his book down, slapping it closed with finality. He leaned back in the chair, crossing his hands high over his meager chest, the tufts of snowy hair peeking up out of his yellowed collar.

"So you want to be a real doctor—not one of these little brats in it for a paycheck," the Old Man said.

I nodded eagerly, and bravely took the seat opposite from him.

He pushed back from the desk, reached over his shoulder into a shelf behind him, and pulled out a thick tome—a paper book. He pushed forward, and tossed it on the desk, where it slid along a landslide of books into my lap. I stooped to pick up part of the avalanche that had fallen to the floor.

"Don't worry about that," the Old Man said. "Just go take care of that patient. In the Index, under C, for Constipation. And tell me how it goes." Then he picked up a pen and waved me out the door with a flick of his hand. I left and found it hard to read the printed pages, but I discovered an electronic version of the same book. The patient got well, and I returned the book.

After a decade of mentoring—an antique volume borrowed, a nod, a sentence here and there—our meetings were just a bit less brusque. I tried to get down to the basement at least once a week. Whenever I did, I felt refreshed, like I was a wide-eyed medical student with much yet to learn. I could tell the Old Man liked me, though he would never admit it.

So there I was, seeking his advice yet again. The basement office's door was ajar. Complete darkness inside.

"Hello?" I said, knocking. "Neal, it's Joe."

A chain tinkled, and an old banker's lamp cast an emerald glow on the ceiling, and a white halo atop the desk. In the shadows behind it, I could just barely make out the Old Man's craggy features.

"Barnes?" he croaked. "Come in, come in."

I came forward and once again sat down in the chair across from him. I could never be sure, but I thought the pile of scattered books on the floor were the very same that had slid off the Old Man's desk that day ten years earlier when he had first tossed me *Diet and the Senior Bowels, Volume 4*.

"Neal, why are you sitting in the dark?" I asked. I felt I could call him by first name, at this point.

"Don't get me started, Joe," he said. "You know I think on Fridays. Sensory deprivation, down here in the dark basement. Keeps the mind sharp, in tune."

"But I thought you only meditated at night," I said.

"It's not meditation—it's thinking, Joe. Little breaks in the middle of the day to harness my inner resources. To find solace amid the raging storm of bullshit," Wetherspoon said. "Sanity's only for the seeker. I've told you this."

I glanced in the corner of the office. Something glinted in the ray of the lamp. I could just make out the fragments of a smashed Atman in the shadows—the third yet the Old Man had destroyed.

"Neal, you broke another one?" I said. "You'd better watch your ass. Kranklein might try to force you to retire again. She's done it for less."

"That woman can do her worst," he said. "Suzanne Kranklein would have gotten rid of me a long time ago if she could. Anyway, she knew that goddamned thingamajigger wouldn't survive five minutes in this office. The cost is hers to bear."

"Just be careful, Neal."

"They're the ones who should be careful. An old man's got nothing to lose but borrowed time. They keep forgetting that. But anyway—you wanted something? I just got done telling you I don't have all the time in the world."

"There was a teenager who died yesterday, and I can't figure out why," I said.

"Someone once sang that only the good die young. But that person grew into a drunken old jackass, so don't believe it."

"This was a severe trauma case—car accident," I said, ignoring his strange reference. "We administered stem cells, he was recovering nicely. The next morning, he was dead."

"This is the hallucinating teenager everyone's talking about? James Cruzen?"

"How did you know? I didn't know you even left this office anymore."

Wetherspoon scoffed.

"I have my sources. The bureaucrats on the fifth floor want to bury me down here, but I have my ways. So you want to know why the kid dropped dead overnight. There's a growing contingent of researchers who suspect that stem cells have heretofore unknown side effects. I trust you tried them?"

"I did. The lead researcher is on sabbatical. In Guatemala."

"Guatemala?" the Old Man said, scratching his chin. "Very interesting."

"Why is Guatemala interesting?"

"Lots of research projects down there," the Old Man said. "Nevermind, nevermind. So—have you checked the patient history, every number, all the contacts in the electronic record?"

"Of course."

"Then check them again." The Old Man paused. A match flared in the darkness, then illuminated the tip of a cigar, the underside of his jagged wrinkles. The smoke enveloped his shadow. "The devil's always in the details, Joe. There's always an explanation, even if it's not immediate."

The cigar glowed bright, the sweet odor of burning filled the room. It reminded me of something far distant in my childhood, a nagging hint of the past.

"Neal, you know the tobacco laws made everything…"

"Yes, Young Joseph, I know they've made smoking anything illegal. They're getting rid of everything fun, law by law and decree by decree. But old habits die hard. If you don't want to smell like an outlaw, feel free to vacate the premises."

I nodded. That was my cue. I stood and stepped gingerly over the strewn books.

"Joe," the Old Man rasped.

I turned around. A plume of smoke glowed with the Old Man's inhale, then vanished into the dark as the cigar disappeared behind the desk.

"Check the room where the kid died," he said. "There are ways to directly access the terminal's full history."

"Neal—that's illegal, too. You know that only the regional health czar has access to that information."

"Sure, it's illegal. So don't get caught when you do it. Especially by that idiotic Kranklein person we report to," the Old Man said.

"Good advice," I said. "Bye, Neal."

The Old Man grunted. I left and went toward the elevators, snapping my fingers as I still struggled to remember where I had smelled tobacco like that last. I pushed a button, the door opened, and I got on. The elevator lurched upward. I smelled at my sleeves, and I could still breathe in the faint scent of the cigar. Of course, the Old Man was right. I had to hack into the system to really figure out what was going on. But the terminals were the most-tightly guarded pieces of equipment in the hospital, even more so than the locked prescription cabinets. Just the slightest glimpse of the database was an indictable crime. I never went into the system unless I had to.

The elevator stopped, pinged. The doors opened. I stepped out onto the third floor, muttering. I would be taking a risk, but long ago I had reached the conclusion that the real doctors in this world had to find a way to hold to the Hippocratic Oath, no matter what the law said. The all-seeing electronic system had all the information a doctor would ever need—the precise amount of insulin the patient needed daily, drug contraindications, psychological profiles. The Bureau of Wellness kept it all confidential—secret even from the attending physicians. Congress had battled over the law since the Great Purge.

But it remained. And at Saint Almachius, the law of the land was enforced by Suzanne Kranklein. As the boss, she had done a great job in uniting the nurses, doctors, and patients in a steadfast hatred of her. Since she had taken over the reins of the hospital five years earlier, she'd picked up a monstrous nickname. Kranklein had come to be known as the Kraken to a disgruntled, mutinous staff. She'd arrived after Wetherspoon had retired for the third time, in the span of a few months when he wasn't around to organize the doctors against the arch-bureaucrat who had never taken a biology class in her life. The scuttlebutt among all the doctors was she had a cousin from Maine in Congress who had gotten her the job, but no one could ever really be sure. Wetherspoon may have started that rumor, considering his dislike of New Englanders from the Nixon II days. Either way, the Kraken slithered into the hospital's cockpit, and slowly but surely tightened her grip on the medical workings of the entire institution. Her opponents retired, died, or—in four cases—were visited in the middle of the night by special agents from the Bureau of Wellness, which ended with moderate prison sentences. All four had accessed the electronic records.

All four had done what I was about to attempt: break the law because the law was essentially killing our patients.

My steps echoed down the intensive-care-unit hallway. I forced a smile at three nurses who passed. They smiled back at me. Breathing hard with each step, I tried to calm my thumping heart. Other doctors snuck peeks at the electronic records. I had done it twice in the last month alone. But it always made me queasy—and something about it this time unnerved me even more than usual. I had no idea why. Maybe because the Old Man had suggested it, and I normally just did it secretly, on my own. After all, the black-market technology was nearly foolproof. I twiddled the thing in my pocket. It was a portable drive, hackers' code built with one purpose. Every doctor had one, everyone used it.

It was only illegal if you were stupid enough to be caught. I took a deep breath.

I walked the final few paces to the room. The door was closed. I swiped my Atman, gently pushed it inward and stepped inside. The door was already closing behind me when I saw the person seated on the bed.

"Hello, Dr. Barnes," said Suzanne Kranklein, glancing up from the screen in her wrist.

Though I recoiled, I did manage to muster a sickly smile at the erect posture of the dreaded Kraken. Her right leg was crossed over her left, black shirt and pants hanging loose off her body. She was a small woman, and there was something gnarled, elfin about her. It was as if a pretty little petite person had gradually mutated—a bulbous flushed nose, bloodshot eyes, flabby rolling gut, ratty hair—from the years of trolling in the sewers of bureaucracy. She and I always avoided looking at each other. We hadn't made eye contact in years.

"What are you doing here, Suzanne?" I asked.

"I was about to ask you the same question," she said. "I suppose you heard the patient in this room is already dead?"

"I heard," I said. "In fact, I came here to check around the room. We still don't know the cause or manner of death."

"'Check around the room' wouldn't mean illegally accessing the electronic Bureau of Wellness records, would it?"

She smiled, that hateful half-smirk reddening the blood vessels in her nose. Lopsided and patronizing, crooked and dangerous, that look of hers. Since the four doctors had been jailed a few years earlier at her behest, I had learned never to turn my back on that repulsive smile.

"Suzanne, I wouldn't even know how. This new system is beyond me," I said.

She looked up at me. Our eyes actually met, and I blinked. I couldn't help it. Her face was more twisted and distorted than ever before.

"Sometimes I wonder," she said, trailing off. She tapped at her Atman screen and stood. "Sometimes I wonder, Barnes, whether you and that Old Man downstairs aren't the same person, just separated by a few generations."

31

"I guess the Old Man and me, we're old fashioned," I said, looking up at the ceiling. "We expect people to say what they really mean."

She stepped closer. And before I could react, she jammed a hand in my coat pocket, and plucked out the portable drive.

"What the f—"

"I don't know why technophobes like you or Wetherspoon would want some advanced piece of technology like this," she said, waving it in my face. "Especially since it's illegal to even own one of these."

The smile spread wide along her thin lips. I reached up to grab the portable drive back, but she quickly stuffed it in her own pocket.

"Doctors can't treat patients if they're flying blind," I said. "You have no right…"

"I know what you and all the other doctors are up to, Barnes. Normally I just look the other way. But with a case this vitally important, everything has to follow the plan."

My eyes narrowed. I pointed my finger in her face.

"What's so vitally important about this case? Some dead teenager?" I said. "And where is this Esmeralda Foyle I'm hearing about?"

She glanced down at her wrist, and, like a zigzagging running back, stepped around me and made for the door. We turned to face one another, like gunslingers. Her eyes shone with that dangerous, sharp glint.

"Every patient is important," she said, her voice flat. "But we obey the rules, Dr. Barnes. You've always been good at balancing the two. Keep that balance and keep your job. There is no patient named Esmeralda Foyle at Saint Almachius, and never has been."

She pushed through the door. It shut. Silence surrounded me. I glanced at the terminal, which was still locked. I had come to Cruzen's room for answers, only to find more questions than ever before.

I left the room. My footsteps rapped down the hall, and I brushed past young nurses whom I barely recognized. The Kraken's words rang in my ears. "With a case this vitally important"—what the hell was she talking about? She never went into patient rooms, since her managerial role was above such menial duties. Something about that dead teenager, Cruzen, made this case vitally important to her. There had to be something in those records, and I had to see them.

I slammed through the stairwell door, and smashed into a person carrying a tray, which upended and sent glass vials of many sizes smashing on the hallway floor. It was Betty. She snarled and punched me hard in the arm. Then she stooped to pick up the shards.

"Betty, damn, I'm sorry," I said.

"Why don't you look where you're going, Joe?" she said. She looked up at me, a few pieces in her palm. "What, you still got your head up your ass about that dead kid?"

"Yes, actually," I said, my voice echoing loudly in the narrow stairwell. I stooped to help her scoop up the remnants of the urine specimens. "The Kraken's hiding something about that kid. And she stole my portable drive."

"Joe, she's a Bureau administrator. She's a pain in the ass," Betty said. "She's just doing her job."

She reached for another piece of glass, and I grabbed her wrist.

"Betty, this is different," I said, pressing my fingers into her flesh. "She's hiding something. Something big. Maybe something criminal. I can feel it."

She just stared at me, a question and challenge crossing her face. A hostile look crossed her face that I had never seen before, and I drew back a foot or so. But I didn't blink. She finally broke her gaze away, pulling from her pocket a shiny new portable drive.

"Take mine, then," she said, picking up more glass. "Figure out what happened to the kid, then get back to work. The last thing we need is you to keep running into people and breaking stuff because of these paranoid delusions."

I grabbed the drive from her hand. It was smooth, and lighter than mine. "Why do you have one of these?"

"Even nurses need them, Joe. How the hell else could we treat the patients?"

I smirked and shook my head. I picked up two more fragments, but she shooed me away, with a wave of her hands.

"Just hurry up. I need it back," she said. "Besides, the Kraken's probably leaving the hospital about now for happy hour. Now's your best chance. I'll run interference. Hurry, hurry."

I kissed her on the forehead gratefully. She rolled her eyes, pushed a button on her wrist, and spoke into her Atman.

"Ladies, it's Betty," she said. "I had a spill over here in the east stairwell, if you can come help me clean up, it would really help a girl out." She shooed me away with her hand. A moment's pause.

"Sure, honey," a voice chirped on the other end. "Be there in a sec."

I stood and turned back through the doorway and walked down the hall. A gaggle of nurses rushed past me toward Betty's mess, and I hurried past the empty nursing station. I ducked into the room where Cruzen died, without anyone seeing me.

I went right to the terminal. There was no time to lose. I plugged the drive in and punched some buttons on the touchscreen. A wealth of information popped up before me, and on the wall monitors. The screen was full of icons and blinking things I had never seen before. Truly, her drive had even better access than my own. After a few moments, the menus started to make sense. I noticed the records of my own encounters with Cruzen, the routine check-ups of Betty Bathory and other nurses. It reconstructed everything—stem-cell booster shot, meal, fluids, vitamins infusion, another meal, a vitals check-up. And everything seemed in order, in tune, and timed correctly.

But then I found what did not belong. I blinked.

The second entry from the bottom: a visit listed at 3:17 a.m. the morning Cruzen died. It was listed as a regular check-in. But there were never supposed to be any non-emergent visits between two and six in the morning.

Most baffling of all was the name listed: Shiro Ishii.

Shiro Ishii. I snapped my fingers, I mouthed the name. It was a name that didn't exist at the hospital, I was sure of that. Even with all the Bureau turnover at the hospital, I always knew all the names, reviewed them and studied them and memorized them. The hospital census was the first thing I checked every morning. I felt it was my duty to know the lay of the land, the complete list of both of patients and staff. I knew I had never seen the name Shiro Ishii before. But still—it struck me as familiar, somehow. I didn't know why, but I felt I had read it before, on some nameplate or in some book, maybe a long time before. Maybe someone had whispered it to me, or it was someone I had met a long time before.

The record showed Shiro Ishii had stayed for thirty seconds and left no other trace, like he had just poked his head in the door, sniffed the air, then left again. This phantom had visited, then disappeared, illegally wiping away nearly every trace. Something creeped along my neck, like an invisible entity had smelled my sweaty skin. I turned. But nothing was there.

I shut the terminal down. I walked out down the hallway to the elevator, which took me up to my office. I hung my coat on the hook, took the token stethoscope off from around my neck, and I swapped it for my lucky test tube off the wise man statue on my desk. I sat down at my desk, rubbing the smooth familiar necklace between my fingers. I rocked a bit back and forth in the chair, which squeaked its well-worn grooves. Shiro Ishii, Shiro Ishii, Shiro Ishii. I couldn't place it, but the name bounced around in my brain. I leaned over the computer and searched my contacts on *Amicus*—I'd reluctantly joined the network after the medical journals started publishing there—but nothing came up. I did a search of the Library of Congress' skeletally reconstructed archives. To my surprise, something was filed there: one short entry for Shiro Ishii, listing him as a doctor who had been part of Japan's Imperial Army during one of the world wars of the 20th century. A doctor who had died of throat cancer in 1959. Nothing more than that—no other information seemed to be left in the archive. I racked my brain to remember which of those wars the Japanese had fought in, and who had won. So much had been lost in the Blackout, that gigantic push of the reset button a decade earlier—everything from holy texts scanned and stored in databases, to symphonies digitized on servers had been wiped clean out of existence in the blink of an eye. Some thousands of years of learning were all zapped by an electromagnetic pulse in the atmosphere, cause unknown. Even the Library of Congress hadn't recovered its priceless treasures of wisdom—and probably never would. Some history just didn't exist anymore. Most of Shiro Ishii's life was lost to history, other than his date of death.

"I guess this can't be our guy," I told the empty office. "Unless he's a ghost."

Betty walked in, her palm extended. It was bandaged from glass cuts. I dropped the portable drive into her hand, and she stuck it in her coat pocket.

"You've got some serious technology there," I said. "Better than mine ever was."

"Of course it is, Joe," she said. "Everyone updates theirs every week to keep ahead of the security changes. Everyone except you and the Old Man. There's a custodian down the hall who does it on the side."

I scoffed.

"We have a janitor who hacks into government security systems?" I said, shaking my head.

"The young guy always tinkering with the JiffySpiff," she said, crossing her arms in front her. "I can't remember his name—but he talks like he's a doctor. The one with the wart on his nose. It's the twenty-first-century Joe, the era of the common man, democracy, crowd sourcing, all that. We'll get you a new drive from him, and we'll keep it updated this time. So...did you figure out what killed the little perv?"

"No idea," I said. "Hey—we don't have a person named Shiro Ishii on staff, do we?"

"No—I would remember a name like that. Sounds familiar, though. Was he that guy on the last season of *How Low Can You Go*? The one who connected the wires to the car battery, kissed his wife, then proceeded to—"

"No, I don't think he was on that stupid show," I said, cutting her short. "He's a man who's been dead for a hundred years. I'm just wondering how he got into that room in the middle of the night for thirty seconds, without any cameras seeing him, just before the kid died."

"Has to be a blip or something. No one has that kind of clearance," she said, turning toward the door. She smirked. "Not even ghosts."

"Where are you going?" I said.

"I have to prep Culling for the night shift. Remember?"

"I forgot. Have a good time," I said. "Hell, he might be a really nice guy once you get to know him. He could even be an eligible bachelor. Husband number two, perhaps?"

Frowning, she held up a ringless hand, showing a discolored band of worn skin around her fourth finger.

"Even if he wasn't a creep, one marriage was enough for me," she said. "You know what they say: 'Once a philosopher, twice a pervert.'"

I laughed.

"I've never heard that before. I like it. Where did you get that?"

"A paper book my grandfather read to me when I was a kid before the Blackout. Some French thing, philosophy or something. Anyway, wish me luck."

She walked out. I turned off the lights and left the room. The hospital cleared out quickly—people in suits and sweatpants, administrators and doctors and patients, all streaming toward their cars in the main parking lot. It was always like this, once the Bureau regulations had limited the hospital's operating hours. I walked to the auxiliary lot, where my little roadster was plugged in to the natural gas port. I removed the hose, coiled the cord into the trunk, got in the car, and maneuvered through the traffic to the ultrahighway.

The news was practically the same as Saxas' broadcast from that morning. The East Asian Federation issued several statements that any interference in their economic sphere of influence would not be tolerated ahead of the big international conference; the debate over the outcome of the War on Cancer continued; the missing-persons epidemic had not been solved over the course of the day; and another fiery crash on the ultrahighway was blocking traffic, dead ahead of me.

I tapped the steering wheel, turned the volume down, and thought about the dead man who walked the hallways of my hospital.

FUNERAL

Japan, 1946

The mourners filed into their seats dutifully. Some even managed to slump their shoulders and fix their faces in grimaces of grief. Only a few snuck looks over their shoulders at the apparition of the dead man staring down at them.

The ceremony was planned with an austere simplicity. The grieving family and friends were expected to arrive in Shibayama by train or bus and walk the half-mile to the house. There they would be greeted by the dead man's wife and his two brothers and ushered to the backyard. Once enough of the invitees had filled the seats, the priest was instructed to light the incense and start the prayers, regardless of attendance. It was all expected to proceed by noon and be over before two. A short lunch would be served, with diced fruit.

But nothing had gone according to plan. Too many mourners had been stopped at the village train station and detained by the American Occupation authorities, the giant men in their khaki shirts and helmets and armbands. Several dozen guests had been left to wait for authorization at a small regional office, as three large Americans carefully inspected their papers and travel passes. By the time two o'clock rolled around, there were still not enough people to fill up any of the rows of seats. The diced fruit sat soggy in the bowls.

But the priest, hands folded across his kimono, kept glancing up to the attic window of the house. Through the hazy windowpanes, he watched the dead man smoking cigarette after cigarette. By the time three o'clock rolled around, the apparition above gave the priest the signal—two strokes of the hand, like a flick-swish of a sword—and the ceremony began.

Lighting the incense, and intoning the prayers, the rest of the mourners suddenly arrived from their detainment in the village. The seats were filled. Everything proceeded, even though the priest's voice kept cracking a key upward, like a teenage boy. He continued on and on, vouching for the departed soul who stared down upon them, inhaling cigarette after cigarette with worldly breath. The priest burned more incense and spoke on. The mourners fidgeted.

Two hours passed, and the rumbling of empty stomachs could be heard in the rows. The priest continued, even as a few American uniforms appeared at the gate to the yard, peering curiously at the proceedings. The priest had his eyes closed, his voice wavering, not seeing the signal from the dead man in the window up above. The deceased furiously waved at him, but the priest's eyes remained closed. Finally the dead man reached out and rapped on the window. The holy man's eyes opened. The signal relayed, he finished his chant, stepped back, and pulled back a shroud, revealing an oven. Through the door the crowd could see a casket. Two men rushed in from either side and lit a fire, which smoked and grew until flames were licking the edges of the coffin. The priest looked up, and the dead man nodded in approval.

The holy man then announced to the crowd that if everyone would please follow him they would adjourn to the porch for lunch. A hum of confusion rippled through the crowd, since the sun had already set beyond Tokyo, and it was much closer to dinner than lunch. But they dutifully followed the priest down the rows, nonetheless. None looked up to see the man smoking at the window of the house, looking down upon the people who had mourned for him for hours. They filed into the house, where they started to pick at the mushy pears, watery berries, and pulpy persimmons.

Once they were safely inside, the dead man softly descended his back staircase, taking a glance into the empty back yard, then stepping outside. He walked to the stove and contemplated it. The ceremony should be enough to satisfy the Americans and the detectives who had come around asking for him. The stupid Americans wouldn't even know him, without his moustache and his uniform. He lit a cigarette as the coffin collapsed into embers and stared at the flames.

"General Ishii?" came a voice, in English, from behind.

The dead man froze. He slowly turned.

"Who are you?" he said.

Four men were there, three of them were Americans in uniforms. The biggest one stepped forward. He was bulky and bearded, with the bloat of the drinker around his jowls. He smiled, and his face stretched taut with natural health. He bowed.

"General, sir, we have been looking for you for quite some months. My name is Norbert Fell, and I come on behalf of the U.S. government. We've come to speak to you."

A small Japanese man at the American's shoulder translated, rapid-fire. Ishii nodded.

"Speak about what?" he asked in Japanese.

"We want to talk about the war," the American said in English, which was translated, too.

Ishii smiled broadly, pulling his kimono strap tighter, sucking on the cigarette with a grimace.

"The war is over, friend," he said. "Not sure if you heard."

Fell laughed.

"And you're not dead—but apparently your friends and family did not hear the news," Fell said, jerking a thumb over his shoulder toward the house. In the window Ishii could see the mourners, some of whom stared out the window at the giant American talking to the dead master of the house.

"Good point," Ishii said. He pulled the cigarette out of his mouth and pointed it at the American. "I stayed in the shadows until now, for the safety of my family. But now I've been seen. Now you know the truth of my survival."

Fell nodded, switching his briefcase from his left hand to his right.

"General, sir, there is much to discuss. Much business to attend to," he said. "If your funeral is still going on, is there someplace we can go to discuss further?"

Ishii dropped the cigarette end and ground it out with a slippered foot, shaking his head. These Americans would not go away easily. And there was nowhere to run.

"I suppose I must play host, now," he said, looking at the people milling through his house. "Perhaps you can return here next Tuesday?"

"We must insist we meet again in Tokyo," Fell said, holding out his hands like he was offering him a large gift in his arms. "We prefer to speak with people at the Occupation headquarters. It takes us too long to get to Chiba, with all the military traffic on the roads. Please do us the honor of coming to us."

Ishii nodded, then turned back toward the blaze, where the embers of the coffin and the effigy inside were burning out. As he and the American watched, the wax and paper figure inside the pieces melted away to nothing. Ishii laughed at the absurdity and waste of it. Fell laughed, too—an empty laugh that was part predatory.

"Life begins anew, you know," said Ishii.

"I suppose it does, General Ishii," Fell said. "I suppose it does."

A FISHING EXPEDITION

U.S.A., 2087

I planned for a quiet Saturday, I really did. I would sleep late, eat a big breakfast, and go fishing with my best friend. But I woke early, to the sounds of retching. Mary was huddled over the toilet, one hand holding her braids back, the other gripping the bowl's rim. Something about her recent struggles with the pregnancy made my gut recoil. She would be shouldering the burden of motherhood, and there was nothing I could do to help her. I could only crouch and stroke her hair.

"Of course I'm alright. Only morning…sickness," she barked, shoulders heaving. "No worse than the vaccines the Corps administered before Iran. Go make coffee or something, just don't let me smell it."

I went downstairs, pressed a button on the wall, and exactly one liter of steaming coffee flowed into the dispenser. I listened to the echoes of my wife puking as I stared out the open window. The pretty birdsong of the summer morning was in a strange rhythm with the sound of sickness above. Retch and tweet; gurgle and chirp. Overhead the shower gushed on. My Atman rang with a videocall. I answered it. A weathered, bearded face with tattoos around the neck and a ballcap covering the burgeoning baldness appeared on the screen. It was Lorenzo Lanza, my best friend since kindergarten.

"My man," I said.

"Hey bro," Lanza answered. He scratched at the thick beard along his jaw. "You ready?"

I shrugged.

"You might have to give me another hour. Mary's sick."

Lanza guffawed.

"Marines don't get sick. Especially Sgt. Mary Smith Barnes," he said. "So do what you got to do. But be outside with your pole in five minutes."

I knocked and shouted into the bathroom door. Over the roar of the shower Mary hollered she was fine, and that I should get out of the house for a while. I didn't argue. I grabbed the old rod my father had given me that last Christmas when I was a teenager who still had parents, a happy memory stained by everything to come right afterward. I angled the pole out the door as the big red pick-up truck pulled into the driveway. I waved and walked up to the cab, slid my gear in the bed and climbed in.

My buddy Lorenzo Lanza sat hunched over the wheel. Six-foot-three, two-hundred-fifty pounds, all muscle. Tattoos swirled on every limb, tribal barbed wire and vine that I knew linked up to a concealed Marine Corps seal inked over his breastbone. The tattoos were so black they stood out on his brown skin. When I closed the door behind me, we punched each other. My arm went completely numb. My friend was unfazed, as usual.

"I've been looking forward to getting out on the river for weeks, my man," Lanza said.

"A cop and a doctor—we're the two busiest people on Earth," I said. "It's amazing we ever get out to the spot."

"It's been crazy since I made detective," my friend said ruefully, nodding, turning down the street and to the west. "One year, and three spree shooters. It's like it never stops. But at least they had the common courtesy to kill themselves so we could wrap up the investigations quickly."

Moments of silence. Lanza cleared his throat.

"So, Mary was sick?" he said. "She's better now?"

I looked over at him pointedly.

"She's great. It's just morning sickness. She's going to be a mom."

Lanza whooped. The car nearly swerved off the road as he smacked my arm.

"Holy shit, man! That's terrific!" he said. "So who's the lucky father?"

"Whoever he is, I hope he pays for college," I said, deadpan.

Lanza laughed and slapped me on the back, a little too hard. It stung, and I marveled once again at his strength.

"Damn, Joe! It's about time—what's it been, seven years of you guys trying?"

"Seven years, three months and one week," I said. "But who's counting?"

"That's great, man," Lanza said. "Having the first kid is perfect. The beginning of everything—so many moments that you wish you could just stop time and live in them forever. You know what I mean?"

"No."

"You will. Trust me—I've been through it three times," my friend said. "Of course, then they grow up to be little brats who run off with their mother to the

West Coast during the divorce, and you end up so broke you can't afford the whiskey to get you to sleep. But maybe that's just me."

I patted his shoulder gently. Lanza took a deep breath, shook his head, wiped at his eyes.

"But for those first few years, it's magical. It actually changes your brain. They've done studies and stuff. You're a doctor, you should know this."

"I can hardly wait for changes to my brain," I said, scratching my head.

We merged onto the ultrahighway, heading west. A holographic condom ad—shaped as a big erect penis—hovered faintly over a strip mall in the bright morning air. Lanza flipped on the satellite radio and found an old favorite song of ours from high school. We sang together. It was something we always did, even though we sounded terrible. Lanza did the silly falsetto parts, I the baritone. Our highway exit came up quick, and Lanza made a sharp turn off the highway. We drove around a rickety fence, rusted and swaying in the breeze, a sign warning trespassers to keep off the last remaining public lands in the Garden State. We passed the still-smoldering acres of trees from the massive forest fire from what Lanza said the cops were calling the Cruzen Fireball. We crossed into the ashen landscape at the heart of the state forest. Utter devastation was all around, ashes and piles of dead things. We turned onto smaller and smaller roads, rutted with the late summer monsoons, driving parallel to the Messowecan River, the blackened tree-husks blurring by and the waterway winding slow beyond. Lanza flicked one cigarette out, lit another. The truck veered onto a washboarded dirt path, winding north and chasing the river farther and further into the skeletal woods. We stopped at a turnoff near a thicket in the bend in the river. The willow tree drooped along the banks, a long survivor of the blaze. It was the spot, our spot. Lanza turned the engine off, then inhaled deeply.

"Smell that fresh air? We're finally back to nature, my friend."

"I only smell burning," I said, sniffing.

We got out, pulling our rods and tackle out of the truck. We went over to the thicket, underneath the sad singed boughs of the willow. It was like only our little spot in the forest was spared the conflagration. We cleared off debris, knocked off some branches, and hauled up the battered yellow canoe from our hiding spot. We shook out the spiders and other critters, wiping away the webs and ashes and kicking away trash, then brought it down to the water's edge. Both of us turned our Atmans onto the alert-only setting. We loaded up and disembarked, myself up front and Lanza in the back, as always, paddling hard in the runoff from the monsoons which had washed down from the worn nubs of the Kittatinny Ridge.

"Come on, Joe. Slubby's Hole is only a half-mile up on the far bank," Lanza said. "The Yah-qua-whee hides there in the summer, the old fishermen tell me. We'll be there in no time."

"A half-mile? It seemed a lot shorter last time," I said, my arms already aching after just a minute of paddling.

"Come on, this was easy when you were sixteen," Lanza whispered.

"Exactly," I said, breathing hard.

After much toil and strain, we made it to the Hole, the cove in the current's shadow. We slipped our poles out and cast a pair of flies out into the current.

"You think we'll see him this time?" I said.

Lanza looked at me silently, his finger raised to his lips. I scoffed at him.

"If there's only one fish, then why are we whispering?" I whispered.

"Because the Yah-qua-whee is smart," Lanza hissed. "I've seen him. And it's not just me. At my Sunday flea market, I overheard a couple oldtimers talking about spotting him in some shallows, a big row of hooks in his lips. He's got huge lips, and double-size fins, they say. The acidity of the Messowecan doesn't affect him. This fish is smart enough to swim off, first thing he hears. Nothing can catch him. Except us."

I shook my head at my friend's irrepressible boyish wonder and watched my fly float along. I let line out, but it when it drifted close to Lanza's, I reeled in. I cast again.

We fished for hours, occasionally snarling the line on the skeleton of the car or some other waste under the waterline. We occasionally put the poles down and dipped our paddles into the current, repositioning ourselves in the calm glassy waters of the cove. We sat in silence, the crack-gush of a new beer the only sound besides the distant whistle of two drones circling high overhead. The day was crisp, silent. The light played all around, seemingly alive on the surface. It was nothing like the deep, dark dream river of the night before. But for some reason, I felt a chill reflecting on that nightmare even in that bright light of day. I readied myself to cast for the two-hundred and sixty-sixth time—I kept count, I always kept count—when Lanza tapped me on the shoulder. I spun around. Lanza's brow was furrowed at me.

"You alright, bro?" Lanza said. "Overcome by the baby news?"

"Something like that," I said. I set the pole down and picked up the paddle to push us away from shore. "I'm thrilled. It's just kind of unreal right now. After everything Mary and I went through, it's hard to believe it actually is happening."

I sighed, and paddled hard away from the bank, stopping the canoe in the middle of the calm water, covered with a shiny slick of industrial fluids.

"But there's something else. A work thing—this kid who died in the hospital," I said softly. "There's no reason he should have died. He was in a bad car crash, but we had him on his way to recovery."

"Joe, aren't there always people who die for no reason?" Lanza said.

"Sure, people die," I said, stowing the paddle beneath my feet. "But we can treat almost anything now. And if we can't, at least we know the reason."

"What did the medical examiner say?"

"There wasn't one. Just the automated O.N.K. autopsy. All tests were normal—his heart just stopped beating. Cause unknown."

"What's telling you there's something wrong? Did you see someone messing with his medicine or something?"

"No. But I did find out that somebody stopped by the room in the middle of the night, using a fake name."

"Shit," Lanza said. "Wait—was this Cruzen? The Fireball kid? The dumbshit who crashed his car and burned down half the state forest just down the road there?"

"One and the same."

"Damn, Joe," Lanza said. "I responded to that call. One of the other detectives processed the accident scene. We thought it was impossible for one exploding car to cause all that damage—even with the natural gas leaks. Even less likely the kid crawled out and made it all the way to the road to be rescued."

Lanza shook his head.

"Weirdest thing, though. There was a stampede of footprints around the car," he continued. "We marked it all down in the notes. But the prosecutors wanted to keep it simple—pressure from above and all that. So we kept it simple."

I turned around to face him.

"Kept it simple? Pressure from above? What the hell are you saying?" I asked.

Beeping—a flittering, unnatural sound—broke the silence around us. Both of us reached for our belts. Each of us pulled out a beeping Atman. The sound of panic—the emergency page. Lanza whistled, long and mournful, like a tugboat's horn.

"If we both got called…" he said, tiredly.

"It can't be good," I said. "I just hope it's not like the last time. February."

"The Bayonne Bloodbath," Lanza said, shaking his head. "Goddamn, that was bad."

Those few words conjured up the horror we had lived through just a few months before, flushing a wave of sweat across my skin. Lanza lit a cigarette, picked up his paddle, and pushed us into the current, back toward the shore.

"So…about this dead Fireball kid. Why do you care so much?" he said. "Don't patients die all the time?"

I picked up my paddle again, pushing the canoe wide of a submerged car wreck.

"Zo, I've been a doctor long enough to know what I'm talking about. I'm pretty sure somebody killed this kid. For some reason I don't know."

Moments of silence passed as we paddled toward the shore. We hit the beach, I scampered out, picked up the tip of the canoe, and hoisted it up onto land. Lanza tossed the gear onshore.

"What makes you think that?" Lanza said.

"There was a person who went in the room. They used a fake name—the same as a military doctor who died a hundred years ago. This dead doctor walks into the kid's room, and the patient drops dead. My nurse and my boss think I'm crazy. So does Mary. But Old Man Wetherspoon thinks there may be something to it."

"Ah, Wetherspoon, the cranky old bastard," Lanza said, stepping out of the canoe, flicking his cigarette into the water. "You know, I could help you take a look into it. But you have to get me some evidence first."

Together we pulled the canoe onto shore, picked it up, and nestled it back in its spot underneath the old willow tree.

"The minute I know something, I'll tell you," I said. "But first let's get to this call."

Both of us picked up our Atmans, turned them on, and got the rundown: shooting spree, in Newark, at the Lockheed-Martin Center, hostages, undetermined casualties. We hung up at the same time.

"It's the Bloodbath all over again," Lanza said.

"Sounds bad," I said.

Lanza flicked on the radio. Saxas' voice was talking about the tragedy at a New Jersey stadium, the latest massacre, and the growing death toll. Her flat tone once again made the unreality of an unfolding nightmare completely surreal. But then her voice cut away to a nasally man talking from the scene, who was panicked, out of breath. I snapped my fingers.

"That's Jim O'Keefe," I said. "The same idiot from February. He's the one who first called it the Bayonne Bloodbath. He got the number of casualties wrong."

"The older guy with the thick glasses—the balding one with the squeaky voice, right? What an idiot. Dude gets every story wrong."

"The Fourth Estate ain't what it used to be," I said, nodding.

We sped east. When we pulled in my driveway, I jumped out, grabbed my pole, slammed the door and ran up the driveway. I waved back at Lanza, but the truck was already careening backward, then racing back toward the ultrahighway.

I dropped my pole in the entryway, went upstairs and threw my fishing togs in the hamper, then whisked on a dress shirt and slacks. I was rushing out of the bedroom when I heard retching in the bathroom again. My heart leapt. Was she still sick in there?

"Dear?" he said. "You're still sick?"

The toilet flushed. Then I clearly heard her breathless voice through the door.

"I was fine for a couple hours. I saw the Newark thing on my Atman. I know you have to go. I'm okay. They need you at the hospital."

I paused a moment.

"Go, Joe," she said.

"I'll be back as soon as I can," I called out, rushing out and down the stairs.

* * *

Swerving between cars and punching the gas, I made it to the hospital in thirty minutes flat. By then a ring of flashing lights had already encircled the hospital. Shouting, running, sirens, chaos all around. I side-stepped paramedics pushing a gurney toward the back entrance. I darted through a hole in the crowd to the revolving door in the front. In the lobby, I pushed through crowds of people, their wails of lamentation like some apocalyptic vision—a dozen bleeding, a few limping, others just mute and collapsed on the floor. I pushed around the crowd to the staff elevator. I got off on the third floor and jogged to my office. I donned my coat, threw on the stethoscope, then headed down the back hallway and the stairs to the emergency room.

Pandemonium. Blood smeared on the white tiles. People howling, crying, and moaning. Doctors rushed from patient to patient, stabilizing them before moving onto the next convulsing form. A man lay in his wife's lap, spitting red globules, before he fell limp, and the woman screamed. An unmoving line wound its way to the spiderlike O.N.K. in the center of the room, everyone waiting their turn. I whisked past them toward the nurses' station, where I found Betty Bathory screaming into her Atman, pounding her fist on a desk.

"...don't tell me you can't get me any more blood. We're out of synthetic, too. We're dealing with mass casualties. Mass casualties, you bastard!" She listened for a second. "Rufus, you damn well know you have extra O-negative somewhere in that dank cave you call a lab." Another pause. "Whatever you say—just don't make me come over there and extract what I need from your still-beating heart, you vampire."

She smacked the Atman. An orderly crashed into me, toppling me forward into the nurses' station, knocking the breath out of my chest. Betty glanced up, and a relieved look crossed her eyes. But she blinked, and it was gone again.

"Joe! Where the hell have you been? We've already got fifteen pronounced, forty more well on their way."

"Fishing on my day off," I said. "I came as quickly as I could. Where to?"

"Come with me," she said.

We triaged. We treated. We saved. The trauma surgeons moved from room to room, and it was up to me to pick out the patients with the best promise of survival and get them prepped on the surgical tables. I had to focus, ignore the screams and the blood. We sorted some moaning patients on a crooked line for the O.N.K. exam. Some were already long gone—patients on gurneys with brains oozing out of shattered skulls, blood spurting from severed arteries. No medical advances could fix the most severe trauma, even at Saint Almachius. As I went along the rows of casualties, I cataloged the wounds and reconstructed the attack in my mind. But I focused on the evidence of what I saw—not the human tragedy playing out in front of me. I couldn't get bogged down in all that muck. From what I saw, and my previous experience, a theory emerged: a lone lunatic with an assault rifle, a barrage of gunfire announced with a few shrapnel explosives clustered close together in the stadium. Mostly younger people—some wearing whimsical uniforms, gold and green and glittering. One guy with a broken leg wore a fake mustache and a sleeveless camouflage shirt. His getup looked familiar, somehow. The guy looked like that Steelman character from that gameshow, the one where people did degrading things for money. Without judgment, I patched the guy up, and moved on.

"Did this happen at that gameshow?" I asked Betty as we approached the nurses' station for an updated list of the living and the dead.

"It was the tryouts for *How Low Can You Go*," she said. "As far as we know, one of the people who didn't make the cut pulled out a rifle and set off some improvised bombs at the stadium."

"*How Low Can You Go*—that show with the guy who bites snakes?" I said. "That's the one Mary watches."

"Everyone in America watches it except you, Joe. It's hilarious."

"I don't find it funny, either," croaked a voice from behind us.

A chair swiveled, and there sat Old Man Wetherspoon, an ancient telephone wedged between his head and bony shoulder, white hair in fluffy tufts like a crown.

"Neal, what are you…"

48

"All hands on deck," the Old Man said, cutting Barnes off. Lifting a glass of something brown to his face, he pointed with a finger toward the far corner of the room. "Go tend to these unfortunates. I'll get you the synthetic blood you need—some people owe me favors."

Betty and I looked at each other, then hurried off. As we reached the opposite end of the emergency room, we spotted a nook we hadn't seen before. Patients were spread on the floor. The Kraken was talking to one of them, a profusely bleeding man sitting with his back to the wall. Her eyes kept darting down from her Atman to the gaping wound in his abdomen, which dripped steadily onto the floor. But then something solid and fist-size slid out of the hole and plopped onto the ground next to him. The man sprawled, atop his own innards.

The Kraken turned away, heaved, and ran for the bathroom. With each step, splashes of her vomit slopped on the floor.

"What an amateur," Betty sneered. "Someone! Anyone! Clean up, east hallway!"

I stood there, watching the entire thing in disbelief. Even compared to the Bayonne Bloodbath, this was true horror. The man who had dropped at least half a kidney onto the floor was already dead. I made the tough call. I pointed to a little girl at the end of the room who was crying over her unconscious mother. Together we went over to the child, and I talked to her while Betty cleaned and stitched an open shrapnel gash on her leg. Orderlies hauled the mother to the front of the line for the O.N.K., where she was quickly pronounced dead, and zipped up in a clean white bag. I watched the girl be led out the door by the hand of someone from child services for a long moment. Another orphan being carried off into the foster system. I knew all too well what would come next. But I had no time to think those thoughts. So, I turned back to the line of patients.

Betty and I went from body to body for six hours. The sweat soaked through my shirt and tie, and then into my white coat. Old Man Wetherspoon worked the phones the entire time, completely ignoring the people inside the room, as he wrangled the extra blood and drugs needed from other hospitals. He succeeded in getting a truckload of O-negative natural blood shipped to Saint Almachius, and enlisted staffing reinforcements from Clara Maass Medical Center, who received only a fraction of the casualties in the incident, for some reason.

Blood, guts, agony, and suffering. It seemed like it would never end.

At last, an insidious quiet blanketed the hospital. Only the janitors' JiffySpiffs hummed on autopilot along the halls, and the stillness was broken only by the occasional outcry of a patient briefly sobering from painkillers. A final tally was taken. Forty-eight people dead, thirteen crippled, and two dozen seriously injured with bullet or shrapnel wounds. The wounded lolled about in drugged stupors or lay in comas, waiting in each of their rooms on the third floor for the final verdict. But hope remained for those still living. Some might even be able to walk again someday with the stem-cell treatments. The surgeons went to the breakroom to snort energy sticks while they waited for the next stitch to break, the next hemorrhage to turn critical.

Betty and I went up a floor and separated: she to the breakroom for a pick-me-up to continue her marathon shift, and I went right for my office, where I hung up my stethoscope after an extremely busy day off and swung the lucky test tube around my neck again. I sat at my computer terminal to check the updated hospital records. The Atman rang, and I picked it up by reflex.

"Hello."

"Yes, hello? Is this Dr. Barnes?" said a man with a wheezy tenor.

"Yes, this is Joe Barnes. Who is this?"

"Hi, Doc. It's Jim O'Keefe, reporter with *Newark FactSecond*. I wanted to ask you a few questions about the terrorist attack."

I pulled the Atman away from my head, cursed softly, then put it back to my ear.

"Terrorist attack?" I said. "Where?"

"The stadium attack. A source told me it's the work of the Intifada in retaliation against one of the groups for the war."

"What source? What group?" I said. "And which war?"

A silence. I could hear the reporter's ragged breathing on the other end.

"An eyewitness told me. It doesn't matter who my source is—that's why I came to you," said O'Keefe. "I need to find out what's going on. I need to confirm the rumors. That's my job."

"I can appreciate you doing your job," I said. "But you're doing a terrible job at your job. Listen, I don't know about what happened, who did it, or why it was done. I don't think it was terrorism, based on the carnage. In my professional opinion it looks like the February one—the massacre down the road there in Hudson County."

"The Bayonne Bloodbath?"

"That's what you called it in the headlines. I'm not calling it that."

I sighed. The reporter was a total moron, totally craven. But he did have a job to do. I could give him at least the basic updates, to make sure the right information got out there.

"I can tell you that we have almost fifty people pronounced here," I said. "And there are a few dozen more who aren't out of the woods yet. I'm just hoping the stem-cell boosters we gave them, and the surgeries and the stitches, keep them together until the bodies can heal. It looks like they will recover."

I could hear the beeps in the background as the reporter recorded the phone call. O'Keefe wouldn't even write an actual story. He'd just play the clip of the interview, like most reporters did. This I was fine with—at the very least, it eliminated the possibility of being misquoted.

"You said that a few dozen are expected to die?" the reporter asked.

"No, I said a few dozen are expected to live. Forty-eight have already died."

"Oh." He coughed. "That's an important distinction."

"Yes. The most important distinction of all," I said.

"What else can you tell me?" O'Keefe said.

"Nothing. We can talk in the morning. Try the Newark police about the stadium."

"Alright. I'll call them, but…"

I hung up. I ran my hand over my scalp. I had had enough of answering questions and solving problems for the day. It was time to get back home to my Mary. The Atman rang again. But I hung my coat, turned off the lights, and walked out.

I went to the breakroom to check on the trauma surgeons. Earlier I had heard the four trauma surgeons telling jokes, swapping stories and comparing notes on the patients, occasionally cracking an energy stick. But now all was quiet. I stepped inside—and immediately saw why. The quartet sat at the same table, around the light from someone's Atman. But they were rigid in their chairs, their heads all turned in the same direction off into the shadows, where a dark figure stood at the sink, banging things. Something metal clattered on the ground, there was a man's voice cursing, and then there was a ripping sound. I approached the surgeons' table, put my hand on the shoulder of one Dr. Stuart Rothenberg, who leapt out of his chair at my touch. He grabbed my sleeve and pulled me down toward him.

"My god, Barnes," Rothenberg whispered. "This man is a lunatic, a danger to everybody."

"Who?" I asked.

"Aye, the night-shift man," whispered Paddy McDermott, the Irish-born Almachius trauma surgeon at the table. "The creepy fuck, he is. Walks in here, without a word to anyone, goes over there, cuts the lights, and starts smashing and bashing things. The knacker."

The two other surgeons, reinforcements from Clara Maass, nodded.

"Did anyone ask him what he's doing?" I said.

"Stuart said something to him about twenty minutes ago. But your man didn't answer. It's like he's in some kind of trance, the freaky fuck," McDermott said.

"The man is a menace, an absolute nut," Rothenberg said.

"I'll talk to the guy," I said, stepping toward the figure. "He's going to have his hands full tonight."

The silhouette came clearer into view, as my eyes adjusted to the dark. The man was standing over the sink, scrubbing furiously at something. I saw the suds flying. I considered approaching and placing a hand on the man's shoulder, but decided better of it. Best not to startle someone who may be holding something sharp at the sink, I realized. Instead I drifted to the other side of the counter, a row of switches near the appliances and the fridge. With a sweep of my hand, the lights for the whole room popped on. Culling stood there, soap dripping, squinting in the new brightness. In his hand was a soaking piece of fabric.

"Hey, Chuck," I said, in my most jovial voice. "What are you up to?"

Culling stood, blinking. For a moment he seemed stunned, like a wild animal caught in headlights. But he shook his head and rumpled the wet fabric.

"Stain on my overalls. Figured I'd work on it a bit before my shift started," Culling said.

"In the dark, ye knacker?" McDermott called out.

"Fluorescent paint. It's actually easier to see in the dark," Culling said, turning to face the darkened panel of surgeons, then turning to the sink. He shrugged nonchalantly. "You bloody mick bastard."

"You bloody—" McDermott shouted, rising from his chair. But the other surgeons leapt to restrain him, shouts erupting. Culling and I were only the ones who hadn't moved.

"Why fluorescent paint?" I asked, raising my voice amid the scuffle.

Culling put the white togs down on the rim of the sink. He turned to face me.

"What is this, twenty questions? My shift doesn't start for another fifteen minutes," Culling said. He placed his sponge next to the overalls and folded his arms on his chest. "What do you really want, doctor?"

I scratched my head, taken aback by the nurse's hostility.

"Just wanted to prepare you for tonight, Chuck. Don't know if you heard about the massacre today."

"I heard something. Innocent people dead. Totally tragic. Et cetera."

Without a change in expression, Culling turned back to the sink, picked up the sponge and the fabric, and started scrubbing again. Something about his body language was off. After a moment's pause, I kept talking.

"It was even worse than February. What some people call the Bayonne Bloodbath," I said. "But you weren't here for that one."

"No, I was not. But we got some of the spillover at my last place. Most of them ended up dying." He scrubbed harder, grimacing downward at his garment. "Lots of sepsis. It was filthy. Disgusting, actually."

I nodded slowly.

"This should be a bit easier, since we took care of most of the initial triage. You just have to keep them alive overnight."

Culling stopped scrubbing, looked at me. His eyes were beady, black, glinting. I could see absolutely nothing in them, like they were those of a wild beast.

"I'll do what I can. That's all I promise."

"That's all any of us can promise."

I flicked off the row of light switches, casting the room back into darkness, and I walked away. As I passed, McDermott's hands gripped the table, his reddened face twisted in a grimace, as his colleagues held his arms.

"Relax, Jerry," said Rothenberg.

"I'll knock that racist fuck's teeth in," McDermott barked, his brogue nearly unintelligible, except for the clear consonants.

As I let the door shut behind me, I heard voices, hateful hissings. They came from around the corner, near the patient rooms. I stepped quietly in that direction. The voices grew louder and more insistent the closer I got. Finally, I reached one of the nurse docking stations at the eastern side of the hospital, when I could make out two voices. The growl of Wetherspoon sparred with the nasty tics of the Kraken. I stopped at the corner to listen.

"…and can't have doctors going around checking on patients whenever they feel like it. It's against the law," she said.

"You're wrong, you've always been wrong, and you'll kill people," Wetherspoon said. "If we don't allow our nurses and doctors full access…"

"Take it up with the Bureau, Neal," the Kraken said.

"It's terrifying that you're in charge of a hospital, you bureaucratic mouthbreather."

The Kraken gasped. I bit my fist to keep from bursting into laughter.

"And furthermore, your hiring practices leave something to be desired," Wetherspoon continued. "For God's sake, Suzanne, you hired that new night-shift nurse, Culling, with that track record? The people at Clara Maass called him Florence the Nightmare."

"I don't even know what that stupid nickname means. He's got a better track record than some of the doctors here," she said. "Better than your golden boy Barnes."

My innards upended at the mention of my name. I closed my eyes. I didn't want to be drawn into this battle of wills. But Wetherspoon just laughed.

"You're delusional. Joe might be the best young doctor on staff," Wetherspoon said. "Even as the supposed boss, you can't just create elaborate fictions."

"Your golden boy. I've got something he may regret," Kraken said, something jangling, and I knew it was the portable drive she'd taken from me.

A moment of silence. I listened, my heart hammering.

"Oh—is that all?" said Wetherspoon. "Well look here, Suzanne."

Something jangled hugely, like windchimes in a gale. Wetherspoon cackled.

"Take a good long look," the Old Man said, "because you'll never get them. And I'll make sure that every ethical doctor and every ethical nurse in this hospital rebels against you every moment of every day if you prevent them from doing their jobs. You stupendous twit."

I could hear the shuffling steps of the Old Man moving down the hallway. I leaned around the corner and saw Wetherspoon walking to the far end, toward the east stairs. The Kraken shook her fists at his back.

"This is the last time, you old bastard," she called out after him. "You think you're untouchable. But I'll have you kicked out and pensionless so fast your head'll spin…"

Wetherspoon kept walking, his gait growing exaggerated and defiant, as her voice harangued him. But I didn't wait to gloat. I turned and rushed back the way I'd come.

I walked past the patient rooms. In one nearest the end, a figure drifted in the darkness. Who could be in there, stalking a patient's room without a light? I stared for a second, then knocked. A pause. The shadow moved.

The door cracked open, and Culling's face leered out at me.

"Can I help you, doctor?" he said softly, his eyes blank underneath the severe Caligula bangs, the bulbous cranium.

"I just want to know why you were walking around in the darkness in a patient's room," I said. "This is not Almachius policy."

Culling stepped outside the room, and then door clicked shut behind. He put his thin hands together in front of his chest, like in prayer. He blinked, long and slow, like a lizard in winter.

"That's one of the recovering patients," the nurse said. "In fact, she's doing so well all she needs is sleep. I left the lights off while I checked the terminal, so I wouldn't wake her."

"What's her name? The prognosis?"

"Nancy," the nurse said. "Substitute French teacher at a local high school. Shrapnel wound to the chest. The hemorrhage stopped two hours ago."

Sounds reasonable, I thought, remembering the patient. We had barely saved her. Still, the night-shift cretin stalking the darkness without supervision was…unacceptable. Alarming, somehow.

"Leave the terminal light on at least, Chuck," I said. "You know—the lamp next to the medicine cabinet. There needs to be light in case something happens. It's hospital policy."

Culling leaned back on the closed door.

"A little light's not going to help the patient sleep," the nurse murmured, crossing his arms.

"Just turn the light on. And leave it on," I said. "Please."

Culling shrugged, hit a button on his Atman, and the room inside was filled with a soft glow. The woman in the bed stirred, her eyes fluttering under her wrinkled eyelids. She moaned in a druggy stupor. The nurse let the door shut. Together we walked to the next doorway.

"You know," Culling said, putting his Atman back in his pocket, "I will never understand how everyone needs lights on all the time. When I was a kid, you had to learn to conquer your fear of the darkness. To feel and listen, instead of just seeing around you."

The nurse swiped his Atman and ducked into the new room. He moved over to the bedside, to a young dude with a thin moustache and no sleeves. From outside the doorway I recognized the patient as the celebrity from the TV show, *How Low Can You Go*. Joe Steelman looked exactly as he did on the screen, except without his trademark sunglasses. Tattoos like inky tentacles swirled up from the collar of his gown to the edges of his jaw, stopping just short of his oversized head, which was still fixed in the cynical smirk that had so captivated American audiences for the past six weeks. I couldn't hear anything through the soundproof window. Steelman spoke hurriedly, gesturing madly with his hands, evidently dissatisfied with some aspect of his care. Nodding, Culling walked to the terminal and tapped the screen.

Room 371. I made a mental note of the celebrity patient's location, then went down to the front entrance. Culling was not the best person to be caring for these patients in need—but we needed every pair of hands we had, in that moment of necessity.

Cameras followed me on my way out. As I walked from the hospital back out to my car and topped off my tank at the natural gas port, I reminded myself to check on the two patients—the substitute French teacher and the celebrity—first thing in the morning.

The ultrahighway was choked with traffic. The sun sank behind the office buildings on the hilltops, aglow in the smog. The holographic billboards twinkled in the twilight. I sat in silence, gripping the steering wheel, watching the other drivers talk to themselves, pick their noses, watch TV.

My body ached—that bone-jarring numbness of a day pushed to the furthest limits of stress and exertion. I'd felt it before—after the Bayonne Bloodbath, back in February. In the aftermath of that massacre, Betty and I had managed to save at least a dozen more patients than could have been considered possible. By the end of that fifteen-hour winter's day, I could barely lift my arms to drive. But I had felt an undeniable satisfaction glowing within, knowing I'd beaten those odds.

This was different. After New Jersey's single worst slaughter since the Great Purge, I felt nothing but disquiet. Betty and I, along with the other nurses and doctors and trauma surgeons, had achieved the impossible. We'd done the undoable, salvaged the unsalvageable. We'd beaten even greater odds than those of Bayonne. But there were so many we couldn't save. The faces of my parents, the dead stares on those dirty gurneys just hours before, came to me—and mingled with those other dead faces of a night so long ago when I was left an orphan.

And somewhere deep inside, there was a feeling, the overwhelming dread, that something was amiss. I clenched the steering wheel tightly.

I turned the radio on, which had two men bickering about something while a third person egged them on. I couldn't follow the debate. It was something about European politics. But my brain was spent. I turned it off and called Mary to ask her to stick the beef-flavored instant tofu in the microwave. No time to give in to thoughts of the past—or a sense of impending doom. I waited for the traffic to clear on the high-speed ultrahighway ahead.

THE MAN, THE WOMAN, THE GIRL

U.S.A., 2087

Everywhere, water crashing. Everywhere, all around. I coughed, I gagged, I choked.

No air, anywhere.

The river flowed around me, through me. Stuck fast in the midst of the current, I was heavy and unmoving as a rock. I couldn't breathe. I saw nothing through the rushing gloom. The dark flow swirled through the unseeing cracks of my eyes and my notch of a mouth. No air. It broke me apart inside, splitting me, washing away fragment after fragment in its turbulence. Something came at me through the murk. Some shape waggled toward me on the current—impossibly fast, dark, growing. No air. I tried to raise my hands to defend myself, but I had no arms. No limbs at all. A gaping mouth—bigger than me, bigger than anything in the world—came at me and swallowed all light.

"…and the Department of Homeland Security has increased its Nuclear Warning to Mauve, in the wake of the Pyongyang Summit and the tensions within the East Asian Federation. Twenty-four-hour fighter-interceptor flights over Korea begin at noon today local time.

"In other news…"

Saxas spoke from deep within the Atman's alarm function. I gasped in the bedroom air greedily. My tired eyes opened and shut. I could not move. The newscaster's voice kept on rattling off the state of decay in the world—untiring, automatic, relentless.

"…and in New Jersey, the gunman who shot up an audition for *How Low Can You Go* at the Lockheed-Martin Center is still at large. The police are withholding all details about the investigation, under the Freedom of Justice Act," Saxas said.

The broadcast abruptly cut to the sounds of gunfire: an advertisement for a weapons manufacturer.

I sat up in bed and flicked the radio off. Mary breathed under the covers, the gust of her Dormus mask the only sound in the room. I leaned down and kissed her soft brow. Then I turned and hobbled to the bathroom.

Forty minutes later I was in my crispest suit, and I cracked an energy stick into my black coffee. Mary appeared at the doorway, rubbing bleary eyes.

"How are you, hon?" she asked, kissing my cheek, brushing past me to the sink.

"Fine, I guess," I said. "Going to be a huge day. All those victims from yesterday." She sipped her water, smacking her lips.

"I'm going to the gym for a couple training appointments. Make a few bucks while I still can, before I get too big to do anything active. I'm swinging by Almachius at noon for my first check-up with Abbud. Don't forget," she said.

"The guards will probably let you in," I said, stepping close, pulling her to me. I gave her a sly look. "You don't look too threatening."

She held a hand over her womb, the outline of her camouflage-patterned nightie. She shook her head, her braids swinging around her shoulders.

"Yeah, I'm pretty unassuming for a Force Recon vet of three tours abroad," she said, poking me playfully in the chest. "But seriously. Make sure you're there. I'm a little nervous."

"I'll be there, dear."

She straightened my tie and collar like she always did and patted the side of my face.

"Okay. Go save some lives, superdoc." She finally kissed me.

I couldn't help but smile. I loved this woman. I picked up my briefcase, then walked to the front door. Outside I started the car and drove off. Saxas' voice accompanied me the entire way, describing a meeting between China, Korea, and Japan in East Asia, complete with a surprise appearance by the U.S. Vice President to help broker the negotiations. She described the ongoing missing-persons epidemic and the results of the second episode of the seventh season of *How Low Can You Go*. The show must go on, and the program will continue, she said. Finally, she spoke of the massacre at the stadium that had interrupted the star-studded competition.

"The *Newark FactSecond* reports that some one-hundred people were killed, but seventy-five are recovering at the hospital," Saxas' voice said.

"That lying bastard," I snarled, pounding the steering wheel.

I replayed the conversation between O'Keefe and myself in my mind. But before I could totally recall everything I'd said, my stomach sank in horror—as my own voice erupted from the speakers.

"But…a terrible job. Listen—I…know about what happened. I…think it was terrorists, based on the carnage. But I can tell you…the stem boosters that we gave them, and the surgeries and the stitches…keep them together until the bodies can heal," my voice said, unnaturally stilted.

The car nearly swerved off the road as I shook with rage. It was my voice, sure. But my words were chopped up, rearranged, perverted.

It was total bullshit. It was libel.

"The police have deferred comment on the terrorist claims, saying the investigation remains privileged under the terms of FOJA. In other news…"

I called Lanza on my Atman.

"Hey, bro," Lanza said.

"I'm going to kill that reporter," I blurted.

"Don't ever tell a cop you're going to kill somebody," Lanza said. "It's not smart."

"Somebody has to take this guy to task," I said. "He just chopped up audio of what I said and remixed it for their soundbite on the news. The national fucking news."

"There's a lesson to be learned here," Lanza said. "Don't talk to the press. Ever. Beware the pen, no matter how dull it is. I learned that in the academy. You best just let this one go, Joe."

We hung up. I pulled into the hospital parking lot. I braked, slowing to a crawl in front of the mob of TV cameras and stunningly beautiful women in suits with low-cut tops—the glamorous reporters for the New York news stations. This opportunistic horde made the trek across the river for each mass-casualty shooting, explosion, and tragic drowning of a child the hospital treated. Everything else in New Jersey went ignored. (All their reporting all got funneled to the Saxas broadcasts anyway, and most would remain unused). These bottom feeders were the last people I needed to speak with. They made O'Keefe seem like an ethical pillar of the community. I hit a button and my window started to roll up.

"Doctor, Doctor," said one of them, a blonde Asian woman in a leopard-print, two-piece suit that bared her midriff, as her heels clattered up to my driver's side, "can you give us a status update on the victims of the terrorist attack?"

"No," I said, the window shutting just as the newscaster thrust her microphone in the gap in the window. I rolled forward a few feet, she shrieked, her arm caught inside. I braked and opened the window enough for her to pull her hand back. Before she could jab the microphone in again, I punched the accelerator, tires screeching, careening around the corner of the hospital. I sped along the delivery road the wrong way, praying no trucks would come. I lucked out—the coast was clear. I parked at the end of the administration lot, a little spot in the shade near the biohazard dumpsters of amputated limbs and expended guts. I only parked in that spot in the gravest emergencies.

I hadn't been back there in more than a year, and I was surprised to notice a new hatch in the building's foundation, shiny and silver. The Bureau seal was emblazoned on it. A sign said "Bureau of Wellness—Special Deliveries" above it.

I stopped and stared. Why would the Bureau need its own chute at the back of the hospital? Since when did they do anything more than hinder the work of real doctors? They never provided anything that needed to be delivered—and particularly nothing "special." The chute looked like it descended to the basement. I tugged on the steel handle. It wouldn't budge. It had to be some kind of new access portal for the pharmaceutical corporations. I stared for a second longer, then walked around the front of Saint Almachius.

I ducked in the front door, behind the TV crews who still faced toward the ultrahighway, waiting for an interview from somebody, anybody. They had forgotten me already.

Inside the hospital, a surreal scene lay before me. I breathed slowly, even though my heart raced.

The hallways of the intensive care unit were lined with gurneys. On each was a body covered in a white sheet, the nose poking up like a tiny peak on a long and morbid mountain range. Dozens of them, the massacre victims who had been alive and sleeping peacefully just hours earlier. Echoes of my footsteps resounded down the long hallway. From far-off, a heart-rate monitor beeped, and a machine rolled somewhere on rickety wheels with a clackity-click-clack. My heart thumped so hard I could hear it. I walked down the west corridor, made a right at the nurses' station, looking for any living person. There was no one. I pulled up one of the sheets. I saw a young face. Red contusions ran down either cheek, with streaks of yellow and green in there, too—it was facepaint. She was a young brunette, maybe sixteen or so. A cute button nose, a pert mouth, dry staring eyes. Dead as a doornail. I replaced the sheet over that face.

I went from one sheet to another. The fifth or sixth was the body of the substitute French teacher, Nancy, alive in bed the night before, now with that same blank void across her face. I stood rooted to that hospital floor, unable to move with all the death surrounding me, taunting me despite my best efforts to have preserved life.

A hand fell on my shoulder. I jumped, and Betty Bathory's haggard face was there behind me, staring down at the body. She pulled the cover ever so slightly back, exposing the pale curve of the substitute French teacher's collarbone, and near her armpit, a blood-soaked bandage which had dried brown.

"What happened?" I said.

"Of twenty-four alive last night, twenty-two dead. The other two are in grave condition," she said.

"Jesus, why?" I said.

She put her hands atop her head.

"We have no idea," she said. "The O.N.K. can't tell us anything."

"They were fine last night. We had them stabilized," I said.

"I know," she said. "And we have no idea."

A door burst open at the end of the hallway, and a squad of nurses and doctors like a mismatched defensive line wheeled a body toward the elevator. Without a word, I hurried after them. The group had emerged from Room 371 and rushed down to the trauma surgeons—I saw the hurried efficiency of their steps, heard their insistent voices barking directions. I caught up with them just as the elevator doors started to close, but between them I caught a glimpse of the celebrity Joe Steelman, beady eyes bulging bloody red, moustache twitching, tattooed arms convulsing under fastened straps. He looked like a cartoon character about to burst his celluloid seams.

I rushed back to Room 371. I swiped my Atman, then walked in. The smell of something burnt—candlewick?—stung my nostrils. The bed was rumpled. Spots of faded blood spattered the pillow. I canvassed the room, scanning for something, anything. The O'Neill-Kane wouldn't be able to determine cause of death in this case, I was already sure of that. Two dozen people stable and recovering from moderate trauma—and every single one of them dies overnight. For it all to happen in one wave of medical disaster was…impossible. This was not a single biological fluke, a microscopic blood clot exploding a crucial artery or a brain lobe swelling to a catastrophic pop against a rigid skull. The O.N.K. would find something like that very easily, something that physiologically ostentatious. No, something had happened that could not be explained by simple biology alone. I had to know what it was.

I went to the room's terminal. I felt in my pocket, remembering suddenly that my portable drive had been confiscated by the Kraken. I needed to inspect the records immediately, before I lost my nerve. I heard the unmistakable squeak of Betty Bathory's sneakers come up behind. I turned slightly and held my hand out.

"Betty, give me your portable drive," I said.

"But Joe, we—"

"The drive, goddammit," I said. "I need it now."

A second's pause. I swallowed hard. The drive fell in my hand. Her sneakers squealed as she rounded the door and went out, her footsteps hard and angry. In that moment, I didn't care.

I logged into the terminal, bypassing the security with the hacker's code on the flash drive. Once again, the screen opened up before me: the entire patient history, the color-coded tests, treatments, diagnoses, and prognoses. It was a personal history without compare.

Joe Steelman's real name had been Joseph Harry Dugash, and he had been a diabetic. But aside from that, the mild obesity and the controlled hepatitis, the 34-year-old celebrity was in good health. The records went further, too. A tab on the side of the screen opened to a background account—education (tenth grade), marital status (divorced three times, four kids), and even a criminal record (shoplifting and marijuana misdemeanors). His profession was listed simply as "celebrity." The medical risks of biting a poisonous snake to death on live national TV for money were not included. But everything else seemed to be: I had never seen such a thorough patient record at the hospital. I clicked through to the most recent updates.

And there, at the bottom edge of the screen, was the entry that bottomed out my stomach.

A person named Shiro Ishii had visited the room before dawn for three minutes, departing without administering any drugs, or logging any activity.

I scanned the records for more data. But there was none, beyond that ghostly visit. A chill crept along my skin. I logged out of the terminal, pulled out the drive, and walked around the room. I scrutinized everything, down to each floor tile. A partial footprint of a surgical booty was smeared in some dirt. I reached under the bed, felt around in the dust. My fingers closed around something soft. I cringed.

And I yanked out...a tattered label. Identical to the one I'd found after Cruzen died. I recognized the same serial number prefix: BOW-137. My brow furrowed. I pocketed it and stood. I strode to the door. I needed to collect my thoughts, understand what was happening here.

I rushed toward my office. But the elevator just pinged, and just as I turned the corner, a set of footsteps echoed against my own in the dead silence of the hospital corridors. I quickened my pace, but the steps hurried after me. I rounded the corner just as the person caught up to me.

"Dr. Barnes!"

I turned around slowly. Standing before me was a gesturing Suzanne Kranklein. She approached, finger wagging like a scolding mother. I jammed my hands in my pockets and braced myself. This time she wouldn't steal anything from me.

"Barnes—what were you thinking, giving an interview to that reporter? Even the nurses know not to talk to that idiot Jim O'Keefe."

"Suzanne, the guy edited the hell out of that interview. He erased some words, spliced the others together to make the whole thing convey the opposite of what I actually said."

She crossed her own arms, staring down at the floor, running her foot along a crack in the floor. Her movement was slow, and deliberate. I steeled myself for whatever may come next.

"I believe you, Barnes. I really do. He did that once to your precious mentor. Wetherspoon got so burned once, he retired for the third time. But that doesn't change the fact that the hospital looks really bad right now. So, I have a suggestion."

I looked at her. The softer tone of Kraken was well-known and feared throughout the hospital. Whenever she seemed to relax, it was simply the executioner's calm, the deep breath before the beheading. I had heard it during my time on the night shift, when I'd seen the same cool fall of the axe time and again on some hapless doctor, nurse or orderly. She stared at the corpse, pausing for effect.

"What do you suggest?" I said.

She smiled. That wan, bloodless smile.

Ten minutes later, I walked out the front door of the hospital, my tie askew. My face was reddened and I could feel a burning sensation as my boss' words rang again and again through my ears as I approached a tiny podium with a big microphone in my face. The crush of reporters closed in on me. There were flashes, the cameras pointed and focused. I blinked repeatedly. O'Keefe was at the front of the line, the loudest voice in the chorus—although the leopard-print woman was trying to elbow around him, shoving her microphone Atman up from the huddle. They would not stop until their questions were answered. So I took the plunge, as the Kraken had instructed me.

"Ask away," I said, nodding at the crowd.

"Dr. Barnes, is it true all the patients from the *How Low Can You Go* audition died overnight?" said O'Keefe, his voice high and raspy.

"We still have one hanging on, but yes, we've lost all the others," I said, rubbing at my eye. "We don't yet know the cause of death."

"What's the cause of death?" said one of the voices at the back of the crowd.

I shook my head, bit my lip. I couldn't say what I wanted to say, that much had been made clear to me by the Kraken.

"I just told you, we don't know the cause of death, or whether there's a link between the patients. The investigation is still underway."

"How is Joe Steelman doing? What is he wearing?"

"We can't confirm that Joe Steelman was one of the injured in the attack," I said, nodding, trying to sound as official as Lanza had always advised me to be. "I'm sure the TV network will issue a press release shortly. If he was a patient here, he would be issued a standard hospital gown. That's what he'd be wearing. Next question."

"What about the terrorism link you made in the interview with the *Newark FactSecond* yesterday? Do you feel like you have egg on your face?" said an older woman, the only person without a microphone, the only one taking notes directly on her Atman.

I shook my head.

"Someone has egg on their face, but it isn't me." I pointed down at O'Keefe, my finger a foot away from the hack's nose. "You all might want to ask your colleague here about his journalistic ethics."

O'Keefe's neck turned red, but he kept his head down and kept fiddling with his Atman. The coward couldn't even look at me. The blonde Asian woman seized the momentary lapse, muscling past him and positioning herself right in front of me.

"You know, doctor, you assaulted a reporter—namely, me—in the parking lot about an hour ago. Do you have anything to say for yourself?"

She half turned from me and vamped at the camera, pouting her botox-plump lips.

"I'll let you know if I ever decide to sue for harassment and maybe file a restraining order against TV reporters who attack my car," I said. "Next question?"

The woman kept speaking to her camera, recording her broadcast without a hitch; she had not heard me. I looked across the crowd.

"Unless there are any more questions, I think we'll conclude for today," I said.

O'Keefe's hand went up. His face had regained its natural pallor. But he still wouldn't look me square in the face.

"I've got one, doc," the hack said. "Were these overnight deaths at the hospital accidental? Were they avoidable?"

"An investigation is underway," I said. "Cause and manner of death have yet to be determined."

"But why did they die, doc?"

I smiled and stepped away from the microphone, waving my arms and bringing the press conference to an end. The throng tried to accompany me into the hospital, but the automatic rotating door brushed them all away. All, that is, except for O'Keefe, who clung to my side like a damned pilot fish.

"Mr. O'Keefe," I said, walking toward the front desk where the two security guards were sitting. "I thought we made it clear. No press inside the hospital when an emergency lockdown's in effect."

"Seeing as how every victim of the massacre is dead, I figure the emergency's over," the reporter told me.

"One patient is still alive."

"Yeah, wonder how long Steelman lasts," O'Keefe said, tugging on my white sleeve. "Doc, this is the story of a lifetime. I couldn't have made up a story this good."

I stopped.

"I bet you could have made up a pretty good one, considering," I said. I narrowed my eyes at him. "You completely edited that soundbite. Why did you do that to me?"

"Can't let the facts get in the way of a good story," the reporter whispered conspiratorially. He nudged my elbow. "Anyway—you should just let me come up and get some visual footage of the scene for my voiceover. What do you say?"

"I'll have to pass," I said, turning toward Stash and Stanislaw, the security guards. "Fellas, please escort Mr. O'Keefe out."

I kept walking on, passing between the gigantic figures of the guards, who lumbered toward the reporter.

"I could make it worth your while, doc," O'Keefe said, as the guards plucked him up by the arms and hauled him like a stuffed doll backward toward the door. "A TV show—the medical mystery of Saint Almachius, probed by Doctor-Detective Joe Barnes. They could make a sitcom. A reality show—solving the riddle of the death of Joe Steelman. The stations would have a bidding war. Millions would watch!"

But he was already thrown inside the revolving door and spat outside the hospital. I watched as O'Keefe was swallowed up in the dispersing crowd. The two security guards trudged back to the desk, their muscled gait stiff. The decorative waterfall behind them gushed down.

"Thanks, guys. I owe you lunch," I said.

"No problem, doc. Just doing our job," Stash said.

"You should come out to happy hour," Stanislaw said. "If your wife will let you." The guards laughed, grunting and elbowing each other.

"She will. One of these days," I said. "Hey—what's that?"

Three police cars careened into the parking lot. The reporters fluttered away like seagulls fleeing a group of children. A van pulled up behind the cars; the words "Crime Scene Unit" were written on the side in squared red letters. The cops exited the cars, and among the uniforms, I immediately recognized Lanza as he gestured at the lingering blonde reporter, yelled at her, then pointed toward the ultrahighway. The journalist scurried off on her stiletto heels. As the group strode to the hospital door, Lanza bumped shoulders with O'Keefe, who toppled into some bushes on the side of the walkway, dropping his case and his hat and keys. Lanza seemed not to notice. The six policemen awkwardly cycled, one by one, through the revolving entryway. Lanza led the way straight up to me. We nodded formally at each other.

"Doctor," he said, holding out his hand.

"Detective," I said, shaking hands with him first and then with each of the cops in turn. I turned again to Lanza. "To what do I owe this honor? I figured you'd still be busy with the crime scene over at the stadium."

"Nah, the feds are taking care of that one now, since whoever it was used an illegal German assault rifle," Lanza said. "And anyway, someone anonymously called us with a tip that the people who died overnight didn't die accidentally."

I stopped. I nodded over my shoulder.

"I've been wondering that myself. Follow me. I'll show you to the ICU."

I swiped my Atman, and we waited for the elevator. I looked at Lanza.

"Who's this anonymous tipster?" I said, blinking at them.

"Honestly," said the grayheaded cop whose uniform said he was a captain, "whoever it was sounded like an absolute nutjob. Somebody with a scratchy throat, using a voice scrambler. But Lanza mentioned you had called with your concern about one of the deaths at the hospital here a few nights ago. So we decided to come take a look."

"Protocol," Lanza said, nodding.

A thunder of footsteps echoed in the distance—growing quicker, louder, harder, closer. From the central corridor burst Rothenberg and McDermott, the trauma surgeons. They ran as fast as they could, donuts in their mouths, bellies bouncing, lidless coffees slopping onto the floor. They rushed toward the emergency room.

"Hey guys," I called out. "What's happening?"

Rothenberg spun around, pulled the donut out of his mouth, and banged backwards through the swinging door.

"The last of the patients is coding," he yelled.

"The celebrity?" I called out.

I got no response. The doctors disappeared. I trotted toward the door, too. The cops were at my heels as I pushed through them. The patient was at the far side of the circular room, and the two surgeons were swinging on their gowns, calling out commands. Three nurses and four specialists were grouped around the gurney like chess pieces, as the machines beeped and rattled, then flatlined. I got a glimpse through the crowd and saw that the patient was none other than Joe Steelman. He had lasted longer than I had expected. The cops and I watched as the doctors used electricity, blood transfusions, tubes, and spongy cloths to try and bring the celebrity back to life. At one point, everything slowed, grew quiet. The sudden silence seemed to bode well. But then the patient started convulsing. Rothenberg pinned him down and barked for McDermott to crack open the ribcage and to try and work directly on the sputtering heart. But he stopped midsentence; the seizure had stopped. Rothenberg brought his ear close to the patient's head. The surgeon tensed, listening intently. Two seconds later, the electrocardiogram droned. The two surgeons stepped away as the nurses brought in the paddles and tried to shock the cardiac muscle back into a rhythm. I stepped back, aware the final reckoning for Joseph Harry Dugash had come, right at the peak of his hard-earned fame.

"Detective," I said to Lanza, who was staring at the face of the fresh corpse. "I can show you the rooms. Most of the other bodies are up there."

"Uh-huh," Lanza said, not blinking, unable to tear his gaze away. "You know…I've never seen anyone die in the hospital before. It's so…clean."

"A bit cleaner than a desert battlefield, I'd guess. But you get the same sloppy result down in a six-foot hole, ultimately."

Lanza nodded, saying nothing more.

The surgeons came out from a curtain, pulling off their gloves with snaps of latex, tossing them in the trash by the wall, then pulling their masks down. Rothenberg stopped in front of me and glared.

"You know someone named Meruda?" he asked.

"Never heard of them. Is that a Latino name?" I said.

"No idea. That's what the patient just said," the surgeon said, shaking his head, the mask dangling at his collar. "I've never seen anything like it before. The guy was dead to rights, no pulse, then his eyes open and he says one word: 'Meruda.' It was barely a whisper, I had to lean in just to hear it."

The surgeon wiped at his hairy hands and arms with a chemical towel.

"That never happens. I've never seen someone die, come back just to say something, then code again."

"Strange," I said. "You have any idea what happened to all these patients?"

"No idea, Joe," Rothenberg said, pulling him a step away from the cops, toward the nursing station in the unit. He looked in both directions, leaned in close to me. His voice dropped to a whisper. "It's too weird to be a coincidence—all those people. But I have no idea what happened overnight. We would have found poison right away, or at least traces of something. The O.N.K. would have found anything in the diagnostic codes. Wouldn't it?"

"No idea, Stuart," I said. "But there is one person who keeps showing up right before patients die, according to the terminals."

"Who?"

"Shiro Ishii."

"Shiro Ishii? Excuse me?"

"A Japanese doctor supposedly on our staff. Or rather, somebody masquerading as a Japanese doctor on our staff," I said. "Maybe it's the angel of death, I don't know. I'm just glad the cops showed up, just in case we're overlooking something."

"Cops are never a good idea," Rothenberg whispered, his eyes darting both directions. He tossed another chemical rag in the trash. "But I've never heard of any Dr. Ishii. Just help them where you can and keep the hospital out of it as much as possible. Namaste, Joe."

The trauma surgeon bowed quickly and stepped away. I walked back to the cops, who were huddled close together. Lanza stared at the corpse of Joe Steelman, as if trying to will him back to life. I patted my friend on the shoulder.

"The man was a visionary," Lanza said, shaking his head, staring at the celebrity corpse. "I don't know if the U.S. will even medal in hot-dog eating at the Olympics without him. And no one else has the courage to bite poisonous snakes— at least no one still alive."

"This way, officers," I said, ignoring him. I tilted my head toward the elevators. "I'll show you the rest."

"Lead the way, doctor," said the grayheaded captain, motioning for them to continue on.

We entered the elevator in silence. Inside, I swiped my Atman. On the third floor, we exited and the cops' bootsteps echoed down the hallway as we neared the line of shrouded bodies along the wall. I lifted the first sheet for them to see; it was the face of a teenaged girl, her eyes open, a tinge of blood smeared along her lips. The youngest of the cops tapped into the device on his wrist. Lanza moved to the next sheet, lifted it, and discovered an elderly man whose mouth hung open, gray and cavernous. Lanza took a small flashlight from his breast pocket, stuck it in the fatty folds of the man's chins, and shut the jaw. But when he removed it, the mouth dropped open again, jiggling the neck's rolls. I walked over and whisked back another sheet. This one was a middle-aged man, wearing a bloodstained rainbow beanie. The other four cops fanned out and investigated all the bodies: children, parents, grandparents, an infant curled like a bloodless little bean on a gurney near the end of the line.

The captain took one glance at the tiny body and covered it again.

"Doc, may I ask what we're looking for?" the captain asked, approaching me.

"We don't know. The O.N.K. says these people just died from natural causes," I said, scratching my chin. "But that makes no sense—it's like they all died of old age in one night. They were stable and recovering after we patched them up. Most weren't even hurt that badly."

"Alright," the captain said. "We'll play this by the book. I'll download the records, take them to headquarters. Doc, you keep playing detective here and let us know what you find."

"Absolutely," I said, pointing at the wall terminal. "Take whatever you need."

The captain went to the wall, opened the glass cabinet with a special Bureau-issued law enforcement key, and punched in his personal code on the screen. He slid out his own special-issue portable drive and plugged it into the terminal. The machine blipped. The captain's brow furrowed. He pulled out the drive, blew on it, scratched at it, then reinserted it. The machine beeped again. He pulled out and tried again, and then again. Each time it was rejected.

"Damnit. Thing's never had a problem before," the captain said.

These cops wouldn't be able to do anything without my guidance. I cleared my throat.

"There have been some strange glitches in the computer system," I said. "Like in Room 371."

I pulled the label from my pocket.

"What's that?" Lanza said, grabbing it out of my hand.

"I found it in Room 371. I'm not sure what's going on, but I heard there may be a record of some person checking into at least two rooms the same night the patients died in them. And I've found those little labels in both rooms the morning after."

"I haven't seen loose paper in years," said Lanza.

With a snort, the captain gave up on the machine. We walked down the hall. At 371, I swiped my Atman and ushered them all inside. Antiseptic air stung our eyes and noses. The cops fanned out along the walls, scouring every corner of the room. The young one with the thin moustache inexplicably dropped to the ground and felt around under the bed, then jumped up and inspected the toilet, sticking his head most of the way in to scrutinize underneath the rim. He was a very excitable sleuth. Lanza and I exchanged a glance and put our hands to our mouths to stifle our laughs. The captain went to the terminal, plugged his drive in and scanned the records for anything unusual. Lanza and I stayed close to the doorway as the team scoured the scene.

"What the hell do you think's going on?" Lanza whispered.

"I told you, I have no idea," I whispered. "Ever since the massacres during the Purge, hospital security's been as tight here as it used to be at the old commercial airports. Technically it's impossible someone could access a patient room without leaving any trace—especially a stranger no one would recognize in the hallway in the middle of the night."

"That's what I thought," Lanza said, shaking his head.

After a few minutes, the captain snarled in frustration at the medical terminal. He slapped the side of the monitor with his big meaty hand, rattling it. The other cops snickered. The captain removed the flash drive and pointed them out the door. But he was the last to leave.

"It's bizarre," the captain said. "I've been called out on at least a thousand hospital deaths, and I've never seen a glitch like this."

"Same here," I said.

"One more thing," the captain said, stopping mid-stride out the door, jabbing a finger at my sternum. "You really have no idea who that guy is, with the strange name you mentioned? These terminals are nearly impossible to hack into, according to our computer guys."

The captain gave me that skeptical cop stare, that unshakeable scowl. I gave him a blank look, slackening my face into the dumbest expression I could muster.

"I've heard how hard it would be to access Bureau information at one of these terminals," I lied. "No one's heard of Shiro Ishii here. But I'll poke around, let you know what I find."

We shook hands, that hardboiled captain and the helpful doctor. I walked the officers out of the hospital in silence. Lanza and I nodded at one another.

"Doctor."

"Detective."

Then the cops went out the door, got in their cars, and pulled away with a flash of lights, a whoop of sirens. As they pulled off into the distance, I cracked an energy stick and snorted it.

Right after the cop cars vanished, two figures emerged from the edge of the parking lot and walked toward the door. One was small, moving slow and measured. The other one was younger and faster, had a hat pulled low over his eyes. As they passed the benches in front of the hospital I recognized George MacGruder, my death-defying patient. After a moment I realized the one in the hat was O'Keefe. They drew even at the door, and MacGruder slowed—but O'Keefe just jumped into the revolving door, the blinking implant in his wrist pointed forward.

"Hey, Doc, I wanted to check—"

I squeezed my temples in frustration. This guy would never leave, he would never stop.

But Stash and Stanislaw appeared out of nowhere. They jammed into the whirling compartment, grabbed the reporter by his arms and dragged him out and toward the parking lot, heels dragging along the pavement. MacGruder shuffled through the door, grinning impishly.

"Who was that guy?" MacGruder asked, scratching his gray pate. "He kept asking me such incredibly stupid questions."

"A reporter," I said, watching as the two guards dragged him off behind a row of parked cars, beyond the view of the security cameras. MacGruder shook his head.

"Joe, that ain't a reporter. When I was a kid, reporters could take down presidents. Now they can't even tell you who robbed the convenience store last week."

We strolled to the elevators.

"So remind me—why are you here today?" I said.

"You said to come in if there was anything seriously wrong with me," MacGruder said.

"What's wrong?"

"Heartburn," the patient said.

"George. That's not what I meant by 'Seriously Wrong.'"

"But you also said heartburn could be a sign of the ulcers returning. And we both know how the last one almost got me."

We stepped into the elevator, I pushed the button for the third floor. The second floor blipped by. We stared at each other like cardsharks over a poker table. A half-smile was etched deep in MacGruder's wrinkles. I shook my head, but I couldn't keep from smiling, too. The man was relentless, and he was the best patient a doctor could hope for, at least most of the time. I sighed.

"I know you wouldn't come into the hospital unless it was really necessary, because you already know your inpatient allotment of days is almost up..." I said, eyebrows raised, nodding my head slowly.

MacGruder nodded eagerly.

"...so I'll put in that I requested an emergent check-up overnight for an irregular heartbeat, and we'll keep you under observation," I continued. "Even though we did the full battery of tests a few days ago, we should still be able to get you one more run through the O.N.K. If the Bureau will allow it—and if it will set your mind at ease."

"It sure will, Doc," MacGruder said. "These are the things my Jody used to treat with chicken soup, maybe a spoonful of cough medicine. But ever since she passed, the same small remedies don't work. I've wondered if maybe she used some special ingredients."

He shook his head, his lips crinkling. I patted him on the back.

"I think," I said, "that special ingredient was love. Or maybe a little whiskey. That's what my mom gave me when I was a kid."

MacGruder got checked in and prepped for the night. I put him in a room on the third floor next to my office, one of the rooms where one of the massacre victims had died the night before. The tubes and sensors and machines were wheeled around MacGruder like a high-tech, beeping banquet. The wall monitors showed steady vitals blipping along. He settled again into the hospital, smiling, gently trying to seduce the prettiest nurses. I watched from afar. I knew the man was probably just lonely and admitting him would open myself up to an official reprimand. But regulations be damned. Patients needed care of all kinds, even if the Bureau wouldn't ever officially recognize it. Especially if the Bureau wouldn't.

As if on cue, my Atman blipped, notifying me of several missed calls. Old Man Wetherspoon had left one page marked urgent—something he'd never done before. I rushed back to the nearest terminal, signed in, and called Wetherspoon's office. There was no answer. So I descended the stairs to the basement, and knocked on the Old Man's door. There was a rustle, a croaked series of grunts, and even though I had my ear to the door, I couldn't make out exactly what his gravelly voice was saying.

I twisted the knob and pushed. But something blocked it. I shoved hard once, then twice. It went a few inches, but stuck fast.

"Neal, it's Joe."

"I know it's you," said the Old Man's voice, clearer, on the other side. "But you can't come in. Not now."

"Why not?"

The Old Man's one bloodshot eye, a film coating it, appeared in the opening.

"Just shut up and listen. You won't be able to find any of the patient records. I know this. Don't ask how I know. But get that patient out of here, or something might happen to him too."

"What patient?"

"The old lecherous bastard. Your friend. The one who has nothing wrong with him, who just wants to hit on the nurses."

"What's going on? Why would I keep a needy patient out of the hospital?"

"That fogey's not needy—he's horny. Just get him out of here. And forget we even had this conversation. These people don't take kindly to people who know too much. And find the girl. Esmeralda Foyle."

The door slammed, missing my nose by an inch. I stepped back for a second, then pressed my ear to the door. Nothing—no sounds. After a few seconds, I knocked. Nothing again. The Old Man was shutting me out for no reason. I kicked the door once, then returned to the elevator. I took it up to the third floor.

The hallways were quiet. I walked into my office and sat down. At the terminal I pulled up MacGruder's information. The vitals were still fine, the numbers normal. I watched the heartbeat monitor fluctuate from eighty beats per minute, to ninety when a nurse came into the room, and then back down to eighty when she left. The breathing rates were regular; everything was on target, from blood pressure down to cholesterol. A healthy old man had taken refuge in the hospital, probably to find a nubile nurse to woo, a May to his December. The Bureau guidelines said patients made the ultimate call whether to stay overnight. MacGruder couldn't be turned away.

I rose from my chair and closed the office door. Sitting again, I plugged in the portable drive I had bought off one of the other doctors. I scanned through the third-floor records. It was foolhardy to use my own terminal, I knew—but it felt safer in my own space than in the rest of the hospital.

The Old Man had never sounded that way before. It scared me, I had to admit. I had no idea what the hell was going on in my hospital anymore.

The terminal search for Esmeralda Foyle still showed a young girl somewhere in the hospital, admitted for some kind of cosmetic surgery. But the bare records told me nothing more. I scoured the records of Steelman and the other patients who had died overnight and came upon the same nearly-blank screen. It had the same brief cameos of the phantasmal Shiro Ishii with each entry. A panic rose in my chest.

Using a button I had never used before—one the Bureau warned never to use, the FrackView status option—I raised the security clearance on MacGruder's room. Now only the highest-ranking administrators—and I—would be able to access the room at all over the nighttime hours. I left a "Do Not Disturb" note for the nurses. I pulled the portable drive out, shut down the computer, and stood up. The Atman rang. I reached out and picked it up—without thinking.

"Joe Barnes," I answered.

"Joe, don't tell me you forgot the appointment," Betty said at the other end.

"I did all my rounds," I said defensively.

"No, you jerk. Your wife's first appointment with Abbud. You know—about the baby she's carrying. Your child."

"Oh, shit."

I tossed the Atman aside and ran out the door, my white coat billowing behind. Panic surged through my veins. Using the back-stairs shortcut I made it to the obstetrician's office in sixty seconds—just in time for Mary to be walking out the door, both braids over her shoulder. She saw me, adjusted the pocketbook strap over her other shoulder, crossed her arms, leaned back on one heel. She seethed. I swallowed hard.

"You actually showed up," she said, lips drawn tight over teeth. "How nice of you."

"Mary," I said, stepping close to her, as she turned away. "I just forgot. There was a lot going on. People sick, people dying, mass casualties, all that."

"Yes. All That," she said. She turned back to me, her brownish green eyes stony and accusing. "I thought we had that talk when we got married. Family comes first, before All That."

"I was trying to save lives—"

"At the expense of your own," she said. She pointed a finger at me, her teeth gritted. "Just know, Joe—in life you only get so many chances to blow it."

Turning abruptly, her braids thwapped across my face. A floral trail from her perfume lingered in my nostrils. I watched her go down the hallway toward the hospital exit. It was no good chasing her, when she was consumed by that kind of righteous rage. I squeezed my temples, a migraine slowly wrapping around my skull. I had blown it—the most important thing in my life.

Abbud, the obstetrician, emerged from the examination room, wiping hands and wrists with a chemical towel. He shook his head.

"I couldn't help but overhear," he said, staring down the hallway where Mary had walked off. "I can at least tell you your child is developing as we would expect."

"That's great to hear," I said.

"Of course, there's still plenty that could go wrong, considering her chemical and biological exposures during her time overseas. But these are statistical improbabilities."

I stared at him. I had never heard a doctor speak like that, like a mathematician. Did he always communicate to patients like that? Abbud shook his head, placing a soft hand on my shoulder.

"Nothing definite in medicine. You know this, Barnes," he said. He smiled.

"Thanks, Abbud," I said, tapping the hand, then removing it gingerly with my own. "By the way, have you seen or heard anything strange the last day or so?"

"I'm sure you mean the patients dying on the third floor," Abbud said. "Can't help you there. I don't work nights, and I've been up to my eyeballs in uteruses and amniotic fluid."

"Gotcha," I said, rubbing my throbbing head. "Keep your eyes peeled, though."

I walked away. Nobody knew anything. There was nothing to know, maybe. And my marriage was in jeopardy. I went upstairs, checked MacGruder's perfect vital signs once more, then shut down my office terminal, walked down the hall, and left the hospital.

On the way home, I practiced what I would say—what I could say—to Mary. How she had to understand I was under serious strain. That I was excited about the pregnancy, but I had no time to bask in the glow like she had. How peoples' lives hung in the balance. How I was too busy preparing financially for a whole family, while keeping my head above water in a hostile, potentially-deadly work environment. How we couldn't, and wouldn't, end up living in her sister's house in Nebraska.

All That. We both knew exactly what that meant. I shook my head, smacked the steering wheel. She was right. She was always right. This time, she would make me pay for it.

We had the talk nine years before, swaying to our first dance as the cameras flashed around us. I was a good man, a good doctor, a hard worker, she had told me. She licked her lips. But I also needed to be able to devote time to a family, she had said. She knew I could do that. That's why she was marrying me, she said. People clapped all around, cheered around our slow circling dance, unaware of our crucial moment. I looked into her eyes and nodded. I made the promise. All That was to come second to our new life together. And it was agreed. She angled her head on my shoulder, her shining hair falling over the lapel of my tuxedo just as the soul singer closed the song with a joyful croon, and the wedding photographers lowered their cameras and let that most perfect moment pass, captured only in a memory.

Even through the years of trying to conceive a child, that promise had been the cornerstone of our life together. I had managed to always honor that promise. Until now.

I turned into the driveway. I still had no idea what I could say. Slowly I got out of the car, and dragged my feet along the walk, up the porch steps.

Inside, I stepped into darkness. The alarm was not activated. But I sensed a commotion somewhere on the second floor. Something was thrown; something smashed. A muffled whimpering. It sounded like violence. It sounded like rape, or worse.

I dashed up the stairs, wrenched the loose banister near the top free—and burst into the bedroom, brandishing it over my head.

Mary sat on her hip, turned away from me, arms bracing her on the ground in the middle of the bedroom, looking down at a picture on her Atman. She looked like a painting I'd once seen with my parents in one of the New York museums, when they were still open. The painting with the disabled woman stranded in a field, leaning on her hands to the side, looking up at a house impossibly far off. It was something about that woman's limited world, a vantage point that only she could see. My wife looked just like that woman in that instant, impossibly beautiful and frail. Mary turned to me, her eyes raw and wet, her hair in a wild mane, unloosed from the braids. Her eyes went wide as I emerged into the light.

"Mary—thank god you're alright…"

"Joe—is that the loose banister?"

"Oh this?" I said. "It's nothing—I just thought you were being attacked and…"

Before I could say anything else she stood and came to me. She grabbed me around the waist. She was sobbing.

Once again, I could hear the sweet tones of that soulful singer, as hundreds watched us sway to our first dance. There, in our shared bedroom in our big overleveraged house seven years later, we looked into each other's eyes.

"Listen, Mary," I said. "I know I screwed up today. It won't happen again. I'll be there for you. I'll be there for this child. For every appointment, for every school bus, and parent-teacher conference. I will be the Tooth Fairy and Santa Claus. I will be a family man."

"Oh, Joe," she said, looking away, trying to smile, wiping her tears with a sleeve. "I know that. You're a good husband. It's just…I'm remembering the streets of Tehran again. I think the hormones are knocking something loose."

"Don't worry. You're going to be a mother. I'm going to be a father. We're going to be parents. That's enough to make anyone crazy. It's not what happened when you were overseas in the Marines. That's all behind you. You're strong, and you survived. You're here with me."

She smiled through the tears, wiped at her cheeks, and laid her face on my shoulder.

"But one thing," she said, her voice muffled by my shirt.

"What, my dearest?"

"I understand you have to save lives," she said, wiping at her face, sniffling. "But promise me you won't miss another appointment."

"I promise," I said, kissing the top of her head, rocking back and forth like we were dancing to the silence.

THE TALE OF THE AMERICAN MAJORITY

U.S.A., 2087

The office was dark and silent, except for the voice of Old Man Wetherspoon. I sat there and listened, as I always did.

"The Great Purge, like any historical epoch, was not known by its rightful name until it was already over and committed to textbooks. After all, you never know if an uprising will be called a revolution or a rebellion until the dust clears, the bodies are buried, and the losers are ground under heel. Frenchmen roasted alive by flamethrowers and Germans choking on mustard gas in the trenches of Europe never heard the words The Great War, much less 'World War One.' It would take a mustachioed villain from Germany another thirty years to bring the concept of a bigger-budget sequel to the whole concept of global conflict."

"What? Who had a moustache?" I blurted out, exasperated. "What sequel?"

I stared in frustration at the Old Man, who took a sip from a tumbler on the desk in front of him. He had called me down to the basement, and I ran down the stairs immediately, sure he was finally going to tell me what he knew after shutting me out from his office. But instead the Old Man had started one of his crazed history lectures I had heard a thousand times before.

Old Man Wetherspoon shook his head. He was in a groove, evidently. Nothing could stop him.

"Nevermind, nevermind. You kids don't know anything. Where was I? The Great Purge. It was nothing at first, really. After the flash-bang of the War on Terror, the United States was fat and complacent. A few iconoclasts from rural areas were elected to Congress. They were united in only one way—hatred of government. They were against public oversight of anything, for dramatic tax cuts for the top half of the country. They promised a hungry electorate they would do anything they could to smash the corrupt machine from the inside out—to build something simpler, better. They flirted with anarchy like a teenager pawing at a brastrap."

I yawned, I rubbed my eyes. The Old Man could talk forever. He hated the world and could delineate its stupidity without end from his dark burrow in a hospital basement. But his voice was even more acidic than normal. I was in for a long one this time.

"They called themselves the Mister Smith Brigade, after a movie from way before our time. No one would have taken them seriously in normal times," Wetherspoon continued. "But these were not normal times. The lengthening, deepening recession lasted into the second half of the twenty-first century. Taxes were out of control, military spending kept increasing as the United States kept sucking at the oil tit that funded the terrorists and their Intifada incursions into America.

"The Mister Smiths picked up a few seats in suburbia, then a few more in the deserted inner cities. Suddenly, they had what is known in democracy as an American majority. Meaning a majority of the people, as opposed to a Russian or Chinese majority, which as we know are based on a plurality of the guns.

"No one knew who the ringleader was," he continued. "The confederation of anti-government politicians would go on the Sunday morning news shows, raving on live TV about the same policy positions at the same time. I remember one Congressman from one of the Dakotas said all we needed was World War III to spring back up on our good exceptionalist American feet. Another Senator from Ohio argued that people with darker skin were at an earlier step in evolution. But when they made these gaffes, the majority would huddle in its caucus for a few hours. They'd reemerge in front of the cameras, six instead of one now speaking the same words, like a hydra of bullshit, fangs bared, unrepentant. In all their intransigence, they could not be stopped.

"Suddenly they controlled the House of Representatives, then the Senate. And that's when the run of bills appeared, at first from the fringe element in the Mister Smith Brigade. They had no names, only numbers immemorial—because numbers mask bureaucratic evil so much more easily. Bill 683, Proposal 713, Spending Plan 1644. They eliminated the social safety nets and funding to public libraries. 'Trimming the tentacles of the monsterpus' was how one Idaho senator described the cuts.

"That was the true beginning of the Great Purge. They got the bills passed during the course of an all-night session of Congress, after the few remaining reporters had left Capitol Hill. And the next week, heads rolled. Figuratively, that is. Millions of workers were cut from the public payroll. Engineers, janitors, lawyers, doctors, garbagemen, blue-collar stiffs. Unemployment doubled, bringing it almost on the level with the Great Depression. The Great Purge name was coined by a news writer who compared the happenings in America with events in Russia from several lifetimes before, with trials and executions, that sort of thing. That was even before my time. Of course, our Purge was never as dramatic as millions being executed by firing squad. But it's tough to top the Russians when it comes to these things. They know drama."

I yawned again. Wetherspoon scratched his unshaven chin.

"In just a few months, the world changed," he said. "Highways looked like the surface of the moon. Schools sprung leaks and went unheated in the winter. Police departments couldn't afford ammo. Fire trucks broke down, sewers flooded streets. Bridges collapsed. A nuclear plant had a full meltdown in the Midwest. It was like a visitation of Biblical plagues.

"Crime rates tripled, people starved in the cities. Garbage fires burned on seemingly every corner.

"Another election approached. One journalist at a gutted metro newspaper—a bespectacled, obese advocate of Darwin, in the tank for the Mister Smiths—went on one of the Sunday morning political shows. He started talking about the need for 'more death' in the lower-income parts of the population. With a straight face, he proposed euthanasia programs in several major cities.

"I can't remember the journalist's name—something with a Q, Quinlan or Quisling or Quigley or Quayle or something," he continued. "The guy was such a cartoonish oaf, the American people suddenly woke up. They recovered their sense of tragicomedy. This Quisling, or whatever he was, became the laughingstock of the country. He went into hiding, but not for long. A week later somebody burned down his house on Long Island, with him still inside. No arrests were ever made. The man had become the great unwitting catalyst, the rallying point for the sane among us. A few weeks later something like ninety percent of the voters in this country rose up, marched to the polls and threw out the Mister Smiths.

"In their place, Joe Q. Citizen voted back in all the normal liars. This time it was the smart decision. The next session of Congress, the usual motley characters voted for across-the-board emergency tax increases, hired back the millions who had been purged, and established the safety nets again. Things started to get back to normal. Of course, the Big Blackout made sure that would never happen…"

I held up a finger.

"Neal," I said. "I'm old enough to have lived through most of this."

"You may have been alive at the time, Joe, but you lack the proper context—the true panorama of history," said Wetherspoon. "You didn't live through the Hatfield era, or the reign of Nixon II. Those quaint nightmares were all prologue to the Great Purge. History bears repeating, again and again and again. Perhaps it's the only thing nowadays—a human voice screaming in the vacuum."

"Neal," I said, measuring each word. "I thought you called me down here to tell me what the hell's going on around the hospital. Not to wax poetic about the futility of human life."

Wetherspoon shuffled some papers on his desk. He took a deep breath.

"Listen, Young Joe," he said. "I know you're appointing yourself chief investigator of everything going on upstairs. But you're out of your depth. Trust me on this."

He pointed a crooked finger across the desk at me.

"Just stick to what you know. Leave the rest to me. Go about your business, do your rounds. Keep your eyes open, and your mouth shut."

I jumped to my feet and pointed right back at him. My hand quaked with anger.

"How dare you say that, Neal," I said, a sweat breaking over my brow. "I can't just let this go. Not on my watch."

Wetherspoon's arms were crossed in front of his chest, his face impassive, unblinking. He looked like the ruler of some ancient land.

"It's for the best, Joe," the Old Man said. "You'll thank me when this is over. There are some secrets bigger than people like you and me. If one person's going to try and confront those, it might as well be an old man who's past his prime. Go home and care for that pretty wife of yours and the kid you have on the way. No reason to get yourself wrapped up in all this."

"That's a hell of a thing to say," I said. "A goddamned hell of a thing to say."

I turned and walked out of the office, slamming the door behind. As I walked down the hallway, I heard Wetherspoon's voice calling out to me. But I kept going, all the way up the stairs.

The Old Man knew something. But he wasn't telling. Wetherspoon himself could have something to do with the rash of deaths. He was always at the hospital. He had access beyond that of any other person at Saint Almachius, except for maybe the Kraken. And his old, cynical brain was probably going senile, perhaps insane. Perhaps even criminally insane. I banged through the third-floor door, not stopping, muttering half-formed curses under my breath that weren't in any human language. My mentor could be behind it all. Shiro Ishii, indeed. Just a pseudonym to throw off the rest of the unassuming medical staff.

But nothing would deter me. I would get to the bottom of it—all of it. As I picked up my keys and Atman from the desk, I was already making plans. I would check up on MacGruder, I would re-examine the bodies of the people who died the night after the shooting before they were taken to the incinerator. I would go over the Kraken's head, maybe call the Bureau's regional administrator and demand a special investigator. I'd check the records and call Lanza. I would get answers. I'd make my voice heard. I took off my coat and hung it on the hook. I straightened my tie in the reflection from the computer monitor. I could handle this.

But first was lunch. I had promised to meet Lanza down at our usual haunt, the Lenni Lenape Automat Diner, on the western stretch of the ultrahighway. Earlier that morning I had regretted even making the plans, since my patient list was long, and I had pledged to make it home to Mary in time for dinner. But now my thoughts brightened at the prospect. I could bring Lanza in on the investigation. My best friend, at the very least, would help me.

* * *

"No, I won't help you," Lanza said, thwapping the packet of InstaSweet, then tearing a corner and dumping it into his cup of coffee. "You can't. We already have an investigation into it. If I let you do that, we'd get in each other's way."

"Jesus, Zo," I said. "It's not like I'm going to steal evidence or hide whatever I find. I just figured…"

"No—absolutely not," Lanza said. He sipped his coffee, shaking his head, looking all around the diner. "Joe, that's like you allowing me to do brain surgery."

"Almost all the cranial laser procedures are automated through the O.N.K. It's actually one of the easiest jobs nowadays…"

"The answer's still no."

We sat in silence. The Lenni Lenape was filled with seniors fitting pieces of toasted tofu into their wrinkled mouths and sipping delicate cups of tea. Bleary-eyed waitresses strode around with purpose, hurrying patrons along, filling cups with hot liquids every few minutes in an endless cycle. Every so often they'd check a screen, then go up to the automated wall, push the big green button next to one of the foggy windows, take the dish out of one of the automat compartments, and bring it over to the customer. A line of TVs near the ceiling showed the President of the United States of America. "Her mouth moved, but the voice of a pundit from one of the networks talked over her speech." It broke to a commercial for the ridiculous Atman Four gadget that everyone was waiting for.

Two teenagers were at the next table over from us, separated by a glass partition about two feet high on the table: a redheaded girl and a boy with piercings in his face, both obese. They were obviously skipping school, drinking neon fluids with straws, their Atmans beeping with alerts. I felt a deep twang of sentimentality looking at them, thinking of our own days playing hooky.

"What do you want to do today?" said the girl. The boy looked down at the beeping Atman in his wrist. His nose rings and earrings jangled on his head. Thirty seconds passed. "What'd you say?" the boy said. More beeping. The girl looked down at her Atman, hit two buttons, then looked up at him.

"I said, 'What do you want to do?'" Both machines beeped, making a strange harmony.

"I don't know," the boy said, gazing into his Atman, smiling.

"I guess we could have another Xtreme InstaBoost," the girl said, nodding. Both Atmans rang.

They both pushed buttons furiously, captivated, numb smiles filling their faces as they stared down at their screens.

"Damned kids," Lanza said, shaking his head, burning his lips on the coffee. "It's not like when we were teenagers. They're not shoplifting from supermarkets or having sex in cars. Now they're hacking bank accounts and taking toilet-cam shots of their friends."

"The obese ones have heart attacks on the street, get their diabetic feet amputated. It's really sad," I said, nodding in agreement. "So—anything on the hospital deaths on your end yet?"

Lanza looked at him.

"Joe," he said, "you know I can't give out classified information while an investigation is pending. However, a piece of pecan pie might convince me to talk— strictly off the record."

I glared at him.

"You're a crooked cop, you know that?" I said, pushing the pie button on the menu. "Now just tell me—has your crack team of toilet inspectors come up with anything?"

"Officially, no," Lanza said, accepting the pie slice from the waitress. "But I can tell you—the powers-that-be have been strangely quiet."

"The powers-that-be."

"Yes," the cop said. "Normally when it comes to investigations like this, in a hospital, there's a whole bunch of oversight from the Bureau of Wellness, down to every detail. That's been the case ever since the Purge. But they haven't even made contact on this one."

"What's your expert cop opinion?"

Lanza raised a forkful of pie to his mouth.

"I'd say it's something big," he said. "Maybe the Bureau of Wellness or even the FBI is onto something, and they need to keep everything quiet until they can spring the trap at the right time. The only thing I've ever seen like it were the Intifada crackdowns in Newark a few years ago. But…"

"But what?"

"But it's never been this quiet. They'll always at least let us know something's going on—a wink and a nod, something like that. This time, nothing."

I tipped the last of my coffee back. I swiped my Atman on the menu interface to pay the bill, then stood from the table.

"I have to get back to the hospital," I said, staring down at my friend with a sullen frown. "But I need help, Zo. Old Man Wetherspoon is the only one who knows what's going on—and he ain't talking."

Lanza looked up at me and sighed. He set the fork down on the bare pie crust. He stood, donning his cap.

"I hate that look, you know," Lanza said. "Ever since we were kids, you've always sulked like that when you don't get what you want."

We walked toward the exit.

"Then just give me what I need," I said.

We pushed through the door, me and then Lanza. We stopped just outside the door, Lanza sucked on his nicotine inhaler. I cracked open an energy stick and snorted in one huge pull. The sun seemed to wobble brightly in the sky, maybe another mirage from the smog.

"Alright," he said, exhaling. "I'll see what I can get from some of the other detectives. It's not going to be easy. I'm not directly involved."

We walked to the lot.

"Anything would help," I said.

Standing by the police car, lost in our own thoughts, the reverie was broken by the digital blip of the police radio.

"Officers in the area—we have Code 810 at the Pinefield Manor apartment complex," the man's crisp voice said. "Neighbors reporting a hazmat situation in the residential buildings. Unknown agent has sickened at least one hundred. Immediate quarantine required. Riot response teams on standby."

"Pinefield Manor—that's the big complex off the ultrahighway," I said. "That's where Old Man Wetherspoon lives."

"Sounds like I might see you later," Lanza said. He opened the door to his cruiser. "Listen—I'll get you something right after we deal with this. Most of the time these Code 810 hazmat calls turn out to be a burning bag of dogshit on somebody's front stoop, nothing more."

We shook hands, formally stiffening ourselves in case anyone was watching. I got in my own car and sped back toward the hospital. A few miles out, I called Betty Bathory. She picked up on the third ring.

"Joe? Where you been? Have you heard?" she said.

"I had lunch with Lanza. We heard something over his radio," I said. "How bad is this?"

"The worst," she said, breathless. "There's probably going to be a quarantine. A hundred patients in one apartment complex. So the doctors and nurses are going there with the whole nine: NBC suits, masks, decontamination, triage tents, all of it."

"Do they have any idea what it is?"

"Not at all," she said. "But someone's been posting pictures on Amicus, and it looks like some of these people have swollen lymph nodes in their necks and armpits."

"You're kidding," I said. "You know, that's the main symptom of—"

"Yes, Joe, even nurses had to study microbiology in school," she said. "And before you ask me how the hell bubonic plague pops up in an apartment complex in New Jersey, all I can tell you is nobody knows anything yet. Just get here—and get ready for a shitstorm."

"Be there in five."

* * *

The hospital entrance was still, quiet. I felt like I was creeping up on another disaster, but I plunged once more into the breach. Stash and Stanislaw, the security guards, calmly waved to me, the waterfall next to their desk trickled. The first hallways were empty, and I almost relaxed. But once I reached the emergency room at the other side of the hospital, it was like an alien world burst open before me. The chaos was more frantic by far than it had been a few days earlier; perhaps because now the nurses and doctors frantically stuffing medical bags with bottles and syringes and gauze and surgical masks realized their own lives were at stake this time. I found Betty shoving a tarp into a bookbag.

"Betty," he said.

"Here Joe, pack this stuff," she said, gesturing toward a pile of mixed devices, medicines, and supplies. "The Kraken said we've got twenty minutes before the buses leave."

"Betty, why aren't the feds taking the lead on this? I thought this was the kind of thing the Bureau was supposed to handle with its agents."

She stopped, mid-movement, ran her hand through her hair, trying to pull it into its normal ponytail. But she hit a snag and yelped.

"Come on, Joe. We all know they'll step in and take all the glory once the work's done. But they don't do anything until we deal with it first."

She walked off, straightening her hair, and I started to stuff the sack. But halfway through, I pulled out my Atman, and called home.

"Hey, hon," Mary said. "Just getting out of the gym. How's your day going?"

"Pretty normal, aside from an outbreak of the Black Death."

"Please tell me you're kidding," she said.

"It's crazy, I know," I said, pinching the corners of my eyes. "We're setting up a quarantine around an apartment complex. The same one Wetherspoon lives in—remember that time we had dinner at his place?"

A pause. Silence on the other end. I could feel her weighing my words carefully.

"It's probably not a big deal. We'll take precautions," I added. "I wanted to let you know I may just be home a little late."

Another pause, as she weighed what she was going to say.

"Okay," she said. "I understand. Just be safe. And get out of going, if you can."

"Bubonic plague isn't my idea of fun, Mary. I'll keep my distance as much as I can," I said. "Love you."

"I love you too, Joe. Be careful."

We hung up. An electronic chime sounded from overhead. Ten minutes before departure. I could only vaguely recall the hazmat training seven years ago, because it was the impossible contingency—the one never supposed to happen. The return of a scourge from centuries before, right here in America. I quickened my movements, grabbed an NBC suit, the spare cotton swabs and syringes, and stuffed it all in the knapsack. A fresh set of scrubs, a surgical mask and cap, and paper booties. I didn't know what else we'd need. I searched around the nurses' station looking for anything else I may have forgotten. I rummaged through the medicine bin looking for some extra penicillin, maybe some morphine, just in case. But I saw only a candy bar, which I snagged instead.

"Hurry up, Barnes. You're holding up the first bus."

I turned and the Kraken stood there. She was looking down at her Atman, eyes half shut, mouth open, scouring the tiny screen.

"Just double-checking things, Suzanne," I said, stuffing an extra bottle into the bag without looking at its label. "Any idea what we're dealing with?"

"Looks like an outbreak of bubonic plague, maybe a few hemorrhagic fevers, some sepsis," she said, tapping into her Atman, as if she was ticking items off a list of Biblical scourges. "As long as we follow protocol, there won't be a problem."

I stared at her for a second. She looked up, an inscrutable look on her face.

"But be careful, Dr. Barnes," she said. "We've never had one of these calls before at Saint Almachius. I want to make sure everything goes smoothly so we keep in the good graces of the Bureau. No telling what they'll do if we let it spread or kill somebody important. They could even cut our funding."

I nodded, turned, then walked down the hallway with the sack over my shoulder. The goddamned hospital funding—that's what mattered to this woman. She was a menace, a tumor within the bowels of the hospital. I clenched and unclenched my fist around the strap of the bag and fought the urge to turn back and scream in her face.

But instead, I silently boarded the long bus. The stairs creaked as I climbed in—it was actually a repurposed yellow schoolbus with peeling paint, a holdover from the Purge's slash-and-burn days—and I sat across the aisle from Rothenberg and McDermott, the trauma surgeons.

"Aye, this is a new one," said McDermott, wiping his brow with a white piece of cloth. "Why in the fuck would they send a trauma surgeon on this call? If there's another Intifada ambush in Newark, who'll mind the store? The allergists? Those two oafs at the security desk? Can they man the scalpel, for fuck's sake?"

"Relax, Paddy," Rothenberg said. "You know they'll call in relief from Clara Maass. We'll get this fixed up as quickly as we can, and we'll be back in time to finish our shifts. It's only a small outbreak. Isn't that right, Barnes?"

The bus thumped hard as it went over a speedbump, and a nurse near the front of the bus fell into the aisle. The lines of medical personnel rocked like we were on a ship in a squall-churned ocean. I shook my head at Rothenberg.

"I don't think a natural outbreak of plague is possible in this day and age."
Silence.

"It can't happen. Not unless someone put it here," I added.

McDermott dabbed at his head with the hanky. Rothenberg scoffed.

"Get off it, Barnes," he said. "There's no one on Earth who would willingly spread plague around just to kill some people at a no-name apartment complex in the suburbs."

I turned and narrowed my eyes at my colleague the hotshot surgeon.

"Stuart, even with the worst sanitation standards in America—say in the Intifada-occupied zone of Newark—an accidental outbreak of plague is impossible. It hasn't happened in hundreds of years. This is not a natural outbreak. I bet they're bringing us in to investigate as much as to stop it from spreading."

"Investigate? Who needs to investigate?" Rothenberg said. "If you're right, let's just keep it simple: save as many people as possible, starting with ourselves. I'd like to avoid anything worse than the flu."

The bus bounced along, axles and panels groaning and shuddering. No one spoke as the ultrahighway passed by. The medical staff on the bus watched the advertisements flickering faint in the daylight air alongside the stream of traffic, which moved quickly. A few minutes later, the bus slowed, exited, and made two quick turns into a garden-apartment complex. The brick rows of buildings opened into eight separate courtyards, each punctuated by a few small stoops leading up to doors cordoned off in yellow tape, which rapped and twirled in the summer breeze. Everything else was silence. The bus made its way to the end of the road, which ended at a small shed lined with shovels, rakes and other tools. A plastic tent was set up to the side of this maintenance house. The bus stopped and the doctors and nurses all filed out, hauling their bags and equipment like a varsity team before a big playoff game. I was the last one off.

"Line up, everyone," Betty said, waving a bullhorn. We all followed her to the back of the tent. "Joe, you and the rest of the personnel get your suits on, and the nurses will come inspect it before insertion."

She walked away, hollering at a clutch of nurses.

"Aye, I'd show her insertion," McDermott said, nodding, elbowing his colleagues.

"Oh yeah," Rothenberg said, making a strange motion with his fist. The two of them grunted in agreement. It was like listening to primates.

"Can we focus here, guys?" I said, rolling my eyes at them. "We're dealing with a deadly contagion that once wiped out half of Europe, for Christ's sake."

The dozen or so of us doctors slid into our hazmat gear. We all struggled with the equipment, because we hadn't done it even once since the last mandatory Bureau training a few years earlier. Betty ran back and forth, yelling through a bullhorn, her hair whipping in the breeze. The physicians were split into four groups of three; the plan was to divide the complex into quadrants, and work our way through each and every apartment, looking for victims and vectors.

"Jaysis. This'll take days," McDermott muttered, voice muffled by the suit. "The fucking knackers."

The teams of doctors marched to their assigned destinations in silence. Rothenberg and McDermott and I were ordered to the northwest corner, the quadrant nearest the entrance. We walked slowly, in our awkward NBC suits, the breeze knocking us off-kilter, step by step. Each step felt heavy, and momentous. I was sweating. Finally, we reached the first stoop of the first courtyard: apartment number nine.

Everything was easy at first. A few patients showed signs of bubonic infection, but they were still in the early stages, and easily treatable. An elderly couple had swollen glands and had progressed a little further, but their lives could still be saved. We gave everybody tetracycline and streptomycin and doled out canned food and water. Then we closed them in their homes with the Bureau regulation sealant we'd been given and moved on.

But something was off. Pinefield Manor, despite some age and a bit of neglect, was immaculate. The synthetic grass was bright green. The concrete was smooth and fractureless. The breeze blew, but everywhere was silence. No birds sang. The others and I poked in corners and combed through kitchens and closets as we investigated. We didn't find the slightest hint of vermin or decay or filth. One apartment was a methamphetamine lab—but even that was spick-and-span, nearly spotless. There were no roaches, let alone contagion-carrying rodents, in any of the places they looked. The place was not a normal incubator of infectious disease, by any means.

I kept an eye out for Wetherspoon. The Old Man lived somewhere in the complex, but I couldn't remember where. I tried to push it to the back of my mind; no use worrying until we all knew more about what we were dealing with.

We moved on to the second courtyard. We found an elderly woman complaining of aches and gave her a month's supply of antibiotics and the special emergency number to call when she needed more food. Then we coated her door with the regulation sealant. In the next apartment we found a middle-aged mom and her young daughter, coughing and wheezing, but who appeared otherwise healthy. The treatments we brought would make them well again, we reassured them. The woman sat on the couch with her child, stroking the girl's soft blonde tresses. We rummaged through her apartment, picking up everyday objects and turning them over like they were alien artifacts: broom, pan, ketchup bottle, toilet brush.

"You do know how this all started, don't you?" the woman said.

I looked up from the baseboard heating vents. With much effort, I raised to one knee, then hoisted myself up in the massive spacesuit.

"We don't know yet," I said. "Do you?"

She nodded.

"It was all in the water," she said. "A few nights ago, as I was brushing my teeth, this weird sputtering sound came out of the tap. The water had a brownish tinge and it tasted weird. I didn't even notice until I had the glass on my nightstand, underneath the lamp. I poured it out, got a new glass—thinking I just hadn't cleaned it in too long—and then looked into the water again. The same brown stuff. It seemed to float, and shimmer. I poured it out. It was fine the next day, the water was clear. But now you're here, and there's some kind of outbreak. One has to have something to do with the other."

Rothenberg and McDermott and I exchanged glances. We gave the woman extra antibiotics and moved on, carefully sealing her door as the little girl waved to us wistfully from her crystal-clear window.

Door number seven was left ajar, swaying gently in the breeze. The hinges creaked a bit with each gust. Inside we came upon two doors: one ajar, another closed. A sign on the closed one said, "MAINTENANCE ONLY." I opened it and peered down a dark staircase. Dust swirled down into the blackness.

"Alright, let's split up," I said. "This one's a basement. I'll check it out. You guys take a look in the apartment. Yell if you need any help."

"Glad to see the brave man taking the safe route," McDermott muttered.

"If it's nothing, I'll come right back up and help you get the apartment sorted out," I added. "Take heart, my dear Paddy."

I patted his shoulder, turned and went down the steps. It was dank and dark. The stone stairs crumbled underfoot, and as I made the turn at a tiny landing halfway down, I took note of insecticide spray cans on a shelf, along with some strange jars that must have been a hundred years old.

I was getting close. I could feel it, a creeping along my clammy skin. A sliver of sweat trickled off my brow.

The bottom was darker still. The only light shone from a streaked windowpane just above the ground outside. Through the shadows and the fogged-up visor, I could see a fridge, a washer and a dryer, and a big old sink at the far corner, a few scattered rusty toys here and there on the concrete floor, and an old oak table right in the center, between two support beams. I felt along the walls, found a switch. But when I flipped it, nothing happened. I walked up to the table, set my satchel down, and pulled out the heavy tongs from the pouch. I went to the fridge, where I found a lidless jar of rancid mayonnaise, one rotting cabbage head, a moldy loaf of bread.

I glanced in the sink. What I saw there baffled me.

Set there were two sealed jars, very shiny, glass and metal, with rubber tubes sticking out of their lids. Dregs in the bottom of the container looked off-colored, strange, organic. I gingerly picked it up, turned the thing over in my hands.

Soft laughter came from behind, and I froze.

THE TWENTIETH CENTURY IN PICTURES

U.S.A., 2087

I wheeled around, nearly dropping the jars. In my other hand I brandished the tongs, ready to strike. Squinting into the shadows, I took one step forward. From the window's weak light, I saw a human shape sitting on the ground, back against the wall. The figure chuckled, coughing.

"Don't drop those jars, man, whatever you do," the figure said. "That would be seriously bad."

I activated the walkie-talkie in the NBC suit.

"Rothenberg—McDermott. I've got a victim and an unknown device down here. Come down ASAP."

"I wouldn't call myself a victim, per se," the man said, laughing, then coughing.

I stepped closer. I finally saw him through the gloom. A young man—short brown hair, glasses, slack jawed, wearing jeans and a T-shirt. An elbow balanced on his knee, he was holding his head in his propped-up hand. His face was drawn and pale. A plump wart protruded from the end of his nose. He smiled at me, and he looked so damned familiar.

"Who are you?" I asked.

"We've met before," the man replied. "It'll come to you. Eventually."

"I'm here to help you, my friend. What is this thing?" I asked.

"Just a little something I whipped up," the guy said. He snorted. "But I think you found your vector. That's what you'd call it, right?"

He laughed again. I placed the jars on the table carefully and stepped closer.

"Who the hell are you?" I said. "What are you doing here?"

"Samuel Lamalade. Nice to meet you," the man said, trying to rise, extending his hand.

I didn't move. The man coughed, a hacking deep within his chest, and staggered back against the wall, sliding back down to the ground.

"Samuel, there's a serious contagion in this apartment complex. Do you have a fever, or swelling, or weakness?" I said, stepping forward carefully.

"All of the above," Lamalade said. "I'm probably too far gone already, man."

He coughed, spitting up a big red blotch of blood on the floor.

"I probably deserve this," Lamalade mumbled. "After killing all those civilians at the stadium the other day, my karma's probably all sorts of fucked."

I didn't move. But I gripped the tongs tighter. Bootsteps pounded down the stairs. Rothenberg and McDermott were coming. I crept closer to Lamalade.

"Tell me what the hell you're talking about," I said, grabbing the man's shirt, tugging him up to his feet.

Lamalade smiled. Blood oozed between his teeth. His eyes lolled in their sockets.

"Oh man...a little experiment," he said, wobbling on his feet, tumbling toward the floor. "I would ask...your friend..."

Lamalade collapsed, dead weight. I tried to haul him back up, but he was too heavy. McDermott and Rothenberg's footsteps came up behind, and then all three of us were scrambling to attend to the strange young suspect. As we dragged him into the small patch of sunlight from the tiny basement window, I got a better look at this Lamalade person. He wasn't more than thirty years old, unshaven, acne on his forehead. But he was deathly ill. At his collar were a few swollen nodes—telltale signs of bubonic plague. Rothenberg radioed in the warning, and a minute later several paramedics hustled a stretcher down the stairs, dropped Lamalade onto it, and hauled him up and out toward the isolation tent. McDermott and Rothenberg followed.

I stayed behind, looking around the room. I picked up the two jars, turning them in my hands. As I looked over the device, I slowly began to understand it. The longer attachment resembled a suction device; it was clear and long and could create a vacuum. The other attachment was threaded to connect to a faucet, a water source. And then there was the brownish muck. If it was properly connected, the reverse-pressure of the vacuum would cause the contents of the jar to be sucked up into the pipes, creating a backflow into all the faucets and toilets connected to the same system.

Delivering some substance—poison, germs—directly into the water supply. The design was simple—just basic physics. But for what purpose? I felt a tingle up the back of my neck, underneath the NBC suit.

I bagged the device in a standard-issue prophylactic sack. I charged back to the medical tent. Lamalade was already gone. The nurses and other doctors had triaged him, taken precautions against the risk of contagion, and then packaged him in an ambulance bound for Saint Almachius. I asked around. No one could tell me why he was evacuated while others were quarantined. I found Betty and showed her the device. I was about to head back to the hospital to question the maniac responsible, I told her. She shook her head, tapping at her Atman for real-time emergency updates.

"Joe, you can't go," she said. "We have too many apartments still to go through. We have people to treat. All-hands-on-deck, as Wetherspoon says."

I shook my head, the NBC suit rustling with my movements. But she grabbed my elbow with her gloved hand.

"Now listen," she said. "Once we finish this last apartment block, you can go interrogate him all you want. But in the meantime, why don't you call Lanza? He's an actual detective. Maybe he can start questioning the guy. If he survives. Give me that thing and let me put it in a hazmat bin."

"I don't know why you're always in charge," I said, half-smiling at her. But she only smirked back and continued her rounds, bossing around the other doctors at the scene.

I used the tent's emergency Atman. Although Lanza couldn't hear me so well at first, I managed to convey the basics: about the device, and the suspect, and the confession, and the outbreak. On the other end, Lanza listened in silence. Swearing, he said he'd head to the hospital right away, and hung up.

Rothenberg and McDermott and I went through the rest of the apartments. The dwellings closest to where we'd found Lamalade had the sickest people in the whole complex. We discovered a dead elderly couple in the apartment right above the basement. In the others we'd opened the doors to eight people just barely breathing in their beds. We did our best with antibiotics and fever medications, and we brought in intravenous fluids and oxygen machines—all to no avail. A middle-aged man died, convulsing, as we tried to move him to a gurney.

But none were evacuated like Lamalade had been—with that same speed and efficiency.

We left when a new shift from Clara Maass arrived on the scene. We were all sent to decontamination in yet another isolation tent, and we all took preventative antibiotics to stave off any germs we might have come into contact with. We took off the suits, washed in the small shower stalls, and carefully followed all the protocols.

"Thank God for Science, right?" Rothenberg said, grinning, throwing a handful of pills in his mouth.

"Aye," McDermott said. "It's a modern miracle we don't die in our own filth, like mangy dogs, it is."

The bus arrived, and we were shuttled back to Saint Almachius. A silence hung over the medical staff. Betty sat next to me this time, and she quickly fell asleep, her head rolling onto my shoulder. Her hand drifted to my thigh, but I pushed it back onto her lap. I rubbed my eyes. Exhaustion had overcome my body, but my mind still raced.

Black Death—a biological weapons attack, with dozens of victims, by the same crazed mass murderer behind the stadium attack. It was almost unfathomable, even after the Intifada attacks of the last few years. What was the possible connection? What inspired your garden-variety spree killer to develop the kind of ingenuity to spread bubonic plague? And why the hell was a random apartment building in New Jersey the target? It was one thing for the Intifada to attack Newark with a dirty bomb, to try and disrupt another major American city like they had done with Seattle and Austin. It was quite another to target no-name middle-class families from suburbia for no apparent reason.

Someone poked my shoulder. It was McDermott.

"You hear? Old Man Wetherspoon's apartment was empty," McDermott whispered.

"I was wondering where he was," I said. "I was worried, but there was no time to stop and ask anyone."

"Your man lives at the back end of that complex," McDermott said. "One of the other teams said they found his place completely bare. Even the rugs were gone, mate. Pretty dodgy bit of stuff."

"I'll find him," I said. "But first I have to talk to the guy we found in the basement. I'll bet he can tell us what happened back there."

"If he's still alive," Rothenberg said, his head popping up over the seat. "Oy, he looked like he was more than half-dead."

* * *

The bouncy ride ended. As I got off the schoolbus and headed into the hospital with the throng of doctors, I called Mary and told her I was still alive, everything had gone by the book, and I just had to finish up my usual rounds. Her voice was bleary, like she'd just woken up. But she said dinner would be ready when I arrived home.

I walked down to Old Man Wetherspoon's office. I knocked, and my heart sank as the seconds passed by without an answer. The door was locked. I cursed and I turned around and went back upstairs. In the middle of the ICU's main hallway, I saw Lanza standing there, hands on his hips, just staring at a wall. He shook his head.

"We got here too late," Lanza said. "Guy was already comatose. The other doctors say he's got an outside chance to survive. But we're not supposed to hold our breath."

"You think this guy's responsible for the outbreak, and the stadium shooting?" I said.

"We're pretty sure," Lanza said. "His DNA matched the shell casings at the stadium. And I take your word for it on the outbreak. But we have no motive. And we don't know whether anyone was working with him. We're interested in talking with one of your colleagues."

"Who?"

"That mentor of yours, Cornelius Wetherspoon," he said, cracking his knuckles. "Wetherspoon has access to the electronic records here, and he lives where everyone just got sick. Also, it looks like he cleared out his apartment and vanished right before this attack. Let's just say it's suspicious, Joe."

I shook my head, reached underneath my glasses and scratched at my eyes. Lanza laid a gentle hand my shoulder.

"Sorry, Joe," Lanza said. "I know you respect the guy. But it looks like he's been up to something. Just let us know when you hear from him, so we can talk to him. He may actually be innocent, for all we know."

"But you don't really think that."

"Doesn't matter what I think," Lanza said. "What matters is the truth. Where the evidence points. You know that, Joe."

Lanza patted my shoulder and walked down the hall where a group of cops with serious faces were huddled in conversation. I turned and went the other way, back toward Old Man Wetherspoon's office. I rattled the doorknob. It was an old-fashioned lock, the only non-electronic one in the entire hospital. I pulled out the stylus for my Atman, and I angled its flimsy shaft in the gap where I thought the bolt might be. I carefully probed, but a few swipes with the tool, it snapped in two. I stared at the door for a second, then turned and went back up the stairs to my office.

The first patient on my list was MacGruder. I walked in the room, and he greeted me with a cheery voice.

"Dr. Barnes," he said. "Long time no see."

"How you feeling, George?"

"Never felt better, doc. I'm actually starting to believe a bit in all your optimism. Since I came back, I feel like I've got a new lease on life."

I checked the terminal. MacGruder's vitals were even better than the last check up: heart rate, blood pressure, and radical carcinogen levels were all perfect for a man half his age. He was a paragon of health, and there was absolutely no medical reason to keep him in the hospital.

"There's absolutely no medical reason to keep you in the hospital," I said.

"But the nurse told me since I got this implant, that I should stay over at least one night, just to make sure."

MacGruder pulled aside some of the monitors from his arm, showing his exposed wrist. Shining there in the middle of inflamed, pinkish tissue was the oval of a newly-implanted Atman. It was the Four—a prototype of the version yet to be released. I recognized it from all the advertisements. The screen glinted in the overhead light.

"Figured I'd keep up with the rest of the world by getting one," he said, squinting at it with ancient, farsighted eyes. "They told me I could have the newest one."

"George, getting that thing implanted is an outpatient procedure. You've already been here too long. You're more likely to get seriously sick in here with all these germs floating around than you are back at home."

MacGruder pointed up at me.

"You know, the other doctor said the same thing," he said. "Really strange. It was like he was warning me to get out of the hospital. Like there was danger or something."

"What other doctor?" I asked, panic raising my voice. "What did he look like?"

"Oh, you know, the old guy," MacGruder said. "Older than me, even—a hundred if he's a day. He's the guy I've seen you around with here and there. White hair, crotchety. The name's Witherfork or something?"

"Wetherspoon?"

"That's the one."

I went over to the room terminal and searched the treatment history.

"When did you see him?" I said.

"Early this afternoon, I think," MacGruder said. "It was just after I got the implant. I was zonked out on painkillers. Right after the nurses settled me down in the bed and went out, he appeared. He was kind of whispering, real close to me. He looked crazy. White hair all over the place, like he hadn't showered in a week. He kept looking over his shoulder, like he expected somebody to sneak up on him. Quite a sight, that guy."

As he talked, I found it, right there on the monitor. A single entry from 1:37 p.m. A person named Shiro Ishii visited for two minutes, then left, without running any diagnostics, or any other check-up of any kind. The phantasmal doctor had again appeared, checked in on a patient, and then left—all in the middle of the day. The video records in the entire wing of the hospital had been deleted from the database, somehow. I turned to MacGruder.

"George, I'm urging you to get your things and immediately leave the hospital," I said. "You could be in danger."

MacGruder waved at the air with a shaky hand, as he settled deeper into the pillow.

"With these painkillers I'm on, it would be more dangerous for me to be driving," he said. "Just let me lay here, doc. I'll push this big red panic button if I feel sick. Sound good?"

I put my hands on my hips, looking down at my patient. We stared at each other. The poker game again. We both knew I couldn't force him out, due to those Bureau regs. He could stay as long as he wanted once he was in the hospital—that was the law. I shook my head in defeat.

"You might die," I said.

"I'm old, doc," said MacGruder. "I could die any moment anyway."

"I'll give you my personal number," I said. "The minute something happens, somebody shows up at the door unannounced, you call me. Got it?"

"Even doctors?"

"Especially doctors," I said, shaking my finger reproachfully.

Hands raised in the air defenselessly, MacGruder chuckled.

"Jeez, doc. What are you expecting, another mass shooting? Relax. I heard they already caught the guy."

I frowned.

"I hope so," I said.

I rushed downstairs to Wetherspoon's door. This time there was no pretense. I rattled the knob once more. I looked in both directions, then I kicked hard at the door. It rattled, but held fast. I backed up, got a running start, and kicked again. The third time something splintered. At the seventh, the door crashed open. I crossed the threshold into darkness.

All was silence—no computer whirring, no working machines. Vague shades of books stood out in the light from the single window like bas-relief on the wall of an ancient tomb. The Old Man's musky cologne still hung in the air. The darkness seemed to stick to my skin. I found the chain to the single banker's lamp and yanked it, lighting up the lower half of the room.

There was the usual mess—the stacks of books, empty glasses and a stubbed-out cigar on the desk's blotter. But the big chair was overturned, and as I came around the desk, I stepped on the crunching shards of a broken wineglass on the carpet. I stooped and felt around; the crimson stain was still wet. I righted the chair, glanced around, and sat. An enormous void was left by the Old Man in that subterranean lair. The far corners of the room were invisible because of the dying light from the window and the weak glow of the lamp; I couldn't see the familiar framed degrees and pictures of his long-dead colleagues on the walls, the pieces of the smashed Atman in the corner, and even the spilled books from my first visit a decade before. I tugged on the handles of all four drawers in the desk, but all were locked. I cursed and pounded the desk with my fist.

What was the Old Man hiding? I crossed my legs and leaned back in the chair. He was not a killer—even if he resented humanity after a century of disappointments. Cornelius Wetherspoon was not a bad man. But he was up to something. I put my feet up on the desk, but I knocked off a huge pile of books that cascaded down to the floor on the other side. I went around to the other side of the desk and stooped to pick up the mound of ancient books.

Again, I marveled at the Old Man's collection of old books, the biggest collection I had seen in years. I noted one of the volumes: *The 20th Century in Pictures*. The old cover had a bright emblem showing it had won some award before the Blackout—before the presses all stopped. Hell, this was all printed in the old alphanumerics, years before the half-pictographic half-acronymic Gliffs had been developed. Although I had learned the old alphanumerics back in my schooldays, after years of the simplified and dumbed down Gliffs on glowing screens had weakened my eyes, like it had for everyone else. Reading off paper was a chore, and not everyone could still do it. But I flipped through the book, looking at the grainy black-and-white pictures from the century before. Minimalist captions were hard to read on the paper, but they apparently told who was smiling, or being killed, what campaign or battle was depicted, and the date. In the middle of the book there were four dog-eared pages. These images were particularly indistinct and out of focus. They showed blurry forms of masked surgeons standing around mounds that I realized, with rising disgust, were eviscerated human forms. Within the pile were amputated limbs and disembodied parts. Several of the indistinct doctors' faces were circled in thick red ink.

My eyes, used to the Gliffs, squinted to make out the caption in the old style. It read, "Manchukuo, 1942." I rubbed my face. I had no idea what that meant.

I shut the book, lifted its heavy bulk, and stood. But I knocked something else over—a folder still on the edge of the desk. Papers flew in every direction. I cursed and stooped again to pick up the contents. But they were so old, they seemed they would crumble.

The documents were full of black splotches, redactions of confidential names and places. The old flimsy sheets spanned back as much as a century. I scanned the places, the dates, the letterhead: 1945, 1955, 1977, 1991, 2012, 2037, Kansas City, Alabama, the Department of Defense, U.S. Army Medical Command, Homeland Security. I sank slowly to the floor, struggling to read the ancient typeface.

But the collection proved to be indecipherable, in the old alphanumerics. My eyes couldn't crack that ancient code at that moment. The few characters I could make out were no help, either. Random words, euphemisms, acronyms, operation titles with free-association names. Letters from one executive assistant official, to another deputy director of something, the sentences were written in incomprehensible bureaucratic language. I stuffed them all back in the folder. At the end were the most baffling items of all. Labels, about an inch wide and half-a-foot long, were stacked in a series. I looked closer.

There were about thirty of them. Two were blood-stained. They only had serial numbers on them, no other identifying markings.

They were the same as the ones I'd found in the rooms where Cruzen and Steelman had died. They all began with the same cryptic prefix, big and easy to read. BOW-137.

On the back of one of them, the Old Man's handwriting had scratched something in the same critical red ink. I stared, squinted, turned it over and around, but I couldn't make it out. Try as I might, I couldn't decide whether it was writing or tiny drawings. I shut the dossier.

It was important, I knew that. The Old Man's secret was in my hands, I was sure of that. I clutched it to my chest, picked up the book, stood, and turned off the lamp. I stumbled and slipped over the fallen mound of books and went out to the hallway. I turned and shut the smashed door as best I could.

I rushed up the back stairwell, from the basement to the third floor. I heard the echo of my own hectic footsteps and tried to slow myself. I heard someone descending from the fifth floor, and I quickly ducked into the door on the third. As I passed, I heard nurses talking with some of the patients, adjusting pillows, administering the last medications of the day. Speedwalking, I kept my head down, even as some of the voices called out to me, asking for an extra hand with a bed or a wheelchair. Normally I would have. But I pretended I didn't hear, banged through the door to my office, and shut the door behind.

The Kraken had sent me a message, which blinked on my terminal. It demanded I stay late to draft a report for her about the bubonic plague cases. I scoffed and deleted it. She would have all the information from the real-time updates from the scene anyway. I swung off my white coat, took the lucky test-tube off the wise-man statue and left the stethoscope in its place, stuffed the book in my briefcase, and turned off the terminal.

I needed to get back home, to be in the silence of my house. I needed to talk things over with Mary, to get a handle on the situation.

Looking both ways down the hallway, I saw the gurneys lining the walls. But all the bodies were gone. A camera trained on me; I turned my face away from it. The muffled echo of talking, laughing, and shouting came from ahead. As I neared, I realized it was coming from George MacGruder's room. I walked to the door, swiped myself in, and entered.

MacGruder was sitting up in bed, watching his Atman, his wrinkled face squished together in laugh lines. It took him a moment to notice me in the doorway.

"Hi, Doc. Ever watch *How Low Can You Go?*" he asked, wiping his eyes with his free sleeve. "Amazing stuff. Some guy just pulled out his own fingernails with pliers for forty thousand bucks. Can you imagine? What an idiot."

I set the briefcase down and went to the terminal. I logged in, using the new portable drive. Gone was the mention of Shiro Ishii. The ghost had vanished yet again. I checked the records two and three times more. I did a triple-take up at the wall monitors, the scoreboard of pulse and blood pressure and breathing rate.

"You okay, Doc? Something wrong?" asked MacGruder, muting his Atman.

I turned to him.

"George, I'm going to have to ask you to leave again, for your own safety," I said. "I don't know exactly what's going on, but I do know people have been dying in Saint Almachius. I urge you to get out now, while you still can."

"I just need one more night on my back, being cared for by some pretty, young nurses," MacGruder said, folding his hands behind his head, a numb smile on his face.

I picked up my briefcase and went for the door. But I stopped at the threshold.

"Damnit, George. Just know I tried. I really did. Remember the panic button. And call me whenever something looks suspicious. Your life may depend on it."

Hand at brow, MacGruder mock-saluted me. I scowled at him and waved my finger at him impotently. I left. As I walked toward the stairwell, I heard the far-off voice of the Kraken reprimanding one of the night-shift nurses on their sheet-folding technique. I quickened my steps and left the hospital before she could find me.

I felt like a coward, retreating from a battlefield. But I had to figure this all out. I had to get home and regroup, figure out what to do next.

* * *

On the way home, the satellite radio played the feel-good hit of the Summer of '87 three times in a row. Now, now, now, baby, now, now, now, the electronic voice repeated again and again, like an incantation. I didn't turn it off. It had a savage rhythm, a pulsing beat that seemed to dull my brain. As I pulled into my driveway, I glanced up at the top floor of the house. Lights danced in the windows. One went on, then off, the next flickered, and then the third stayed on. Then a large dark shadow whisked across. Someone was inside the house—someone was attacking Mary.

I jumped out of the car and rushed up to the front door. It was ajar. I burst inside and rushed upstairs, again grabbing the loose banister rung.

Under the master bedroom door was a bright line of light, broken by the play of shadows. I took a deep breath.

I burst into the room, cocking the banister pole like a club. But I stopped short. Mary sat there on the floor with a circle of Atmans around her, glowing like ceremonial candles. She was wearing her reading glasses and her camouflage nightie. There was nobody else there. She tapped at her Atman and lowered her wrist. She smiled at me, eyes arched over her glasses.

"Did everything go alright?"' she said. She sprung up from the floor and grabbed me in a hard hug. But when she caught sight of the spindle of wood in my hand, her brow furrowed.

"Joe, did you break the railing again?"

"Oh—this," I said. I half-hid it behind my back. "The front door was ajar. I thought you might be in trouble."

"Oh, honey," she said. "You're getting overprotective. Like a crazy daddy-to-be."

She clutched me around the neck, touching her lips to my cheek and neck. I didn't move—I eyed the screens flashing on the floor.

"What's all this? Looks like some kind of strange Unified Three ritual."

She smirked at me, her lips parting to a smile.

"Very funny, Joe. This is all of the baby stuff," she said. "This is all the documentation Adam gave me."

"Adam?"

"Dr. Abbud. You know—the obstetrician? Your colleague at the hospital?"

I squatted to look at some of the screens, all different Atmans on loan from the hospital. There were applications about breastfeeding and maternal nutrition, with checklists so simple a child could learn how the sexual act could mix together a new person, like a cocktail, in a lady's organs. One was titled "So How Did I Get Pregnant?" with journalistic edge.

"Seems pretty thorough," I said, shaking my head.

"It sure is," she said. "Still lots for us to do, Joe. I start the Tough Mothers Pregnancy Boot Camp at work tomorrow. And then there are the supplemental nutrition waivers Abbud had me sign."

"Waivers?"

"He said it would be best for me and especially for the baby if I took some iron and folic acid supplements. He said it's no big deal. You already initialed them, remember?"

"I did?" I asked, scratching my chin. "Well, I trust Abbud. He's a good doctor. He was in the top ten in our class. Just behind yours truly."

"Yes, I know, hon," she said, rolling her eyes. "I know our baby's in good hands."

Looking down at her, I watched her brow furrow as she pored over the Atmans. The maternal instinct had already taken on a kind of spiritual possession. I loved this woman—I could feel it tingle across my chest. We were making a family. This time, finally, after so many years of failure, it was going to work.

"I'm proud of you. I'm proud of us," I said. "It took a long time. But we'll be better for it. We're going to be great parents."

A moment of silence. I stared. She glanced up at me. She blinked.

"Did you say something, hon?" she said, her eyes unfocused. She had not heard a word I had said.

"Nevermind," I said, dipping forward to give her a kiss on the forehead. I walked back toward the door, swinging the banister up onto my shoulder. "By the way, when's the next appointment with Abbud?"

No response came, as she pored over Atmans in each hand. Shaking my head, I walked out of the room. Dinner had not been made, after all. Down in the kitchen I fixed up a NutriFast bag. After a while she came down the stairs, explaining she was not hungry because she had eaten a late lunch. We talked over the kitchen counter about finances, and about choices: whether we would pick a boy or a girl or just leave it to genetic chance, and what we would do if there was a congenital defect. We agreed to let nature take its course, come what may; we would love our child, no matter what. She asked about the Black Death outbreak and I told her the things I'd seen over the course of the day, the precautions, and the delirious lunatic we'd found who claimed responsibility for a biological weapons attack. Later, we lay in bed and talked some more, until our words drifted past one another. She turned out the lights after midnight. I hit the broken Dormus with my open palm, but after a few minutes I gave up and fell back on the pillow. I lay there for hours in the empty dark, thinking about the dossier sitting on my desk back at the hospital.

A DREAM WITHIN A DREAM

U.S.A., 2087

The dream washed over me once again. The water rushed past, the drowning dark and the breathless pain as I splintered in the current. Once again, the black mouth approached, swallowing the prisms of light from above. But this time the cavernous maw clamped over me. A bone-cracking chill pierced me, and I felt myself swallowed alive in the infinite black.

I awoke, with the air-conditioning vent in the ceiling gusting an icy gale directly on my bare chest. Dawn cracked through the window. I rubbed my face, crawled from bed, and went to the bathroom.

As I shaved, the dreams faded from my brain. No one dreamed with the Dormus—it was one of the perks of the technology. I barely remembered ever having to shake away the orphan's nightmares of my youth. I prepared for my day like in a trance, shivering under the blast of the shower, even though it was scalding hot.

Downstairs I told Mary about my underwater nightmare. She shook her head. She'd already put in two service calls for my Dormus, she said, but we still were far from the top of the list. I shook my head tiredly, my brain seeming to slosh in my skull. I kissed her, then headed out to the car to begin the day.

Hectic energy buzzed around the hospital when I arrived, but it was a strange quiet bustle. No mass casualty incident was taking place, the plague victims were still alive, and some were even recovering. But a weird dread hung in the air. A meeting had been called by the administration for the early afternoon, and the heads of the hospital's various units disappeared mid-morning. Even though I ran the third-floor rooms, I was technically not a unit head by title and I was not part of the gathering. Relief washed over me when I found the dossier still on my desk, unmoved and unopened. I slid it into a drawer, locked it, then started my rounds. The administrators reappeared after an hour or so, treading the hallway in file, haggard faces hanging.

"I bet it's something bad—something from the top," Rothenberg said, snapping an energy stick into his espresso, watching the suits march past the breakroom.

"It can't be good, that's for sure," I said.

"I heard—" Rothenberg said, before a violent fit of hacking and coughing overtook him, doubling him over, splashing the espresso over his lap, on the floor.

"Jesus, Stuart, are you alright?" I said.

"I'm okay," he said, standing up straight. A weak smile crossed his white lips. But then his eyes rolled back in his head—and I caught him just before he hit the floor.

Bubonic plague was the diagnosis. It was still in its early stages—though we weren't sure any of the antibiotics left in the hospital's supply were strong enough to treat it. And since Rothenberg had already taken preventive antibiotics before and after the visit to the apartment complex, basically nothing was left in our arsenal to save him. But we gave him doses of the two we had, and Betty sent a request out to the Bureau of Wellness to requisition a few more exotic varieties from Clara Maass. McDermott and I watched the nurses minister to the fever as Rothenberg lay unconscious inside a glass-walled isolation room in the intensive care unit. The machines beeped. We all stood outside, staring in, groaning.

"Jaysis, the man's got a bad dose," McDermott whispered, carefully watching the shallow rise and fall of his fellow surgeon's breathing. "You think any of us've got it?"

"No," I said, watching the tubes up Rothenberg's nostrils. "We would already have symptoms. Besides, it was a total fluke that Rothenberg contracted it. He had protection, he was careful. It was just the luck of the draw."

"I can hardly believe it, mate."

"Poor Stuart. He's got to pull through. Just think of his family."

"Rothenberg, a good man if there ever was one," McDermott said, shaking his head. He tapped on the glass with his fingernail. "At least the poor fucker's got a break from the Kraken."

We chuckled.

"Yeah, at least he's got that," I said. "Although this is all her fault to begin with."

Hands grabbed our shoulders. We froze.

"Having a good time, gentlemen?" said Suzanne Kranklein, her voice creaky. "I understand your concern for your colleague. But a schedule is a schedule. Time for our meeting."

We nodded, and followed her down the hallway, up a flight of stairs. We entered the big auditorium with stadium seating. It was the space for the biggest, most important staff meetings. All the seats were filled, and murmurs rippled along the rows and aisles as Kranklein entered ahead of us. McDermott and I lingered at the back and leaned against the wall, cups still in hand. The Kraken advanced to the lectern at the front of the hall. She tapped the microphone twice, sending a rip of feedback all the way to the top tier.

"Hello, everyone," she said, flashing a fake smile that was all teeth and no eyes. "Thank you all for setting aside some time."

The crowd grumbled. I noticed that all the nurses and doctors on the Saint Almachius staff were there. Nobody was minding the store, keeping patients alive throughout the rest of the hospital. Betty Bathory was in a cluster of nurses huddled together and whispering, and at the last seat in the back corner I spotted Nurse Culling's oversized head, his eyes staring unblinking at the stage.

"As you may know, we've had quite a busy time in the last week," Kranklein continued. "We always plan for the worst—but hope for the best. We've gotten a little bit of both, between a horrific shooting, saving a bunch of patients, then losing them, and then responding admirably to an outbreak no one could have foreseen."

She cleared her throat.

"But I think we've all done a great job keeping our spirits up, our outlook positive. We'll keep on ministering to the sick and dying, and we'll do the best we can. To that end, we have an announcement."

Total silence filled the auditorium during her brief pause. She pulled a hidden glass of water from the lectern. The woman was clearly in control, a born bureaucrat, and she relished the moment of total attention. I elbowed McDermott, and he nodded. The Kraken took a slow, theatrical sip. She nodded as she set the glass down again.

"The Bureau of Wellness has taken note of the way in which Saint Almachius has handled some of the toughest situations a modern hospital can face. Especially over the last few days. So they've chosen us to helm a prestigious new study."

"What kind of prestigious new study?" called out McDermott.

Whispers hissed among the aisles.

"Good question," she said. "It's a program on the use of vitamins in the course of normal treatment."

Here she turned her head and looked straight at me. I smiled and winked at her. She seemed to take no notice, though.

"The regional administrator informed us we were in a unique position to try additional infusions of vitamins for people who are undergoing a whole span of treatments—cancer, knee surgery, whatever," she said. "They want to measure the net benefits. It's going to be done discreetly, and we're going to administer it as a double-blind study."

"Don't the patients have to consent to this kind of thing?" hollered one of the gastroenterologists.

"Not if it's not dangerous," Kranklein said. "If there's only minimal risk, it's legal by Bureau standards. And we are 'doing no harm,' for those of you with hangups about the Hippocratic Oath."

The audience went silent for a second, then a cluster of hands went into the air with more questions. Kranklein easily answered all of them, as she pored over her Atman—what must have been the talking points she'd been given by the Bureau. Just as she was about to wrap up the speech, I raised my hand.

"Suzanne," I hollered, not even waiting for her to call on me. "Does this program extend to everybody, and every unit? As in, is obstetrics going to be part of it?"

"Yes, Joe, it does," she said, brushing her hair back off her shoulders. "With a difference—most of the expectant mothers are being informed of their participation. The Bureau decided it was best to notify them, so that if the patients were already taking supplements, we wouldn't be malnourishing the unborn children with double doses of vitamins."

"So," I called out again. "Is this program mandatory?"

"Mandatory is such a strong word, Joe," she said, looking down, consulting the Atman again. "But really, it wouldn't be scientific if we weren't able to get a full cross-section of the patients. And the mothers don't have to come to this hospital to have their babies. So they do have a choice.

"Now, folks," she said, turning, cutting me off, ignoring my still-raised hand, "we all know that this is another program run by the Bureau of Wellness, and there will be some additional regulatory forms to fill out."

Groans filled the auditorium.

"But," she continued, "you also know that this administration will be backing you up, making sure you get it all done. And it will be funded by the feds, so that means another year of solvency at Saint Almachius. Maybe even raises, when all is said and done. So go back to your posts, and we'll distribute instructions as the program progresses."

She winked and gave a crooked thumbs-up.

"Just know that we're here for you."

With a wave of her hand, everyone was dismissed. The crowd rustled and broke free from their seats, as nurses hurried back to their stations, and the doctors clustered to gossip about the new study.

"I wonder what the hell this is all about. I'm not missing my Saturday tee time because of this bullshit," said one young male doctor voice.

"I guess the Bureau of Wellness sees us as a possible test group for a big program," said another doctor, a bespectacled middle-aged woman. "It could be a great opportunity for the hospital, and for all of us."

"It's fucking shite, whatever it is," McDermott whispered to me, leaning in close.

"Just another way for the Kraken to kiss the Bureau's ass," I said. "But at least vitamins are harmless. At least she can't get people killed that way."

McDermott and I went down the hallway, pushed open the next door, and Betty Bathory stood there. She pushed past the Irishman and grabbed my sleeve.

"Lanza's looking for you," she said. "He's in your office."

I nodded and followed her. Lanza was sitting in my chair, feet up on the desk, buffing the badge on his chest as we walked in.

"You're getting to be a regular around here, Zo," I said. "What is it today—another Biblical disaster? Are the locusts on the wing?"

Slapping his feet down off my desk, I sat in one of the two patient chairs. Lanza leaned forward in the doctor's chair, waving at Betty to sit, too.

"I don't know what you're talking about. Just listen to me," Lanza said. "We don't think your Old Man is responsible for either of the attacks. Now everybody at the department thinks this Lamalade guy is the lone actor."

"That's what I was trying to tell you," I said.

"That's what the motherfucking scumbag said himself," Betty said.

We just stared at her. She shrugged.

"I just calls it as I sees it," she said. "I came to tell you guys—Lamalade's coming along. He's conscious, and he can even talk a bit. Some guy in a suit came to visit him and ask questions. He flashed a Bureau badge at me, and he said he was part of the investigation."

Lanza slammed his fist down on the desk.

"Goddamnit, we're supposed to do the interviews. I want to talk to him now."

"He might be asleep," Betty said.

"We'll wake him up," I said, jumping to my feet, ending the debate.

The three of us walked in silence down the hallways to the intensive care unit, and to the room in the farthest corner. Lamalade lay blanketed, in a pool of light from an overhead lamp. He wore a surgical mask over the bottom half of his face. The visible skin was nearly translucent. As our footsteps echoed into the room, the patient opened his eyes. Betty and I went to the foot of the bed. Lanza sat down in a chair next to the patient but leaned back as far as he could.

"Officer," Lamalade said, his voice muffled by the mask. "Don't be scared, man, I'm not contagious—this is for my own protection."

"And this is for mine," Lanza said, tapping the camera on his epaulet.

"Hey man—I want a lawyer," Lamalade said. "Isn't there some kind of due process here?"

Lanza laughed.

"Don't be stupid. All that went out the window with FOJA."

Betty elbowed me.

"FOJA?" she whispered.

"The Freedom of Justice Act," I said.

"Oh—that one," she said.

"We spent a little time reading up on you, Samuel," Lanza continued. "Quite a fall from grace. Promising scholar, star athlete. But a few years later you dropped out of med school and embarked on a life of petty crime. Been jailed at least four times for short stints. Owner of several very illegal German assault rifles. And we know you were a janitor at this very hospital, on duty the very same night your victims from the stadium massacre died in their beds. What we want to know is, why? Why did you do it?"

Betty elbowed me in my ribs again, but I shrugged it off. I was watching the sick patient. Lamalade was utterly strange and seemed on the verge of total collapse. From his bed, he stared at each of us. His crazed eyes narrowed to slits, mask crinkling as his smile widened.

"I shot those people, and I started the outbreak," he said. "But I never had access to the patient rooms. I was the janitor—I was cleaning shitstains and puke puddles, man. I was shining the floor just so thousands of filthy germbags could get it dirty again. Ask anybody here—I didn't finish those people off. I have better things to do with my time, man."

"Like plan another attack?" Lanza said, a little louder. "Kill more people?"

Lamalade laughed.

"I'm not much of a planner, man." He shook his head weakly, his glassy eyes shut slowly. "These things are just a product of bigger social forces at play. It's all statistics, man."

A moment of silence. The madman's words hung in the air.

I cleared my throat and everyone in the room turned to me. I glanced at Lanza, and then looked at Lamalade.

"Did you have anyone working with you?" I said.

Lamalade opened his eyes, then blinked. His gaze flicked to the window on his right.

"I had no help aiming and pulling the trigger at the arena, if that's what you're asking," he said.

"But with the outbreak, how did you do it?" I said. "Did you learn how to do all that at med school? Or while you were here at the hospital mopping floors?"

"That was easy," Lamalade said, eyelids fluttering. "It was just a vacuum in a jar, and if you hook up the right fixture to the right faucet, it back-sucks the bacteria right up into the water system. Instant outbreak. It's not rocket surgery, man."

Lanza had his arms folded, and he glared at me. I bit my lip. This was his show, and I was ruining it. But I had to know more, and I knew he wouldn't ask the right questions.

"But why?" I asked the patient.

"Oh, come on," Lamalade said, limbs pulling for the first time at the restraints under his bedsheets. He stared hard at Betty. She looked away.

"Nobody has any real idea why they do it," Lamalade continued. "Some say they were abused as children, or that they get sexual gratification from snuffing another person's life. I just wanted to do it. I got the idea, I got curious, and I tried it. I liked it, I did it again. There's no big reveal, man."

"Mm-hmm," I said, stepping toward the door. "Sounds sane. Well, good luck with the rest of the interview, and with a speedy and fair trial under FOJA. The nurses will drop in on you periodically. Tomorrow I'll come myself to check if you're still breathing."

I opened the door and walked out. Betty followed behind, and when we rounded the first corner, she yanked me by the arm into the alcove of the emergency exit.

"Joe, what the hell are you doing, butting into a police interrogation?" she said. "Are you nuts? Even if Zo is your friend, there's protocol."

"Lanza's good at many things, but one of his fatal weaknesses is a faulty bullshit detector," I said. "When we were kids, I put things over on him all the time. He still doesn't even know I lost my virginity to his sister in high school. And I know this psychopath Lamalade is lying."

"You slept with Juliet?" Lanza roared, coming around the corner, stopping just a foot away from me.

"Yes, Zo, it was her idea," I said, holding up my hands. "But that's not important now. That guy in the other room is full of shit. He's just a patsy. Someone put him up to this."

"How do you know that, Joe? You a trained detective or something?"

"No, but I do know the signs when someone's lying. It's been proven time and again that peoples' eyes move up and to the right as the brain accesses the part of their cerebral cortex using imaginative powers. The bullshitting part of their brain. While he was delirious, he talked about others being 'in on it,' meaning the attacks—it says that in the medical case file. Plus, this guy's too much of an idiot to put that device together. Even a talented engineer couldn't do it without some serious outside help. He had plenty of assistance—from somewhere."

"You have the medical case file?" Lanza asked. "I thought it was against the law for doctors to have…"

I glared at him.

"Zo, don't ask me a question if you don't want to hear the answer," I said.

Lanza nodded. He snapped his fingers and his face brightened.

"Could your Old Man be the guy?"

"Truth be told, I bet he can't be totally ruled out at this point," I said. "But I'm pretty sure this is beyond him, too. I think this person has some heavy-duty backing. Professional, corporate—maybe even government."

Betty and Lanza looked at each other. They burst into laughter.

"Government?" Betty said, rubbing her eyes. "Joe, you can't be serious. You know what you're saying?"

"Yeah, I do."

I folded my arms and glared at the two of them, from one to the other. They stopped laughing. Betty looked down at the ground, shaking her head; Lanza put his hands on his hips and stared at the ceiling. He sighed.

"You're nuts. But let's just say for a minute you're right," Lanza said. "Let's say there is some vast conspiracy to kill innocent people. Tell me one thing: Why?"

I looked from one to the other.

"Just think about it. Any lone gunman, no matter his IQ, can take out a crowd of people. We see that all the time—we know that profile, that modus operandi," I said. "But killing the survivors at the hospital, as if he was trying to eliminate all witnesses, and spreading plague at the apartments? That's something totally different. Not just any homicidal maniac has the patience and execution to pull that off. They need to have help—even just to get the bacteria. If it's not the government, it would have to be a biological facility or some expert. Maybe an academic. A true pro."

"I need to talk to your Old Man," Lanza said, shaking his head. "He lives in that apartment complex. He's a doctor."

"Wetherspoon doesn't have that kind of access to the big labs anymore," Betty said. "Besides, why would he shit where he eats?"

I nodded.

"I've got a hunch," I said, patting their arms. "You guys have to give me a day or two, but I have an idea who could have been behind this—or at least someone who would damn well know."

"Just don't get yourself fired, Joe," Betty said.

A loud beeping came from the opposite end of the intensive-care unit, followed by a rush of white coats. Instinctively, Betty and I rushed toward it, too, joining the flow of doctors and nurses.

When I was close enough to see the fray, I could see they were at Rothenberg's bedside. Rothenberg lay there, tubes askew out of his nose, mouth agape. I realized immediately my colleague was dying. Tears sprang to my eyes.

The nurses and doctors bellowed back and forth like a religious ritual, a call-and-response prayer of medical science. The rhythm continued as a big strong nurse pounded on his chest. Betty grabbed my arm tightly. I wanted to leap in and help. But there was nothing I could do. I wiped my eyes. The electric paddles came out, the barks grew louder, tubes were attached and then unattached, one drug and then another were administered.

Minutes passed. The movements slowed, ground to a halt. Then…silence. Everyone looked at the lead doctor, who shook his head. Lanza groaned, Betty shook her head. I wiped my eyes again.

The whole ceremony broke apart. Nurses left the isolation area, pulled off their masks and walked away. Doctors checked the monitors and the clock on the wall, a handful of others stood there for a moment, glanced at the body, then walked off to other duties. The door shut. After the crowd cleared, one remained, tapping into his Atman, noting the condition of the body, triple-checking instruments and measurements, completing the record before the body was moved to the morgue. I wiped my eyes and stared blearily, the unreality of Rothenberg's death washing over me in waves of horror. How could this happen—to a doctor who was my friend, no less? Had we done everything we could? Is this another person I could have saved?

"Hey, is that Culling?" Betty said, nudging me. "What's he doing on this floor, during the day shift?"

"I saw him before," I said. "I don't know why he's here."

I sniffled and wiped my eyes clear. And then I recognized the tall, slouch-shouldered nightshift nurse. Indeed, he wasn't supposed to be there. I reached forward and rapped on the glass. Culling raised his head, looking around for the source of the noise. I knocked again—this time harder, more insistent. Culling spun around, his eyes squinting devilishly over his mask.

"What are you doing here?" I said, loudly.

Reluctantly, Culling came over to the other side, tapping some words into his Atman. Then he held his wrist to the glass so we could see the message on the tiny implanted screen.

"WORKING OVERTIME FILLING IN FOR ONE OF THE TRIAGE NURSES WON'T MISS MY SHIFT TONIGHT," it read.

"You're not supposed to be here, you weirdo," Betty shouted.

Culling just shrugged. He turned and went back to the body, continuing his vulture circle around the body, the documentation of Rothenberg's slide into nothingness. The son of a bitch shoved one of the doctor's lifeless hands out of the way as he circled the gurney. I banged my fist on the glass. But he didn't turn around.

"He—is—supposed to be here," said a voice behind us. The Kraken squeezed herself between us, taking her own notes on her screen as she watched Culling's ritual around the body. "We have to record how the patient died. Charles has that experience with postmortem environments."

The Kraken just stood there, taking notes, watching Culling's perambulations. I angled my head to sneak a peek at her screen, but from my angle I only saw strange symbols I couldn't understand.

Betty stared at me. Her deadened eyes told me to say something, make a move, do something. But before I could do anything, the Kraken turned and marched toward the elevators.

I hesitated a moment. But then I charged after her, catching her in a few strides, grabbing her shoulder a little too hard. We both slid on the slippery tiles, still wet from the janitor's JiffySpiff. We caught ourselves—Kranklein grabbed a gurney, and I clung onto a nurses' terminal on the wall. Her face was flushed, livid.

"Doctor, what is your problem?" she said, straightening her brown suitjacket. Her twisted face looked all the older and uglier at that moment. I jabbed my finger at her. I felt a migraine building, the rush of rage through my head.

"Isn't there something you want to say?" I roared. "That wasn't just any patient we lost. He was one of our best doctors, goddamnit. And Wetherspoon has vanished. Isn't there something you need to tell the staff?"

She actually smirked at me. Her fingers did a little dance on her Atman.

"This is a hospital, Dr. Barnes," she said. "People do die, and diseases do spread. We can't be perfect all the time. I will send out a note on the passing of Dr. Rothenberg, and we will make sure his family is financially solvent. Apart from that, is there anything else you want me to say? Should I send everyone a card? Bake some cupcakes? Don't be a goddamned child."

My temples throbbed, my hands shook. I stared at her as she turned. Her heel slipped a bit, but she caught herself and continued down to the elevators.

"Oh, and Barnes," she said, without turning. "If this leaks out to the press, I want you to handle all the calls. Since you're sensitive to the subject, you can tell the world about how valiant your colleague was in giving his life to save others. Something poignant like that. Make it good, I don't care. Just know: any more scandals, and I will have you fired."

The Kraken barked something at a nurse folding towels, then walked away. That slow strut of hers was unpanicked, unhurried, at ease with the world—it was not the stride of a leader of a hospital in chaos. I felt a hand on my shoulder, then another.

"Your boss is a heartless tyrant," Lanza said. "I'd love to have a reason to pepper-spray her."

"It's as if she expected someone on staff to catch an eradicated disease and die on the job," Betty said. "What an asshole."

"Zo," I said. "I want you to check up on her. She's hiding something, and I think it may have something to do with all the insanity around here."

"Not going to be easy with the Bureau's regulations," Lanza said. "But I can do it. I'll call in a favor from some guys down in records."

"Good," I said. "I'm going to look into something myself. I'll let you guys know what I find."

Back in my office I flung open the dossier, releasing a puff of dust over the desk. But just as I ran my fingers over the first page, the Atman rang. I let it ring four and then five times, then finally picked it up.

"It's Jim O'Keefe with the *Newark FactSecond*. Don't hang up."

"You've got some gumption, calling me again, you jackass."

"Just hear me out," the reporter said. "I understand one of your colleagues was killed by bubonic plague. Isn't that the medieval disease? Where did he get it?"

"Listen, O'Keefe," I said, feeling my voice quake. "There's an investigation underway. There were multiple victims, but we don't know for sure how they contracted it. One of the doctors who responded to the scene was infected, and he died less than an hour ago. I don't know how you know that already."

"Doc, I have my sources. But I was hoping to find out—"

"And you will find everything out in due time," I said, cutting him off. "You know as well as I do, O'Keefe, that we can't put things out there that would panic people. We don't want to spread mass hysteria, right? So I'm sure there won't be any misquoting or fabricating stories or splicing together soundbites to take things totally out of context this time. Right?"

"Doc, I don't know what you're—"

"Yeah, you do. So that's it for now. Talk to you later. Or maybe never."

I hung up. As I pored over the page, the Atman rang once again, and I grabbed it.

"You goddamned sonofabitch," I barked into it.

"Honey?"

It was Mary's voice.

"Oh," I said. "Sorry, Dear. Thought you were somebody else."

"Joe," she said. "Did a doctor just die in the hospital?"

The silence hung. It was accusatory, seething. I loosened my tie.

"Yes. It was Stuart Rothenberg. You know—the surgeon who has the pool party every summer," I said. "The one with the back hair. He got plague. We couldn't save him."

She gasped.

"Joe, I thought everything was safe."

"He contracted it when we were all at the apartments the other day," I said. "It's safe. It was a total fluke he got sick."

Silence. I continued.

"We can't be sure everything always goes as planned. But we have to try and save people. What am I going to do, Mary, just walk away at a time like this?"

"It's all over the news, Joe," she snapped. "Everyone knows there's some kind of outbreak, and now it's killing doctors. Apparently I'm the last person to know. The wife of one of them."

"But Mary, it's just the media sensationalizing—"

The connection clicked dead. I punched in her number, but her Atman wasn't receiving calls. What could I have told her—that I had taken a risk in doing my job? Only Rothenberg got sick, and only because of a fluke. No one could even have known enough about it to publicize it.

Except for one person. I lunged for the terminal.

DEADLY VIRUS KILLS DOC, THREATENS THOUSANDS, screamed the headline of The *Newark FactSecond* story across my computer screen. I read through it—a story more or less accurate, except every number was inflated tenfold, the plague was referred to as an airborne virus instead of a bacteria transmitted by water, and the sense of panic was palpable in each and every word, each extra adverb flung gleefully into the mix. As I read through it, a voice started speaking through the computer. After a few seconds I realized it was my own voice, then that of O'Keefe. It was the completely unedited recording of the conversation we'd had just minutes before. I listened with horror as I heard myself threaten, then cajole, and hang up on the reporter. It looped back, repeating every syllable. I sounded bad—like an inside man hiding something. I could feel a tingle across the back of my neck. I picked up the Atman.

"Hello, *Newark FactSecond*," O'Keefe said.

"You son of a bitch—that conversation was private," I said.

"Doc, Doc," said O'Keefe. "You know as well as I do that I was interviewing you—and that you said all those things on the record. As my old editor used to say, 'That's baseball.'"

Insouciance colored the journalist's voice. He was eating on the other line, crunching something, chewing slowly. My hands shook with rage, my head thundered. He grunted once—then hacked deep in his throat, the unmistakable cough of a smoker of illegal tobacco. He gasped for a few moments. Then he laughed.

"At any rate, I'm ready to throw this whole conversation on the website as part two of our exclusive interview."

"You wouldn't."

"Still recording," the reporter said, still chewing.

I smacked my head. But I took a deep breath. The flush of defeat upended my stomach.

"Alright, turn off the recording. What do you want?" I asked.

"Thought you'd never ask," he said. "You know the Double-L Diner? Meet me there in a half hour." O'Keefe hung up.

What else could I do? I had no other choice. The Lenni Lenape Automat Diner was a forty-minute drive, including traffic. I got McDermott to cover my rounds, then sped down the ultrahighway heading east. I banged on the steering wheel the whole time, cursing myself for being outwitted by a sleazy reporter. When I walked into the diner, fifteen minutes late, O'Keefe's huddled form was already sitting at the table Lanza and I always shared. The same two teens, obese boy and girl, were sitting in the same place, tapping away at their Atmans, not looking at one another, muttering, playing hooky from school for yet another day. I gave them a glance, then sat down across from the reporter.

"Well, hello, Doctor," O'Keefe said, punching his order into the touch-menu.

"You unethical piece of—" I said.

But O'Keefe shook his head and raised a finger to his lips. He held up his wrist, where his Atman was blinking patiently, recording.

Grabbing the other menu from between the salt and the ketchup, I tapped a few buttons, then slid it back to its slot. O'Keefe smiled.

"So, Doc," he said. "I understand you'd like to continue our interview."

"Turn off the damn recorder now, or I'm not saying a word."

O'Keefe shrugged, then pushed a button on his wrist. The Atman light went off.

"Alright, what did you have in mind?" the reporter asked.

"You tell me what you're after."

O'Keefe held up his hands.

"Doc, you're the one that's been saying stuff on the record. You have nobody to blame but yourself. I'm just here to get the story."

"Even when you fabricate it," I said. "You know—after that editing job you pulled on the other one, I could sue you for libel."

"Come on, Doc," O'Keefe said. "Don't be dramatic. We can settle this like adults, without going to court."

"You've got some gall, talking like you have the moral high ground here," I continued. "You're just a lowlife blackmailer. Before we continue this conversation, you have to admit to me, right here and right now, that you're an unethical piece of shit."

A smirk crossed O'Keefe's face. He glanced around the diner. He shrugged.

"Yeah, sure, Doc," he said. "I'm unethical."

I shook my head.

"Repeat after me: 'I'm an unethical piece of shit.' Say it."

"I'm an unethical piece of shit. I'm a scumsucking gutter dweller. A two-faced lying rat bastard. Sure. Whatever you want," said O'Keefe, grinning wide. "But I'm just giving the people what they want. They crave soundbites, they want to see things for themselves, video and audio, graphics, cartoons. Shiny pretty things. They don't want to read anything. How can words about a murder possibly compete with raw footage of somebody's brains splattering against a windshield?"

I pulled out my Atman underneath the table, where O'Keefe couldn't see, and checked the time. It felt a little warm to the touch. The screen flickered, went blank. Strange. I shook it, then put it back in my pocket. But I was pretty sure it was still recording the conversation—my own little insurance policy I had prepared for the interview. I looked at the reporter and smiled.

"So what do you want?" I said, as pleasantly as I could.

"I heard you've got some actual paperwork from that older doctor in the hospital there," O'Keefe said. "Don't ask me how I know—I can't reveal my sources."

Hot panic slithered along my skin. I wiped a trickle of sweat on my brow.

"Yeah, I found a bunch of old papers. Why do you care?" I said.

"I want to know why they're so important."

"Who said they're important?"

"From what my source says—and I quote—they're the 'key to everything.'"

"Interesting," I said, cracking my knuckles. "So I give these files over to you, what are you going to do?"

"First, I would delete all our combative interviews," O'Keefe said. "Then I would inspect the papers. Then maybe I can help you with things back at Saint Almachius."

"If I don't give them to you?"

"Then this all becomes part of a messy story published this afternoon. Probably within the hour. I'm sure your boss will be pleased. What do they call her—the Kranker or something?"

I was silent. How had I become trapped in this situation? I remembered the Kraken's threats from just an hour earlier. My head swam with her grating voice still ringing in my ears.

"Come on, Barnes, let me take a crack at these papers," O'Keefe said, smiling, head shifting strangely on his neck. "Maybe I can help you while I'm helping myself."

A moment of silence, as we stared at each other like boxers in opposite corners of the ring.

I stood and walked out of the diner. Muttering to myself the entire way back out the front entrance, I returned to the car. I took the package off the front seat—the brown dossier. Tucking it under my arm, I turned on my heel and walked right back into the diner. I glanced at the waitresses, the same two obese teenagers from the last time at the Double L, the geriatric patrons lining the small tables along the walls. None of them looked suspicious—none of them seemed like they could be Bureau agents. So I slid the dossier across the table.

"You found it," the reporter said, pulling it over.

"It was in my car," I said, still glancing back and forth. "I didn't know what to do with it. I can't even read most of it. It's impossible to make out those tiny little letters. But I can tell it's old—and official."

"I know how it is, trying to read off paper," O'Keefe said, ruffling the sheaf beneath the table. "But I have some software for this kind of thing. It'll be able to digitally scan the old typeface. From there it's just a matter of picking through these redactions."

We ate, listening to each other chewing. The two teenagers to our right made some muffled, halfhearted conversation. The TV in the corner of the room celebrated the latest results of *How Low Can You Go*. Apparently, someone had eaten their own shit and had advanced past the first round; another had divorced his paraplegic wife to win the bonus round. (She would be able to take double or nothing by attacking him with a chainsaw the following episode). There was analysis of the Vegas odds, how many thousands of gamblers had beaten the spread and had won millions of tax credits. I tried not to listen, but someone had turned up the volume. After my fifth bite, I pushed the plate away. The reporter devoured his fried Twinkies, apparently unaware of the TV. When he finished, bright white cream was smeared through his gray beard. I didn't tell him.

"So, Doc," he said, picking up the coffee cup, the steam rising over his face. "Now that we're in this together, what do you think is going on? Do you think this shooter was also the guy who pumped the germs into the apartment complex?"

I cracked an energy stick and snorted it. With a rush, my brain seemed to vault back into action.

"We're not friends, O'Keefe," I said, rubbing my nose. "We're not in anything together."

"Come on, Doc," the reporter said. "May I call you Joe?"

"No."

"Fine, fine. This is all off the record, between business partners."

"In answer to your question, I don't know yet," I said. "Could be one rogue sociopath. We have them every few months. But I've never even heard of an overnight die-off like this before. Other patients at Saint Almachius are perfectly healthy. It makes no sense."

O'Keefe reached across the table and smacked my arm.

"That's why you need the power of the press!" he said. "Like the old-time watchdog role, the way it used to be! I'll see what's in these files, I'll ask around and see what we can dig up."

Sipping the coffee, O'Keefe stared off toward the TV, puckering his lips. He scratched at the dossier on the seat next to him, nodding.

"Let's agree—going forward we'll work together to figure it all out," the reporter said.

"I'm not your friend, O'Keefe. We're working along parallel lines, nothing more," I said. "And that's because I have no other choice."

"That's the spirit," O'Keefe said, reaching across and smacking my arm again. He rose from his seat, tucking the dossier under his arm. "Desperate men make the best investigators. You go talk to that maniac locked up in the hospital. In the meantime, I'll get to work on these pages. We'll talk in a day or two."

O'Keefe tapped the documents, flipped on his cap, and stepped toward the door.

But he turned and stooped with a graceless lurch near my ear. He wheezed hot breath down my neck.

"And just so you know: a source tells me the cops are looking at you as a suspect," O'Keefe said. "So watch your step, my friend."

GUATEMALAN SABBATICAL

U.S.A., 2087

The form was amorphous, throbbing, as Abbud waved the wand over Mary's womb. The white ultrasound mass floated in and out of view. Mary squeezed my hand as our child took shape, vanished, then reappeared on the screen. My heart leapt with each new ripple before my eyes.

But it appeared strange. It looked unreal, somehow. I had seen a million of these images, but my unborn child looked different, for some reason. I rubbed my eyes.

"All healthy and normal," Abbud said, nodding and smiling. "A little bit on the big side for the first trimester. But still normal."

Mary smiled and nodded, rubbing her abdomen dreamily.

"Boy or girl?" she said.

"Well now," Abbud said. "I could tell you, but both of you would have to sign the standard waiver—"

"Let's just be surprised," I said.

"But why keep it a secret?" Mary said, sitting up a bit, knocking the sonogram off-kilter so the screen went black. "I'd rather be able to plan ahead. Start painting the bedroom pink or blue. Things like that."

"I'd like to have a little old-fashioned mystery along the way," I said. "Let's at least wait until we talk this over at home. It's something we can't unhear."

She rolled her eyes, then looked at Abbud and nodded.

"Maybe the next appointment," she said. "I'll work on him."

"You're the boss," Abbud said, nodding. He readjusted the wand, so the bulbous, pulsating fetus again came into view. He nodded. "Everything looks good. But just one thing—keep in mind that this pregnancy may not be typical in some respects, considering Mary's exposure to the agents in the Middle East during her time in the Marines. There may be some vomiting of blood, and nausea, and other side effects."

"Vomiting blood?" I asked, my head starting to spin.

"Yes, Joe," said Abbud. "But as you know, Joe, nothing is definite in medicine."

Sweat pooled in my palm as I held Mary's hand. As I watched the squirming image, I saw—or thought I could see—vestiges of a life to come. The outline of my own chin, Mary's cheeks, what appeared to be relatively big hands the child could only have inherited from his or her father. But it changed and mutated, like a psychedelic dream. It looked like paint smeared by a brush on an easel. I stared and it changed back and forth, first becoming my human son who was just ready to burst into this life—then transforming to a softer-shaped daughter, a blob of cells, a primordial monster. Every time I was unsure of what I was looking at—a hand, or a foot, or a head—I stared all the harder to reassure myself there was a human being in that image before me. But then I'd blink and squint, unconvinced. Why was the kid so big? Both Mary and I had been born premature, and underweight. Was Abbud giving us the whole prognosis? Did he even know what was going on? How could bloody vomit be normal? I closed my eyes and breathed hard.

As the sweat pooled in my hand, the pulse in my thumb—the princeps-pollicis artery—throbbed hard. Then the same rhythm boomed in my temples, the superficial-temporal vessel. I withdrew my hand from Mary's and rubbed my head. The pain amplified tenfold, in a single moment. I almost screamed, but my mouth made no sound.

"Honey, what's wrong?" she said, laying a hand on my shoulder.

"Migraine," I said. I stood from the stool. The room wheeled around me.

"Overcome with seeing your child for the first time," Abbud said, nodding, his form blurry and distorted. "The realization you're going to be a parent takes over, and it can be overwhelming. I've seen it hundreds of times."

"Or it's too many of those damned energy sticks, Joe," said Mary, grabbing my arm.

Abbud stood and walked me toward the door. Everything around me was a maelstrom of light and color.

"Go back to your office—the rest of the check-up is just a formality," the obstetrician said, patting my back. "You already know the important things. Your baby is healthy, even if it's a little big. Everything is coming along."

I heard all this as a far-off echo. The pain seared through my head, a build-up like a complex symphony. I hadn't had a migraine in years, and it was worse than ever before. But this was important to Mary, so I swallowed and closed my eyes, and tried to stop the spins.

"But what about the nutritional supplements? We have…to know what…those are," I said, stopping at the threshold, fighting through the pain.

"Honey, don't worry," Mary said, wiping down her greased belly. "I've been reading up on everything, and Dr. Abbud and I have been going over all the fine print. This is only going to make the baby healthier. Just go sit down in your office and get a glass of water. I'll be up after we're finished."

Nausea crashed over me in waves as I turned and stumbled down the hall. I made it to the end near the elevator. I stopped and braced myself against the wall. Dozens of stingers attacked my skull, a pain that widened, then sharpened. I went through the door and ambled up the stairs as fast as I could, then down the hallway. The motorized ceiling cameras whirred, tracking me. I rushed into my office, swiped the Atman across the front of the drug cabinet, fumbling the codeine bottle on the lowest shelf. But just as I shook the pills out, I gasped once and closed my eyes. A vision of the drowning river, of my nightmare, washed over me—and then vanished.

The pain vanished. It disappeared with the vision, as quickly as it had come. I didn't move for a moment, waiting for the spikes to stab pierce my brain again. But nothing happened. I waited a moment. Nothing. So I shook the tablets back into the bottle, and set it back in the cabinet, which I locked.

What was happening to me? Rocking back in my seat, I kept my eyes shut and breathed. It was absolutely baffling—the violent queasiness had passed so quickly. I had never read about anything like it in any of the medical records before, let alone experienced something like it myself. But still I waited. I rubbed my temples to calm myself, put everything back at ease. Was I getting the mystery sickness that killed the Cruzen boy—or the plague that had killed Rothenberg? I snapped an energy stick, snorted deeply, and allowed the silence to envelop me.

It didn't last. Footsteps echoed down the hall, coming closer to me. I took a deep breath. There was a knock at the door.

"What do you want?" I snapped.

There was a beep, a click, and then Betty Bathory walked in, her scrubs rustling between her thighs.

"Joe."

"What is it, Betty?" I said.

"Seeing your unborn child for the first time too much for you?" she said, laughing. "Just think of all the afterbirth and fluids to come. The steaming diapers in your future."

"Shut it, Betty. I can't deal with this now."

She sat down in the guest's chair. Her grin contracted into a small smile.

"I'm just messing with you, Joe. How is Mary?" she asked.

"She's already the perfect mom," I said. "It's like she's possessed by some exotic Third-World fertility goddess. She's doing all this research, she's doing exercises and calculating her nutrition. She's got her head straight, too. That former Marine is going to make one excellent mother. It's incredible."

Betty's eyes narrowed at me.

"But also disconcerting," she said.

"Not disconcerting—just a bit overwhelming," I said. I shook my head, and folded my hands on the desk, like I was about to pray. "Betty, I haven't told anybody else this. But I've got to tell somebody, or I'll go crazy."

"What, Joe?" She leaned forward, an eager look on her face.

"Mary and I always talked about having kids," I said. "But it had been so long, I thought it would never happen. I just got done paying off one mortgage, and I wanted to build up a nest egg—just in case. We have all the money we'll ever need, but it's all caught up in things I can't touch for a little while. So there's no cash. I had a plan. It was all going perfect. And then she got pregnant. The miracle happened, and I'm not ready for it."

"So this is a roundabout way of saying you're in a financial hole," Betty said.

"Not a hole, exactly," I said. I opened my mouth to say more, but I couldn't.

"But the finances are not good," she said.

"Yes. That's a better way of putting it."

"Is this just a we-might-have-to-cut-back-on-eating-out kind of thing, or is it a we-might-not-have-food-on-the-table-at-all problem?"

A pause. I rubbed my eyes.

"Food might generally be a challenge," I said.

She sighed, rubbing at her own eyes.

"Damn, Joe. Does Mary know?" she said.

"Not really."

She sighed.

"You know you have to pay the birth tax," she said.

"I know. I'll figure something out," I said.

"Are the baby's health costs covered, at least?" she said.

"Yes. But only because everything's covered under this new vitamins study. Mary's been reading the fine print on that, checking everything out. But if we weren't part of the program, we'd be delivering the kid at home on the couch with blankets and kitchenware."

"That's good. But I would read that fine print yourself—not that I don't trust Mary," Betty said. "With things like this, it's always good to have a second pair of eyes checking everything out. And you're a doctor. She's just a jarhead, no offense meant to her."

"She's more than just a jarhead, Betty. But I will. I haven't had the time. You know how it is lately around here. Maybe I'll check with Abbud now. Mary might still be there."

"That'll have to wait, Joe," she said. "Because the psycho wants to see you."

"Kranklein?"

"No, not that psycho," she said, chuckling. "The janitor. Lamalade. He's been asking for you ever since my shift started. He's got a wild look in those googly eyes of his."

I rose from my chair and tugged at my collar.

"I wanted to talk with him anyway," I said.

She came over, slapped my hands away, and straightened my tie. She was close. Her sweet perfume rose to my nose.

"So go give him the third degree before the cops come back," she said, holding up her hands. "They've been relentless ever since he got here. Especially your friend Zo."

I opened my eyes. She looked up, and our eyes met. We looked at each others' lips, and a quick thought, and memory, were exchanged. But we glanced quickly away, and I stepped aside.

"I'm going. Just start on the rounds. Check on MacGruder, especially."

"Why MacGruder?" she asked.

"I'm just…worried," I said. "I couldn't say why. So just keep up on him. And tell him I'll be by later, if I can."

"Aye aye, Doc," the nurse said, giving me a mock-salute. "And don't worry about Mary—I'll make sure she gets home in one piece."

I turned to go, but she grabbed my arm.

"And I won't say anything about the money," she said. "But you have to tell her. The sooner the better."

"I know," I said, turning away from her.

The cameras tracked me, with their whirring gears, as I walked down the hallway.

Again there were no guards outside Lamalade's door. The chances of an escape in his weakened condition were not good, and apparently the authorities weren't worried about retribution from the victims' families. Lamalade sat up in bed, reading on the Atman in his wrist, some tiny spectacles perched on his nose. The mask was gone. The big wart on his nose was clear to see. He looked like a ghoul. When he saw me walk into the room, he smiled and snatched the glasses off his face.

"Dr. Barnes, to what do I owe this honor?" he said.

"You asked for me."

"Did I? I guess I did. Man, I've been so out of it ever since I came down with this bug that's been going around. It's all been a blur, man."

"By bug you mean bubonic plague. From your own biological-weapons attack," I said, pulling a chair to the bedside.

"I wouldn't say 'attack.' And for most people it's just a passing thing. It's not like we live in Dark Ages Europe or something. Antibiotics kill infections, people get better."

I sat down, leaned forward, elbows on knees.

"That's rich. Twelve dead, five more on the verge. You're smarter than the average psychotic, Sam," I said, shaking my head. "But you never gave me a straight answer. Why kill these people at the talent show? Why infect an entire apartment complex?"

"'Talent show'—that's funny, doc. Let me see if I can give you the 'straight answer' you're looking for," Lamalade said, folding his hands across his lap. "First off—have you seen this so-called 'talent show'? '*How Low Can You Go*'?"

"I've heard of it, but I don't really watch TV."

"I knew I liked you, Doc—I knew you were a sensible man," Lamalade said. "'*How Low Can You Go*.' It's right there in the name. It features people taking dares from the audience, the more outrageous the better. People eat insects, fight wild animals, disfigure themselves, and perform live sex acts on strangers for a chance to win sums of money. I saw a father inject his nine-year-old daughter with heroin—he won a couple thousand bucks for that. And that lowlife who bit poisonous snakes—he was a real winner."

"You're saying you punished people who liked a TV show. Innocent fans of a TV show."

"Not really. I'm punishing the culture itself."

"Bullshit. You murdering innocent people does nothing to the culture."

"Not necessarily. But if someone has to go on a killing spree, why not pick the place with the lowest common denominator?"

I held out my hands.

"What do you mean, 'if someone has to go on a killing spree?'" I said. "Did someone put you up to this, Sam?"

But the younger man said nothing. Scratching my brow, I shook my head. I felt so tired—so incredibly tired, speaking with this unhinged patient I had to keep alive, yet who valued no life in any way.

"You're talking to a doctor, Sam," I said. "My whole existence is about saving lives. In my world, you're just one little human tumor in the midst of an otherwise functioning society. And even still, I'd like to save your life."

Lamalade laughed. His rail-thin frame lifted higher in the bed, like he was ready to jump out of his leg restraints onto the floor, perhaps even spar with me.

"Listen to yourself, man," Lamalade said. "Your self-righteous platitudes just make my point. These people who died in the last few days, weeks, whatever—what did they do to help the human condition? You'd say everyone's innocent, everyone has a right to live, blah blah blah. But you don't see any of these people doing anything to better the world. People starve in Africa, terrorists bomb every city in the Middle East. These sleazes watch clips of it all on TV and make jokes. A few blocks down from this depraved 'talent show,' people are living on the Newark streets, unable to feed their children, and these social parasites do nothing. They zip past on their way to an audition for a show called '*How Low Can You Go*,' where they compete to debase themselves for a few crumbs more. These people were not innocent. Most of them were probably Mister Smith voters. They were all guilty as hell. And they deserved punishment."

I stood, walking slowly toward the window, my steps slow as I carefully worked through the words of this killer. I worked through a spot diagnosis from my memories of psychology. Lamalade was not insane, necessarily—but perhaps he was a psychopath. I had to tread lightly in this conversation, because he was no fool.

"So what you're saying," I said, "is that these people deserved to die because they were fans of a despicable popular culture."

"Last season's winner had sex with a horse on live television, man," Lamalade said. "But the guy couldn't collect his winnings until after he got out of the hospital. And you should have seen the horse."

"Sam," I said, affecting my most professorial tone. "Even if these people were not innocent—what does it solve, really? What does killing random people do to improve anything?"

Lamalade grinned, and for the first time, I could see the lopsided nature of the man: the crooked teeth, the shiny-eyed glint, the splotchy cheeks, the glee in the premature wrinkles, and that bulbous wart. He was only thirty or so, but at certain angles he looked like a man twice that age. I cringed a bit looking into that visage.

"Oh, you think it doesn't improve anything," the patient said, settling back on the pillow. "But you can't see the forest for the trees, man. You can't see that by saving a single life, you might cause a thousand to die. Or by killing fifty who deserve it, you can save ten thousand who deserve to live. You can't see my point."

"Alright," I said. "Make me understand."

With a coy smirk, Lamalade turned away, like a flirtatious young girl.

"I'm not supposed to tell," he said.

I sat back down.

"So someone gave you orders."

Lamalade scoffed.

"Listen, man, I don't take orders from anybody. Nobody's pulling these puppet strings," he said, pinching at the shoulders of his hospital gown, wires from his fingers dangling. "But we all have to answer to somebody in this lifetime."

He paused, glancing up at the ceiling. I felt around in my pocket to make sure the Atman was still there, still recording. Lamalade sighed, breath rattling in his chest.

"Man, we have to be willing to do some bad things for the greater good," he said. He labored to inhale. "Occasionally, you've got to take a great leap forward by being a person of courage and character. Not just obeying what you were taught in preschool, or what you read in a religious book. You can't just be a couple of claws scuttling across the floor of the ocean, man."

Those words unlocked something in me, like an incantation. They were so familiar, from somewhere deep in my past. I could hear the echoes of my father's voice, from his chair in the old house, a lifetime ago. This psychopath hadn't gotten them exactly right. But I could nearly remember their pattern, that rhythm. Where had those words come from?

"I don't even know why I'm telling you this—I'll probably get in big trouble," Lamalade said. "You see, it's all an experiment. Everything is an experiment. It's all trial and error, man."

I shook off my reverie and pointed at him.

"What do you mean, an experiment?" I said. "What are you saying?"

"Man, you don't even know. You don't even know."

Lamalade yawned, slowly. He closed his eyes and sank further into the pillow, with a strange little shudder. In a single moment, his skin flushed to a patina green.

"Mer-da," Lamalade mumbled. His jaw fell limp, mouth agape.

"No. Wake up. We're not done talking yet," I said, springing forward, shaking the patient's shoulders. Lamalade's head rolled limp on his neck. He wasn't asleep. I felt for a pulse at his jugular. There was none.

"Nurse!" I yelled, running to the door, looking both ways down the hallway. I rushed back to the bedside and pushed the red panic button on the wall. It started blinking. Footsteps tipped, tapped, slapped down the hallway. Three nurses and two emergency doctors burst into the room. I pointed at the patient, directed them to fetch the paddles. The doctors opened Lamalade's eyelids, shone a light in, and opened the patient's shirt. The oldest nurse came over with the defibrillator, slathered with gel.

"We've still got a chance. He's been gone less than a minute," I said.

The other doctor, a bespectacled young woman, pulled Lamalade flat on the bed.

"What the hell happened?" she said.

"I don't know. He has plague," I said.

"Then what the hell good is the defib?" said a third doctor, also young and unfamiliar to me.

"This man can't die," I barked. "He needs to live."

The male nurse among them charged up the paddles and waited for the order. I gave it. The nurse shocked the heart, and Lamalade's torso bucked up violently. Nothing. I gave the order again. Again, a convulsion—and again nothing. The nurse looked at me. I nodded. A zap, and nothing more. Cursing, I waved them off. They scattered.

Culling, who observed unseen from the edge of the room, emerged from the shadows in the corner to document the death scene, to download the data from the patient's monitors. He moved around the body like a wraith, slow and silent. I stared at him in disbelief, like I was looking at the angel of death itself.

The young doctor with the glasses came around the bedside to me. She had a shock of curly hair and the youthful face of the perpetual intern, the seasonal worker of the hospital.

"Dr. Barnes, did you say this patient had plague?" she said, pushing the glasses up her nose.

"Yeah, he was the suspect found in the apartment complex a few days ago," I said.

The young doctor looked at the bedside, where Culling took notes on his Atman. Her brow wrinkled, she shook her head.

"Everybody around here knows this patient," she said. "But I was with the treating doctor when he said the stem cells had worked. His blood was clear of *Yersinia pestis*. They were taking him to the county jail tomorrow. He was cured, the treating doctor said so."

"What treating doctor?"

A young male doctor at her shoulder shrugged.

"Asian guy. Never seen him before. Middle-aged. He didn't talk much, but he muttered some affiliation with an Ivy League school. Very quiet."

The mention of an Asian doctor from an Ivy League school sent a jolt through me. I held my finger up, my mouth open like I was about to say something, but I turned and dashed off. I reached my office on the third floor in a minute flat, and frantically scanned through my computer looking for the name and the number of the stem-cell researcher. It had to be a coincidence; it couldn't be that big a deal anyway. It's not like doctors with Asian names were scarce at Ivy League schools, after all. I myself had worked with dozens matching that description during my time as a student. At the bottom of the screen, I found a small entry for the call weeks earlier: the doctor who had written the study on the premature deaths from stem-cell treatments, the one on sabbatical in Guatemala.

The name was Yoshiro Fujimi.

I checked the roster of doctors and nurses in the hospital's database. And at the bottom of this list, like a speck of gold on a riverbed, were the same two words, although they were backwards. The shock of recognition hit me.

Fujimi Yoshiro; Yoshiro Fujimi. The same exact name.

I said it over and over again, practicing the pronunciation like it was some incantation, syllables meshing together like a sing-song spell: Yo-she-ro-fu-ji-mi, Ro-fu-ji-mi-yo-she. The words spiraled out of control, took on their own swirling life in my head.

Mi-yo-she-ro-fu-ji.

Head spinning, I picked up the Atman and called the Ivy League office number I had on file. No-one picked up. But the recording of a young female voice said the same thing I'd heard before: Professor Fujimi was on a lengthy sabbatical conducting research in Guatemala, and he was out of the office indefinitely. I hung up.

But still it continued. Fu-ji-mi-yo-she-ro. Ji-mi-yo-she-ro-fu…

I took a deep breath. Sitting back, I held my head in my hands as I slowed my brain's revolutions. There was no reason to believe it was the same person. No name was unique any more, not after the world's population had reached eleven billion, way ahead of predictions. Nothing new existed under the sun. Yoshiro Fujimi or Fujimi Yoshiro—either way it could be a common enough name among the Japanese. No reason to jump to conclusions. I calmed myself, thinking of all the Joes I knew, all the Steves and Michaels and Claras and Patricias, and even the Blaines and Blakes and Jesuses, monikers which were unusual enough. I knew at least three of each and every name, and they were of all different colors and creeds. Hell, I knew a LaQuan who was redheaded Irish—and a José who was a hulking Russian. There could be any number of Yoshiros and Fujimis in the world, and they could be from any corner of the mixed and matched medley of the 21st-century global village.

But Meruda. That was a name I hadn't ever heard—except on the lips of dying men. Who was this woman who so captivated the flickering lives of men on the brink? I had to know.

Turning away from the terminal, I thumbed absentmindedly through the paper book I had taken from Wetherspoon's office. I came upon a picture of screaming children walking down the road, away from a blackened, burning sky. Soldiers talked in the background. In the center of it all was a naked girl howling, her arms held out at her sides, like her seared skin was balanced atop her arms and would fall off with any movement. Her mouth was impossibly wide, like she could swallow the world. I knew it was old, but there was no caption. For some reason the picture made me think of my unborn child. I picked up my Atman, tapped a message to Mary, and waited for her to respond. Stowing the book underneath the desk, I leaned back, with my hands behind my head.

And in walked the Kraken. She rolled her eyes at my relaxed posture. I had to smile at her timing.

"Thought I'd find you here," she said, sitting down in a chair. "Dogging your rounds again, Barnes?"

"Suzanne, do we have a new doctor on staff here?" I said, ignoring her question. I sat forward, folding my hands atop the desk.

"Actually, that's what I came to see you about," she said. Her eyes were pointed down at her Atman. "Perhaps it was a mistake to designate you as our spokesman over the last few weeks."

"I thought I handled those responsibilities remarkably well," I said.

"You've been talking to that reporter—what's his name, O'Creep or something?"

"Jim O'Keefe. You told me to handle the press. I talked with him a few times. I had to."

She looked up and nodded, biting her upper lip to keep from smiling as she savored some delightfully-bad news. My heart sank at that executioner's joy, the barely-suppressed mirth. Something heavy was coming. She was moving in for the kill, and I was the prey, I knew.

"Well, the administrators were told that was not the case," she said, slowly. "We have reports of you being seen with O'Keefe over coffee at a local diner."

I could feel my skin turn warm and clammy. They had seen. They had eyes everywhere.

"Just a short interview," I said quickly. "We ran into one another. He recognized me from the time I had him thrown out of the hospital."

"The hospital's cameras show you receiving a call, then hurriedly leaving on the ultrahighway in the direction of the Lenni Lenape Automat Diner. The eyewitness also says you handed the reporter a pile of old papers stolen from the hospital."

I shook my head slowly. She was grinning.

"They were only some documents shared between myself and another doctor," I said.

She shook her head.

"Dr. Barnes, we know you took those files from Cornelius Wetherspoon's office," she said. "You stole hospital property and made it public. It's not only an ethical violation, it's also a legal violation, according to Bureau regulations. I could have you arrested and charged by the end of the business day."

"It was not hospital property," I said, scoffing. "It was my property Wetherspoon gave me before he disappeared."

"Yes, Doctor. I'm sure he also authorized you to kick in his door."

Now she was positively beaming. I smacked the desk, once, hard. My temper simmered, a dangerous feeling I struggled to tamp down. I had to maintain control.

"Well, I guess you trust your spies more than your own employees," I said. "So where does that leave us?"

"Funny you put it like that," she said. She paused, gazing down at the Atman as if it was a crystal ball. "Really, it's out of my hands. The federal code says you must be suspended indefinitely." She looked over her shoulder at something. Something black. I squinted. It was a camera in the corner. I'd never seen it before in all my years in that space. It had to be new. She snapped her fingers at it.

Sweat beaded my brow. I looked at her face. She stared at me with dead eyes, appraising me as if I was just a broken gear to be yanked out of the machine. But I fought down the tremors in my voice.

"Some Asian guy is taking my job?" I said, guessing.

"When you say it like that, Barnes, it sounds racist. But in a word—yes," she said. "Dr. Fujimi came to us highly recommended from the Ivy League school where he teaches. He's an icon in the Bureau's experimentation division. We figured while we had to fill an open slot, we might as well upgrade."

A shiver ran through me at the sound of the name. But she didn't notice—she was staring at a few of my diplomas on the wall. She frowned thoughtfully.

"Of course, if you were to return the stolen property back to the hospital, the Bureau might consider reinstating you." She smiled, and she put her hand in front of her face, covering the wide smile, the hateful joy.

I stared at her. I leapt up and lunged toward her, jabbing an index finger in her face. My hand quivered with rage. I had lost my battle for control, and my anger had taken over.

"I don't know what part you're playing in whatever's going on," I said. "But I will find out. I will expose you."

She snarled, standing, eyes wild. She jabbed her finger in my face. We looked like two ineffectual fencers, with tiny swords pointed at each other. The ceiling camera rotated a bit, focused on us.

"What'll you do, team up with that idiot reporter? Don't threaten me, Joe Barnes," she said, sneering. "Your patients died, and you are a failure. You compromised hospital security. I'm going to ensure your medical license is revoked."

She smiled.

"You can pack up your things, Doctor. And if you get the stolen property back, you can crawl back here, and grovel. Maybe I'll consider—just consider—bringing you back on board."

I snarled at her, grabbed my necklace, picked up my briefcase, and walked to the door. I didn't glance back once at my office. She walked behind me, step for step. Waiting in the middle of the hallway were Stash and Stanislaw, the security guards, looking at me with apologetic faces.

"Come with us, Doc," Stash said.

"You can pack up some things first," Stanislaw added, nodding sadly.

I shook my head and gestured them onward.

We walked down the hallway. The Kraken stayed at the office door, tapping into her Atman, which blipped brightly. We reached the elevator, went inside, and Stash pushed the button. But as the doors closed, I noticed a white coat and a dark mane of hair whisk by. I stuck my hand out in the closing slot, opening the doors. I stepped forward and peered out. Suzanne Kranklein looked up and said something inaudible to the fast-approaching man in the white coat. The two shook hands. She ushered the stranger inside my office. Just before he entered, he swiveled his head to me. I squinted, and could just make out the pinched, academic face of a man. The man waved a strange farewell. I started to step forward and opened my mouth to call out.

But big hands yanked me back in the elevator. The doors shut.

"Sorry, Doc," said Stash. "We have our orders to make sure you get out of the hospital safe and sound. And fast."

"Yeah, sorry, Doc," Stanislaw said. "Once you're in the elevator, we have to get you out of the building."

"We have to go back," I said.

"No can do, Doc," Stash said.

Two floors ticked by, and the elevator reached the ground. I waited for the doors to open. After a moment, I slammed my fist into the wall of the elevator. Pain seared through my fist, and I sucked in breath through my teeth.

"You'd think after years of slaving away at this goddamned place, I could at least talk to the scab replacing me."

The doors still hadn't opened. There was some kind of delay. I glanced at the guards. Stash had his finger on a red button, holding the door closed. His brow wrinkled.

"Not for nothing, Doc," Stash said. "But this wasn't any normal kind of suspension. I mean, Slav and I haven't thrown many people out before. We've seen violent criminals walk out of here on their own. But for you, there was a notice…"

Stash looked at Stanislaw, who nodded.

"We got this notice on the terminal downstairs," Stanislaw said, nodding eagerly. "It was from somebody way up. Way beyond the Kraken. Someone from the Bureau of Wellness, with the holographic seal authorization on it and everything. It was marked 'Urgent.'"

I nodded. I tapped Stanislaw on his massive shoulder.

"Not to worry, guys," I said. "You're just doing your job. I'll get this all straightened out. It'll be fine."

They nodded at me, meeting my eyes. Stash took his finger off the elevator button, and the door opened. Together we all walked out into the lobby, neat as you please, like nothing was wrong. The two guards were on either side of me, cramped into the revolving door. We all stepped a few paces out onto the front walk.

"Best to you and the family, Doc," Stash said.

"I hope you get this all sorted out," Stanislaw said. "And be careful, for chrissakes."

I nodded and shook both their hands.

"Take care of the place while I'm gone," I said.

Three cameras followed my march to the parking lot. I paid them no mind. I got in the car and drove away without looking back. Just before the onramp for the ultrahighway, I stopped the car. I attacked the steering wheel, punching it, elbowing it, headbutting it in a primal fury. Years of work at an end, everything was over because of a worthless bureaucrat and the faceless scab now settling into an office I had earned after years of slaving away in the ICU. I had earned everything, and now it was gone. I punched the rearview mirror off the windshield, and my hand exploded with pain.

It had happened. It was all done with. There was nothing I could do. I was finished. Breathing in and out, pulse racing, I pushed myself to a kind of calm. What's done was done. Time to get home. I pressed the accelerator and pulled away.

As I drove west, I flexed my throbbing knuckles and listened to the radio. Saxas rattled off the latest in the world-at-large: a new topic every fifteen seconds, a few sentences, then on to another continent. Her voice seemed quicker, higher than normal—perhaps the advertisers were pushing for quicker news broadcasts. But the unflappable cyborg voice had a tinge of foreboding, somehow. Maybe it was a software glitch, I thought.

The came the featured story. I twisted the volume knob gingerly with my aching fingers.

"Breaking News. In Asia, a shocking turn of events. Just as an historic accord between Korea, China, and Japan was about to be reached at the Pyongyang Summit, a lone gunman breached security and shot and killed the U.S. Vice President.

"The American dignitary was having a lobster dinner with the other heads of state, when a waiter reportedly approached him, and asked in perfect English whether he would like a glass of red or white wine.

"The Vice President answered red, and the waiter tapped the order into his Atman, pulled out a handgun, and shot the second most powerful man in the world four times in the head, then put one bullet through his own. Although the rest of the delegation rushed both the leader and his assassin to the hospital, both were dead on arrival.

"Within minutes of the announcement of the Vice President's death, all parties involved in the region blamed one another for the assassination. The Pyongyang Summit is effectively canceled, all travel between the countries is shut down, and trade between members of the East Asian Federation has ceased," Saxas said. "The United States has not yet issued a statement on the assassination, but the President has called for a press conference this evening to discuss 'matters of grave importance.'

"In medical news. A coalition of experts who contradicted the War on Cancer findings have dropped their objections to the Bureau of Wellness' declaration of victory over the disease. However, none of the coalition's leaders could be reached for comment.

"And in other Bureau of Wellness news, the federal agency unveiled a new vitamins study looking at a cross-section of the U.S. population. The study's already been in progress for several years. But officials now say they're reaching out to the public in an effort to bring more volunteers into the unprecedented research. The agency says they're focusing on prenatal health, but otherwise declined to elaborate further about the triple-blind study."

I looked at the radio. The vitamins study had to be the same one Kraken presented. I hadn't been listening intently, but the words "triple-blind study" sprung out at me with sudden familiarity. I'd heard the term before but had no idea what it meant. Double-blind, sure—but triple-blind? Who was the third party kept in the dark? What did it mean?

The radio recycled itself, Saxas speaking of the world catastrophe in the same tone of voice and inflection. No further information, no elaboration on the world's movements and happenings—the intrigues and tragedies of the day. Chaos without resolution for another day, and another cliffhanger ending. I flicked the radio off. The highway sped by in silence. My hands took me home, automatically, without a conscious thought.

It was only when the car was parked in the driveway when the panic hit me. I frantically grasped for ways to tell my wife I had lost my job. I phrased the questions and answers carefully in my mind. Conversational dead-ends popped in my head. The air inside the car got hot, I started to sweat. I would have to tell her everything, the unvarnished truth. I knew it. What other choice did I have? She would discover everything anyway, and the best way was to just tell her. Visions of yelling and divorce proceedings spun through my mind. I sweated through my shirt.

But I couldn't tell her about the money. That would be the breaking point. I had to tell her everything—everything but that.

Taking a deep breath, I stepped out of the car, walked up to the door and went inside. Sounds from the kitchen—pots and pans clacking. I tossed my briefcase next to the umbrella stand, unknotted my tie, took another deep breath, and went through the hallway.

She was at the stove. She looked up from a boiling pot and smiled beautifully at me. My heart nearly broke in that moment, and my lips quivered at the sight.

"Hiya, hon," she said.

"Rough day," I said, coming up behind her, giving her a kiss on the cheek. "Dear, there's something I have to tell you. About the hospital."

She banged a spoon on the pot, nodding, her smile vanishing.

"I already know," she said. She placed the spoon down and turned to face me, locking onto my eyes. "I called Dr. Abbud before, and he told me."

"You called Abbud. He already told you."

"Yes. You doctors gossip like a knitting circle."

Mary reached out and hugged me, patting my back. I felt drained, lifeless on my feet. We said nothing for a few minutes. She just held me. Nothing moved other than the systole, diastole of my heart for that time in her embrace.

"I can get my job back," I said, my voice choking. "In a few weeks. Once everything settles down."

"Just take it easy," she said. "Everything will be fine."

"I have to make sure the health costs are covered when the baby comes. Kids don't come cheap," I said.

"It's all covered, remember? Abbud and I went over it," she said, gently patting me on the back. I pulled away, so I could get a good look at her.

"Everything is still covered? I thought I had to be in good standing with the hospital."

"We're still covered, hon. Abbud reminded me to look at the waiver I signed at the first visit," she said. "It's part of the vitamin trial—no matter where you work, no matter what insurance you have, they guarantee to cover you 'through the birth and for the first two years of the child's life.'"

"Really," I said, staring off at the boiling pot, thinking. "So that leaves only us to worry about."

"That's not a worry, either. The waiver covers all three of us," she said.

She smiled. I scratched my head, turned and walked a few steps. All the health costs were covered for an entire family—what did that mean? They'd never offered a deal like that at Saint Almachius before. They'd never offered a deal like that anywhere, I was sure. A triple-blind trial in which everything and everyone was covered, without any insurance at all…

"So who fired you? That Kraken bitch?" she said, turning back toward the stove.

"Yeah," I said. "They're accusing me of stealing hospital property."

"What kind of property?"

"Papers."

"Papers?"

"Papers from Wetherspoon's office."

"Did you take them?"

"Yes."

"Were they yours?"

"Not really."

"What did you do with them?"

"I gave them to a reporter."

"Goddamnit, Joe. Why would you do a stupid thing like that? Were they important?"

"I think they're important. I think they're a clue to the unexplained deaths. They were old and unreadable, but they mean something to somebody."

"Why didn't you just give them to the cops? To Zo or somebody over there?"

"They would just gather dust. Some of them are from a hundred and fifty years ago, Mary. Cops only care about what happened last weekend. They forget about most crimes after a few days. Why the hell would they care about ancient history?"

"Alright," she said, setting the spoon down on the stove-top. "So these papers—what's so important that it's worth losing your job over?"

"I couldn't read most of them, I'm telling you. They were all in the old alphanumerics, no Gliffs at all. I haven't read ink on paper since I was a kid, and these pages were smudged, anyway."

"Why did Wetherspoon have them?"

"If he was around, Mary, I would ask. But he's been missing since the plague outbreak at his apartment complex."

"Neal can take care of himself," she said. She grabbed both my arms. "They can't just fire you without having good proof that you harmed Saint Almachius, that you were doing really improper things not in the best interest of the hospital."

"I was doing something that wasn't in the best interest of—some people— at the hospital."

"Yeah, but did you do something that would hurt the patients?"

"No. I'm trying to save the patients."

"See? You're a healer, honey. A good doctor. You'll get your job back. Or you'll get another one. We'll be fine."

We hugged, the timer on the boiling pot went off, Mary finished fixing the NutriFast sack for dinner. Mary said something about buying a crib with one of her credit accounts. The unsaid thing—the crippling debt—hung over me in the silence. Later we went to bed. We lay awake for some time, talking about what our child would be like—whether he would be tall, or she would be pretty, whether the kid would do well in school, what sports the child would play in high school. After awhile, Mary's Dormus hummed peacefully on the other side of the bed. I stared at the ceiling above my head without seeing anything other than shadows, and an old stain I hadn't noticed before.

THE STARES FROM UNSEEN EYES

Japan, 1946

As dawn broke over Shibayama on the third day, the three Americans again approached the Ishii house. But this time they walked with a fourth man—a tall thin doctor puffing a cigar. A rooster crowed off to their left, from behind the house, and they jumped.

"What a fucking country," said the doctor, shaking his head, pulling at his collar. The ash tumbled off his cigar. "It's like a dollhouse that just spreads on for miles."

"A dollhouse filled with people who hate us," Fell said. "Keep moving—I want to make sure we get to him as early as possible for the check up, Phil. Especially before the Russians get there."

"Word is they'll arrive before lunch," Stanger said, nodding at the doctor.

Slawson lit a cigarette with trembling hands.

"No time to lose," Slawson said, tilting his head down the street.

The other three men nodded, and they went shoulder to shoulder down the tiny thoroughfare. Fell strained to hear anything in the houses or the side streets of the village, but there was only silence. That's the way it had been since the beginning of the Occupation, when the tall Americans in helmets and khakis began streaming down every street, poking into every doorway on every island. The Japanese hid in their homes, just waiting for it all to pass, like an illness. And wherever the Americans went, they could feel the glares, the stares from unseen eyes in the windows up above, from doorways and alleyways in smoldering cities from Hokkaido to Kyushu. Fell knew any of these small alert people could ambush him on a darkened street on the way back from the bars each night, like samurai materializing from the shadows.

At the door the four men lined up. Fell reached forward and knocked. A minute passed, and the door creaked inward slowly. Nothing more—no one appeared at the threshold. Fell went in first, followed by the other three. Broken shards littered the ground underfoot—pieces of ceramic and glass, the fragments of a telephone, with cord still attached. The fern lay shredded in a wide puddle of water. Slawson whistled, long and low.

"Must have been a hell of a party—" he said.

But as he turned around, his voice choked in his throat. Fell turned too, and his jaw dropped. Ishii's wife stood behind the door. She looked away, only her profile visible. But Fell took a step forward, and gingerly tilted her chin upward. She did not resist him. Her right eye was encircled with a deep purple bruise, surrounded by a sunset of bloody contusions.

"Jesus, chief," said Stanger.

The Americans closed in tight around her, but she cringed, and backed toward the wall. She was completely turned away from them, her slight shoulders shaking. She waved her hand in the direction of the bedroom. The Americans stared at each other. Then Fell led them in that direction, and the only sound was the clap of their heels on the wood floor.

Ishii still sat in the middle of his leafy bed like a croaking frog on a lily pad, smoking two cigarettes. He was still in his smooth kimono. But the green sheets were in wild disarray, and he sat at the edge, his knobby knees bare. He faced the translator, who sat against the wall, his clothes rumpled. When the two of them saw the Americans, they started speaking in machine-gun syllables, hurriedly cramming in a discussion.

"Are we interrupting?" said Fell.

Ishii shook his head. He stubbed out one of the cigarettes, reached over to the pack, and lit another.

"We are…" Ishii said in English, "on alert."

"I'll be a monkey's uncle," said Slawson, slapping Stanger's arm. "The son of a gun speaks English."

Ishii nodded, sucking on a smoke.

"I traveled in your country during my studies," he said. "But we can't discuss. We have no time."

He stood, and paced the left side of the bed, in front of a print of a pleasing forest scene. The smoke trailed behind him, then he was lost in the cloud, back and forth, back and forth. Fell coughed, but it sounded like a laugh. Ishii stopped on his heel, turned and pointed at him.

"What is so funny?" he said.

"Dr. Ishii, you just appear spooked, is all," Fell said.

Ishii's eyebrows twisted as he mouthed the word spooked. He turned to the translator. The translator nodded, started speaking in Japanese. They said the word 'spooked' a few times. Ishii stared, stopped in thought, then turned to Fell.

"Yes, spooked," he said. "We are spooked. By Russians."

The look of amusement drained from Fell's eyes.

"The Russians were here?" he said, frowning.

Ishii shook his head and toppled back on the bed. He held his head in his hands.

"The Russians did not come in house," he said. "But the phone rang all night. Heavy breath, no one spoke. Scratching at roof. Lights in windows. All night."

The translator nodded.

"All night long."

Fell looked at the other Americans. He nodded at the doctor, who stepped forward and swung his bag up on the bed next to Ishii. He opened its clasp, and pulled out a stethoscope, the thick cuff of a sphygmomanometer. Ishii glanced at him wearily, then loosened the kimono and held out his arm. His knee bounced as the doctor leaned to him, and Fell noticed there was a trembling to his fingers, too.

"We need you healthy, General Ishii," Fell said. "We know you've been feeling unwell, and we figured maybe you caught something when you were with your Unit out in Manchuria."

Ishii, whose arm was cuffed in the stiff fabric, frowned at him. He spoke Japanese softly, and the translator answered him, and they had some kind of earnest conversation as the doctor pumped the air into the cuff, then released the pressure and listened to the systole, diastole beating of the man's heart. The doctor removed the cuff and placed the stethoscope on the chest of the patient, who took the deep breaths without any instruction, clearly no stranger to the steps of the routine exam. Then he stood and opened the front of his kimono all the way. The American doctor glanced down, then looked up into the face of his Japanese counterpart. They stared into one another's eyes. Fell stifled a laugh. Shrugging, the American reached for his gloves, slid them on and performed a hernia check at the sides of the general's testicles. Ishii waved with a hand back at the translator, who snapped to attention.

"Dr. Fell," said the little lackey. "General Ishii understands you want the secrets. Everything with his Unit. Seven-thirty-one. But he needs protection."

Ishii nodded as he turned his head and coughed, his hand impatiently urging the translator on as he the doctor felt his crotch.

"The General…had some unwanted calls overnight," said the translator, his eyes searching the faces of the Americans. "The Russians have located him. We believe they have agents in the neighborhood, who are conducting surveillance on this house. They might be listening right now."

Fell shook his head, grunted. Now was the time to set the hook and reel them in.

"We know for a fact the Russians are interested in you, General," Fell said. He paused for effect.

"But what secrets are we talking about?" Fell continued. "We are now allies. Allies cooperate with one another. They tell them things. We need to know what you know."

He stared at Ishii, who had his tongue extended far down his chin, saying "ah" as the doctor peered down his throat for imperfections. Ishii rolled his eyes and snapped his fingers. Fell couldn't help but laugh out loud, this time. They all looked at him, but he did not care.

"What the general wants you to know, Dr. Fell," said the translator, standing, "is that there is much you don't know. But a deal will have to be struck before he tells you what he knows."

The doctor wrapped his stethoscope and put it in the bag, nodded once, relit the cigar, and left the room. The door shut behind him. Fell looked from the translator to Ishii, who was re-wrapping the kimono tightly around his torso. The American stepped forward, around the other men, and sat on the edge of the bed.

"Finally we're getting somewhere," Fell said. "Sit down, General. Let's make a deal."

Ishii eyebrows arched. Fell patted the rumpled sheets next to him.

"We need to know about the patients," Fell said. "The lumber mill, General Ishii. The logs you cut up. We know almost everything already."

Silence. Stillness. Barely a breath.

"The rats. The experiments. The vivisections. Everything," Fell said.

Ishii nodded, his head tremoring. He stubbed out two cigarettes and lit one more. Fell stared long and hard into his Japanese counterpart's eyes. There was finally real understanding there, something that bridged two worlds an ocean apart, and even years of a war of extermination. Fell nodded.

The four Americans left three hours later. The doctor led the way down the Shibayama street, puffing cigar smoke over the three behind.

"That man is healthy as a horse," he said, waving his cigar. "I mean, his heart rate was elevated, he was clearly nervous, but the man could probably run a marathon."

Fell blew across the fresh ink of the signatures on the documents in his hand. He folded them and stowed them inside the pocket of his jacket.

"Of course he's healthy," Fell said. "The man is one of the most eminent doctors in this country. He gets the best treatment possible."

"I still didn't understand the paranoia he had about the phone calls, and the noises," the doctor said. "Can't we protect him?"

Slawson snickered. Stanger just shook his head.

"What's so funny?" the doctor said, stopping short, turning from one to the other.

The other three continued walking, not even breaking stride. The doctor pulled the cigar out of his mouth and hurried after them. He tapped Fell on the shoulder.

"Yes, Doctor?" Fell said.

"Are the Russians really going to get ahold of that man? It seems like they know where he lives, his phone number, everything. It might be best to get him some protection."

The three laughed, out loud this time.

"The Russians have their hands full sifting through the rubble in Manchuria," said Fell.

"The Communists weren't making the threatening calls," said Slawson, turning around, walking backward for a few paces. "We made those calls, you dolt."

Fell backhanded his arm. Slawson cringed and turned around again.

"Wait—you guys were the ones making the threatening calls?" the doctor said. "Why?"

Fell stopped walking, and the entire group stopped around him. He glanced at Slawson and Stanger, then extended a hand toward the doctor.

"Listen, Doctor," said Fell, shaking the doctor's hand. "Why don't you go on ahead? Thanks for coming out on short notice. We needed to make sure that General Ishii was not indeed as ill as he had been claiming. But I must ask you to keep this entire visit confidential. This meeting is of the strictest national security. American MPs are already providing the general security as we speak."

The doctor nodded, stepped back, and pulled the cigar out of his mouth.

"I understand, Dr. Fell," he said, tipping the brim of his hat. "If you need me again, you can reach me through the embassy."

They all shook hands. As the three American operatives lit cigarettes, they watched the doctor amble down the road.

"Is he a loose end?" said Slawson, his voice deadened by an exhale of thick smoke.

"Everyone in MacArthur's office assured us he was discreet," said Stanger, tapping the dossier with his fingertips.

"Yes, the doctor is a patriot. We can count on him," Fell said.

He nodded in the direction of a side street, and they headed in that direction.

"Let's go clean up the surveillance post, and clear back to Tokyo. By the time the Russians actually do show up around here, we want to be clear of the area. We got everything we need. We can take all of the data back to the Project. The Commies will never catch up."

The three slapped each other on the back. They walked, ties swinging in the soft breeze, smoke billowing behind.

WORDS IN THE DARK,
TROUBLE ON THE RIVER

U.S.A., 2087

Dim lights overhead. Seated on the waiting room chair, hospital-hard and unforgiving, my legs numb. Listening to voices all around, the people rushing and shuffling by, each at their own speed and volume. Nurses shoving a blood-stained, empty gurney past. A woman somewhere behind me, raspy voice wailing about the blood in her urine, lamenting a three-hour wait. A man to my left moaning from a kidney stone. To my right a child much smaller than myself just sobbing, alone. Doctors rushing by with lab coats billowing. The solemn elderly hobbling unsteadily by on canes.

But I was removed from it all. Nothing escaped me, but I was no part of it—I was a black hole in the midst of the shimmering, bright panic all around. Sucking it all in, emitting nothing. The other room—where it was happening, where the horror was unfolding—none of it crossed my mind, none of it broke the plane of my perfect focus. It couldn't. I just absorbed it all around me, down to tiniest details—the smoker's rasp in the woman's throat, the tortured twist of the man's face, the musky smell of the boy.

But the veneer broke when something dropped in my lap. A hand squeezed my shoulder. I remained still, not looking to see what I had been given. Instinct told me the person was friendly, the hand's grip somehow comforting, a protective gesture. But I didn't look to see who it was. I wanted only to be that black hole, that untouchable, empty thing, crushing within me whatever came close. The hand left, the person walked away, trailing a doctor's lab coat behind. It was only then that I glanced at my lap. A miniscule test tube, twinkling in the light, lay there. Turning it over, I watched the sparkle of a liquid, a tinge of green. I looked off in the direction where the giver had gone—and only saw the terrified scurrying of people back and forth, hurry and not-hurry, arrival and departure. The friendly presence had vanished.

Then—splashdown and submergence in the black river. The drowning, the darkness coming at me, this time noticing that it was a cavernous mouth—a fish mouth—swallowing me whole. Cold terror clamped down, I screamed without sound.

Drenched in slimy sweat, I awoke to a ringing sound. My eyes opened, I angled out of bed and reached around in the dark for the lamp switch.

The ringing again—the digital call unfamiliar, resounding in the dark.

My hand found the switch and flicked it. Light filled the bedroom. Mary did not stir, her Dormus gusted slow and rhythmic. I slipped on my Kevlar moccasins, swung on my robe, and shuffled out into the hallway.

The noise had stopped. I waited, listening to the pipes and the settling of the house. The windows were lit by moonlight. Empty silence.

It struck again, a ding-dong of something up above. I looked up and saw the shadow of a dusty speaker in the overhead corner. The doorbell, I realized with relief. The unfamiliar sound I'd only ever heard a handful of times, and then only when the damned Unified Three missionaries came calling. Then it rang again—insistent this time.

I scratched at the thin beard along my jaw. Who would ever come to my door during the day, let alone in the middle of the night? I crept down the stairs and grabbed the loose rung of the railing, trying not to make too much noise. I went straight into the dining room, trying to get an angled look through the windows at whoever was on the porch. But I couldn't see—the dark figure was too close to the door. All I could make out was the person's back. The doorbell rang again. I heard a muffled voice from upstairs—Mary was talking in her sleep again, through the oxygen mask.

Cursing softly, I went to the front door. I waited. Just as the person reached again for the doorbell, I edged the door open a crack. I angled my eye at the opening to get a look.

The shape was backlit from the moonlight. I couldn't see the face, but the silhouette was stooped, not tall, hands hovering at the beltline, like a gunslinger. The person stood rigid. The picture was ripped from a nightmare. My heart hammered. I pulled my face back and shut the door.

A tiny knock, a little rap of knuckles.

"Joe. It's Neal. Open the door."

I reached forward, twisted the knob, and cracked it open a few inches.

"Neal?" I asked.

"Nice dark yard you have here. Let me in, damnit," the Old Man croaked.

I opened the door and the shape shuffled in, and I saw from a weak ray of moonlight that it was indeed Old Man Wetherspoon, wearing a ballcap and a sweatsuit. I stifled a laugh but ushered him in and closed the door. I led him into the kitchen, flicking the light switches on along the way. Wetherspoon turned each one off as he followed.

"Let's just stay in the dark," the Old Man said. "Mary has to be asleep."

"We have to have a little light in the kitchen, at least," I said, tapping the little light over the stove. "Want a glass of water?"

"God, no," Wetherspoon said. "Never drink from the tap, Joe. Trust me— you'll live longer. But if you offered me a whiskey, I'd have a whiskey."

I rubbed the sleep from my eyes. Wetherspoon looked all around, as if he expected an ambush from the dark. The Old Man seemed unhinged—he would have to be handled carefully. I smiled at him.

"Okay, whiskey it is," I said, nodding. I walked into the dining room, opened the cabinet, poured two fingers' worth into two heavy glasses. My foggy mind wondered why the hell the Old Man had appeared at my home in the middle of the night. But I would have to play it cool, keep him talking. I returned to my spot at the counter and handed one to the Old Man. Wetherspoon took a sip, smacking his lips. A strange smile I had never seen before on his face crossed his lips—like that of a tired man who had finally reached his bed at the end of a long arduous journey.

"God, it's been so long," he said.

"Neal, you've been gone for weeks. Where were you?" I said. "And wait a second—I thought you didn't drink?"

Wetherspoon swished the tumbler in his cupped hand, watching the amber liquor lap up near the rim, leaving a film sliding slowly down the side. That narcotized smile was still spreading across his face.

"I was somewhere safe," the Old Man said, ignoring the second question. "You know, nothing's safe unless it's secret. And a secret is only a secret if it's absolute. So you'll forgive me if I don't tell you, Young Joe."

"Fair. But why are you knocking at my door in the middle of the night? And how did you get my address?"

Wetherspoon grinned.

"Even if you're unlisted, the hospital records have it all. They have to," he said. "At least the good, classified ones have to."

"You still have access to the hospital's database."

"Of course I do," Wetherspoon said. "I was there before there was a database, so I made sure to carve out my own little electronic niche in the whole thing, right from the start. In case of catastrophe."

Taking a slow quaff of the whiskey, I pointed at him with my upturned pinky, the cheap liquor wrinkling my face, burning deep in my chest.

"You're saying this is a catastrophe," I grunted.

"An unmitigated disaster," the Old Man said, nodding. "And we're smack-dab in the center of it."

"Does this have anything to do with the documents in your office?"

"Ah, the documents you stole, then fenced to our wayward journalist friend," the Old Man said, shaking his head. "The documents that got you fired. Quite a beard you're growing there, by the way."

"Fired?" I said, the panic rising in my chest against the whiskey burn. "The Kraken told me I was just suspended."

"No, you're done at the hospital. Sorry to tell you this way, Joe," said Wetherspoon. "The reason I'm here is because we're both outsiders, and outsiders have to stick together to survive. And those documents are the key to everything at Saint Almachius."

The Old Man tipped back the glass and drained it. He plunked it down on the marble countertop with finality. His face was taut in a grimace. Breathing hard, trying to keep myself calm, I went in the other room and returned with the whiskey bottle. I poured Wetherspoon another glass and topping off my own. I set the bottle down and watched as the Old Man began in on the other glass, savoring every drop. I swished my own on the countertop without drinking it. It was too late, or too early, to drink. Normally I'd be pulling off my Dormus, readying myself for work. But the machine was still broken—and I had no job to go back to anymore. Nightmares and hellish daydreams were all I had remaining to me. And the Old Man had reappeared standing there in my kitchen in the middle of the night. That seemed like a strange dream itself. I took a hesitant sip and recoiled again at the sting in my throat. I pointed at my guest.

"Goddamnit, Neal," I said. "What's the catastrophe? What's in the documents?"

"You already know, to some extent," Wetherspoon said. "You know people have dropped dead inexplicably in that hospital. You know there are some new staff members suddenly appearing out of nowhere. And you know some strange new initiatives are starting."

"And it's all connected," I said.

"Yes. But you don't know exactly how connected they are, or how far back these things go. If we hadn't had the Big Blackout—quite an appropriate term, take it from this old drunk—then we'd all have a better handle on how deep these roots really run."

"Stop with the cryptic bullshit, Neal," I said.

"The Bureau of Wellness has been performing medical experiments on the general population and has been doing it for more than a hundred years."

Wetherspoon drained the rest of his glass, then slid it across the countertop. I caught it, somehow. In a daze, I splashed liquor in it, and slid it back.

"Joe, we are witnessing the largest human-experimentation program since World War II. There's an open-air lab all around us. And every one of us is a guinea pig."

"Bullshit," I said, shaking my head.

Wetherspoon sneered.

"Joe," he said. "Do you really think the bubonic plague just appeared out of nowhere? And how about that mass die-off at the hospital that you oversaw? And the convenient death of the suspect implicated in both? Does this all sound like a coincidence?"

"I don't know."

"You don't have to believe me. Everything was in the documents you stole."

"I couldn't read them. They were on smudged old paper, in the old alphanumerics. No one could read them."

"You kids nowadays—those goddamned Gliffs on those glowing screens have made you illiterate," the Old Man said, shaking his head. "You need to know this: a vast program of experimentation has been right under our noses for years. It's been going for decades. And no one's ever been able to stop it."

"Neal, this sounds insane," I said.

"How else do you explain Lamalade's actions—the bubonic plague, the die-off?"

"A lone psychopath, gunning for glory and infamy," I said.

The Old Man shook his head.

"This janitor was just a tool intended to serve his purpose. He was like a Bunsen burner or a scalpel, used for a while and then thrown away. How far this extends, where it goes from here, no one has any idea. And Lamalade dropped dead just as he was pulling back a corner of the curtain for you. You heard it yourself. And then they fired you, to get you out of the way."

The Old Man coughed, tipped some whiskey down his throat. I pointed at him again.

"I'm assuming you know about Lamalade because of your all-knowing hook-up to the hospital records," I said.

"I have my sources," the Old Man said. "Over the years, I knew there were studies going on. But most were benign."

"What else do you know?"

"I know the documents. A list of studies too long to remember."

I snapped my fingers. It suddenly occurred to me—the physical thread linking all of this.

"What about the labels?" I blurted.

The Old Man's white eyebrows arched high.

"You found labels," Wetherspoon said. "Did they have the Bureau seal?"

"Yes."

"And a long serial number?"

The Old Man seemed to know everything. Down to the last detail. I watched him for any sign that he was lying to me. But I saw nothing.

"Yes," I said.

"They mark the experiments. They catalog the patients, and disease."

I walked over, picked up my Atman and gave a voice command to call the hospital. The Old Man rushed over, joints creaking, and yanked the device out of my hands.

"What in God's name do you think you're doing?" Wetherspoon said.

"I was going to call McDermott over at the hospital. Maybe he can help."

Wetherspoon's veiny, gnarled hand placed the Atman on the counter. He shook his head.

"No. He might be part of the whole thing. Anybody could. Everybody could. Don't you realize that?"

"Then I can call Zo Lanza. He'll know what to do."

Wetherspoon returned to his spot at the other side of the kitchen island, except this time he pulled out a stool, sat, and pounded his fist on the granite countertop. I recoiled from him.

"That would be even worse," the Old Man barked. "You can't trust any of them. All this goes way above us—way above anyone at Saint Almachius. What's one cop going to do about that? Write them a summons?"

Shaking my head, I sat on the stool across from my mentor.

"Can I at least call Betty Bathory and warn her?" I said.

Wetherspoon shook his head.

"Betty is a wonderful woman," he said. "But you can't tell her anything, either. Everyone at the hospital knows she's close to you. If she knew anything, there would be all the more reason to target her. Better for her to know nothing."

"You think something big is coming," I said.

The Old Man stopped pounding the countertop. He deliberated, chewing his lip, rocking his head back and forth as if physically weighing the options. He had never seemed jittery like this before. He was like a man possessed, a soul consumed.

"I do," the Old Man said. "Besides that, I don't know much. This Lamalade character…"

"The guy dropped dead, mid-sentence, while he was talking to me. Never seen anything like it."

"What exactly was he saying?" the Old Man asked.

"He was saying something about others being involved. Then he mentioned a woman's name." I scratched my head, trying to remember. "Meruda, I think it was. Yeah, that was it."

Wetherspoon narrowed his eyes and groaned. I pointed at him.

"You ever heard that name, Neal?"

Wetherspoon quickly shook his head, but he was looking off to his right, toward the windows. The signal of a liar, totally unmistakable. He swallowed slowly, bobbing his head.

"Never," he said.

I stared at him. I knew he was at least holding something back. But I said nothing; it was not the time yet to confront him. The Old Man swished the amber liquor, then drained it.

"Anyway—Lamalade wasn't acting alone," Wetherspoon said. "He told you as much. So it figures someone knew he was a weak link, and they silenced him."

It made a kind of sense. The Old Man's face was twisted in a horrific grimace. A thought hit me, and I raised my finger at him.

"If any of this is true, you don't suppose the Kraken could be behind it all?"

The Old Man scratched at his chin, shaking his head.

"Suzanne Kranklein," he said. "Well, now. She is the de-facto head of the hospital now. And I'm pretty convinced she's evil incarnate, based on my years of working around her."

The Old Man paused, waving his index finger like a lecturer.

"But she's not behind this. She's not creative enough to pull all this off," he said. "She's a middle manager through and through. Only bureaucratic stuffing in that thick skull of hers."

I pointed at him.

"So we have no idea who or what this program really is," I said.

Still clutching his whiskey, Wetherspoon walked around the room. Halfway through the third lap, he stopped next to me and leaned on the countertop, breathing hard. He smelled like mothballs and sweat mingled with the tangy booze.

"You get those papers back. They'll tell you what you need to know," the Old Man said. "Then we wait. But in the meantime, don't say anything to anybody. Your life could depend upon it."

Silence enveloped the kitchen. We drank in the half-dark.

Wetherspoon left as the sun crested the treetops to the east. After making mutual promises of secrecy—over four more tumblers of whiskey—I walked him out the door, hoisting his drunken old bones back into the station wagon. Even before the door was shut, the vehicle was rolling backward out of the driveway. The Old Man's wagon—one of the few old gasoline guzzlers still on the road—lurched forward and sped toward the ultrahighway. I shut the door and clicked all three locks.

Sleep was out of the question, I knew. Too many thoughts reeling through my mind, the dawn pressing down upon me. I headed inside, closed the door behind, started the coffeemaker with a spoken command, and drank cup after cup, as I watched the television. My eyes were heavy but stayed stubbornly open.

It all rushed at me in a blur through my insomniac fog. Non-updates about the assassination in Korea, the simmering Pyongyang Summit, a wrap-up of the previous night's episode of *How Low Can You Go*. A new snake-eater who had replaced Joe Steelman had edged out the self-immolator in the bracket (the latter turned out to be a one-trick pony), and the clips showed a bunch of the lesser competitors all getting verbally abused by the celebrity judges. An ad for the new Atman flashed by, naked dancers shimmying under a strobe. The ticker along the bottom of the screen mentioned something about a maniac with a bazooka killing dozens in a shopping mall just outside Washington D.C. The glare of the screen reflected off my dull eyes as the coffee sobered me up. I turned it off, returning the room to silence.

The day was underway—but there was no job to go to, and nowhere to go. I thought of the long dragging hours ahead. For some reason, my mind drifted toward the yellow canoe in the river miles to the west, and the wily old trout stubbornly surviving, against all the odds. The Yah-qua-whee. Even with madness breaking around me, a possible conspiracy closing in, I couldn't tear my mind away from the memory of the peaceful spot along the Messowecan, and the creature surviving in the toxic depths, against the brutal odds. I remembered my nightmare of the suffocating water, the darkness drowning me each night in my half-sleep. The Yah-qua-whee gave me a twisted kind of hope. In the dawn the nightmare had no true power over me.

Instead, the empty hours ahead held their own horrors. Snorting an energy stick, reaching for the Atman, I dialed Lanza, who picked up on the third ring.

"Bro."

"My man," I said. "You free to talk?"

"Yeah. Everything alright?"

"I got suspended from the hospital. I haven't told you. So, no, not really."

"I heard. I talked to those two big oafs at the front desk when I went to get the results of the Lamalade autopsy yesterday."

"Autopsy?"

"You were right—the O'Neill-Kane didn't find anything. The guy's heart just stopped."

"I told you," I said. "You around for a trip down to the river today? I could use it. If you're not on-call."

"You're in luck," Lanza said. "Since the Lamalade investigation's been closed, I've got the day off."

"Pick me up in an hour, and we'll take a ride out. I'll tell you all about it on the way."

I showered, and as I was dressing in the bedroom Lanza's truck pulled into the driveway. The horn honked three times. Mary jolted upright in bed, her eyes raw and bleary. She pulled the Dormus mask off.

"Wha' happen'?" she asked.

"Dear," I said, buckling my belt, stooping to kiss her sweaty cheek. "I'm going out with Zo for a little bit."

Mary's mouth contorted. Her eyebrows arched, the color drained from her cheeks. She bolted out of bed toward the bathroom, the door shutting behind her. Retching sounds echoed, muffled, from inside. I went to the door and knocked softly.

"Dear?" I said.

A pause—a flush of the toilet.

"Dear?" I said again. "Are you alright?"

"I'll be fine," she growled. "Go. Have fun. Tell Zo I said hello."

I hesitated at the door, listening. But the horn honked outside again. Silence in the bathroom. She was a grown woman, a warrior who had beaten everything that had ever challenged her. I had to believe she knew when she needed help. With a slow movement I grabbed my ballcap off the hook near the door, and went out to Lanza's truck, which had kept honking every few seconds without pause.

"You trying to wake the whole neighborhood?" I barked as I climbed in.

"Aren't we grouchy this morning," Lanza said, lighting a cigarette, backing out the driveway. A sensor on the dashboard beeped, detecting the illegal smoke.

"Yes, a little bit," I said. "I lost my job, people are dying in droves, and I've got a lunatic conspiracy theory that would get me kicked out of a UFO convention."

"Sounds like a bad week," Lanza said, whacking my arm affectionately with his huge hand. "Lay it on me, bro."

As we drove west, I told him about the late-night meeting with Wetherspoon over whiskey, the deaths, and the rumored government program of rampant medical experiments. Lanza drove in silence, smoking. The dashboard sensor beeped on and on.

"So…some kind of experimentation program is going on at Saint Almachius, but I can't find out any more, because I'm not technically an employee anymore," I concluded.

Lanza flicked his cigarette butt out onto the ultrahighway. The dashboard sensor beeped once more and finally went silent.

"That's crazy," he said. "That's crazier than the shit I hear from kids overdosed on Fantasia-B who say they can fly and jump off roofs."

I sighed.

"This is real, Zo. I have documents. And Wetherspoon says he remembers how it all started," I said.

Lanza sighed.

"If you're telling me this to enlist my help, I can tell you patrols already swing past the hospital every fifteen minutes, and detectives are looking for anybody connected to Lamalade," he said, lighting another smoke.

"That's not going to do any good," I said. "They won't find any hard evidence."

I snapped my fingers. There was some evidence, after all. I kept forgetting.

"Except for the labels," I said.

"Labels?"

"I told you about them. The ones I found in the rooms after the two patients died. They were diagnostic labels with a serial number. They're connected, somehow."

"It could be a break," Lanza said, scratching his chin. "So where are these labels?"

"I gave one of them to your captain," I said. "The other is in the dossier I took from the hospital."

"The dossier," Lanza said, softly, patiently. "So there's a dossier. With documentation of some batshit conspiracy. This dossier is where?"

I sighed, looked out the window, and flushed with embarrassment. I knew I had to tell him.

"I gave it to the reporter," I mumbled.

"What?"

"I gave it to goddamned Jim O'Keefe," I said. "I gave the goddamned dossier to that goddamned reporter so he could translate the goddamned thing."

Lanza shook his head. Then he pounded the steering wheel with his fist. A pause. And he slammed it again.

"You gave the only evidence to a reporter. The same reporter who already burned you twice. Joe, for being a brilliant doctor, you're really a goddamned idiot."

He rubbed his face with agitation.

"And what about the money situation? How the hell will you pay for the kid?" Lanza continued. "Whatever happened to your big plan to get away, to go west? All that's gone now, bro."

I pinched my chin, elbow planted on the armrest of the car door. I watched the hologram billboards along the ultrahighway whisk by. We were nearing the exit. We sat in silence, as we had during our rare fights over the years, whether it was on the playground, or in science class, at a teenage house party or a wedding. We were the oldest of friends. We could measure each other's thoughts, balance each moment on what we would say, like we were having a telepathic chess game. Lanza tossed his cigarette butt out the window and lit another. He turned onto the country road parallel to the Messowecan. But the silence continued, as the car bounced and rattled over the rain-washed ruts in the road. A half mile later, the truck rolled into our nook beneath the spreading willow tree. Without a word, we got out and went to the canoe, prepped the gear, dropped the craft into the river and pushed off from shore. Again I was in the front to power us, and Lanza was in the back to steer—the way it had always been. The silence hung between us—but we continued our ritual, the rhythm of water off the paddles we'd repeated ever since we were kids.

"Let's head to port," Lanza said quietly. "That's where the Yah-qua-whee will be. I've got a hunch."

"Upstream?" I asked. "I don't remember the last time we headed up there."

"It's been a while," Lanza said. "All the more reason to go. Maybe that thing is up there."

A few strokes more, and the current pushed us. We paddled hard against the flow. After a few minutes we were fifty yards upstream, at a cove neither of us remembered. The banks were curved and tidy, like they had been carved out by an ice-cream scoop just minutes before. A semicircle of canopy trees lined the edges of the bank. I had no idea how they had survived the Cruzen Fireball. The canoe edged into the still and deep water, and we quietly grabbed our poles. Lanza cast, then I did. The only sound was the whip-whoosh, whip-whoosh of our fly rods. No birds sang, no bugs buzzed, no fish blubbed in the water.

Hours passed. We made cast after cast. The sun hit its apex and started down the other end of its inevitable arc. No sign at all of the Yah-qua-whee. The sweat soaked through my clothes. My Atman was on, but there was no call from Mary. Still, I thought back to her kneeling on our bathroom floor.

So the day dragged for me, as it always did on the river. It wasn't a bothersome boredom; it was the soothing sense the world was revolving on its axis and you were going along for the ride, no matter how hard you strived for the horizon. It was the same on the canoe as it was in an airplane or two feet on solid ground. I settled back and watched the clouds and the haze of the smog, and the blackened trees bending and creaking in the breeze. The forest was rippled with shadow.

But something caught my eye, out in the immolated forest. I squinted. A green stalk stuck up from the ground—but it had a conical little roof on it. It looked absolutely out of place in midst of the rows of carbonized trunks. I set down my pole, picked up the paddle and pushed us toward the shore.

"What are you doing?" Lanza whispered, his line still out in the water.

I paid him no mind. I stroked toward the shore, then clambered over the side, trudging through the sucking mud. I made it to the burnt woods, and the green protrusion. The carbonized odor nearly knocked me backward, but I trudged on.

It was a pipe four feet high and about a foot around. I ran my fingers across its surface, and it was cold to the touch. I went around to the other side. A yellow sticker was emblazoned with big black writing.

"WATER TRIAL INTAKE VALVE NO. 1644. PROPERTY OF BUREAU OF WELLNESS, U.S. GOVERNMENT. IN INSTANCES OF CONTAMINATION, PLEASE CALL 1-800-731-1644."

I scratched my chin. The pipe was stained with dried mud, but the label was new, the writing bright and fresh. I reread it twice more, memorizing it, thinking about what it could mean. A Bureau water intake in the middle of the only preserved natural space left in the Garden State? The source of the drinking water for millions of people?

"Joe, you coming back?" Lanza called out. "Or are you going native?"

I repeated the number once more, then stepped away, slowly picking my way around the dead rotting branches and fallen logs. I slopped through the mud on the banks, dislodged the canoe, and stepped in with a splash. The vessel drifted back from land, back out into the cove.

"What were you doing?" Lanza said.

"I saw a pipe out there. Weird-looking thing."

A pause.

"Was it one of those green Bureau of Wellness pipes? With the warning?" he said.

I turned slowly in my seat.

"Yeah—how did you know?"

Lanza grunted, pushing back into deeper water.

"Those pipes are a matter of security. National Security."

I stared at him. Lanza stopped paddling. We drifted out, silent, to the darkest and deepest part of the pool. I kept glaring at him, and he couldn't meet my eyes. He wiped at his brow and shrugged.

"I don't know really any more than that. The local cops are ordered to keep an eye on some things. Those pipes are one of the biggest priorities. They're marked on our patrol displays. I don't know why. Basically, we're supposed to make sure the Intifada can't get at them, that teenagers don't mess with them. That kind of thing."

"But you have no idea what they are?"

"Above my pay grade, bro. I'm on a need-to-know basis when it comes to anything with the Bureau of Wellness. You know that."

I turned fully around to face him.

"Same here. At least when I was gainfully employed."

A whip-whoosh, whip-whoosh-splash sliced the air as Lanza cast into the still water.

"I know this dossier's lost," Lanza said, now at full volume. "But what was in it?"

I pivoted back in my seat and picked up my own pole.

"I really don't know, Zo," I said, swooshing out the line, sending it back toward a fallen log in a shallow part of the pool. "Papers. I couldn't read most of them, the print was so old. Army files, most from way before the Purge."

"How did Wetherspoon get them?"

I watched the fly lay still on the water, sending ripples outward. There was something to Lanza's voice. Something suspended in my old friend's tone. I didn't like it. I selected my words carefully.

"I really don't know, Zo," I said. "I'm just the out-of-work sawbones. You're the crack detective. Why don't you figure it out?"

I glanced back and saw Lanza scowling.

"You bastard—"

But Lanza's words died, stopped short by a strange swooping sound above. We craned our necks to the left, upstream. Two shapes flew low in the distance. They looked like big vultures soaring down the river toward us. My heart hammered.

Horror swept over me as they kept getting bigger and bigger. They came fast. Their shapes seemed to change. Finally, I saw they weren't birds at all—they were airplanes.

Low-flying drones, angular, diving hard and straight at us. Lanza and I could only watch in stupefied horror as the roar increased, the full-winged forms grew, and strange circles dropped out of the bottom of each. The planes soared by, just feet above our heads, and I turned to watch their wings disappear low over the trees to the east.

"Joe, look at that," Lanza said.

I turned back. The two spherical objects floated down to the water on small parachutes that had deployed. A few seconds more, and they touched down in the current, about a hundred yards upstream. Quietly both of us put down our rods and grabbed our paddles and angled the canoe in that direction.

As we approached, the globes bobbed brightly on the surface. But when we came within twenty yards, the one toward the farther bank sank slowly beneath the surface. And then the closer one reached some kind of tipping point and submerged too.

I looked back at Lanza, who shrugged. We drifted forward a bit, but the current slowed the canoe. We peered deep into the swirling waters of the Messowecan.

Emerging as if from a nightmare, unnatural green plumes suddenly bloomed below the surface. I froze. The neon streaks spread outward like radioactive tentacles. They came right at the canoe, seeming to reach for the hull. I thrust my paddle in the water and hacked frantically at the water to turn us around.

"What is it, Joe? I can't see anything," Lanza said.

"Paddle hard, damnit!" I shouted. "Hard, damn you!"

Just then, a ray of sunlight glinted off the green water. A tiny hint of greenish vapor wafted off the water. I held my breath. The boat rocked as Lanza spotted the cloud and recoiled, boat lurching, then slapped at the water with his own paddle.

I watched in terror as the green water passed within a foot of the side of the canoe. But our vessel broke free and jerked quicker and quicker from the billowing streams of jade. In moments we were yards away from it, cruising toward the bank.

Soon we were out of reach of the spreading cloud, but we paddled harder and harder, arms aching, terrified adrenaline driving us onward. We reached the shore and scrambled out into the water, splashing, dragging the canoe up frantically onto land.

"What in the motherfucking…cocksucking…hell…was that?" Lanza said, breathless, fumbling the rods and tackle.

Looming across the water, we saw the green mass reflected in the sunlight like an enormous plug of floating mucus. Smoke hovered on the water. A long plume stretched downstream, but I saw the biggest cloud was headed toward the opposite shore. And from this side of the bank, I watched it flow straight at the green intake pipe.

"I don't know," I said. "But you've got to report this. It's going toward that Bureau intake. Whatever it is, it's going to kill somebody."

We threw the fishing tackle in the back of the truck. I stole glances at the glowing cloud, which shrank quickly at the intake. How did a chemical travel upstream? I thought about the warning label on the pipe and my stomach bottomed out. We got in the car. Dialing with shaky hands, I called the emergency number from the green intake I'd memorized—but there was a busy signal. Lanza picked up his Atman, and it beeped loudly. He held it up to his ear.

"Chief, I was just about to call. You're not going to believe—"

But he stopped short. His eyes grew wide. He nodded.

"Affirmative," he said with finality. The thing beeped again. He placed it on the dash.

"What was that about?"

"A plane crashed into a school," Lanza said, grim-faced, putting the truck in reverse. "I couldn't really understand him, but he said something about green smoke everywhere."

"Green smoke," I said, looking out over the river. "The drones…"

Lanza took a cigarette from the center console and lit it. The sensor began to beep, but Lanza clubbed the dashboard with a heavy hand, and it stopped. We peeled out. The truck bounded along the rutted road, and then we were on the smooth ultrahighway, speeding east.

"I need to get right over to that school," Lanza said. "I don't have time to drop you off."

"That's fine—I'll stay in the truck," I said.

"You better, or I'll have to arrest you," Lanza said.

"You'd better radio in that green stuff on the river, too," I said.

"Are you kidding? Who cares about some green shit in the river, when there are kids burning alive in a school?"

We drove in silence, except for the dashboard's insistent smoke alarm.

"When we get there, you have to promise me you'll stay in the car," Lanza said, as they took the exit. "You can't do anything stupid. No doctor playing detective, that kind of shit."

Lanza reached into the console, pulled out a small black Glock, and laid it on the dash.

"You've got it," I said.

But I was lying.

SCHOOL DAZE

U.S.A., 2087

The SallyAnn Salsano Elementary School was a two-story brick building atop a little hill, surrounded by quaint streets of old colonial houses, all built after smallpox had killed off the Lenni Lenape tribes in the area centuries earlier. The neighborhood was a few miles from my house—it was the school where I believed my unborn child would someday learn to read and count.

The pickup truck pulled into the row of handicapped spots in front of the school. Emergency plans were already in effect. A line of students marched away from the building, hands on the shoulders of the one in front of them. The young faces were tear-streaked, the mouths open as they howled in terror. They reminded me of the horror of the little naked girl I'd seen in the Old Man's ancient history book. But this horror was multiplied, manifold. The heads kept bobbing by: little freckled cheeks, dimples, girls with curly hair, and boys with cowlicked crew cuts. Several wore T-shirts with the image of Joe Steelman emblazoned on the front. Among them walked bigger figures in stark-white NBC suits and gas masks. A few of these pallid forms patted the kids on their heads, reassuring them there everything was normal, there was nothing to fear, as their school burned. I almost laughed as they stooped down in their alien-looking suits and tried to assuage wide-eyed fears with big, scary faces shaped like anteaters from hell. The last few kids along the evacuation route lagged far behind the others, staggering sporadically, punching at their Atmans, seemingly oblivious to the pandemonium. I sighed.

With a roar, flames punched through the roof, flinging tiles and shingles down to the ground. I saw then that the air over the school seemed to ripple in mirage from the heat, and a greenish haze seemed to hang, mixing with the black smoke. The line of kids wasn't the only part of the evacuation. Throngs of teachers and janitors streamed off in every direction away from the school, toward every side street putting them at a distance from the burning destruction. Far off at the northwestern corner of the school, more white figures clustered around a tent.

"I guess they were ready for this," I said.

"What do you mean?" Lanza said, shoving his gun down the back of his jeans.

"Think about it. We saw the plane fly over, we saw the green plume in the river, you got the call, we came here. It's been less than a half hour. They've already set up the biohazard tent, the full disaster response. It's almost like they had everything prepared ahead of time."

"I guess it's a testament to the planning of the Saint Almachius staff," Lanza said. I scoffed.

"The hospital is the lead agency? Why not the Bureau of Wellness?"

"My chief doesn't tell me any of that kind of stuff," Lanza said. "Just stay in the car. Since you're not a hospital employee anymore, you can't technically be here."

"They might need help with the victims," I said.

"They'll be fine. You have other things to worry about. Like getting that dossier back from the reporter. Getting your life back on track. Being arrested at an active disaster scene won't help you or Mary or the kid. So sit tight."

I just nodded. Lanza narrowed his stare at me for a second. But then he turned and walked purposefully toward the school, the loosened straps on his fishing hip boots jangling like spurs. I watched him walk down the sidewalk, toward the flashing lights of the cop cars.

Once my friend was out of sight, I leapt out of the truck and strode toward the big tent. As I approached, the white-suited figures brought boxes and gear out of the front flap. My mind cycled through things I could say if I was suddenly confronted by one of those gasmasked faces. I might say I was a doctor at Saint Almachius, but anyone would recognize me and know I had been suspended. I could explain I had arrived with the police, but I didn't have a badge. I could just force my way past, saying I was a Bureau of Wellness administrator doing a spot check. All were bullshit stories, but I decided upon this last course as my best bet. It was just farfetched enough to work.

Just as I approached, a suited figure lugged a big plastic baggy containing some viscous green glop out of the tent. The person stopped at my approach. My breath caught in my chest. I nodded sternly at the figure. The person paused for a second but, just as I neared, stepped aside and vanished around the corner.

No one inside. The mobile-operations post was set up the same as at the plague outbreak: the three cubicles set up for equipment, staging, and triage. I paused for a second, and then headed straight for the equipment locker. Stark white NBC suits were stacked neatly there. I grabbed one and quickly pulled it on, around my body and over my head. These were bulkier and heavier—they felt like armor as much as biohazard protection wear. I triple-checked the fitting, and while I was doing so, two people walked in. The muffled voice of the shorter one was unmistakably Betty Bathory, carrying her bullhorn with a regal kink to her wrist. I nearly froze but busied my hands. The other suited figure was talking to her, mumbling a muted protest of some kind, but she shook her head, denying the person whatever it was. The talking stopped. Her head swiveled in my direction.

"Sergeant, why aren't you out there inspecting the wreckage?" she barked.

Sergeant? Baffled, I glanced through the mask's visor down at my shoulder and saw distinct military chevrons on the white material. Betty clapped her hands and barked some kind of order. I gave her half a salute and ducked outside.

Within my heavy mask, the scene was unearthly—sight constricted, sounds smothered, face nearly smothered by plastic. A group of white figures huddled around a generator which chugged, spewing smoke. Another cluster of the suits yelled at one another, gesturing madly. I gave them a wide berth and trudged toward the side of the school. I stepped like a man on the moon, slow and cautious, toward a closed door. I saluted a pair of passing soldiers with assault rifles on their shoulders. I passed them with gritted teeth and moved on.

I shook my head in the enormous suit and glanced around the schoolyard. Why was the military working with the hospital at a plane crash? What did it have to do with the Bureau? The federal agency avoided entanglements, ever since the Purge. Something was different this time.

I grasped the handle of the school door. With a quick tug, it opened.

The inside was dark, lit only by weak sunlight from an old corner window. It was a small antechamber before the school gymnasium to my right. I walked along the marble floor to the entryway ahead and shoved at the handle. It gave.

Smoke rushed at me. I stepped inside, shut the doors behind, and clicked on the miner's headlamp in the suit. Sweeping it back and forth in front of me, shapes of stacked desks and flashes of neon children's drawings on glowing screens along the walls emerged from the gloom. The haze was green in my little beam of light. I stepped cautiously forward, expecting the shadows to leap out at me at any moment.

Stupid, stupid, stupid, I told myself. Rushing into a burning building with soldiers swarming all around. Without a medical license, I'd end up in jail this time—or shot on sight, I thought. Sweat beaded on my brow, my bladder felt full. But I kept going.

Doors appeared on both sides of the hallway. I peered in to each classroom window with the light, little desks and chairs and blackboards frozen in the weak rays from the tinted windows in each room. They reminded me of Mrs. Bopp's classroom from a lifetime before. Except everything seemed impossibly tiny, the desks coming up just over my knee. And things were missing—no bookshelves, no papers or crayons or pencils like we still had in school when I was a kid. Instead, there were little Atmans on each desk, screens glowing eerily in the dark since their users had fled their desks in panic.

I walked farther down the hall, scanning each classroom for a second, then moving on. The arches of the main office in the center of the building opened on my left, a few sunbeams casting hard angled shadows across the hallway. The clerical offices were empty and quiet too, except for one computer, beeping continually. A few more classrooms were just as empty. I came to a door marked as a library, and next to it, the stairwell to the second floor.

The library was empty. A sweep of my headlamp showed white walls bare up to the high ceilings, broken only by holographic images every few feet: animated scenes of fantastical swordfights, kisses of princesses bestowed on their rescuers, drone strikes on a cluster of tents in a desert during the Tenth Crusade. Rows of low desks with computer monitors blinked out of sync with one another. The scene was bizarre, a place I never would have recognized without the sign on the door. I turned back and went out to the hallway.

Lights bounced and swung at the far end of the hall. A half dozen white figures approached. Voices barked military orders. I cupped my hand over my own light and retreated through the door to the stairwell heading up.

The smoke thickened. The green mist swirled around me, and I felt some kind of pulsing energy above. Hairs on my neck stood on end. I climbed. Sweat trickled down my eyebrows, tumbled to my cheeks and neck. The heat intensified. The doors at the top of the stairs were splintered in dozens of pieces of glass, each reflecting the flickering flames within. I pushed through the door gingerly, kicking aside some of the bigger shards.

The second-floor hallway had imploded, it seemed. The walls had crumbled into mounds of sheetrock and pebbles. No appreciable architecture stood after forty yards. I took cautious steps forward, trying to visually dissect what I was seeing. At the far end of the rubble, I made out the triangular shape of a drone's tail rudder. The flames were hottest around it, but they were no ordinary flames—they were sparkling, twisting emeralds. The air thickened with green particles at each step forward. Even within my protective membrane, my skin crawled.

Survivors—survivors and victims were the objective. I took a deep breath. I had to find the people inside, if there were any, and carry them away from the disaster. The possibility of dead children in the debris had become real. I sucked in the suit's sterile air and stepped forward.

Three classrooms stood between me and the awful slide of rubble. I scanned the first and second. Both were dark, their windows covered by soot. The floors were covered with debris and garbage, but the walls and desks were somehow intact, untouched by the fire and the plane's explosive impact. I crossed the hallway to the third classroom's open door and peered inside.

I gasped.

A figure in an NBC suit stood over two tiny figures who sat against the wall. I was about to call out, but something in their postures stopped me. The seated people were kids, arms crossed over their heads.

It took a second to see the restraints around their little wrists. I held my breath. I had to do something.

I stepped closer, edging around glass shards underfoot. The suited figure, indistinct through the green haze, loomed over the children. He stared down at some device in his hand, bigger than an Atman, waving it all around, like he was measuring something in the air. I heard a voice, a man's guttural rumblings under the crackling of the flames and the falling of debris and the zap-pop of live wires. It sounded like an incantation, something religious. I stepped closer. Then the figure's words became clear.

"…levels are slightly elevated. Contagion not yet spread to Meruda," he said. "Subjects restrained. Estimated time of transmission anywhere from ten to fifteen minutes."

I went closer. The two kids appeared to be in some kind of drugged stupor, as they wriggled and coughed. Their eyes were shut.

"Subjects appear to be half-conscious at minute twenty-eight, which will make test controls easier," said the man.

The voice suddenly sounded so familiar, so serious.

I took one more step forward. Something beeped.

"Readings of the agent are now elevated…" the man said, his voice rising.

Another step. But I didn't look down this time, and my foot came down on something that went pop, then crunch—a lightbulb. I froze. The man kept punching numbers into his device, recording his data, oblivious. He had heard nothing over the roar of the flames.

But one of the kids—a little blond boy—had heard. He raised his head and opened his eyes. They glimmered like jade in the light. The boy stared. He opened his mouth as if to say something, maybe to scream at what he probably believed to be another tormentor. The boy tugged on his restraints. I waved at him frantically to be quiet, but it was too late. The restraints made a sharp sound in his struggles, and the man in the NBC suit looked up and then spun around at me, hand grasping a black gun holster at his side.

"Sergeant, this is an isolated Bureau of Wellness study area," the man ordered. "Show me your credentials."

That voice. I knew this man, from somewhere. But I didn't dare move. The man's gloved hand tugged at the holster—but he couldn't unsnap the clasp with the thick latex gloves.

At that split second, without a thought, I rushed forward. I angled my shoulder low and hard into the man's center of gravity and slammed into him. The man toppled, legs splayed out over a low desk next to the wall. But still he struggled to rise, still tugging at the gun in the holster. I bullrushed him with my shoulder again, smashing his head against the wall, bowling him over to the side. The figure was still trying to rise. I stooped down and slammed the man's head against the concrete once, then again, and he went limp.

I stood over him. I looked down at my hands, wondering what I had done, whether I had killed him. But it was self-defense. I couldn't tell who the person was, whether it was a Saint Almachius employee or some rogue researcher who tied kids up in a burning building contaminated with biohazards. The vinyl visor was tinted, and it was impossible to see the face inside. I could rip off the protective suit. But I knew that patrol was coming, and it would take time I didn't have. I went over to the kids, loosened the restraints, and lifted them to their feet.

"Don't worry, we're going to get you out of here," I told them.

They weren't drugged at all—they broke out into terrified sobs as I ushered them out of the classroom. Once we hit the stairwell, the one in front ran off down the stairs. The other one—the smaller, blond boy—stuck close to me, a bit wobbly over the debris. I steadied him with a hand on his shoulder and held the door open for him at the bottom. A thought hit me.

"Is your name Meruda?" I asked.

The boy looked up at me with a blank stare and shook his head. I ushered him through the doorway. As the kid went through, I noticed something stuck to the collar of his shirt. It was a piece of paper. I peeled it off, turned it over in my hands. It was a label.

A jolt ran up my spine, prickling the hairs on my neck.

But before I could inspect it, three headlights appeared behind us, through the glass of the first-floor door. I clicked my own headlamp off and urged the kid onward through the darkness.

We kept going. The kid led me down a black passageway and out a different door, at the opposite end of the gymnasium. The sunlight blinded the two of us for a second. But I pushed the boy around the corner, to the basketball courts in the middle of the U-shaped school. We ducked behind a dumpster.

I tore off the NBC suit, first unzipping the helmet, then pulling off the sleeves and the legs. Then I noticed the kid just standing there, staring at me. Terror twisted his face, and he looked like tears were about to burst from his big eyes.

"What's wrong, kid?" I asked.

"Are you going to rape me?"

I stared at him, unsure at first if I heard him correctly. I stepped out of the NBC suit.

"No, kid. I'm not going to rape you," I said, peeling the suit off my shoe. "Why would you say something like that?"

"My mom says bad guys rape kids when they get them alone."

"I'm not a bad guy. The people in the white suits are bad guys."

"But you were wearing a white suit, too," the boy said. "And a mask."

I shook my head.

"No, I was just pretending so I could save you," I said. "I'm not a bad guy."

"Oh," the kid said.

"Do you know who Meruda is?"

The kid just shrugged and shook his head.

"Alright," I said, crushing the NBC suit into a tight ball, "let's get you back to your teacher."

Just before I threw the suit in the dumpster, I noticed the label still stuck to the glove—the one I'd taken from the boy's shirt. I peeled it off, then held it up in the light. My heart skipped a beat. It was the same label I had seen at the hospital, the same serial number and bar code I had discovered in the rooms of the dead patients.

BOW-137.

I held it up to the kid.

"Where did you get this?" I said.

"The bad guy put it on me," the kid said, face crinkling like he was about to cry. "He said it was like a name tag, so he wouldn't forget me."

"He was one of the bad guys," I said, nodding, patting the kid's back gently. "Don't worry. I'll get you out of here."

I pocketed the label. We walked away quickly, across a cracked basketball court and an overgrown baseball diamond, to a fence at the edge of the schoolyard. The patrol of hazmat-suited soldiers was nowhere to be seen. The kid went right toward a one-foot gap and squeezed through. I squeezed to fit through, got stuck, then backed up and vaulted over it with a huge effort. We looked at each other for a second.

"You're not going to ebduck me, are you?" the kid said, blinking up at me.

"No, kid—I'm not going to abduct you," I said. I slapped at my pants, and a puff of green dust drifted off on the breeze. "I'm one of the good guys. I'm getting you back to your class."

The kid lifted his wrist, and typed into the Atman implant there, one of the miniature models.

"What are you doing?" I asked.

"Messaging my teacher," the kid said. "Telling her I'm with a stranger. Just in case."

"Just in case what?"

"Just in case you ebduck me. Or rape me."

I could only shake my head. What the hell were they teaching kids nowadays? We walked along the eastern side of the school, back in the direction of Lanza's truck. I changed the subject, trying to assuage his fears of my intentions.

"What is your name, by the way?"

"I can't tell you," the kid said. "My parents told me not to tell strangers. My dad's in the government."

"I'm a doctor. You can trust me," I said.

The boy shook his head. I didn't push the issue. We walked on—me ahead, slowing every few steps to let the kid's tiny legs catch up. I noticed the intersection where the other class had turned away from the school, and I turned us in that direction.

"What happened at the school just now?" I asked.

The boy shrugged, still staring down at the ground in front of him.

"It was a big crash, and everyone hid under desks, like in the active-shooter drills," he said. "Then there were two men in white clothes who pushed everyone out. They kept me and Timmy behind. They said we needed to help them find some of the kids from the other classes. Then the bad man who you hit covered our faces with something that hurt my nose and face. It made us sleep and when we woke up, we were tied up. The man acted really weird. He kept talking into a radio about some lady. But then you came and untied us."

"A lady?"

"Yeah. Some lady. That lady you asked about. Mary Two—that name. I don't know her."

I shook my head. Meruda. Whoever or whatever it was, it was everywhere. The kid scratched his head, stumbling a bit back and forth, like an old drunk, as he talked.

"The man was really weird," he continued. "He kept looking at this thing in his hands. He walked around us. He looked at the thing. It was like an Atman or something. He stuck something in our mouths for a while."

"He stuck something in your mouths?" I said, alarm rising in me.

"Yeah, I think it was a ther-mom-et-er," the kid said. "But it was bigger than that. He kept pushing buttons on it after he took it out. It would make beeping noises. It was like…"

Here the kid trailed off. We were cresting a hill, and I could see a group of people—a school class—at the side of the road, underneath a willow tree. The boy walked faster.

"It was like what?" I asked. "Tell me."

"It was like the guy was doing a speri-ment or something. Like how we did a science speri-ment with the cricket and the pins and knife in class last week."

The kid shuddered at the memory. I patted him on the head. Heading down the slope, practically jogging now, we drew closer to the group.

"He didn't touch you anywhere—he didn't do anything to you?" I asked.

"No," the kid replied. "Just the ther-mom-et-er. In my mouth. No rape or ebducktion. Just the speri-ment."

I pointed the kid in the direction of the crowd, and then walked quickly across a yard in the direction of Lanza's truck. When I reached the corner, I caught flashing lights out of my peripheral vision, off to the west. I walked quicker. When I rounded the corner, Lanza was leaning against the back of the pickup, exhaust swirling around him. He glowered at me as I approached.

"You left the truck," Lanza said.

"I just took a look around the school," I said. "Curiosity got the better of me."

"There was a report of a non-authorized person abducting a child in the evacuation zone," said Lanza.

"No abduction," I said. "I just took a walk around the perimeter, seeing if I could put my medical license to good use."

"Your suspended medical license," said Lanza, shaking his head, as we climbed in the truck. "You know, Joe, there are stiff penalties for messing around with a Bureau of Wellness investigation. Stiffer than losing your job. Stiffer than losing your house."

"There were two kids inside the school. They were tied up. They were part of an experiment, Zo. They were left there to die."

"So you actually went inside an unauthorized, potentially-biohazardous accident scene."

"I put on an NBC suit before I went in."

"And you stole an NBC suit. From the Bureau, while you're suspended. Then you went into the tightly-controlled scene of an investigation. And abducted a child."

"I didn't keep the suit or anything," I said, my voice rising despite my best efforts to keep it calm. "Something had to be done, Zo. Those two kids were tied up by some rogue researcher. God knows what he was up to."

Lanza turned the truck off the curb, and we drove to the ultrahighway.

"I don't want to hear any more," Lanza said. "Since I helped you flee criminal trespass and abduction charges, I'm not saying anything. I saw nothing, and neither did you. You weren't there. We don't even know each other."

"Fair," I said. "You know what happened? What brought the drone down?"

"It's all in the jurisdiction of the Bureau of Wellness. They're the only ones who know."

"But I thought the hospital was the lead agency," I said.

Lanza scratched his brow.

"You know—that was weird," he said. "Some of the people were Bureau, others were military. But I didn't get a good look at them—they were all wearing NBC suits. Never seen military and Bureau work together like this."

I said nothing. Lanza lit a cigarette, and the dashboard sensor began beeping again. Lanza coughed, then spit out the window. I opened my window and held my breath against the smoke.

PROPHYLACTIC FUNERAL

U.S.A., 2087

TWENTY-EIGHT CHILDREN PERISH IN SCHOOL DISASTER, the *Newark FactSecond* headline screamed. But the number was inaccurate, as usual—and O'Keefe reported no cause of death. The victims were all cremated at a special undisclosed facility within days, McDermott told me over a brief call. He told me all the nurses and the rest of the doctors were asking about me, and some had taken up a petition demanding my job back. I told him not to worry—I'd find a way to beat the Kraken, in the end.

Rothenberg, the trauma surgeon, was buried two weeks after he died. No one could understand what the delay was, especially since Rothenberg was Jewish and for thousands of years they buried their dead as soon as possible—as Rothenberg continually told me over the years. Friends waited for an obituary that never appeared, and then hundreds of Atmans received a two-line message over Amicus on a Thursday, saying the wake and funeral would be held the very next night, honoring their beloved husband, father, and friend. It gave only a time and an address for the funeral home—no pictures or any personal messages about the doctor who had given his life for his patients, the friend and colleague with whom I had worked with for ten years since we graduated medical school together.

All this Mary relayed to me in the bathroom the day of the funeral. She had returned from Tough Mothers Pregnancy Boot Camp, showered, and shaken me awake. It was already late afternoon. I'd been sleeping the day away in the weeks since my suspension, the sun streaming in unfamiliar angles into the bedroom until it breached my lidded eyes, finally jarring me awake. I would start looking at some of the Bureau files I still had access to, before dinner. But this was the latest I'd started the day yet—Mary had already started simmering the tofu and vitamins for dinner.

I stumbled to the bathroom and stood in the shower, soaping and rinsing, my blood warming under the hot stream. She was on the other side of the curtain, detailing her face at the mirror with rouge and some black touches of mascara. I watched her blurry form through the clear plastic and could smell jasmine fill the room as she sprayed perfume on the nape of her neck, the tender undersides of her arms.

I couldn't keep hold of the slippery white soap. It dropped once and twice, then once again. The last time I stooped to pick it up, and my foot gave way. I grabbed hold of the steel bar on the wall, but only after banging my heel on the hard side of the tub. I howled in pain.

"Everything all right?" she said.

"Yeah, I just dropped the soap," I said. "I can't get a grip."

She pulled aside the curtain, looking my naked body up and down. She shook her head.

"I'm not talking about the soap," she said, "You've been a zombie recently, Joe. Is there something you're not telling me?"

I lathered and rinsed off my chest. I shook my head, sending suds flying. I gave her the best smile I could approximate, then turned to the wall and kept scrubbing.

"I lost my job, Mary," I said. "A decade of my life down the drain. I've got to start all over again. Maybe I'll do housecalls—that could be the future. Or maybe I could become a lumberjack or something. I've already started the beard."

She reached over, ran a palm across my stubbly wet cheek.

"Honey, the Bureau doesn't certify anyone to do housecalls. And there aren't enough trees left to cut down for you to be a lumberjack," she said. She shut the curtain and drifted back to the mirror. Her voice hardened, an empty echo on the bathroom tiles. "Why don't you get those papers back to the hospital, and see if you can pull some strings to get your job back? It would be so much easier. Neal Wetherspoon could help you out."

I turned off the spigot. Swishing the curtain aside, I met her eyes and reached for a towel. I stepped out of the tub.

"He's not with the hospital any more, either," I said.

She turned around, uncapped lipstick raised.

"He retired again?" she said.

"No," I said, toweling my hair roughly. "Just in hiding. Mary, something's going down at the hospital. We're better off staying away from all that."

She stared at me, eyebrows arched. I blinked, drying my face.

"I didn't know what to tell you before. But now I'm sure," I said. "There's something criminal going on at Saint Almachius. Wetherspoon and I aren't exactly sure what it is—but it's the reason we were forced out."

"You're a whistleblower, you mean," she said. "And you're being retaliated against."

"That's one way to put it," I said, plumbing my ear canal with a pinky finger.

"Then why don't we get a lawyer? Honey, if you're doing the right thing, then you need to make a stand. Any court would side with you on that. Any judge would see reason."

I bent toward her and kissed her cheek.

"Mary, the courts don't work that way. Not anymore, they don't."

Her mouth twisted. Color drained from her face. She yelped.

"Oh God, Joe," she said, shoving me at the door. "Go—get out!"

She pushed me out, slammed the door, and the retching began. Still naked and dripping on the floor, I pressed my ear to the door. Each heave echoed louder off the tiled walls than the one before.

"Dear, are you alright?" I said.

"Get…ready…the funeral," she barked.

Ten minutes later, I was totally dry, my suit was on, with the tie and cuffs adjusted. I went back by the bathroom, and just as I was about to knock, she opened the door. She looked perfect in her form-fitting black dress, a hint of pregnant plump at her middle, and her lipsticked mouth a deep crimson. But a red streak ran from her mouth's edge to the middle of her cheek.

"I'm ready—let's go," she said, smiling tiredly.

"I think you missed a bit," I said, licking a finger, wiping at the rouge smudge with it. It wouldn't come off—it was thicker than lipstick. It was dried blood.

"Oh—that," she said. "That's fine. I'll get it."

"That's blood, Mary. That's not normal."

"Don't tell me about my body, Joe. I know what the references say, and I know that this is not unheard of with the vitamins program. And Abbud said I have a special case."

"Mary, I don't think—"

"Joseph! Enough!"

Whenever she called me Joseph, it meant I should stop talking. So we walked out. Outside, I got behind the wheel, and she slipped in the passenger's side door. I tried to start the car, but it only clicked. Sighing, I fastened my seatbelt, then blew into the hole on the steering column. It started at the third turn of the key. Mary's car had all the new standard safety features.

"Why do you always drive?" she said.

"Because I'm more aware of the dangers of the road. I have better road awareness."

"You're paranoid, you mean," she said.

"I'm not paranoid," I said. "I've just reached a point in my life where I realize that everyone is out to get me."

"That's very funny, Joe. Haha."

We cruised onto the ultrahighway. The sun had slid behind the clouds on the horizon, and the holographic ads off the roadway started to glow brighter in the dusk. Saxas announced some developments in the Asia situation and an outbreak of unknown disease in a small town in western Iowa. But Mary reached over and flicked it off.

"I wanted to hear that," I said.

"We need to talk, Joe," she said.

"Can it wait?" I said, my hand on the radio knob.

"No."

My hand fell to my lap. A moment of silence. The road hummed underneath the car. My mind raced for a moment. She had found the bank statements. She knew the numbers, the bottom line. I braced myself. This could be the moment that she asked about our money and absolutely everything fell apart. I felt the air fragment all around me.

"What's going on at the hospital? You have to tell me," she said.

I breathed, and it was almost a sigh of relief. But I switched lanes and swallowed hard, trying to look casual.

"If I could tell you exactly, I would, dear," I said. "But I don't know, exactly. I can tell you people are doing things they shouldn't be doing, and people are dead because of it. I promise I'll tell you when I know more."

"Like how you told me about the plague right away."

Another moment of silence. She shook her head.

"But that's history," she said, shaking her head.

Silence again. I didn't want to say anything more. I couldn't say anything more. I was just glad there was no talk of the money.

"So—what I really wanted to talk about," she said. "Do you ever get the feeling we're not ready to be parents?"

I shook my head. I drifted over to the fast lane, punched the accelerator.

"Why would you ever say that?" I said.

She raised her hand to her temple, like she was battling some pain inside. With her other hand she rummaged in her bag for something—a rattling bottle of pills.

"Migraine?" I said.

"A weird one," she said. "Just part of the morning sickness. They weren't kidding about these hormones. It's like being possessed."

She popped two tablets, then washed them down with a tiny bottle of water. She dabbed at the edges of her crimson lips with a napkin. She applied more lipstick to the smeared spots. She did this meticulously, with the precision of an artist, in the reflection of the visor's mirror. I changed lanes again and slowed as our exit neared. I had to say something to her. Something soothing, at that moment.

"So why are we going to be bad parents?" I said.

She capped the lipstick, puckered her mouth, and closed the mirror.

"I don't know," she said. "It's such a huge responsibility. And watching you turn green in the hospital at that appointment…"

"Hey, that was just a momentary case of…"

"I know you, Joe Barnes," she said. She touched my thigh. "You had no siblings, you lost your family so young. You haven't experienced these things. It's not your fault."

Silence, for a moment. She continued.

"All I know is we're bringing another human into this world. And for some reason, I feel impending doom. It's like those premonitions people get before a big heart attack. Things have been going crazy—all those patients dying, then that outbreak, then the plane crash at the school. You lost your job. The world is spinning out of control. Don't you ever feel that way?"

Before the traffic light at the top of the exit ramp, I steered the car over to the shoulder of the road. I put the car in park and turned to her. I reached for her hand. It was clammy and cold, the skin raw and rough, but I held it fast. I had to.

"Dear," I said. "We're ready to do this. We might be nervous, the world might be insane. But it's always a crazy place, this world. We love one another, and we'll love our child. And that's all anyone can ask for."

She smiled. A tear trickled down her cheek. She gazed again into the mirror and dabbed at her face, pulling out another tool from her bag to work at the newest blemish.

"You're right, Joe," she said. "I guess it's just hormones. They're so…overpowering sometimes. I just want everything to be so perfect, but there's always another loose end.

"I get this vision sometimes right before I fall asleep," she continued. "Total darkness, except a dangling rope in front of me, whipping in the wind. It comes apart. I fix that strand, but then other braids unwind, and I can never stop the wind from working its invisible fingers at the knots holding everything together. The rope frays, undoing everything. Chaos wins out."

She breathed. She shook her head, swinging her hair braids.

"I have no idea why I see that rope. Christ, I sound like such a nutcase," she said, closing the mirror.

I glanced over at her, looking for the signs like she was getting bad again. This was the way she talked when she got bad.

"Dear," I said carefully, "is this different than when you got back from the Middle East?"

She turned to me.

"Yes, Joe," she said. "That was trauma. That was PTSD. My soul had been ripped to shreds. This just feels like everyone is out to get me. Like I'm paranoid, like you are. Completely different."

She rubbed at her mascara.

"Have you talked to that reporter to try to get those papers back?" she asked. "Because I have to admit, Joe—I wasn't worried about you not having a job at first. But I started thinking about what would happen if we went through all the money in the accounts. Remember: I only make hourly wage at the shifts at the gym. We would have to sell the house, move to Omaha with my sister. It makes me short of breath just to think about it. I hate Nebraska."

She glanced over at me.

"But it won't come to that, will it?" she asked, a hopeful lilt to her voice.

"We'll be okay, dear," I said, nodding. "No Nebraska. I promise."

I grabbed her hand and squeezed, smiling at her. I clicked the car back into drive, pulled back onto the ramp and took a left turn.

Sweat flushed on my neck and forehead. I had to lie to her. Strange forces were at play, and my livelihood—probably even my health and safety—were caught in something much bigger than Mary and me and our growing family. In truth, her vision of a rope fraying wasn't crazy—it was prophecy. We were indeed a flimsy rope unraveling in a gale. But it would do nothing to voice my own fears—her own were enough of a burden to her. I watched her out of the corner of my eye, remembering how she had kept her composure, her cool, through all the big decisions in our life together—a wedding, the years of living hand-to-mouth during medical school, saving up to buy a house, caring for and burying her parents. She had never panicked, never broken down, after she put the memories of the Corps behind her. Whenever I felt like I was ready to burst at the seams, she had always been there at the end of a long day with a smile, a reassuring word, a glass of wine, a goodnight kiss. It always made life livable—even if she was only offering template platitudes from a blind faith in the future, as I had always secretly suspected. But all that had now changed. Her knee-jerk optimism was gone, that invisible well run dry. The weight of bringing another person into the world had become too heavy for her. So I knew I needed to be that rock for her this time instead—even if I was terrified of what the future held.

Or it all could be paranoid delusions. There were no larger forces, no conspiracy, no danger threatening me and my family and Wetherspoon—it was all just a product of my own tortured imagination. The scariest thought of all hit me: that the only threat was my own crumbling reality, and the only thing to fear was fatherhood. I watched Mary dabbing at her nose, and I shook my head to push the thought away.

Either way, I could not tell her about the money. Not now, not amid all this, on a drive to a memorial service for a dead friend.

The mortuary was on a hill, the oldest of its kind in the area. I drove up the driveway, past the big sign that shone "Funerals" in mustard-colored neon script. A line of mourners processed toward the lit doorway, where a dark figure stood, eclipsing the lantern over the entrance.

"I've never heard of a funeral at night," I said, suddenly feeling the night around me.

"They won't bury him in the dark, will they?" said Mary.

* * *

I parked in the last spot on the far end of the lot. We left the car and walked toward the entrance. Her heels clicked in time on the pavement, mine dragged slowly across the hard concrete. She took my arm. I squinted at the dark figure as we approached. And I recognized who it was. Within five feet, I made out the shabby outline and frizzled hair of Jim O'Keefe. The reporter's face widened in a smile.

"Evening, Doc. Mrs. Barnes," the reporter said, doffing an imaginary hat.

"And you are?" Mary asked.

"Dear, go get us a seat—I have to have a word with this gentleman," I said, guiding her past with a hand at the small of her back.

Mary took one blank look at the stranger, and then continued inside. When she was through the door, I looked at O'Keefe, then jerked my head over toward the shadows at the corner of the building. When we got to the spot, I jabbed a finger in his face.

"A funeral?" I hissed. "Harassing a grieving family at the sendoff for a dead loved one? You're a goddamned vulture, O'Keefe."

"It's news," said O'Keefe, nodding. "A doctor dying from an outbreak of the Black Death is news."

"I can't stop you," I said, through gritted teeth, shaking my finger at him. "But so help me God, I will physically restrain you from approaching that family." I stepped toward the door.

"I'm not here to see them," O'Keefe said. "I'm here to see you, Joe."

I stopped in my tracks.

"What about?" I said, without turning back.

"The documents. I finished translating them. I'll give them back to you, you can hand them over to the hospital and get your job back and all that. Then everybody's happy."

At this I turned. O'Keefe pointed at me, and he stepped close.

"But Doc, you've got to seriously consider whether you'd ever want to go back. When you read everything we've got, you'll want to steer clear of the whole place."

I grabbed the reporter's threadbare sleeve. His eyes were wide and unblinking.

"Tell me right now. Just tell me what's in those papers," I said. "I need to know."

O'Keefe gazed beyond me, at the doorway, a shadow of something flitting across his face. He pulled away from my grasp.

"We can't talk here," he said, sidestepping me toward the entrance. "But it's huge, I promise you. Meet me out here after the service. We'll go somewhere safe we can talk."

Before I could grab him, the reporter strode away, through the lighted door, and into the crowd. I had to go inside and just pay my respects to Rothenberg—there was nothing else I could do at that point. So I followed him inside.

The line of people in black ran down an ornate hallway wallpapered in flower patterns, lit by low lamps. Whispers drifted for just a second as they all took stock of the new person—me—entering. My face felt hot. I recognized a dozen doctors and nurses. I waved at one or two of them. Betty Bathory appeared and grabbed my elbow; she wore a slinky dress without sleeves that ended at her ankles. Mary was suddenly at my other elbow.

"Glad you two made it," said Betty, pushing herself up to peck me on the cheek. She and Mary kissed hello and embraced.

"Let's go pay our respects," Mary said.

"After you," I said.

A few minutes of handshakes and sad smiles brought us to the viewing room. Mourners sat in rows, staring ahead at the open casket, leaning and whispering. Soft organ music piped in from a speaker somewhere overhead. We stepped up to the end of the line—right behind the white tufts of Wetherspoon's head. I leaned over the Old Man's dandruff-flaked shoulder. I smelled whiskey, and a tang of musk.

"Good evening, Doc," I whispered.

"I thought you'd make it," the Old Man mumbled, not turning. "We need to talk."

"Hello, Neal," Mary said softly.

Wetherspoon swiveled at the sound of her voice. A rare smile crossed his lips.

"Well now, you made it, too," Wetherspoon said. He leaned in and kissed her cheek gently. "Looking every bit the glowing mother-to-be. How are you?"

"Pretty good," she said. "Some rough parts to this whole motherhood thing."

"Don't worry about that," the Old Man said. "I've seen some pregnancies so difficult, they look like terminal cancer. I'm sure you're fine.

"So, Joe," he continued, turning to me. "We'll talk…afterward?"

Mary shook her head at both of us, rolling her eyes.

"Sure, I'll be right behind you," I said. "Let's just pay our respects to Stuart."

The line had vanished in front of us. Wetherspoon stepped up to the casket and bowed his head, without kneeling. Then he walked away, after only a moment or two. How rude, I thought, as I walked up to the coffin.

But just a glance told me why the line had moved so quickly through the mourners, why no one had prayed for long by the side of the box.

Inside the casket was an envelope of thick, opaque plastic. The light glinted off the thick milky material, and it extended to either edge of the coffin. The dark shape hermetically sealed within was barely discernible as Rothenberg's dead face. Red blotches dotted his cheeks, and there were black smudges high on his rotten scalp. The whiteness of the skin outshone the plastic. The eyes were open, dry and desiccated. His mouth was sewn shut with thick dark spool. Half his nose had already rotted away around one nostril. It was a nightmare vision, and it was right there in front of us. Mary's hand slipped into mine. We bowed our heads for a moment, then we too moved on.

"Can you believe…" Mary whispered, grabbing his wrist.

"No," I said. "We'll talk about it later."

Rothenberg's family—the widow and two young, plump teens—hugged each and every person in the receiving line. Their puffy and raw faces stared, their heads nodding like off-timed metronomes. I embraced the widow Shelley for a few extra seconds, our eyes locked for a moment upon withdrawing. Nothing was said, a look was exchanged, nothing more. I never knew what to say at such moments. Then Mary and I moved on, finding Betty and Wetherspoon talking over a water cooler in the adjacent sitting room. We were the only ones inside.

Wetherspoon was in midst of one of his more intense diatribes. Betty just nodded along. Mary went over and gave her a hug. Wetherspoon stopped and shook my hand. All four of us were fidgety, shaken by the nightmare in the coffin. Mary laid her head on Betty's shoulder, and the nurse stroked her hair, saying something softly. I grabbed my mentor's elbow and pulled him aside. We were in a darkened corner of the room, near a dust-covered piano. I thought it would be safe to talk.

"Why is Stuart sealed up like that?" I asked. "He looks like a NutriFast dinner, for Christ's sake."

"The Bureau of Wellness released the body on the condition it would stay in a prophylactic sheath, and would be incinerated immediately after the services," Wetherspoon said, scratching at his eyes.

"Bullshit. They can't just demand that. The Rothenberg's are Jewish, they probably don't want to cremate him."

"Don't believe me? Take a look at that warning label on the coffin."

The Old Man pulled me by the sleeve to the doorway, so I could see the foot of the casket in the adjacent room. A yellow-and-black label was affixed to the edge. I couldn't read it; it was too far away.

But curiosity pulled me closer, and I approached the coffin. From a few steps away, I saw it was the same Bureau of Wellness emblem I had found on the intake pipe at the river. I drifted to it, the horrible fascination drawing me within feet, until I could read it clearly.

BOW-137—that same serial number, yet again.

It was the same call number, too. I repeated it over and over again, committing it to memory, because I didn't dare to pull out my Atman and type it in at that moment.

Just then, the soft electronic piping of the organ grew louder. A stream of people crushed into the room closer to the body—though the front of the crowd kept a good fifteen feet away, a force-field of horror repelling them all. Wetherspoon edged us in closer to the threshold, and I could feel Mary and Betty behind us, straining to look over our shoulders.

The crowd hushed. A screen descended from the ceiling. It rotated to face the audience of mourners. The face of a holy man, black-clad and spry, wearing the blue collar of the New Church of the Unified Three, beamed out of the high-definition 3-D pixels.

"Friends," the reverend's head said warmly, as it swiveled the crowd. "We gather here today to hail and farewell our dearly departed friend. Would we be so kind as to silence our Atmans and make time for our final reconnoiter on this earthly plane?"

Hands came out of pockets, blips hiccupped around the room and screens flickered through the crowd. The minister pursed his lips knowingly, an affected grace tempering the movement of his lips and brow. He pulled a pair of FocalSpecs from a breast pocket. Squinting, I watched the off-screen teleprompter reflected backward across the top of the lenses.

His baritone droned for a long time. The holy man mouthed the typical platitudes about a life free of death. More words—a better future, a calmer place beyond everything mortals could ever know. The same syllables of empty solace, of hollow pathos, which an orphan had committed to memory at his parents' funeral two decades before. My mind wandered over that night I had been left so alone, and I got so lost in my past I was unsure, for a moment, whether I was an adult or a teen.

The voice kept on, the holy man's eyes tracking back and forth, back and forth. I pulled my mind back from the memories, and I scanned the crowd of faces, the prim mouths and hard stares of the mourners around me. I recognized almost all of them: colleagues, Rothenberg's family, the occasional acquaintance within the hospital's social circle. I saw a local politician leaning over and laughing as he whispered into the ear of a pretty aide—until he caught me watching him, and his face quickly twisted with crocodile tears.

"There are no Gods but Allah…and Yahweh, and the Lord…and there are no messengers other than Muhammad…and Moses…and Jesus."

The holy man paused, nodding at the ground, swept up in his own performance. Wetherspoon snickered, leaned to me.

"Never understood how this Church unifies all three," the Old Man whispered. "Back when I was a kid, they all hated each other. Wars were fought. Millions died."

I nodded. The broadcasted face of the holy man glared at the two of us. I averted my eyes toward the crowd, where a few family members were dabbing at their eyes with white tissues—a white that punctuated the rows of black suits and dresses like seagulls in a night sky. Except—there was one splash of color, a single red kerchief in a suit's breast pocket at the back of the room. I squinted.

It was Yoshiro Fujimi. My replacement. The crimson cloth disappeared. The doctor's expressionless eyes glared forward. Next to him was the grimacing face of Suzanne Kranklein.

I scratched my beard and stared hard at Fujimi. The scab's moustache was a thin dark arc over his lip, his glasses squared and severe at right angles. His black-and-white hair was cropped short at the sides, but his bangs were gray and long. His face was pinched with intelligence, wrinkled with the long stress of thought and exertion. It was an unkind face, and I struggled to reconcile this hard visage with the far-off figure who had waved a fond farewell down the hospital corridor at me. Fujimi had Asiatic features—but something in his haughty grimace and upright posture made him distinctly American.

179

The holy man's amplified voice lifted, filling every corner of the room. In the front row, just feet away from me, the widow sobbed. It was uncontrollable; an utter primal despair raged from deep down inside her. It was a kind I remembered from that night a lifetime before when I had lost everything I ever had. The minister paused for a melodramatic second, then closed with a five-second prayer. The holy man's face on the screen ascended into the ceiling. Everyone rose from their seats and grouped around Rothenberg's wife, consoling her. I kept a short distance away, watching the crush of embracing hands and arms around the wailing widow.

None other than Suzanne Kranklein pushed her way through the crowd, edging people aside with her elbows, rubbing her face as she tried her best approximation of humanity. Fujimi was at her heels.

"Watch this—this ought to be good," Wetherspoon said, nudging me.

The two hospital bosses reached the throng and pushed their way to Mrs. Rothenberg. Suzanne reached out with both hands to offer solace.

With a roar, the widow slapped the Kraken's hands away. The grieving woman hissed through the snot covering her face, blinking through the rivulets of mascara. She snarled at the Kraken.

"Get out of here!" she shrieked. "It's you that did this to him! He'd still be here if it hadn't been for you!"

The widow's hand connected hard with the Kraken's cheek. The crack of flesh froze the room. The widow lunged, gripping the Kraken's throat. But the arms all around quickly pulled her off and back toward the coffin. Fujimi grabbed his cohort by the sleeve and yanked her toward the door.

"You animals," the widow snarled, voices and hands soothing her, shielding her once again. "You keep your filthy hush money. You goddamned butchers."

Wetherspoon nudged my arm again.

"It seems Suzanne Kranklein's particular charms extend beyond the hospital," the Old Man said. "Anyway, let's get out of here. Let's see where the dreadful duo goes."

We walked toward the exit, Wetherspoon and me with Mary and Betty behind. But Abbud emerged from a side doorway. A broad smile tilted his handsome face lopsided, like a deflated ball. For the inside of a funeral home, it was a scandalous expression.

"Guess Rothenberg's wife isn't holding up so well," he said, whisking past his two former colleagues, kissing Betty on the cheek, then taking Mary's hand, as he inspected her up and down. "So how is my number one patient?"

I thought I saw my wife turn a bit red, but I couldn't be sure in the weird low light of the funeral parlor. She twirled one of her braids like a schoolgirl, though, and smiled wide.

"I don't know, I've been feeling okay, Adam," she said. "Except I get these stomach pains sometimes, and the morning sickness is an all-day thing."

"Forget it, my child," Abbud said, mimicking the Unified Three reverend's booming holy-man voice. "This too shall pass."

She laughed, tapping his wrist, shaking her head. I hadn't heard her laugh in days, maybe weeks. I stared at the two of them—Mary and this Adam person I'd only ever known as Dr. Abbud—and I have to admit a jolt of jealousy ran through me. It was an acidic sting I hadn't felt in years. I watched as the neonatologist inquired after her health, asking questions, nodding, smiling, responding, and reassuring. I tried to hear what they were saying, but they spoke softly, and Wetherspoon was talking insistently in my other ear.

"The baby doc has taken quite an interest in your wife's well-being," the Old Man murmured.

"I'm sure Abbud—Adam, whatever—is just doing his due diligence," I said.

"Hmmm," Wetherspoon grunted, his arms crossed. "Due diligence. I wonder."

Two men with stark white NBC suits emerged from a doorway on the other side of the coffin. They looked like cartoons amid the sober misery of the mortuary, but no one else seemed to notice. They walked around the coffin, checking for something. One went to the foot of the coffin and scrutinized the label, his rubber index finger tracing the letters. The other one closed and sealed the lid, using a power drill to tighten the screws. Something about the finality of that electric whinnying of the screws going in sent a shock up my spine.

"Anyway," I said, over the whirring of the tool. "Let's go see where this Fujimi character and the Kraken are headed."

Yes—let's go see where the monstrous Kraken and her nefarious partner are headed." Wetherspoon said, grinning.

As we neared the exit, rays of color sparkled through the glass door. Red and blue and white lights flickered and flashed in the dark. Outside, we saw a line of a half-dozen cop cars on the northern side of the funeral home. Their emergency lights blinked in different tempos. Wetherspoon and I stopped and stared at the strobing chaos. My head started to thrum; it felt like another migraine coming.

"What the hell's going on?" I said.

Bright spotlight beams whisked up to us, brushed across our faces for a second, then swept across the parking lot and into a dark copse of trees.

"They're searching for someone," the Old Man said. "I don't see Fujimi or the Kraken anywhere."

We watched the beam of light, which whisked by the black thickets, along a line of cars at the far end of the lot, but then edged back toward the shadows. It stopped, hovered in one spot. I squinted, and I caught the dark shape of a man edging through the brush. The figure froze. The line of cops closed in. The man panicked and bolted out in the direction of the funeral home, tie flailing and hat falling as he sprinted for his life. But he wasn't going fast, and his steps slowed after the first ten steps or so. The cops quickly rushed in and wrestled the man to the ground, putting in some quick kicks and jabs for good measure. The man went limp, and they hauled him up. A group of four of them carried him, one with each limb. Their path to the patrol cars was directly past the doorway. Wetherspoon and I watched in silence. Only when the group passed did I recognize the man's face. I gasped.

"O'Keefe," I said.

O'Keefe's head turned, and our eyes locked for a second—mine wide with surprise, the newsman's swollen with fear. O'Keefe flailed one last time to free himself. One arm came free from an officer's hands, and something shiny flew off to my right, glinting in the light for a second, then vanishing in the gloom. No one else noticed. Other hands quickly grabbed the newsman's free limb. The officers tightened their grip for the last few yards to the back of a cop car. O'Keefe's eyes looked up, his face upside-down, pale.

"Find Meruda," he said to me. "That's the only way. Find Meruda. Down below!"

A cop whacked him in the stomach with a baton, and O'Keefe's howled, his eyes rolled back in his head. He was carried off into the flashing lights. I shielded my eyes. I turned to look at Wetherspoon. His hand was at furrowed brow, his eyes narrowed.

"That was the scribbler, wasn't it, Joe?" he said.

"Yeah, the guy who has your documents."

O'Keefe's limp form was slammed against the patrol car, his hands cuffed behind his back, chest against the back window. Rough cop hands frisked him. He started to try and push himself up by the shoulders, but the cop conducting the search banged his skull against the metal roof, a sound that echoed off in the darkness. They opened the door and shoved the dazed reporter into the backseat.

Footsteps approached from the dark part of the parking lot. A shadow emerged from the line of cars. The figure sharpened as it came into the light. It was Lanza. He smiled at me.

"Figured I'd catch you here," he said, hiking up his belt. "Damned shame about your doctor friend. My condolences."

"Stuart was a good guy. He didn't deserve to go like that," I said. "Hey, Zo—that was the reporter, right? What did he do?"

"It was Jim O'Keefe, the reporter," Lanza said. He unwrapped a piece of nicotine gum and stuffed it in his mouth. "For this one we're on a need-to-know basis. We're just backup. The Bureau is calling all the shots."

"Need-to-know basis?" Wetherspoon scoffed. "Just more fascist stooges following orders, eh?"

Lanza shook his head. He looked at me, then at Wetherspoon. A poisonous little smile spread across his lips.

"Joe," he said. "Would you tell this Old Bastard to take it easy, so I don't have to enforce those outstanding warrants in the database?"

I held my hands up and stepped between them.

"We don't need any trouble," I said. "Neal's just been under a lot of strain lately. Isn't that right, Neal?"

"Maybe 'fascist' is too big a word for this stooge to understand," the Old Man said, sticking out his stubbled chin. "Maybe 'pig' is a little easier to comprehend."

Lanza took one step closer. I stood fast between the two of them, the shrunken centenarian and the towering cop.

"I'll bet you've been under a lot of strain," Lanza said, his voice low, menacing. "Dodging a manhunt for weeks, and all that. And getting those homicide warrants changed to misdemeanors, somehow. It must have been exhausting. But I guess it pays to have friends in high places. Somebody could get away with murder."

Wetherspoon shook his head and walked away, face dark with rage, hands on his hips. Lanza tapped my arm with his gloved fist.

"He's the one you ought to be watching," Lanza said. "He's the one who's been around forever, who knows everyone and all that. Think about it. He must know more than he's telling you."

"Come on, Zo," I said. "Cut the guy a break. He's innocent until proven guilty, even under FOJA. We're going to get out of here. I'll talk to you later."

Lanza nodded, took a long glance at Wetherspoon, then slowly walked off. Once his footsteps had faded out of earshot, the Old Man stepped next to me.

"Your friend is a buffoon," he said. "Just another foot soldier goose-stepping into history."

Without another word, Wetherspoon walked off into the darkness. I heard a door open and shut, the roar of the old gasoline engine, and lights splintering the darkness at the far end of the lot. I watched in silence as the station wagon pulled out. At the line of cop cars, Wetherspoon honked three times, cursing, and one of the black and whites rolled aside to let him through.

Quiet and stillness surrounded me. I peered back through the glass of the funeral home door. Mary was laughing at some joke Abbud was telling, her hand lightly gracing his wrist. I watched as Abbud placed his hand on her stomach and felt for the baby. They laughed again. I felt the sweat on my neck. So much for professionalism from the baby doc. I forced myself to look away, scanning the darkness. Empty silence, and I was all alone.

Now was the time. I crouched over in the bushes and felt around for the shiny object O'Keefe had thrown in the bushes. My hand closed on something metallic and sharp—a jumble of keys. I picked them up, careful not to jangle them. The keys were all different sizes, but the largest was a car key.

I found the reporter's old gasoline-burning model Rasul parked in the darkest corner of the lot, where O'Keefe had been hiding. The door opened, and the smell of burnt tobacco was pungent on the inside. Food wrappers and empty plastic bottles covered the seats and floors. I turned on the overhead light, and there it was, practically glowing at me. The dossier of ancient papers. I picked it up and thumbed through it—it felt like everything was there. I breathed hard and nearly cried from joy.

Collapsing on the seat atop the litter, I paused, lost in thought. Excitement coursed through me. Everything could go back to the way it was, now. I could get my job back, even if it meant pulling horrible shifts. I could work at the hospital again, and so could Wetherspoon. I wouldn't have to worry about finances or struggle to afford to keep a child alive and healthy. Whatever was in the documents wasn't insidious. It couldn't be—that was crazy. This entire series of events was just a delusion of circumstance. I rubbed my eyes. What was the use in going against the flow, seeing things that weren't there; if no one else saw anything either, then it didn't exist.

There was no conspiracy. No great buried truths. People died inexplicably—the human machine breaks down every day, like it did for Cruzen. Hearts fail, even young hearts. Terrorists got ahold of guns and bombs and killed innocent people for no good reason at all, as had always been the case. Drones dropped chemicals into rivers and crashed into schools. Shit happened in the land of the deliriously free, the home of the foolishly brave. But the statistics and probabilities were the only true conspirator. There was no grand design of evil, no overarching collusion of forces. I laughed and shook my head, shutting the car door. I turned.

A shadow blocked my path. I recoiled. A man just slightly taller than me stood there, but I couldn't see anything else about the figure, backlit as it was by the light from the funeral home. It was like a black hole in midst of the void.

"Dr. Barnes," the stranger said, syllables clipped. The man stepped close, eclipsing the light.

It was my replacement. Fujimi.

"Yes?" I said, swallowing hard.

"So nice to finally meet you, Doctor," the man said, his words precise. "I have followed your work for years. My name is Yoshiro Fujimi."

I said nothing, but I clung tighter to the dossier.

"You must know it was not my decision to have you terminated from the hospital," Fujimi said. "It was a Bureau of Wellness diktat. And you know you can return, if the conditions are met."

"Conditions?" I said.

"I assumed Suzanne Kranklein informed you. A series of conditions to prove your good faith efforts toward the Bureau."

I waited, said nothing. I couldn't tell this man anything. Fujimi continued.

"First, you need to give me those papers you just recovered. Second, you need to cooperate fully with the hospital's new initiatives," he said. "Third, you'd need to abandon all these subversive activities you've been undertaking with Cornelius Wetherspoon."

"Subversive activities?"

"The trespassing, the stealing, the commission of crimes," Fujimi said, leaning so a stray ray of light glinted off his glasses. "Wetherspoon is a paranoid old man. Do not let some deranged coot like that destroy your promising career, Dr. Barnes. Whatever your curiosity may be, it will be satisfied in due time."

"If I abide by these rules, I get my job back. Everything goes back the way it was?"

"Yes, except you'd be reporting directly to me—and no longer Suzanne Kranklein. The Bureau studies would be your primary responsibility."

"Which studies, exactly?"

"They're triple-blind studies administered by the highest Bureau officials," Fujimi said. "They've been an ongoing undertaking since the turn of the millennium."

"Like the vitamins program. Why haven't I heard of these studies before now?"

Fujimi chuckled. It was a mirthless sound, like the rap of a scalpel on a surgical table.

"They are classified, Dr. Barnes. These studies will never be written about in a medical journal or broadcast on the news," he said. "They're much too important for that. The researchers are all hand-picked. It should be considered quite an honor to be asked, I would add."

"Was Lamalade part of these studies?" I said.

"Who is that?" said Fujimi.

"Samuel Lamalade. The janitor who shot up the talent show and started the plague outbreak."

"I hadn't heard anything about that," Fujimi said, shaking his head coolly. "I can assure you, we wouldn't hire just any madman to carry out our work. The Bureau is very serious about getting results. We have too much invested, and there's too much at stake for our country."

"But you are saying you would do such things."

"I never said that, either."

"What about James Cruzen?" I said, changing tack. "Was he part of the studies in any way? He was a patient who died at the hospital a few weeks ago."

Fujimi shook his head. He looked off somewhere into the shadows and chuckled.

"A person died at the hospital. Aren't we all going to die at the hospital, if we aren't so fortunate as to die at home, peacefully, in our sleep?"

"How about Esmeralda? The girl with the tattoo on her neck."

Fujimi visibly flinched at the mere mention of the girl, and I knew I had hit upon something. But he recovered quickly—the shadow's voice again smooth and level.

"Dr. Barnes, we could talk about any number of people whom you know, and whom I don't. But this is all beside the point."

I nodded. I lowered the dossier to my hip.

"You know, I tried calling you months ago," I said. "You were in Guatemala. Your secretary told me you'd still be there on sabbatical. Conducting population research. Or something."

Fujimi stiffened at the mention of Guatemala. He brushed at the lapels of his suit.

"That was a research trip—it was nothing," he said. "We compiled our results well before the clinical deadline. I was going to go back to New England, but once I saw the opening at Saint Almachius, I jumped at the chance. Nothing more to tell."

"You stopped years of groundbreaking research abroad for a job at a local New Jersey hospital," I said, crossing my arms. "Isn't this Bureau initiative just a continuation of whatever you were doing down in Central America? Wasn't that a 'triple-blind' trial of some sort, too?"

"You really have been listening to that crazy old man too much, I'm afraid," Fujimi said. "Take a deep breath, Dr. Barnes. Just consider our offer. It would be best for everyone involved—you, your wife, the Bureau—if you would accept. Think of your unborn child."

I stared at the dark figure. I cleared my throat.

"Are you threatening me, Dr. Fujimi?"

"Only stating the obvious, Dr. Barnes."

Silence. I readjusted my hold on the dossier.

"I'd like a night to think this all over," I said.

"That is acceptable. I know you have to consult your wife. I met her inside. Charming woman. She practically glows, even in a funeral home," Fujimi said, extending a hand.

I shook it—the flesh dry and cool. Then Fujimi turned and walked away, without another needless word.

I stepped slowly in that same direction into the lights, my head spinning. Something about Fujimi was kinetic. The man gave off a crackling energy, like he was draining the atmosphere around him. As Fujimi strode down the driveway, I realized how much I had forgotten to ask.

Fujimi stopped a few feet from the patrol car holding O'Keefe. He paused, reached into his pocket. He pulled out something small. He pointed it at the back of the cruiser. I cringed, and ran toward him, expecting the pop of a tiny pistol or some weapon. But nothing came. Fujimi stuffed the object back in his pocket and continued walking confidently away from the funeral home.

I stopped. Was this man insane?

But then a noise came from the cop car. Someone banged on the car windows—from the inside. O'Keefe's hands and head slammed against the shatter-proof glass. The cop in the front seat burst out of the car and dashed around the side to the back door. I sprinted forward. A few papers fell out of the dossier, and I stooped and stuffed them in my pockets and ran forward.

"Suspect in cardiac arrest," the officer said into his shoulder-radio. "Requesting ambulance immediately."

He yanked open the door and O'Keefe spilled out headfirst to the pavement. His mouth was frothing, white eyes rolling back in his head.

"Officer, I'm a doctor—what happened to this man?"

"I don't know—he was demanding to call his lawyer when he just started to shake and vomit," the officer said, laying the reporter out on the asphalt.

"Let me see him."

The cop backed off, and I set the dossier on the ground and crouched over the reporter. O'Keefe's heart had indeed stopped. I began chest compressions and mouth-to-mouth, the life-giving rhythm. But the reporter was dying. The heartbeat had just ceased—the body was burning up. I felt at the jugular for a pulse, then pulled up the sleeve.

The Atman in the wrist glowed with a strange light. Lightly I touched a fingertip to it, and recoiled, cursing. It had burned me with heat, like a frying pan, on contact. I angled the wrist over. The screen was flashing, without a pattern at all. It was just a miasma of swirling colors, a visual chaos. It was doing something to O'Keefe. It was killing him. I stared for a second, but then I came to my senses. I tried a few more compressions and deep breaths, but it was no use.

The Atman kept flickering, like it was possessed. I had an idea.

"Officer, do you have a knife handy?"

"What do you need a knife for?" he said.

"I need to remove the man's Atman. I think it's killing him," I said.

The cop frowned, then walked back to his cruiser. He came back with a jagged hunting knife, which he handed over.

"This is crazy, Doc," the cop said.

I grabbed the blade and plunged it into the flesh around the Atman. Since O'Keefe's heart had stopped already, the blood came as a mere trickle onto the pavement. I incised an inch beneath the skin, then angled the blade and sawed sideways. As I proceeded along the bone, I pried the device upward. Finally, at the edge of the machine, I yanked, and it came free with a sickening suctioning of flesh and muscle. The cop retched, covering his mouth with his hands. I tried to tug the Atman free of O'Keefe's arm, but part of the implant was stuck fast. The blood was flowing faster again, hot and heavy. I glanced up. O'Keefe's eyes were open. He blinked once. His mouth moved.

"What is it, O'Keefe?" I said, drawing close.

"Check...dossier," O'Keefe said. "Meruda...experiments..."

"Take it easy, Jim. We need to get you to the hospital," I said, shaking him. "But who is Meruda?"

O'Keefe's eyes went wide, then blank, his face dropped limp. The blood stopped coursing out of his arm. I felt for a pulse. It was gone again. But now the Atman dimmed, slowed down, then went black. I did a few more chest compressions, but it was useless. Shaking my head, I reached out and closed the reporter's eyes.

My hand brushed against something papery at his collar. I felt around, squinting in the half-darkness. My fingers closed on a familiar strip—it was another label with the same damned serial numbers.

BOW-137.

I yanked it off and pocketed it. Standing, I looked around. The cop was on the other side of the police car, doubled over, vomiting from the sight of the impromptu surgery. No one else was around; all was silent. I took a few steps toward the funeral home. But then I remembered the dossier I had left on the ground and turned on my heel.

It wasn't there. I retraced my steps. I walked in a circle around the reporter's body, listening to the cop's sickening heaves. I searched the darkness for thieves in the shadows. I scoured the nearby bushes, I canvassed the slope of the lawn, looking down the rushing lights of the ultrahighway. But there was nothing—not a single stray page anywhere.

Someone had stolen it. I balled my fists and roared at the sky, I spat on my own face. I flailed back toward the funeral home. It could not be happening. The documents would have gotten me my job back, made life normal again. Who had taken them? Who had robbed me of my reprieve?

A shiver crested my spine, lighting up my brain. Only a few reasons could make someone interested enough in an old dossier of papers to steal them. They were important. They were damaging to someone or something. They held unnamable secrets. And they had to be removed. Someone had to make sure I didn't even have the chance to try to read those old alphanumerics. Someone had been watching and waiting. They'd used O'Keefe's death throes as the perfect distraction to swipe them from me. Someone had killed O'Keefe because he had decoded their secrets. Was it Fujimi's weird gesture that did it—and if so, how? I held my head in my hands, mulling over the possibilities.

With a bustle, Mary came through the funeral-home door, laughing, glancing over her shoulder at Abbud, who followed her with a youthful spring in his step. She glanced at me, and the smile quickly melted off her face.

"Joe, what's wrong?" she said, coming over to me. Her hand brushed my damp forehead.

"O'Keefe—he's dead," I said, gesturing behind me at the body.

"What?" she said, her hand covering her mouth.

"Is there anything we can do?" Abbud said, starting down the driveway.

"Absolutely nothing," I said, ushering Mary toward our car. The big crowd of mourners started to stream out of the funeral home, and a crowd clustered near the reporter's lifeless body.

"Come on, let's go," I whispered in Mary's ear.

"Shouldn't you wait for the police to take your statement?" Abbud hollered.

"I don't think that would be wise," I said, pointing at the vomiting officer, pulling Mary toward the car.

We climbed in the car and took off. As I pulled out the back exit onto a side-road, I noticed Abbud frantically waving his arms in the rearview mirror. But I only waved with the back of my hand and drove out the back exit, and onto the eastbound stretch of the ultrahighway. The sparkling holograms streamed by. Adoring *How Low Can You Go* audiences shimmered in the broadcast onto the night sky, their roar like an ocean. Every other ad sparkled with the vision of the release of the new generation of Atmans.

"You know you want it," echoed Saxas' voice across the valley.

"Joe, was that the reporter? The one who stole the Wetherspoon files? What happened to him? You didn't…"

"I didn't do anything to him," I said. "He gave me the papers, but they were stolen by whoever did that to him."

"Call the police, Joe! Call the hospital!"

"There's nothing I can do, Mary. The reporter just died. I have no better explanation. But I will find out, I promise you that."

She smacked my arm.

"Joseph Aloysius Barnes! Go back and find those papers! Right now!" Mary said. I shook my head.

"They're long gone, honey."

She continued yelling. There was nothing I could do. In a way, she was right. Those papers were everything. But I knew they were gone. And I knew what I had to do. As I switched to the fast lane, a blotch against the black sky drifted across the rearview. I adjusted the mirror and glanced back. A gray plume of smoke was drifting upward from a thin high chimney on the funeral home's roof. After a mile, it faded into the depth of the night.

THE MONSTROUS INSTANTS OF HISTORY

U.S.A., 2087

The Atman blipped and pinged as with each finger stroke. I had never noticed the noises before. But as I sat in my first-floor bathroom, the door closed, those tiny tones suddenly seemed thunderous, soundwaves bounding off the tiles, breaking the trance of dawn. Mary was fast asleep upstairs, hooked blissfully into her gusting Dormus. I did not want to wake her; she needed her rest.

But I had not slept. Without my own Dormus, my body could not relax. My limbs were cramped, kinked in every position, with each toss and turn, over every minute of the interminable night. Each breath felt labored as I tried not to keep shifting, talking to myself. All I needed was a few hours of rest. But the reality of the past day corrupted every moment. There was no way to shut it all out. My neck tensed, and then I grew physically tired as my mind raced, still wide awake. Even as my muscles fell limp, the thoughts bounced and whirled in my brain. The nightmare of drowning in the river was gone. It was replaced by new hellish visions—these not dreams at all, but wakeful knowledge of the world I could not escape even for a night's respite.

It was an unceasing kaleidoscope. The burning rubble of the school. The pallid bodies of plague victims in tiny apartments. The contorted death grimaces of Cruzen, Lamalade, and O'Keefe. The sonogram blob, my unborn child. The impassive glare of Yoshiro Fujimi. The sobs of Rothenberg's widow over her husband's freeze-dried corpse. The bureaucratic fingertapping of Suzanne Kranklein. The ominous bloom of green ooze flowing on the river current. The strange labels on dead people, on water-intake pipes and caskets. The stolen dossier—and the three pages I'd tucked and crumpled inside the pocket of my suitjacket.

And Meruda—whoever the hell she may be.

Finally, I gave up and left the sweaty bed. I went down to the kitchen, past the bay windows framing the sun's rise. When I flipped on the kitchen light, I realized I was still wearing the suit from the funeral. My belt was still fastened. The only piece I had removed before crawling into bed was the jacket, which was still hanging on the back of a chair. I reached into its breast pocket.

The strange pages came out in my hand. I straightened them. The edge of one slit my finger, and I cursed, sucking at the sliver of blood as I held them up to my face. The papers were written in bureaucratic doublespeak, acronyms and euphemisms. I tried to read the old typeface with a rising sense of helplessness. A timeline, a newspaper clipping, and the blurry facsimile of an ID card. They may as well have been artifacts from an ancient civilization, words of a dead language gouged in a clay tablet. As my eyes rushed headlong through the pages they seemed more and more inscrutable.

I slammed my fist down. I walked over to the liquor cabinet, poured a whiskey, took a long swallow. Pulling an energy stick from a drawer, I cracked it and snorted deeply. I closed my eyes and breathed. I went over to the chair, sat down, took a deep breath, and tried again.

The first page was headed "Project 137." It was the easiest to read, and as I focused, the daze of insomnia lifted. My eyes, so used to glowing screens, slowly were starting to reaccustom themselves to the old alphanumerics of the typewritten official documents in front of me, even as smudged as they were. But it was still a slog; the enumerated entries, the truncated words, the grand sweep of lost 20th century American history. At least there was a kind of guide: the handwritten annotations written in O'Keefe's shaky ink along the margin.

And I started to understand. This was the key to absolutely everything.

1946 to 1948—Guatemala. U.S. government doctors intentionally infect hundreds of psychiatric patients with syphilis to watch the speed of their deaths, read the first entry.

"Nobody cares about lunatics. Especially foreign lunatics," O'Keefe wrote in the margin.

Mid-1950s—St. Louis. Motorized blowers installed on city rooftops. Zinc cadmium sulfide and other undetermined agent spread among population. About 10,000 rare cancer cases determined by year 2000. Virtually all are poor African-Americans, read the second.

"Army project designed to test BW attack on impoverished Russian city, using Saint Louis ghetto as a model for Soviet Bloc housing," O'Keefe added.

1960s—Project 112. DOD and CIA collaborate on BW and CW research formally for the first time, read the next one. *Project is one of a numbered series; later officially shut down by the administration. But subsequent Projects retain essential superstructure for subsequent work. Gas release and dosing of water systems with psychotropics and spores carried out at intermittent times in scattered locations, including South Dakota, Nevada, and New Jersey. Murders, psychotic episodes, and suicides result from exposure.*

"New Jersey is center of water dispersal tests of contagion starting in 1982, causing thousands of undocumented cases of physiological and psychological disease," O'Keefe added, underlining every other word. "Autism and birth defects, and unexplained deaths, increase steadily. Garden State becomes known as a toxic wasteland, the butt of comedians' jokes."

My hair stood on end. New Jersey was in the middle of it all, reaching back to my parents and even my grandparents' time. I swigged the whiskey, and I cracked another energy stick. I snorted and read on.

1970s—San Francisco dispersion experiments, New York subway population trials. Control group bacteria released in open city and in enclosed subterranean space to define control group of the spread among a mobile population. No effects studied initially. However, bacteria commingle with pollutants to become carcinogenic compounds. Cancer clusters and autoimmune ailments proliferate in 1980s. Death estimates conservatively placed at 375,000. But they likely exceed 2 million.

"Millions dead within cancer clusters—even as U.S. wages a 'War on Cancer,'" was the trembling annotation, cut in thick ink, rage gushing from O'Keefe's pen. The reporter had really given a shit about the common good, after all, I mused. I raised my glass to the ceiling and took another hit of the whiskey, saluting the now-deceased journalist. But I read on.

United States signs updated versions of Geneva Protocol in 1972 and 1993 banning research into Chemical Warfare and Biological Warfare—CW and BW.

"Liars had their fingers crossed behind their backs," O'Keefe footnoted.

From 1980s onward into the first decades of the millennium, it continued, *CW and BW research in the U.S. continues and expands, with mass aircraft dispersion of lithium particles also beginning in 1982. Funding increases in multiple sections of the defense budget, tucked within other fiscal items, and never as a single category scrutinized in audits. Research is described as defensive—first in the interest of counter-balancing the perceived threat of the Soviet Union at the end of the Cold War. But then the Iron Curtain crumbles, and it's another decade until Terrorism replaces Communism as the major threat to World Peace.*

"One—ism is as good as another!" O'Keefe scribbled underneath.

Starting in the year 2001, Food and Drug Administration controls are relaxed by several successive acts of Congress, it continued. *New frontiers in ingredients and synthetic additives are opened to the big manufacturers. Corporations progressively employ more dyes, taste enhancers, substitutes, preservatives, thickening agents, and emulsifiers which go untested just as long as side effects remain unreported. Using new electronic health databases, blood samples are surreptitiously taken and cataloged, creating an extensive pharmaco-anthropological study of the Americans' serum from region to region.*

"Strange they all got the same idea to study human serum at a population level at the same time…" O'Keefe wrote.

In the fall of 2018, Project 137 goes fully operational. Latest in the line of the Projects combining the CW and BW research, and the ambient population effects of air toxics, water purity and nutrition—all are conducted now at the most classified levels. The possibilities of determining environmental effects on disease, such as dietary effects on cancer, are nearly endless. The newly-christened Bureau of Wellness becomes lead agency. They announce massive research into population-level health indicators. But behind it moves Project 137, sole inheritor of the U.S.'s work in BW and CW.

"The game is afoot," O'Keefe wrote.

To be noted—the U.S. programs into CW and BW only really started with the end of World War II. Although limited research was conducted prior to 1945 at Fort Detrick in Maryland in response to the global Axis threat, it was only after the end of hostilities that the funding and the staffing began to envelop significant portions of the national defense budget. Use of hemorrhagic smallpox during the Korean War is first instance of American deployment. The sudden gains in technology and know-how in BW and CW starting in 1945 remain unexplained in official channels.

This board's recommendation is to keep this information privileged in perpetuity.

The signature beneath it all was indistinct and faint, like it was a copy that had faded with reproduction after reproduction over the years. But I held it up to the light, squinting.

And I gasped.

Executive Summary prepared by:

Cornelius Wetherspoon, PhD, gastroenterology and geriatrics,

Saint Almachius Hospital, N.J., Bureau of Wellness satellite office, March 17, 2019.

The bastard had been playing me all along. He was in the thick of it more than anyone. I read the name again and again, as if I could be wrong about the name, or that it could be another Cornelius Wetherspoon. I balled my fist and thought about punching something. But instead, I tipped the glass back. I refilled it, drained it, and refilled again. I snapped an energy stick under my nose. I turned the page.

The second page carried the reproductions of two news stories. They were from the days of newspapers; my eyes had even more trouble with these blurrier items. There were no dates—but they clearly came from before I was born. Small headlines and tiny typeface. I could remember the last remaining newspapers from when I was a child, and I knew the editors had decided these were unimportant stories. They were afterthoughts; castaways tucked away in the throwaway back pages, stranded somewhere behind the obituaries and in front of the flimsy supermarket coupons.

SICK FAMILY'S CLAIMS AGAINST GOVERNMENT DENIED

PHILADELPHIA— *A federal appellate court today dismissed the claims of a New Jersey family who claimed government experiments with their water supply gave them rare cancers.*

The court ruled the government did not purposefully give the residents of the village of Chooser's Mill chronic diseases.

Federal agencies were simply dosing a standing water supply with toxins to gauge the effects, and were not necessarily trying to cause any deaths, the judge said.

"These officials simply created a set of conditions, stepped back, and objectively observed the effects," said Hon. Dickinson DeLarder, the circuit judge who wrote the opinion.

Some 400 people were diagnosed with various immunodeficiencies in the wake of the experiments, the defense had claimed.

The Bulsara family also alleged in their lawsuit that the trials, run by the Army under codename Project 137, were part of an extensive biological and chemical warfare weapons program that began during World War II, when technology and expertise was seized from the defeated Axis powers of Germany and Japan, and then turned against the American people for research purposes.

"We know what they did, and they know what they did," said Freddie Bulsara, who accuses the government of causing his ruptured spleen, hemorrhaging rectum, and late-stage prostate cancer. "The shame of it is—it will take a whole lot of other people getting sick before the truth of the government's crimes against the people are revealed. Mark my words—this is a crime against the American people and someone will uncover it, eventually."

Jim Frick, the U.S. Attorney handling the case, said he was pleased—but not surprised—at the outcome.

"Just another conspiracy theory gone too far," he said. "Occasionally people catch unlucky breaks and look for someone to blame. In this case, a family took the initiative and sued the government. Thankfully, the judges saw through their motives. The taxpayers have been saved of a needless burden."

The judge ruled that all court costs are to be handled by the Bulsara family, because the suit was deemed frivolous.

Frivolous—that final word was underlined once, hard, with O'Keefe's pen.

The second one was barely a blurb.

SICK FAMILY WHO SUED GOVERNMENT FOUND DEAD

> TRENTON—*A family that accused federal agencies of poisoning their water supply and sickening them as part of a massive biological- and chemical-weapons program was found dead in their rural New Jersey home Monday morning, authorities confirmed.*
>
> *The Bulsara family died of unknown causes in their new home in Old Rimrock, state troopers said. Autopsies are pending, but local detectives have already deemed the five deaths non-suspicious.*
>
> *The Bulsaras were assessed legal fees by a federal circuit court last year, after a judge threw out their claims that the federal government had poisoned them. The family filed bankruptcy weeks later, according to sources.*
>
> *The family's case had been the centerpiece of a class-action lawsuit for families in the affluent nook of Chooser's Mill, where dozens of citizens claimed they contracted a wide spectrum of diseases through the alleged government experiments. The Bulsaras were the lone family to take their case all the way to court. The others settled for undisclosed sums. But the court ultimately found the claims frivolous.*

Frivolous. Again, O'Keefe's pen cut an emphatic line underneath the final word.

The last page was an old photocopy of an ID card—the kind of credentials for government locations with the tightest security. The whole thing was blurry. But I could just make out the words "Research Team."

The blurry name was Cornelius Wetherspoon. The picture was shadowy, indistinct, but the shape of the head and the prominent nose were all those of my mentor, a few decades younger, his jowls plumper. He looked threatening, somehow.

And at the bottom was a familiar logo. The same Bureau of Wellness seal, the two snakes coiled around the staff, the quiver of arrows fanned out at the taloned feet of the screaming eagle. Below the seal ran the same serial number prefix I'd seen for weeks, on the collars of dead men, at the water intake valve on the dead river, on the foot of Rothenberg's casket.

BOW-137
Bureau of Wellness
Project 137

I stared at it for a second. Then I put the pages down, taking a last quaff of the whiskey. I snorted an energy stick. I stared at the bright window as my mind wheeled. Wetherspoon knew it all, back all the way to an unknown and undocumented century. And what had happened to the Bulsara family was just the beginning. Was there a link between a vast research program, an ongoing push for weapons of mass destruction, and the unexplained death of an entire family in their rural home decades earlier? Between ancient history and the rushing present? The possibilities made my head hurt.

Wetherspoon would be able to answer. At best, the Old Man had been withholding information about the Bureau of Wellness. He knew more than he was telling. At worst, he was a murdering puppetmaster.

Either way, a liar. Potentially a thieving, murdering kind of liar. I had been wrong about him the entire time, and I felt like I could kill him myself at that moment.

I went to the bathroom and sat on the toilet. The Atman in my hand beeped and pinged at each touch, echoing off the tiles. I dialed the toll-free number for the Bureau of Wellness. As it rang, I could see the light of dawn breaching the window blinds. I'd just let the phone ring, and then listen to whatever the prerecorded message told me.

"Operator," burst a woman's voice. "What is your emergency?"

I was taken aback. The voice was so familiar. Who was it? I didn't know what to say. A moment of silence passed.

"Operator here. Do you have an emergency to report?" the voice repeated.

"Yes," I said.

"City, state, and zone, please," the operator said.

"Yes—there's been a chemical spill in the Messowecan River, in New Jersey, Metro Zone. It turned the water green, and it infiltrated a Bureau water intake."

The operator typed, clicked and verified, from her cockpit on the other end. Something beeped loud, stinging my ear.

"We will note your report, sir," the voice said. "We are sending investigators out to examine your claim and take the appropriate response. Are you in imminent danger, sir?"

Suddenly I knew where I'd heard this voice before. It was the synthetic, brusque tone of Saxas. Somehow, I was talking to the cyborg herself. Or had she always been alive, a human creature? Stunned silence paralyzed me.

"Sir, are you incapacitated?" she asked.

"No, no, no," I stammered. "I'm not in danger."

But then, on the other end of the line, the clicking stopped—the process of noting and reporting halted.

"Sir—when did this chemical spill occur?" the voice said.

"About ten days ago," I said.

"And sir—how did you come to learn about this chemical release, as you call it?" she said. "The Messowecan River is twenty-three miles west of your current location, by my coordinates, and it is a prohibited preserve. Only Bureau of Wellness personnel are authorized to visit that location. But you already know that, don't you, Dr. Barnes?"

Recoiling from the Atman in horror, I slapped it off with a wave of my hand. I stared at the thing, then put it aside. At the sink I splashed some water over my face and toweled off.

The Atman rang. It hiccupped with that electronic babble, bouncing off the walls, seeming to grow more and more insistent. I tossed the towel on the rack. What had I done—what digital triggers had I tripped with a single call? I pushed the power button, turned it off.

Ten seconds later, amid my hammering heart, it rang again—without even being on. Rearing back, I hurled the thing against the wall, but it only resounded with a thud and tumbled down the tiles to the bottom of the tub. I reached in, picked it up again and walked toward the kitchen.

As I reached to put it on the counter, it rang again. With a desperate roar, I tapped the screen and the figure of a man popped up—a man coughing. It was MacGruder, hacking, doubling over. He looked terrible, like a monster from a pre-Purge horror movie. I breathed hard, temporary relief washing over me. I rubbed my face.

"Christ, George, are you alright?"

MacGruder held up a finger, pausing the conversation, as his other hand covered quaking coughs rattling deep in his chest. After a few moments of choking, my patient gasped harshly.

"Doc, I hope you don't mind me calling," he croaked. "I don't feel well."

"You sound terrible," I said. "You don't need me—you need a hospital. Don't go to Saint Almachius, though. Go to Clara Maass."

"Can't you make a housecall, Doc?"

"I've been fired, George. I can't treat you."

"That's just the thing, Joe," MacGruder said. "I know you were suspended. But every time I go to the hospital since you left, I end up feeling worse. I can't explain it."

MacGruder wheezed high-pitch, like some tiny part inside him somewhere was broken. It ended with another hacking cough.

"I only…trust…you, Doc," the patient said, wheezing. "The other specialists and nurses…don't even look at me. They plug their recommendations into the O'Neill-Kane, and then go off on their rounds. It's like I'm not even there…" He hacked again.

"Alright, George," I said. "My license is still technically in good standing outside the hospital, so I can come by, maybe even prescribe something. But if something's really wrong, we'll have to get you an ambulance somewhere better."

"Thank you so much—thank you so much," MacGruder said. "When do you think you can get here?"

"I can leave in ten minutes. I just have to wash up," I said.

"Oh, thank you. Thank you," MacGruder said. "See you soon." His coughing began again.

I touched the screen off. The man was in bad shape—it sounded like pneumonia, or worse. I had to hurry. I went upstairs and pulled off my dirty suit, which had begun to emit an odor, then went in the bathroom. I washed my face and brushed my teeth. Then I went over to Mary, whose face was still hooked into her Dormus.

"Dear, I'm leaving for a bit," I said. "There's a patient who needs my help."

Her head stirred on the pillow. Her mouth opened. She pulled the mask up onto her forehead.

"What?" she said, her eyes opening to narrow slits.

But before I could answer, her eyes went wide. Her face contorted, and she clapped her hand over her mouth. Flinging the Dormus apparatus aside, she scrambled out of bed, lurching to the bathroom. The door flew shut behind her.

"Dear," I said. "Are you alright?"

A retch. A splash. A retch. A spit.

"I'm fine," she said, voice echoing from deep in the bowl. "Where are you going?"

"There's a patient from the hospital who needs help. It might be nothing—I just need to check on him. I should be back in an hour or so."

Behind the door, the toilet flushed. I heard the gurgling—all the morning sickness sounds I'd come to know so well at that point. But for some reason, this time, I was afraid.

I forced myself to turn away. But before I left the room, I realized I was missing something. I checked my pockets—and I found my Atman wasn't there. I'd left it behind in the bathroom. Hesitating, I knocked once. No response. I quietly pushed the door inward.

"Sorry, dear," I said, my hand shielding my eyes. "I've got to grab my Atman."

The Atman was at the side of the sink. I stepped forward, averting my sight. I grabbed it and slid it into my pocket. I tried to leave without looking. But I glanced at her. And I was stopped dead in my tracks.

Blood. There was bright red blood in the bowl, and when she pushed the handle, it swirled around the edges, and then flushed down. But a pinkish tinge still stained the water.

"Jesus, Mary! Are you okay?" I said, rushing over, crouching by her side.

She pushed me away.

"I'm fine," she said. She gestured weakly, but her arms fells limp on the toilet seat. The wispy strands of her hair spread out over the edge of the toilet.

"Dear, this is not normal," I said, feeling her forehead with the back of my hand. "We need to get you to the hospital. To a real hospital like Clara Maass. Not Saint Almachius."

She shrugged my away, stubborn but sluggish. I stood.

"I'm fine," she said. "My mother always said…difficult pregnancies…run in the…family."

"They very well may run in the family," I said, "but this is something else. I'm a doctor, Mary. You've got to trust me."

Her face angled up to me. She blinked twice.

"Joe, I'll be alright," she said. "Remember, Adam said to expect this. You go and take care of your patient, and we'll talk when you get back." Her pale lips spread to a weak smile.

"When I get back we'll go right to the hospital, right?" I said.

She nodded, and hiccupped.

Everything inside told me to stay and care for her. Her face had never looked that deathly pale. But MacGruder was sick, alone in that house. A helpless old man just sitting there, gasping for air. I had to do something. I'd be back in a less than an hour, I figured. With a slow deliberation, I stooped down, kissed my wife on her warm forehead, and walked toward the door. When I turned, her head was back down in the toilet.

"If you have any problems, call me," I said. "I'll come running."

"I'll call if anything gets worse," she said. "But I'm a Marine, Joe. Nothing's killed me yet. So go save your patient."

Our eyes met, and we knew what we were saying without any words at all. I simply turned and trotted down the stairs, the echoes of my wife's sickness following me with each step that brought me farther away from her.

* * *

The drive to MacGruder's was just a short distance, five miles or so. But the traffic on the ultrahighway stalled again and again. The red tail-lights in front of me stopped, started, then slowed again. I could have run it faster. I cracked another energy stick under my nose. Saxas talked on and on, spilling all her data across the airwaves.

"Asia is at a standstill this morning as the breakup of the East Asian Federation continues," Saxas explained. "Japanese drones, backed by U.S. satellites, are conducting flyovers of Korea and Eastern China. Both countries have marked the aircraft with tracers. But no shots have been fired. U.S. diplomats in the region are trying to arrange a conference between all the heads of state in an effort to stave off an impending war. But the Administration continues to refuse comment."

Saxas sounded tired. The ending syllables of each sentence seemed to drop off, ever so slightly. The perfect voice sounded worn and frayed—almost human. My ears still rang with that same voice—that of the Bureau operator. Was Saxas a real person—and had I spoken to her? Had she informed the authorities on me?

"In other news, the War on Cancer debate is now effectively concluded," Saxas continued. "The doctors opposing the Surgeon General's declaration of victory have formally withdrawn their challenge. The declaration is expected to be ratified by Congress in the coming weeks. A ticker-tape parade down Broadway in Manhattan is scheduled for next month.

"In other medical news, the Bureau of Wellness announced a new line of inquiry within its triple-blind vitamins research project unveiled last week," said Saxas. "The agency has announced they are now investigating birth defects—and their link to pathogens during pregnancy."

My stomach plunged. Pregnancy, vitamins study, Bureau of Wellness, medical experiments. My head spun. It had to be a coincidence. Only that, and nothing more.

Saxas started to repeat herself, looping back on the news cycle.

"Asia is at a standstill this morning as the breakup of the East Asian Federation continues. Japanese drones, backed by U.S. satellites…"

I flicked it off and took the next exit. Storm clouds were collecting far-off in the sky, dark, and so plump they looked ready to burst. The Atman blipped as I pulled in front of MacGruder's home. I took a deep breath and got out of the car.

The solid Tudor house was nestled under large oaks, protecting it from the acid rains and the ultraviolet sun and the years. Broken shards of the stone walk crunched under my shoes. The door was open, offering a view of silent shadows inside.

"Hello? George?" I called.

Eerie déjà vu washed over me as I stepped within. A neglected order ruled. China dolls and commemorative plates and desiccated flowers lined crooked shelves, Oriental rugs soft underfoot. But everything neatly arranged with a woman's touch was now coated in a widower's dust and neglect. Even the sunlight was muted by filthy yellowed windowshades. A painting of George and his wife, young and carefree, standing in front of the New York skyline was coated in cobwebs. Pictures of children long since gone were hung in skewed rows. Dust motes drifted lazily. I smelled must, maybe mold.

"George—it's Joe," I said, tiptoeing forward.

A groan came from far-off. From the back half of the house. I crept in that direction. I entered a dark room—which flashed with a lightning bolt from outside. But after a few moments of blindness, I realized the shades of the small room were drawn. It wasn't lightning. The TV was shorting out. It flashed again. The encore of *How Low Can You Go* from the night before was playing. The strobe light showed the outline of a lamp—a couch—a mantle—a china closet.

And a sprawled body on the floor.

"George?" I whispered.

I stepped toward the prostrate form, which was right in front of the flashing television. I hesitated after each and every burst of light, as I drew closer, and closer. My pulse raced faster with each foot forward.

"George?" I said, standing over the body.

No answer. The TV stopped its flashing. I paused in the dark. My heart pounded, listening for the slightest reply. The dark was impenetrable, the silence total. Crouching down, I waited for the television to flash again. It didn't. After a minute I went into my pocket for the Atman's light.

A hand grabbed mine. I yelped in terror.

"Doc," said a dry voice.

"George?"

I pulled my wrist away and hit a button on my Atman. The pale glow lit the face of MacGruder, who was stretched out on the carpet.

"George," I said. "Where is the light switch?"

MacGruder's crooked finger pointed feebly at a corner. I followed it and found a switch behind the china closet and flicked it. The glare was blinding, but gradually I could open my eyes. MacGruder lay halfway between an easy chair and the television.

"Doc," MacGruder rasped.

"Yes, George?"

"The damned thing burns," MacGruder said. "They're...killing me."

He gestured vaguely toward his left forearm—where the Atman had been implanted. I went to him and lifted his sleeve. The device was blinking—flickering with the same strange incomprehensible digits that had appeared on O'Keefe's Atman. The device was scalding to the touch, whirring with unstoppable energy.

"Please, Doc," MacGruder said. "Please get it out. It hurts…it's…killing…"

"Just hold on a second, George," I said. "Everything will be fine. Let me think."

I stood and drifted toward the next darkened room. A rotten smell hung. When I hit the lights, a dirty kitchenette appeared before me. A knife was what I was after—I needed anything sharp to carve out the Atman. There was no time to panic. In front of MacGruder, I had used that skill of mine—to casually downplay the gravest dangers. But in the kitchen my hands shook. MacGruder wouldn't be alright. I had seen the ultimate outcome twice now. I pulled a fishing knife and a grapefruit spoon from the drawer. They were the only implements I found which would work for the job at hand. I also grabbed an old stiff towel and returned to the living room.

MacGruder was already unconscious. Losing no time, I pulled off the old man's shirt, tied the towel tightly around his bicep. I pulled over a chair from a corner, and placed the arm atop it. Then I sawed with the blade through skin and muscle, around and under the device, which grew hotter and hotter to the touch. Halfway through the incisions, I ran to the kitchen and grabbed a thick oven mitt to grapple the sizzling metal. The TV flashed on and on and on.

MacGruder moaned. But I gritted my teeth and kept going.

"Just a little farther now, George," I said, using my calmest tone.

I incised for another few minutes, cutting around the soft flesh, but it wouldn't come free. The metal was anchored, probably to the bone. Thousands of implants of the X-rays had never shown anything like this. I tugged and yanked— the stubbornness of the machine in the flesh was sickening. The blood kept flowing, soaking through the whiteness of one towel, then another I grabbed from the kitchen. I howled. I was losing another patient. I was losing George MacGruder, who was also my friend. I needed help, any expertise, another pair of eyes.

I knew where I could find that help. Even if I loathed the thought of calling him. I pulled out my own Atman, I swiped on the screen, and I waited. On the second ring, I heard the voice I needed.

"Hello," Old Man Wetherspoon croaked.

"Doc, I need your help," I said.

"Joe? Is that you? You sound like shit," said the creaky voice. "I hope you haven't gotten yourself arrested at that damned hospital."

"No. Doc, I'm at a patient's house. I need your expertise," I said.

The single mention of expertise seemed to awaken the Old Man. I heard rummaging and grunting on the other end, like the Old Man was sitting up in bed for the first time that day.

"What kind of expertise? Personal? Professional? Romantic?" he said.

"I can't explain now," I said. "It's an emergency. It's about the thing we've been talking about. Can't talk over this line."

I gave him the address.

"Hurry. Get here as soon as possible," I added.

The Old Man grunted again, then hung up.

Ten minutes was all MacGruder had. Although MacGruder's life was not violently spasming out of his body like O'Keefe's had, it was still slipping away. The device was still attached to him, even though I had severed most of the connections. Despair welled in me. His pulse was faint, his breathing shallow, and though the bleeding had slowed to a trickle, it was still going. I tried once more with the grapefruit spoon to pry out the device, started the red flow again, then set it aside and stanched the wound. The towel had been scorched by the Atman's heat. I found a new one from a kitchen drawer. I knelt at the body, pressed, and stared up at the ceiling, trying not to feel the weight of each second ticking by.

"You'll be fine, George," I whispered. "Help is on the way. Just hang on."

MacGruder only groaned, through his fever and delirium. Thunder rolled far off outside the house. The television flashed. But this last time, it stayed on.

I paid no attention at first, focusing instead on the pressure on the blood vessels of my patient. But then it was simply unavoidable. I turned my head and watched the intro of *How Low Can You Go* screaming on the screen, though it was on mute. I had never really sat down to watch the show before, and a curiosity simmered within me, I must admit. A woman was offered a pink envelope by the host, a razor-bald man with pirate earrings dangling from each lobe. She accepted the envelope with a slim delicate hand. But she looked apprehensive. On the screen behind both their heads, a man was strapped down to a strange gurney with metal restraints. He cringed as medieval-looking tongs dangled something writhing and alive, but out of focus, over his head. I cringed, too.

I reached down, felt for MacGruder's pulse. It had weakened to a throb. I cursed Wetherspoon, willing him to drive faster in his stupid old gasoline car.

And then I lost myself in that depraved TV show.

The *How Low Can You Go* host said something, eyebrows bouncing provocatively. The woman glanced in the direction of the camera. She turned toward the imprisoned man, obviously her husband. Her head tilted to the floor in shame. She placed her hand to her face. The camera zoomed in to a close-up of her lipsticked mouth.

Yes, the pink lips said, very visibly. Yes.

The camera flashed to the full shot of the captive man. The tongs lowered, and the television showed very clearly the walking gnarly legs and wicked stinger of a scorpion descending inch by inch.

Then a split screen: the man's horrified face from above, underneath the airwalking claws of the creature, and a sideview of the distance between the nose and the descent of the scorpion. The creature stopped falling, two inches from flesh. The stinger lashed downward, narrowly missing its target. Any further descent would have the poisonous creature within striking range.

The camera flashed back to the host. An amusement arched his eyebrows, pursed his lips. His perfectly-plucked eyebrows jiggled. He asked her something.

Then a shot of the woman, who had her hands on her face, not even looking at him. There were seconds—moments lasting ages—as she shook with some kind of indecisiveness. She shook her head. A pause.

An intense close-up of her moist lips. Darker and closer than before, trembling. They parted—a glimpse of the teeth, a hint of tongue.

"Yes," she said. And she nodded.

"ONE BILLION DOLLARS!" the screen flashed. The letters glowed. A flash to the woman, who grabbed another envelope from the host, this time big and gold. They embraced, he kissed the crown of her head. Balloons fell from above. Strobing lights all around. The crowd went wild. A shot of the woman again, wiping away the tears of joy tumbling down her face.

Then a cut to deepest black. A fade-in to the nose, the scrambling claws and the stinger, descending and unavoidable. The tongs widening, releasing. The screams.

I left MacGruder's wound, stumbled to the television, and hit the power button just as the scorpion landed on the man's screaming face. I took a deep breath.

The doorbell rang. I ran to the door and opened it. Old Man Wetherspoon stood there, at the entrance, sopping wet. A jagged lightning bolt broke the sky. Rain fell in torrents, splashing up from the porch in the dark morning light.

"Storm came through just as I left," the Old Man said, stepping inside, brushing sheets of water off his rubberized sleeves. "Even twenty years ago we didn't have these goddamned flash monsoons. I'll never get used to them."

He stopped in the hallway.

"So…whose house is this? What's the emergency?"

"MacGruder's. That's him on the living room floor," I said. "He's about to die."

The Old Man's jaw clenched. I pointed toward the back of the house. We walked to MacGruder. Wetherspoon stooped to the body and inspected it, lifting the eyelids, feeling at the jugular, gingerly pulling the towel away from the Atman and the wound. At a touch, the device singed his fingertip, and he recoiled with a curse. He stood up and rubbed at his face with his open hand. Focus fell across his face.

"Did he butcher himself—or was that you?" Wetherspoon said.

"That was me. I had to. The damned thing's killing him."

"Now he's dying of blood loss, Joe."

"But I had to do this. I saw this happen before, Neal," I said. "That journalist with your papers—Jim O'Keefe. He died right in front of me. His Atman heated up, he went into convulsions, and he fell into some kind of septic shock right outside the funeral home. Died in minutes."

Wetherspoon stared at me, hard, for a few seconds. His arms crossed, he looked calm. But that businesslike grimace on his face was something I have never seen before.

"Do you have a pen?" he said.

I laughed and pointed at him.

"Goddamnit, Neal. What, you want to record a dying man's pulse? Is this your part of Project 137? What goddamned paper can you even find outside your office?"

Wetherspoon didn't blink. He held out his hand.

"Joe, give me a pen," he said.

I noticed a desk across the room. I reached inside a cup and pulled out a dozen ancient ballpoints. I thrust a fistful of them at the Old Man.

"You want pens? Here are some goddamn pens," I said.

The Old Man inspected, then plucked a single black one out of the bunch. He held it up between his index finger and thumbs, looking at me pointedly. Then he stooped to inspect the body again. He pulled aside the towel and glared at the Atman.

"Knife," the Old Man said.

I searched around, found the fishing knife next to his foot, and handed it over.

The Old Man used the knife to pry up the device. The blood started flowing again, but Wetherspoon's hands worked slowly, they worked with assurance. Holding the opening at the side of the Atman, he probed around with the sharp end of the pen until there was a soft click. He pushed inward. Something beeped. Then he removed it, wiped the blood on the carpet, flipped it around, and used it to push a button on the interface. The device's light faded and died. Wetherspoon replaced the towel, wrapping it tightly to stop the bleeding, then stood.

"Well, that's that," he said. "And now…you probably have questions."

"We don't have time for questions—the man's dying," I said. "We've got to get him to a real hospital."

"The Atman is off," the Old Man said. "We just have to make sure he doesn't lose too much blood, and then we stitch up these wounds from your botched surgery. We'll get him somewhere safe—maybe Clara Maass. Not Saint Almachius."

Wetherspoon pulled out his own Atman and sent a message. He stuffed it in his pocket and walked toward the back of the house, feeling his way around the rooms in the twilit house. I stooped to check MacGruder's vital signs. They had improved, and the device was cooling down. I stood. My older colleague was rummaging around in the kitchen. I glanced around the corner. A bolt of lightning back-lit the Old Man's shadow. I went toward it.

Wetherspoon found the switch for the kitchen just as I entered. The Old Man searched through cabinets and pulled out a glass. Then he walked right past me and back to the living room. He staggered a step or two, swaying over the carpet.

"What the hell are you doing?" I asked, rushing forward to catch him if he fell.

"I thought I saw it somewhere…ah, here," the Old Man said, pulling out an amber-colored bottle from a collection on a nearby table. He poured some into his glass, downed it, and poured another. "It's a good brand—a good year." He held it out to me.

Anger jolted through me, and I slapped it out of his hand, and the glass thunked on the carpet. For a moment, Wetherspoon stood there, his fingers still spread, holding empty air.

"I don't want a goddamned drink," I said, through clenched teeth. "I want to know what the hell Project 137 is, and how you're involved. You goddamned liar."

Wetherspoon stared at me for a second, wide-eyed. A transformation came over his face, softening his features. Fatigue sagged his jowls. The Old Man seemed to age in mere moments. He nodded, and reeled back onto the nearest couch, like the drink had immobilized him. Setting the bottle at his feet, he held his head in his hands.

"You read the dossier. What else do you need? A diagram? A flow-chart?" he said.

I sat in a rickety wicker chair across from him and leaned forward.

"I read what I could," I said. "I read enough to know that you've been lying to me since the first day we met."

"Now that's where you're wrong," Wetherspoon said, holding up a crooked finger. A fire flared in his eyes, for a moment, the contrarian look I'd always known and expected out of my mentor. "I've never lied to you. I respect you too much for that, Joe."

Those words were too much, at that particular moment. I shook my fist at him.

"Goddamnit, Neal," I said. "A far-flung conspiracy was right under my nose, and you've been involved in it for decades. Now it's killing people."

"Conspiracy—now there's an interesting word," the Old Man said. He picked up the bottle, set it on the ground between his feet. "If it's just the powers-that-be playing their normal games—and everyone's in on it—is that a conspiracy?"

I had no answer. I just stared at him. Wetherspoon continued.

"So you only read part of it. Tell me what you know, and I'll fill you in on the rest."

"Some sweeping program of human experiments, involving what I take to be biological and chemical weapons," I said. "Gassing subways, inundating streets and homes with germs, without warning or clear documentation. It's been going on for almost a hundred years. And you were there from the very beginning."

The Old Man stared at me. I shrugged. But he smiled.

"If only it was that simple," the Old Man said. "There's so much you don't know…"

Thunder rumbled, followed by a flash of lightning outside as the monsoons rattled the windows. I growled at him, a sound emerging from deep within I could not control.

"You've known the whole time! And it's not like this is history—this is still going on. My patient is dying on the floor here because of it."

My hands trembled with rage. I stood. I stepped toward Wetherspoon. My fist closed tight. I felt the urge to wind up and deliver a haymaker on the jaw of a man triple my age, a gnarled relic from a century before. Wetherspoon held up his hands, reading my thoughts. But his face was slack and impassive.

"Now, Joe," he said. "I was no guiding hand in any of this. I've been against the Project since the turn of the millennium, and I've lobbied to get it discontinued. Why do you think they were after me? Why do you think I went into hiding? I wasn't on vacation—they knew I was against the program, and that I had too much information to be able to just quietly slip away. So sit down and have a drink—I'll tell you everything you need to know. Trust me—at least for the time it takes for me to tell you my side of this sordid story. At least you can give me that."

I sneered.

"You've got five minutes, Old Man," I said, using the nickname I'd never uttered to my mentor's face before. "Five minutes. And then I start beating it out of you. And if you think I'm kidding, just try me."

I paused. We locked eyes.

"Just try me," I repeated, without blinking, clenching both fists with whitened knuckles.

Wetherspoon took a pull off the whiskey bottle. Releasing one finger off the bottle, he pointed at me.

"You've always had spunk, Joe," he said. "That's why you deserve nothing less than the unvarnished truth."

"Do we need to move MacGruder?"

He shook his head.

"The bleeding's stopped. He'll live. We, on the other hand, might not. There's not much time, Joe. I'm sorry I have to rush this explanation. What do you know about Maruta?

"Don't know her," I said.

"It's not a person, Joe. It's the Japanese word for 'logs,' Joe," said Wetherspoon. "You know what the Bureau calls the basement of Saint Almachius? The lumber mill."

"What are you talking about?" I asked, my stomach bottoming out.

"Back before either of us were born, during a kaleidoscope of horrors once called World War II, the Japanese had a biological warfare unit. They called it Unit 731," said Wetherspoon. "Its leader was Shiro Ishii."

"Shiro Ishii?" I said. "Like the one who's been logging into the hospital terminals?"

"Not exactly, Joe. Let's just say Ishii made sure he'd be around a long time after he died," Wetherspoon said. "So, when Unit 731 struck a deal with the Americans, and crossed the Pacific, Joe they just flipped it. It became Project 137, Joe."

"Project 137?"

"Yes. And now the Project is playing its ace in the hole, Joe," said Wetherspoon. "The Tojo Virus."

BECAUSE WE CAN'T BE BEAT

U.S.A., 1951

Shiro Ishii shook his empty glass, and the crisp ice cubes rattled. A young American reached across the interior of the limousine and splashed two fingers of Bourbon into the glass. Ishii nodded. The Maryland countryside whisked past the window in a blur of green.

"Dr. Ishii," said an older man, facing them, his back to the driver. "I've been meaning to ask you—how are your accommodations?"

Ishii took a deep drink, smacked his lips, shrugged.

"It is not like home," he said, each English syllable taut. "But I am comfortable. There is whiskey. Women."

The young man snickered, turned and saw his boss' glare. Cringing, he slid the Bourbon bottle back in the limousine's mini bar without another word.

"You left your wife back home in Japan, did you not?" said the man in charge.

"Yes, Mr. Stapleton. Too much work. Too much play. In America," Ishii said, toasting them, then downing the rest of the liquor. He smiled at the two Americans.

The younger man grabbed the glass, started to refill it, but Stapleton lifted his hand an inch off his knee, shook his head once. The younger man nodded and stowed the glass away in the bar with the bottle. The Americans were in a clear disorder of rank. The younger one was a coward, the older one a fool. Ishii wiped at his mouth with the sleeve of his tweed jacket.

"And Dr. Ishii, we are looking forward to having you on the team at Fort Detrick," Stapleton said, scratching at his jaw. "We could certainly use your expertise, now that the Chinese are across the Yalu River."

"Yes, Mr. Stapleton," Ishii said. "More of Chinese than of you."

Glancing at the limo's minibar, he shrugged and produced a flask from his jacket pocket.

"But we can make things…fair," he said, unscrewing the cap. With a salute, he tipped it back to his open mouth.

The two Americans turned away, their eyes darting out the window. Ishii looked out at the passing landscape too, the trees and green fields, a split-rail fence zig-zagging alongside. He liked to watch the wide-open American spaces, the huge expanse of the land. It looked nothing like Japan. The rolling farms, the lazy river bordered by scrubby little trees to the east. Ishii capped the flask, and as the liquor slid down his throat he slapped a clumsy martial beat on his spread knees. The openness of America was enough to inspire hope in anything—even a new life, he knew.

Buildings appeared, blocking the river and the sky, and the highway entered a town. A right-hand turn off the road brought them into the heart of apartment blocks. They rolled up to a gated guardhouse. A sentry saluted, then waved them in. The limo circled through a few brick buildings, and then it pulled into a dark garage and stopped. The driver got out and opened the door for the three passengers.

The Americans shook hands, offered drinks, and inquired continuously about his health. They smiled at their esteemed guest. They were all fools—but they were hospitable and welcoming fools.

An hour later, a scientist stood next to Ishii. Both doctors stood with their arms crossed, looking up at a web of metal piping over their heads. The ducts all connected up to the great steel sphere above them. It was like nothing they had ever developed in Japan. Clearly, the Americans were serious about pushing the work forward, and Ishii nodded approvingly.

"Meet your specifications, doctor?" asked the scientist.

Ishii smiled, but shook his head.

"I need to see results, Dr. Olson."

The American scientist smiled, shaking his own head, running a hand over the thin film of hair on his head, then reaching up and grabbing a pipe.

"We don't have results yet, Dr. Ishii," he said. "We're still in the experimental phase."

Ishii walked forward, putting a hand on the curving steel. It was cool on his fingertips.

"You have test group?"

"We have a test group," Olson said, tapping the pipe. "It wasn't easy, but we have one."

Olson waved at a guard in the corner. On cue, a group of young men came through the door. Crew-cutted, shirtless, they shuffled on stiff legs, covered only with tiny briefs. They marched in a single line past the two doctors. Only a few glanced up. They rounded the sphere and stopped. Twelve of them, waiting, shifting from foot to foot with a nervous bounce. They reminded Ishii of nothing so much as a line of pitiful prisoners standing at attention in the yard back at Ping Fang, unwittingly waiting to serve the Emperor.

All these Americans stared straight ahead—except for one, whose almond eyes caught those of Ishii's. Clearly of Asian descent—Korean, if not Japanese. The young man glanced away quickly.

"This is our test group," said Olson.

Ishii walked around the sphere, inspecting the line, but keeping a wide berth away from the line of ragged patients. Their youth, their vitality, was fascinating. The file of young men curved around, seeming not to notice him, silent, just staring ahead. At the front of the line was an elevator, a helmeted man ushering the first three on board, then shutting the gate and taking them upward. Ishii stepped back, watching it ascend to the loft above, the three alighting, the elevator descending again to take up more. Ishii stepped back for a better view of the second floor: a loft surrounding the sphere. Strangely-shaped holes lined the steel surface. Each of them was fitted with a mask, with soft rubber and tight straps.

"I see," Ishii said. "Very efficient operation."

"Yes, Dr. Ishii, we were thinking about all the data that came from Japan, and it took us years to come up with our own way to further the work of your Unit," Olson said.

"Where did you get prisoners?" Ishii asked.

"These subjects are all volunteers," Olson responded.

Ishii's brow furrowed.

"Why do subjects agree to tests?" said Ishii, watching another elevator of volunteers ascend.

"Seventh Day Adventists," Olson said, arms folded, watching the elevator come back down. Ishii shook his head, uncomprehending. "Seventh Day Adventists, Dr. Ishii. A religious group. They believe the end of the world is coming. They think Russians will start dropping H-bombs any day now. They all would rather be part of our tests than get out there and fight."

Ishii smiled, shook his head.

"We had kamikazes. Everyone wanted to defend the Emperor," he said. "But we lost the war. I will never understand America, Dr. Olson. How you people win."

Olson nudged the arm of his Japanese counterpart.

"Can-do spirit, Dr. Ishii. It's what separates America from the rest of the world. We don't believe in losing. It's why we won the war. Because we can't be beat."

Ishii slowly drew back from Olson's touch, as if he was contagious. The elevator ascended again to the second floor, and the final men, including the Asian runt who had to be Korean, were getting off. Three more helmeted soldiers spread out, delivering them to their stations around the sphere. Ishii ambled to the elevator, and Olson followed at his heels. The gate opened, they were taken up. As they stepped onto the loft, the volunteers sat on stools at each of the holes, their faces pressed into the portholes in the sphere. The helmeted men went from man to man, lashing straps on arms and legs, around necks. Ishii walked by them all. The subjects stiffened, grew still. The guards rustled around, making final checks.

"We're all ready, Mac!" hollered one with markings on his breast pocket. "Turn it on!"

Nothing moved. Absolute silence for a moment. But then, from far off, a clanking came, rattling through the pipes as if a furnace had just kicked on. The sound grew louder, getting closer, and then entered the sphere. A hissing, just a whisper, replaced it in the surrounding silence. There were groans all around. Ishii looked across the line of volunteers and realized the sounds weren't human—it was the leather straps straining, the wrenching of the materials as the subjects tensed silently, young wiry muscle and sinew struggling against the bonds. Ishii's fingers trembled. No sounds came from the mens' mouths, their chests, as the veins in their necks bulged. Olson squirmed a bit, turned away, and braced himself against the railing. The helmeted MPs stood ramrod straight, their hands clasped behind them. Ishii scratched at the razor burn on his upper lip, his eyes unblinking. A smile rippled across his mouth, as the bodies wiggled and shook. An MP checked his watch.

A minute passed. Ishii stepped forward. The helmeted soldiers glanced at him, then at Olson, who nodded in approval. Ishii walked along the lines of the convulsing soldiers. He felt twenty years younger, like a commanding general once again. As he walked, his smile widened. Like a leaf blown up in a strong wind, his hand fluttered off his hip and along the air, tracing along the quivering shoulders of the young men. He stopped behind the Korean, who was shaking more than the rest. Ishii grabbed the scruff of the neck. He held it there, squeezing the flesh.

One by one the men slumped forward in their bonds, their faces still pressed into the sphere. The Korean held on and seemed to be flex against Ishii's grip, but he too crumpled after another thirty seconds of struggle. Ishii let go, wiped his palm against the leg of his pants, and backed toward Olson.

"Very good," Ishii said. "When will we cut them open?"

The helmeted men's mouths fell open. One gasped.

Olson yanked Ishii away from the line, to the elevator, pulled the gate down behind and pushed the down button. As it crept down, Ishii stared at his American colleague in puzzlement. What had gone wrong? Silence hung between the men. The elevator reached the bottom. Olson opened the gate, and pulled Ishii, who moved compliantly, like a leashed dog. Together they walked out. Ishii slowed underneath the pipe joints, touching the cool fittings and molds, but Olson urged him on with a gentle hand on his back.

Olson seemed to be a in a hurry. They walked down smooth gray hallways, under bare lightbulbs, to the outside. They pushed through a big heavy door with a hollow sound. Ishii turned on him, his arms folded in front of his chest.

"Don't we need to witness experiments?" Ishii said. "We need to see results."

Olson looked over his shoulder, up at the corners of the building, all around them. He shook his head, stopping to light a cigarette.

"Dr. Ishii, there's nothing to see," he said. "We will know the results once the reports are finished. They're aerosol dispersion experiments—visual observation alone won't tell us anything."

They walked along a brick wall toward a line of bushes. Olson directed him around the corner of the brick wall. They were walking in a narrow space between trees and bushes, a dark space.

Suddenly Ishii was shoved against the wall. Olson's face, eyes bloodshot and cheeks covered in sweat, was pressed close to his. Ishii turned his cheek, but he inhaled Olson's cologne, the chemical stink of it. They were out of sight in the growth, invisible within the heart of Fort Detrick.

"You must understand, Doctor," Olson said, cigarette flapping in his taut lips. "This is not Manchuria. This is America. There are rules. No vivisections. No amputations. No rape. And most of all—no talking."

His face was twisted, sweaty. He scratched at his receding hairline, shook his head, and he seemed to calm himself.

"I know you remember the war, all the possibilities," the American continued, running his hand over his head. "But you have to realize that this is completely different. We have to keep things secret."

Ishii gave him a calm smile and nodded. This American was weak. Clearly, he had been appointed to be a middle-manager of the operations—a lackey, and nothing more. He would certainly have no say in the coming Projects. And he would be expendable, Ishii realized.

"Secrets," Ishii said, reaching up to a branch, snapping off a green sprout of a twig. "I understand secrets. But it was understood America wanted my skills because of Manchukuo. Because of the advances we made. Because of the Russians, because of what's coming. Because America needs me."

Olson nodded. His mouth opened, then shut, and then he took a drag off his cigarette. He turned and walked out of the leafy canopy of the trees. Ishii snapped the twig in his hands, smelled the fresh scent between his fingers. It smelled different than the trees of Japan, of home. He dropped it on the ground, and followed the American back toward the laboratories, all of which were hard at work.

215

THE ORPHAN'S GIFT

"The Tojo Virus is not exactly a computer virus, and not exactly an organic hemorrhagic fever," said Wetherspoon. "It's both, and they're spreading it through these Atmans you damned kids use all the time."

But I was only half-listening—because I had stooped and was feeling for MacGruder's jugular.

"Neal—George is dead," I said.

"Not possible," Wetherspoon said, kneeling beside me. Cursing, he tried feeling for the artery. Pulling away the towel on MacGruder's forearm, he touched the device—and drew back his hand with a hiss. He stood, shaking out his burned finger.

"Jesus."

"What is it?" I said.

"You're right. He's dead," the Old Man said. "And it wasn't blood loss. The Atman re-booted. They've developed new software."

"Let's get him to a hospital," I said. I started thrusting down on MacGruder's chest, but before I could place my mouth over MacGruder's, Wetherspoon grabbed my shoulder. His hand was strong, a viselike grip suddenly like that of a man seventy or eighty years younger.

"The patient's dead, Joe," Wetherspoon said, pulling me up with a forceful yank. "There's nothing we could do. Whatever they gave him already ran its course. I shut the damned thing off. It still killed him. It seems they've perfected the Tojo Virus far beyond anything I could have imagined."

"What are we supposed to do with a body we mauled with home surgery?" I said. "This looks like we killed him."

"Don't worry about that," Wetherspoon, slapping me on the back. "Leave it to me."

The Old Man stooped and picked up both ends of the throw rug underneath the body. With two quick moves, the body was wrapped, like a burrito with bloody salsa spattered on top.

"Listen—I'll take the body to a safe hospital," the Old Man said. "I know people. I'll make sure they hear what I have to say. You take my dossier and drive west. Keep going. Find a motel with Mary and wait to hear from me. I'll let you know when it's safe to come back. I can't imagine you'll be gone for more than a week."

"Wait, Neal," I said. "About those files."

"What about those files?"

"About those files," I said, rubbing my face with both hands. "About those goddamned files. Shit."

"Oh, Christ," Wetherspoon said. "You weren't kidding. You lost them."

"They were stolen while the reporter was dying in my arms."

Silence. Wetherspoon's eyes flickered to the corners of the room. Then his arms began flailing, curses echoed off the walls, words vaguely Germanic but not part of any earthly language. A lamp flew off a table, a vase sailed to the wall and exploded in shards. The Old Man grabbed a fire poker and speared the glowing TV screen, which sparked and flashed and died. I watched in silence as Wetherspoon reeled toward me, still seething.

"You took two decades of work," the Old Man said, "and you threw it to the wolves... You took a carefully laid plan to end a war against the American people, and you threw it away in a single moment."

"I didn't know, Neal."

"No, how could you have known," the Old Man said, lip curling in a sneer. "How could the young hotshot physician with his whole life ahead of him realize there was everything to lose, including his own family?"

A moment of silence. What the hell was that supposed to mean? I shook my head.

"What do you mean, lose my own family?" I said.

Wetherspoon recoiled. He shook his head. But he suddenly looked sad, as well as angry.

"You didn't really believe that your parents died of food poisoning, did you?" he said.

Something in the Old Man's eyes softened, his voice was muted.

"Joe, your parents didn't die of food poisoning. It was the Tojo Virus."

Just as those words started to make sense to me, the room whirled all around. I raised my arm to steady myself, but I found I was falling backward, and then Wetherspoon's hands were guiding me downward onto the couch. Everything felt black, like I was that orphan in a chaotic hospital waiting room once again. But I was still awake.

"Listen to what I'm saying," the Old Man said, his voice slow and distorted. "I thought you would have figured it out by now.

"It wasn't an accident, Joe. It happened the night the Blackout started. The Project dispersed some of the Tojo agent," Wetherspoon continued. "It wasn't painful—they were dead before they knew what hit them. It was during one of the field trials I voted against. I only found out after the test was completed. They ate some of the Tojo samples served in the hors d'oeuvres at a restaurant. It was the salmon mousse. They were part of the experimental group."

A moment of stillness, of silence. Then I lunged, grabbed the Old Man's wrinkly throat. Anger blinded me. I saw nothing but the cold black abyss beyond the light.

"You...bastard," I said.

My hands squeezed. The Old Man's trachea clamped shut. His eyes bulged with the pressure.

"Just...understand...Joe... Not...coincidence...you at Almach... There was...reason you...got offer at the hospital... I made sure...you...survivor...someone who...could understand...the monstrosity...would be...on...my side..."

My hands loosened on the Old Man's throat. I didn't know why; I felt like they had decided on their own to try and murder my mentor, and then relented of their own volition. I stepped back, flexing the strange fingers that seemed so different from my own. Wetherspoon's head rolled back with a thud on the hard back of the couch.

"I was trying...tell you..." he said, gasping. "I made sure...you were hired by Saint Almachius, no matter the cost. I was...one of the doctors triaging the deaths during the Blackout. Dozens, maybe hundreds, in those first days... But I wasn't supposed to be there anyway...we had gotten word there was to be a mass-casualty incident planned by Project 137. I don't know why I went...why I was complicit. At that point, I just figured I could help treat the people who were already sick... There had been experiments conducted in the area before, and no one had died. They had all been tests to analyze how things spread, how to protect against a biological attack from a terrorist group, things like that. But...when they started bringing in the bodies from the neighborhood, covered up in sheets and wrapped in plastic, I knew something had changed."

He held his face in his hands, scraping his cheeks raw with his fingernails.

"Chaos. Pure chaos. Four planes went down in the area that night, due to the wholesale electrical failure from the Blackout. Almost every doctor in the place scrambled to save the people with lost limbs, massive bleeding, third-degree burns, souls barely clinging to life. The hospital was entirely dark, except for the emergency lights which cast long shadows down the hallways as medical staff rushed from room to room and bed to bed.

"I was one of the few left to tend to the bodies. I was already considered well past my prime, and the dead, someone figured, were more my speed than the living. I suited up and checked the remains, making observations and taking down the data by hand as I pored over each corpse by flashlight. I quickly realized this was something totally new. I couldn't pick out the exact cause, but I knew it was some kind of fast-moving hemorrhagic virus that burned the patients up from the inside. I suspected Ebola immediately, so I was careful to take all the precautions. There were four men and three women in my room. Two of them were married couples, one of them young and one of them old. All from the same restaurant.

"Except I wasn't ready for what I saw out in the ward's waiting room. I walked down the front hallway of the hospital—ready to have a well-deserved pinch of snuff outside, catch my breath, get a grip on the swarming multitudes of the dying and panicked. That's when I noticed one unmoving center amid the bedlam. A teenaged boy sat there in one of the chairs, hunched over, hair over his face, elbows on knees, hands clasped together as in prayer. I asked one of the triage nurses who the kid was. She told me it was the sixteen-year-old son of the younger married couple I had just been tagging and bagging. The kid was now an orphan, she said, shrugging.

"I nodded and headed toward the door. The kid was on my right. It was obvious he wasn't looking, or seeing, anything. He didn't even know he was breathing. He had forgotten he was even alive—because something inside him had just died. It wasn't my job to talk to him, to deal with the patients after the experiments were 'concluded.' Project 137 expressly forbade that. But I watched from afar. I felt ill. I hadn't felt that since I buried my very first patients.

"I had to do something. I started walking toward him. He didn't notice me. I stared for a second.

"I reached into my pocket and pulled out the tiny test tube I had collected. I still don't know why, but I dropped it in his lap. Then I melted into the crowd. As I peered back through the throngs of panicking people, I could see this shaggy-haired kid slowly pick up that thin glass cylinder and turn it over in his hands. He looked around in every direction—other than my own. I kept walking out the revolving door, snuff pouch in my hand. He never saw me."

Old Man Wetherspoon pointed at me.

"I gave you that test tube so you would never forget that night," the Old Man said. "As the years went by, I kept tabs on you with some help of my friends in academia. I made sure you got into the best classes. I had the hospital roll out the red carpet when you got your degree. I sheltered you a bit when you first came here. I always stayed in the background—I had to be sure you were never forced down the path I wanted for you. But you never disappointed, and soon you were my most trusted colleague. And now here we are, the day when you and I find ourselves partners in this mad escapade."

"You mean—that test tube…" I said.

"It's the specimen I collected from your mother that night. An attenuated sample of the prototype virus that killed them. The prototype of what killed MacGruder here. The Tojo Virus. It's got the antigen that can cure any form of the virus, even the latest kind."

I rubbed the test-tube still hanging around my neck. Wetherspoon pointed at it.

"It's a talisman, Joe," the Old man said. "Even in this cold, sterile world, there's still magic in some things."

"I didn't know," I said. "I never remembered how… I never really knew what…"

The Old Man smirked, rubbing at his sore throat.

"I remembered," he said. "Somehow, I knew it would see you through."

As I stared at him, the Atman rang. I stood and reached into the pocket of my jacket, and I saw a familiar number. It was coming from my house. I pushed the button to answer the call.

"Mary, is everything okay?"

"Joe!" said a man.

"Who is this?" I said, alarm bending my voice upward.

"Joe, it's Adam. Adam Abbud."

"Abbud," I said. "What are you doing in my house?"

Wetherspoon smacked his forehead and walked across the room.

Abbud cleared his throat, as if he was making a prepared speech.

"Joe, I have to tell you…your wife is ill," Abbud said. "We're bringing her back into the hospital for observation. I wanted to let you know we're doing everything we can."

My stomach plunged.

"No, no, no," I said. "I'm heading there now. I can get her to a hospital in twenty minutes."

Abbud clucked his tongue.

"No need," he said. "Mary called me, and I'm personally taking her to the Saint Almachius quarantine. She's in good hands."

"Quarantine?"

I checked my Atman—only two hours had passed since I had left Mary.

"Abbud? Why are you in my house?"

Perfect digital silence.

"Why are you in my house? Why didn't Mary call me?" I said, my voice now roaring. "What quarantine?"

"Mary didn't think to," Abbud said. "She was in some medical distress, the readings on her Atman set off an alarm, and she called me. We made a house call. She's under careful medical observation. No outside interference. We need to catalog everything, you know."

I was speechless in that moment. The Old Man, who had come close to lean in and listen, only nodded. A sad nod of recognition. He squeezed my shoulder, but I shrugged him away.

"What do you mean—you need to catalog everything?" I yelled. "Abbud, leave my wife there. I'm taking her to Clara Maass, not Saint Almachius."

Abbud guffawed. His voice was suddenly cold, sharp over the digital connection.

"You should pick your affiliations more carefully," Abbud snapped. "You decided to make trouble. The Project will move ahead, no matter who's on the operating table or holding the scalpel. You should learn from this experience, Barnes. You've been warned."

The Atman beeped. Abbud had hung up. I went to the door.

"Where are you going?" the Old Man said.

"I've got to go get my wife," I said. "Abbud's got her—she's part of the experiments. Goddamnit, Neal. She's a guinea pig for those bastards."

Wetherspoon grabbed my elbow.

"Joe, they're already long gone," he said. "They know you're against them. Mary is a hostage. They know we've got the evidence, and they want it back."

"Goddamnit, Neal," I spat back at him. "What could I possibly have that they want? No one would believe a story like this. The one person who might have had the platform to expose all this—O'Keefe—is dead. We don't even have that dossier any more, for Christ's sake. How could we even prove any of it, at all?"

The Old Man nodded.

"We've got three things," he said. "I have a backup copy of the documents. And we've got the body of unfortunate George here, of course."

"You have an extra copy of the dossier?"

Wetherspoon nodded, rolling his eyes.

"Not my first rodeo, son," he said. "It just might take awhile to find it."

"Alright," I said, holding up two fingers. "The dossier, and George's infected corpse. But what's the third thing?"

"The test tube around your neck. That's the most important thing of all."

PROCEDURE

We made a plan. It wasn't the best plan, but it was order amid chaos. Covered in polymer ponchos to protect us from the monsoon, we carried the body of MacGruder wrapped in the rolled-up rug to the back of Wetherspoon's car. Then I drove off in my own car, accelerating hard through the puddles, praying Mary was still home and not in transit to whatever slaughterhouse awaited in the basement of Saint Almachius.

As I cruised the wet and uncertain miles through herky-jerky traffic, the radio voice of Saxas rang hollow out of the speakers. Her voice sounded even higher, pinched somehow, like the supercomputer feeding her the script was straining to process it all. Or perhaps her programmer had sped her up to fit everything into the time slot. I turned the volume up anyway. Even though my mind was consumed by my mad dash to save my wife, the news was a shocking alarm rattling me to my core.

"Tensions in Korea touched off by last week's assassination of the U.S. Vice-President at a meeting of the East Asian Federation continue to escalate," Saxas said. "China and Japan and the United States have confirmed they are all deploying troops. The *U.S.S. Donald Trump* is speeding west from Hawaii to support Japan but will be later than required in the century-old alliance, due to the closure of Pacific bases from the Great Purge.

"However, the U.S. is sending a team from the Bureau of Wellness as part of what it's calling a "peacekeeping mission" in the wake of last week's assassination," she continued. "Chinese forces are already mobilizing divisions along the Yalu River, and are awaiting orders to march south toward Pyongyang and Seoul. Japan itself has nearly the entire fleet of the Self-Defense Forces off the southern coast, waiting to strike at a word from Prime Minister Sogo. Korea is readying all its defenses from Wando to Onsong, with particular strongholds on the Inchon peninsula and a line of surface-to-air missile defenses along the Yalu River, barely a half-mile away from the massing Chinese forces. Korea, still undergoing reunification, has issued terse warnings of "wholesale destruction" to all nations converging on its borders.

"The military buildup includes the nuclear arsenals of all four nations—which are on highest alert. The Bulletin of the Atomic Scientists has moved the Doomsday Clock forward to one minute to midnight. The United Nations, which is not in session, remains silent and has only said it condemns the first use of weapons of mass destruction. Strangest of all, record-breaking swarms of some kind of biting insects with pincers have beset every square mile of the Korean Peninsula and seem to be spreading disease and wholesale death in the cities of Seoul, Busan and Pyongyang."

A pause.

"In other news, the Knicks lost to the Miami Heat, 101-97…"

I stared at the radio, waiting for something more. But Saxas went on with the pre-season basketball scores, and then rattled off a few items about a mass shooting in the Midwest, another outbreak of plague in Oregon, another in Nebraska. The rain beat down on the car's roof.

I flipped off the satellite connection. I had to focus. She had to be home—she had to be at home. Mary had to be safe, I kept repeating the words in my mind like a protective mantra. I twiddled the test tube around my neck. There was no time to consider a world war. There were plans to focus on—to concentrate on saving my wife, on stopping the Bureau's insane program of experimentation.

The front door of the house was open, creaking a bit in the monsoon gusts of warm wind. The alarm blipped as I stepped inside, but I breezed right past it. I searched every room. But Mary was nowhere. Inside the bedroom I found the half-dozen Atmans with blinking screens strewn on the floor and across the bed.

"Mary!" I called out, my voice hoarse, beginning to break.

In the toilet, I found a thick, near-black stew of blood and bile. My heart pounded hard, salty sweat stung my eyes.

"Mary!" I screamed, and my throat gave out to a rasp like sandpaper rubbing against itself.

I walked slower down the hallway to the stairs, scrutinizing long scratches and wet footprints on the sheen of the red-maple floorboards. There were many tracks, clustered and smeared. A section of one looked like a heavy boot. But I couldn't tell who or what had left them—or how many of the intruders there had been. I scraped one with my finger; the mud was still moist. The scratches looked the like the point of something incredibly sharp had been gouged angrily into the wood. Like a scalpel.

In the kitchen I went to the house terminal and checked the last number dialed. It was mine, twenty minutes earlier. I punched in Mary's number, but it didn't even ring. I dialed Wetherspoon's number, but there was no answer. I went to the sink and splashed cold water on my face, trying to calm my quaking heart.

It was my fault she had been taken. I had put her life in the gravest of dangers. By leaving her alone at a critical moment, I had doomed her.

She was still alive, she had to be. There was no time to panic. Even the most medically-unethical experiments would take weeks, if not months, to finalize. Nothing would happen in the few hours it would take to find her. But the blood in the toilet… A horrible thought occurred to me. Rushing back to the bedroom, I dropped to my knees and flipped through the Atmans on the floor. I scrutinized one, glanced at another, tossed aside a third. Nothing made sense.

But a clue appeared. It was one waiver form allowing any treatments deemed necessary by the Bureau. Then another waiver, and another. Together the pieces fell into place. It all had been directly in front of me—hidden in plain sight. How could I have missed it? A supposed population study on vitamins—but it was really a Project 137 experiment on pregnant women. Everything had been signed by Abbud—and I noticed the Bureau of Wellness seal on everything, with the same serial number prefix, BOW-137. It was all in there. Nameless injections and regimens listed as "placebos." The triple-blind study disclaimers on every screen. The clause at the absolute bottom guaranteeing the Bureau of Wellness would in no way be held liable for any eventuality. At the bottom, she had signed each and every form with her personal signature code.

And there, next to it, was my own neat set of electronic initials, pin number confirmed.

Without reading the fine print, I had signed my wife's death warrant. She was a guinea pig for Project 137, which I'd allowed with my tacit, stupid consent.

I clawed at my face, praying to wake from this nightmare. But I knew I was not asleep.

Standing, I looked around the cluttered room, now shadowy as the dusk settled. I surveyed its contents. Nothing—nothing at all.

I took a step forward. Stepping on the edge of an Atman, my ankle twisted underneath me. I toppled toward the floor, panicking upon the fall, until my head crashed against the bedpost.

Blackness swallowed me.

Again the river rushed over me, I splintered, the cold darkness enveloped my limbs and my brain. I knew I was inside the Yah-qua-whee, the mythical fish that didn't even exist. I knew it didn't exist; I knew I was still within a dream. But still I struggled for freedom against the innards of the beast. My arms wouldn't move, as I sank lower and lower into its depths, and I froze solid, my limbs shattering, icy knives slicing my guts.

The next moment, something clamped down on my shoulder. I was shaken awake. A pale face loomed in the darkness over me.

My heart nearly stopped. Neither of us moved for a second. My eyes finally pierced the shadows of the gloom.

It was Lanza. I tried to rise, but I found I couldn't move my hands. At my belt, links of a tiny chain tinkled. My wrists were cuffed tight. I was helpless.

"Zo?" I said. "Get these off me."

"Sorry, buddy," Lanza said. "But the law's the law. I came here after the alarm tripped. You're a wanted man—there's a full-blown manhunt for you and that Old Man."

"What—why?"

"Bureau of Wellness, my friend. Broke my heart to hear there are murder warrants out for you."

"Murder warrants?" I scoffed, propping myself on an elbow. "Who did I kill?"

"Better question is who—didn't—you kill. They put twenty-two counts on the warrant, mentioning specifically the school attack, and the death of the reporter outside the funeral home."

I laughed.

"You've got to be kidding. You and I were fishing the entire time the school thing went down. And the reporter was in police custody when he died. How could I have killed him?"

"I'm not the one you have to convince," Lanza said, shaking his head, pulling me to my feet. "The feds signed the FOJA warrants. It's all over the news already. Saxas called you the 'Men-Gulla of modern medicine,' whatever that means."

I snapped my fingers. I had to make him understand.

"Listen, Zo," I said, bringing together my cuffed hands like in a prayer. "You have to know this doesn't make sense. How the hell did I do it? Was anyone killed with a fishing pole?"

Lanza stared at the ground, waiting for me to finish, weighing my words. His eyes slowly titled up toward me. I could tell immediately that decades of friendship meant nothing in this new context of crime and punishment. An ice clutched at my veins I had not felt since the death of my parents.

"I could believe you, Joe," he said coldly. "But that doesn't change the fact I have a job to do. I have to follow orders. And that's what I'm going to do."

Motioning toward the doorway, Lanza unclasped the holster of his service pistol. But he didn't draw the gun—instead he stepped aside to let me pass. We walked, one-and-two, down the hallway. We started down the stairs. I groaned as the cuffs seemed to tighten on my aching wrists.

"So all the years we grew up together mean nothing. Everything we've done, everything we've gone through. All that is nothing," I said.

"It's not nothing," Lanza said, pushing me, making me descend quicker. "But you know how it is, Joe. It's a job. If I don't do it, they'll find someone else who will. Someone's always watching—and listening."

Lanza tilted his head to the side, toward the standard-issue camera on the epaulet of his uniform. Everything was being recorded, in real-time, and monitored in some far-off bureaucratic office. We neared the bottom of the stairs.

"Sure," I sneered sardonically. "Makes sense. I understand."

"You know how it is, with child support and alimony and everything," Lanza said. "If you're as innocent as you say you are, you don't have to worry. Judges and juries don't just go off half-cocked."

I stumbled a bit, and Lanza went around me to steady my walk. It was then, or never. In one swoop, I shoved him and yanked at the gun in the holster. But the clasp had been refastened. Lanza easily brushed me aside and pinned my neck to the wall with his forearm.

Face mashed against the wallpaper, I felt the hard barrel of the pistol jammed into the base of my skull. I could feel a different kind of blackness seep into the corners of my senses—but this was a dangerous, complete nothingness.

"See…where…coming from," I spat. "But…listen… You're…like…brother."

Lanza released me, and I gasped for breath. He holstered the gun and snapped the clasp. He shook his head at me.

"We can talk on the way to the hospital," Lanza said. "But don't do anything stupid like that again, bro."

I shuffled behind him to the door. I wouldn't try anything again—escape was out of the question. Outside Lanza's patrol car waited, idling. My best friend pushed me to the back of the car, stuffing my head down inside like any other perp, slamming the door behind. Lanza climbed behind the wheel.

"About these cuffs," I said. "The least you can do is toss me the keys. I can't run or anything."

"No can do, bro," Lanza said, looking past me as he backed out of the driveway in the street. "Protocol."

The car cruised along the suburban streets. At first, I stared at my friend's eyes in the rearview mirror. But then I turned to the window, watching the yards passing by, house after house with the same dimensions, setbacks, shutters, and color—all exactly like mine.

"You wanted to talk," Lanza said.

"I was going to tell you about how Mary is a guinea pig for some psychotic doctors engaged in a massive conspiracy, and how I needed your help to save her from them. But that's a moot point now."

Lanza pressed a dashboard button. Pinpoints of light there and on his epaulet flicked off. He nodded at me in the rearview.

"Alright. We've got a minute or two before dispatch notices the cameras are off."

I took a deep breath. This was my last chance to get my friend to understand, to help me save myself, save Mary.

"Mary was taken to Saint Almachius," I said. "She's part of a Bureau experimentation program in the hospital basement. They take missing persons there, runaway teenagers and homeless people and prostitutes who just vanish. Thousands all over the country disappear every year. A lot of them go into that basement, and ones like it, every single day across the country."

Lanza was silent for a moment. He snorted and started to laugh.

"Joe, I don't know what you expect," Lanza said, shaking his head. "You've got twenty-two counts of murder against you. I've been around long enough to know that where there's smoke, there's fire. Nobody's ever charged for no reason. They have your fingerprints all over the scene at the school and at the apartment complex. Video of you at each place."

He rubbed his hand over his face and breathed hard, struggling.

"They said you were the only one who could have had the expertise and opportunity to put together the attacks, goddamnit. They're even saying you poisoned that poor bastard you framed for the plague outbreak and the school bombing. What was his name—Le Mallard?"

Lanza paused, catching my unblinking glare in the rearview.

"You've been acting crazy. You just need help," Lanza continued. "And if you're really innocent, you'll have your day in court. Justice will be served."

Moments of silence. I breathed deep and laid down in the backseat.

"Nothing to say?" Lanza said, glancing over his shoulder down at me.

"If my own best friend, my only family I have besides my wife, won't believe me," I said softly, "then why should I bother? It's over. There's no chance for Mary or the baby. None at all."

Lanza banged the steering wheel with his fist.

"You're delusional, you know that?" he said. "Your wife is in the hospital because she's sick, and your baby is sick. Nothing more. There's no big conspiracy out there, Joe. How could something like that even exist?"

I remained silent in the backseat. There was absolutely nothing left to say.

"I get it," Lanza continued. "You've lost your mind. The old Joe I know never would have gone off the deep end like this. That's why they sent me to pick you up and bring you to the hospital first, before the jail. So you can get treatment."

I sat up straight in the seat. Our eyes locked in the rearview.

"See—they want you to bring me to Saint Almachius," I said, my voice rising. "When's the last time you heard of anyone wanted for murder taken to the hospital first?"

"I arrest injured suspects all the time. We take them to jail after they're stabilized."

"Exactly," I said, thumping my chest, my arms, my face like an ape, with my handcuffs rattling harsh and metallic. "Where's my injury, Zo? Why do they need to take me to the hospital when they could just take me right to jail and start due process? Under FOJA's grand jury rules, they could have me indicted before midnight. Why wait?"

Lanza glanced at me, then turned away, shaking his head, his brow furrowed.

"Your injury's in your brain, you maniac," he said.

Lanza pressed a button, and the lights came on again on the dashboard and on the shoulder of his uniform. The gray shutter between the driver's side of the window and the backseat whirred shut, separating them. I was shut in. I couldn't even hear the police radio crackling.

It didn't matter. The cop cruiser was almost to Saint Almachius anyway. The familiar streets and traffic lights passed by, and then the hospital was dead ahead. My breath caught in my chest.

TO FREEZE TIME ITSELF

U.S.A., 1968

The limousine came long and low around the turn and rolled toward the armed guard. It slowed as it approached the checkpoint, then stopped at the gate. They always stopped the limousine, no matter how many times their seniormost expert Dr. Fujimi had come through, day after day and year after year. A moment's pause, and the driver's window lowered with an electric whir. The guard raised his hand to his brow—but not quickly enough for Fujimi's liking.

"Morning, Sam. Morning, Dr. Fujimi," said the guard, saluting the blacked-out windows in the back of the limousine.

"Morning, Corporal Grimes," said Sam, smoke rising around his beefy face, up to the brim of his cap. "How's the girl?"

"She's doing a bit better, Sam," Grimes said. "She sleeps through the night, at least. The bleeding stopped. The neighbors have stopped complaining."

Sam smiled, stretching the folds in his face as he blew smoke out his nostrils.

"That's great to hear, Mike," he said. "Really great."

Grimes smiled and scurried back to the guardhouse, reached in, and punched the button. The bar of the gate started to lift. Grimes squared his shoulders to the limousine and saluted again.

"My regards to the doctor," Grimes said, looking again to the black windows. "And please thank him again for me. I don't know if he can hear me."

Sam touched the brim of his chauffeur's cap, smiled sympathetically.

"I'll get him the message," he said, as he raised the window of the limousine.

Fujimi heard him, but only glared through the blacked-out windows. The car zoomed through the gate. It rolled through the base, past the signs for the laboratories and the euphemistic facility names—cleaning, grouping, the recreation center. From the back of the limo Yoshiro Fujimi—née Shiro Ishii—watched it all pass, as he had done every day for years. Ever since he arrived in America for his new life, with an entire facility at his disposal. All he had to do was be this new person Dr. Fujimi, and he could continue his work. A guard standing on the corner of Ditto Avenue stopped and saluted the limo. Ishii fought down the urge to scratch the unending itch under the scarf around his neck. He glanced up and Sam's eyes were staring at him in the rearview mirror.

"Doc, I don't know if you heard, but Cpl. Grimes said his daughter's doing better. He thanked you," Sam said, making the turn, touching his cap at another guard who stood there saluting.

Ishii waved his hand dismissively. The itch in his throat had vanished as quickly as it had come, and relief washed over him. Perhaps the narcotics were finally kicking in.

"I wanted to make sure you heard, since I know you took a keen interest in the girl's case," continued Sam. "A lot of people really appreciated what you've done for the infected kids."

Ishii just nodded. The limousine slowed, made another turn around the edge of the low brick building, and went all the way to the back, stopping at the usual spot next to the dumpster with the Bureau seal on the side. That seal let the rest of the Fort Detrick know this was a place for the Project—and no one else. It was the secret center of it all. The secret of secrets.

"Here we are, Doc," said Sam, getting out.

Ishii struggled to pull himself out of the seat, but Sam opened the door and his powerful hands lifted him and propped the doctor up on his feet, with no more effort than if Ishii was a plush doll. Ishii nodded again, held out a one-dollar bill with a tremoring hand. Sam pushed it back at the doctor.

"How many times do I have to tell you, Doc," said Sam. "No tips."

He ushered the doctor to the low green door, which Ishii unlocked with a key off his belt.

"I'll be right here, Doc," said Sam, patting him on the shoulder. "Take your time. There's no hurry."

Ishii nodded and hobbled inside. Lurching down the smooth gray hallways under the bare lightbulbs, Ishii made the three turns to the stairwell, then carefully stepped down, clinging to the railing with his damned shaking hands. It grew with each step. Then he was under the emergency lamp, which cast its faint glow at the door. Ishii used his key and went inside.

The hallways were bare, the doors all shut as the experiments proceeded. Ishii glanced through each eye-level window. Inside were gowned and masked surgeons: one washing up at the sink in one room, another donning gloves, another calling back to a nurse, a still-silent drill dripping blood onto the sheet atop a subject, a nurse in another room turning a wet spattered skull over in her gloved hands philosophically. Ishii glanced in at each, then kept going, the routine of a Monday morning. Business moved on as usual. The work proceeded—and would continue without him, he thought absently, still shuffling forward.

From far-off, he heard music. The tinny echo of Frank Sinatra's voice cut by the whine of a power tool and the mechanical whine as it ground through bone. Ishii smiled for the first time that day. The troops liked their work, and they were making progress. That much he could always be proud of.

His office was the one at the end of the hallway, a room only slightly bigger than an American jail cell. This too had become part of his new life in this strange new American world.

They had put him here on his third full day at Detrick. He had taken one look at it and turned on his heel. Still carrying his box of books and papers from the Manchukuo days, he had marched right to the commander's office, and he had yelled—in Japanese—about how dissatisfactory the working conditions were and how was he expected to get any work done when they stick him in jail like a common criminal, and so on. The commander tapped his cigar in an ashtray and nodded. He pushed a button on the intercom next to him and barked something in muddled English. He had barely taken his finger off the button when two MPs arrived, threaded their arms underneath Ishii's elbows, and carted him off. The struggle was violent. In a few minutes they arrived back at the same bare room with the single small desk. The two grunts dropped him in the chair, turned, and walked out. Groaning, Ishii dropped the box and slumped to the side. His ribs ached. He held his hand to his nose. It came back bright red with blood. He reached for the tissues at the corner of the desk and stuffed one up each nostril to stanch the flow. Without another word he unpacked some of his boxes, his hands shaking in rage as he placed each binder and book on the empty shelves in perfect chronological order, preparing for his new job. There would be no further bargaining. He was employed by the Company, and they would give him the tools he needed, and nothing more.

Almost twenty years later, Ishii's hands shook with age and illness as he packed up that same box, now yellowed and tattered. His weak fingers slid small sheaves of yellow brittle papers with Japanese characters into the small box. The newer, whiter papers were written in English. They had been removed on handtrucks by personnel over the weeks Ishii had been on sick leave. He wasn't surprised. The last news they had of him could not have been promising. They must have assumed the worst. But like everyone else before them, he had proven them wrong. By sheer dint of will he had again triumphed where only defeat had been possible.

He laughed—but no sound came, only the pain again. He pulled down the scarf and lay his neck bare, finally giving in to the urge to scratch around the raw hole in his throat. He lightly fingered the tender flesh around the bandage and felt the soothing sensation of his fingertips sating the dying nerves within.

No good in being a medical researcher if you didn't strive to further the work; what better place to start than on oneself? His subordinates at Detrick had fought him at every step, but eventually even they had to admit he had a point. If a doctor was willing to give his own body for science, then he deserved to be able to make that sacrifice. Ishii placed the last of the papers in the box, and he lashed it together with twine, triple-knotted.

The papers he'd leave to the Unit. They would need them, with all the competition from Naito and Kitano, those reckless fools and their damned organization. The audacity to call it the Green Cross, to organize it as a corporation in plain sight. And all while working on the pandemic retrovirus…and negotiating with the Russians. The Unit—the Project, whatever the idiots in America called it—would need everything he'd left behind, to keep ahead of those morons.

A tiny knock at the door. Ishii felt a tingle through him as he heard it—the same knock as every morning for five years. He shuffled over, leaning on the chair. He twisted the knob, and slowly pulled the door inward.

There stood Leslie, blonde bobbed hair, white lab coat open to reveal a green dress sheathing her buxom hourglass figure. She held some files in her arms.

"Dr. Fujimi," she said, her jaw dropping open, her stupid eyes bulging wide. She set the files aside on a nearby shelf, and then grabbed his arm, pulling his weight onto her shoulder. "Yoshiro, you need to sit down."

She pulled him and, without complaint, he shuffled in her direction toward the one chair left in the office. She helped him ease down into it. The perfume off her breasts caressed his nostrils. As she slowly withdrew, his hands lingered at the small of her back. She froze in place, compliant and tense, willing, but his hands fell at his sides. She straightened, her dramatically circumscribed eyes wide as they searched his face. She reached out and touched his cold hand, which lay on the armrest, but he could barely feel her warmth. She kneeled beside him. Her eyes stared into the hole in his throat—she couldn't meet his gaze for more than a moment. A tear tumbled down her cheek. Her lips, pasted with pale lipstick, trembled.

"Yu," she said softly. "Yu, I love you. I didn't know if you would come back, if you would get out of the hospital. They wouldn't tell us anything. I called the house but hung up before she answered. I prayed…"

Her pinky rubbed his thumb. He could feel that, at least—the warm touch that had sustained him for five years. But he withdrew his hand. There was no time for any of this—he had no time left. He stood, knees unsteady, and he shook his head at her.

The years of working together, in the lab, in the conference room, and even those hours still on the clock in the plastic-sheeted motels. All of that seemed to surge through those pale blue eyes of hers as she stared at him, the eyes narrowing, turning to glass. This woman was the last one who would ever love him.

Well, he was glad all that was over now, at least.

As if sensing his thoughts, her face crinkled.

"Just as well that you can't talk, Yu," she said. "You'd probably just say something hateful to me, or about America. How Shibayama is so much prettier this time of year. I'm so sick of hearing about those fucking cherry trees. That fucking country."

She ripped the handkerchief out of his breast pocket and threw it on the ground.

"I guess you need a wheelchair so you can get out of here?" she said, sneering, half-smiling. She wiped her eyes. "Well, let that be my parting gift to you, Dr. Fujimi."

With that, she shoved out the door. Ishii stood, savoring her scent for a moment, knowing he'd never see her ever again. He stooped slowly and picked up the handkerchief, fingering the monogrammed Y and F at its embroidered corner. He turned to the box and pulled out the bottle of Scotch he'd packed from the shelves. Backing up with small steps, he lowered himself into the seat again, facing the sole window high in the wall, just above the ground outside. The bars blocked most of the sunlight.

What do you need, what could you possibly need when the end is so near and there is nothing left to hope for? No great horizon ahead, just the abrupt edge of the abyss. The hole in his throat contracted, convulsing, the pain shot through his neck. He scratched harder at the ragged surgical hole. Being a doctor meant that there was no room for illusions, the hope for miracles.

But then he looked at the refrigerator. It hummed there despite his silence, quietly preserving everything inside. The samples, the DNA, the instructions for when the technology would be advanced enough. Cloning wasn't far off. It wouldn't be long at all; a way of freezing time itself. Maybe in a decade, maybe twenty years.

A smile spread over his face, the first of its kind in months, and the last in this lifetime for the man born Shiro Ishii, who would die as Yukio Fujimi. How did the Americans say it—wherever there was a will, there was a way? And there was always a will. Science provided the way.

He would return.

BENEATH, A WORLD

U.S.A., 2087

The police car cruised around the rear of the hospital. It neared the silver hatch in the wall with the bright Bureau of Wellness seal emblazoned on it and stopped. The engine died. The door opened, and Lanza stood there. I blinked up at him, the rain blinding me.

"Why are we at the back?" I said.

"Dispatch told me you wouldn't have clearance anymore, so you have to go down the supply chute," he said. "After that, I'm supposed to walk around the front and start the intake procedure for the psych ward."

I knew this was truly the end of the line. Cuffed hands grasping the edge of the door, I struggled to remain in the car. I pulled and I struggled. But Lanza yanked me out with minimal effort, placing me on my feet and then brushing me off like a wayward puppy heading to a dog show. I tried to pull away, but Lanza held me fast.

"And you see nothing strange about this?" I said, giving up, out of breath. "The fact that they want you to take me to the hospital, push me down a chute, then walk around to the front to commit me to some psych ward. Which doesn't even exist at Saint Almachius, by the way."

Lanza paused a second, his brow furrowed ever so slightly. He grunted. But then he shoved me forward, toward the silver chute, the Bureau seal that seemed to glint in the gloom. A camera overhead angled away from us, as if it didn't want to make a record of this decisive moment.

"I've got orders," Lanza said, thrusting me with two hands. "Besides, it's not like you're the first. Last time was a couple of weeks ago. They had me deliver some teenage girl who started that big forest fire. She had a tattoo on her neck, some blob of ink. At least she was unconscious. Much easier to handle than you, bro."

Lanza was pushing me closer and closer to the hatch, which beeped, and yawned open automatically, a yawning metal mouth. My eyes widened in horror.

"Zo, wait—" I said.

But as I tried to dodge him, I tipped backward through the panel, hurtling downward, heels dragging overhead, faster and faster in that tight tunnel. A few seconds of falling, and then I shot out into a bright room onto a material that softly enveloped me. Rough hands grabbed me and dragged me across it and I flailed my elbows against them. But these were two orderlies—and they were even bigger than Stanislaw and Stash. Their hands were like vices at my joints, hauling me across the room and to the door. It slid open automatically, and I was in a dimmer corridor, the two grunts dragging my knees across the tiles. Terror closed in. I couldn't breathe, like I was under water. Just like in my nightmare.

To the right was a window. I twisted toward it, and I saw a line of people in a waiting room, seated, reading magazines. It was the charity-care wing in the basement. Wrenching myself, dropping my dead weight, I managed to fall to the floor and out of the orderlies' grasp. I landed hard but lunged past them, slamming both cuffed wrists on the window, screaming until my chest would burst. But no one looked up, or even flinched. Two of the young teens were facing me, but their faces showed nothing—no recognition, no surprise. And I could see that the other side was lit differently—it was a two-way mirror. A thick one—a soundproof one.

The orderlies grabbed me again, one gave me a quick shot in the kidneys. Blinding pain crippled me, and I crumpled. They grabbed my limp body and hauled me to the end of the hallway. I had never seen these men before, their sweaty swollen faces. Their skin was pale, their black eyes deep-set like cave-dwellers. Their blows fell on me, quick and remorseless. The pain flared like an amphetamine rush through my body.

"Remember, we can't hurt him—could ruin the results," said one of them.

"This one keeps fighting," said the other, giving me a shot in the gut. "Besides, we've got to have our fun now and then."

"Fine—just no bruises," said the first orderly, kicking both my tibias with hard kicks.

They dragged me through another door. A bright room with green walls, bare. An examination table stood like a cenotaph in the center of the floor. One of the orderlies ripped off my belt, tossed me on the table, then turned back. The door clicked shut behind them. I sat there bewildered, the antiseptic smell emanating from every surface. The room was one I'd never seen before. I had been down in the charity-care wing—the opposite side of the basement from Wetherspoon's office—only a handful of times in my years at the hospital. But I had never seen any of this before: the chute, the intake room, the secret hallway, the waiting room behind the two-way glass, this pale-green patient room.

This wasn't simply a hospital basement, I realized suddenly. This was the Project's facility—the dark hub of their insane machinations. A chill ran along my sweaty skin.

Standing from the table, I went over and inspected the two doors. The one I'd come in was locked, and the one opposite it was, too. Between the locked exits, there were two recessed parts of the wall. I banged on them with my cuffed fists, but they sounded solid. I tried the doors again and kicked one of them hard. Nothing—no furniture, no pictures, no wall-mounted devices. No cameras, either. My eyes caught a series of vertical lines on the back wall at waist-height, behind the examination table. I walked over and discovered painted-over gouge marks the size and shape of human fingers, like someone had clawed away at the plaster. But that was all. After a few minutes searching for any sign of an escape route, I acceded to my aching legs, and I sat back down on the table.

The door opened, the orderlies rushed inside in a blur of white. This time they wore surgical masks. I stood wobbily, trying to maneuver around them to the door, or at least defend myself, but they pounced on me and threw me down. They unlocked the cuff from my left wrist. I stopped struggling for a second—but they seized the unclasped cuff and locked it over a bar on the side of the examination table. I flailed at them. They released me and walked out, the one stepping over my wild kick at their knees. I yelled out after them, but my voice died in my throat when I saw my next visitor walk in: a short figure sashaying slowly forward in nurse's scrubs.

The figure pulled the straps of a surgical mask back behind the ears…and it was Betty Bathory.

I gasped. She smiled, flashing sharp teeth, as she pulled her hair back into a ponytail.

"Well, Joe," she said, pulling the mask tight over her nose. "It's been a while since your last checkup, hasn't it?"

Too dumbfounded to speak, I just stared.

"Oh, come on, Joe. Don't look at me with those puppy-dog eyes."

She pulled a hypodermic out of her pocket and flicked it with a fingernail, knocking the air bubbles out of the chamber filled with a tinted liquid. Fluid spurted from the needle's tip. She walked over to the wall, where she pulled up her sleeve and tapped with her free hand into her Atman. My head swooned as I watched her nonchalant fingers move the same way I had seen every day for a decade—but this time for a very different purpose.

"What is this place?" I said, voice dry. "I've never seen this part of the hospital."

"Oh, this is the basement—part of the charity-care wing. But it's only for the special charity cases. The Project's charity cases."

She turned to me, her eyes squinting in a smile over the sterile mask. I shook my head.

"Betty?" he said. "You, of all people?"

Her hands went to her hips, the attitude of the Jersey girl I'd always found so charming in her before that moment. It was not charming now—it was horrifying.

"Why not me—just because I'm a nurse? Let me tell you something, Doc-tor-Bar-nnn-esssss," she said, dragging out impossible syllables. "Nurses are everything. We're the ones changing bedpans, talking to patients, drawing blood, calming fears. Why wouldn't we be as important in research? Especially something as important as the Project?"

"No, I mean—how...could you?"

"Oh, you mean ethically." She laughed, capping the syringe and tucking it back in her pocket. "But what you're really asking is, why haven't we continued doing medicine in the same way for the last hundred years? Why haven't we been content to repeat the same mistakes, instead of taking the risks that make us better?"

Tapping into her Atman, something beeped. Two recessed parts of the wall started to rise, panels lifting slowly. Slowly I saw two brighter rooms, in each a patient lay on a table with feet raised in stirrups. I could not see who they were yet, but my skin crawled at the sight. I had a good idea what would happen next.

"The Purge strengthened our resolve," she continued. "Made us remember we need to progress as a society, and not just as a collection of individuals. We realized the importance of the greater good."

Her eyes narrowed, she smiled behind the mask.

"You know, I believe if we'd told you about the Project, you would have appreciated its importance, its scope and ambition," she said, still tapping into her device. "There's national security to think about, sure, but there's also the research. If we hadn't made mistakes in the past, where would we be today? If the doctors in the ancient world hadn't had the foresight to cut open a woman's womb, would we have ever succeeded in saving millions of children and mothers with caesarians?"

The panels had risen to the gowned shoulders of the patients. One was a wraith, the other a woman with knees up, nude underneath. But I couldn't see faces yet. I yanked at the handcuffs, trying to free myself, heart hammering, panic rising.

"I told you to read the fine print, Joe," Betty continued, glancing at the rooms on the other side, nodding. "And I don't think you listened."

The panel vanished upward into the ceiling. I squinted, and I could finally see. The seated patient in the left room, strapped into a papoose, was the emaciated form of Cornelius Wetherspoon. He wiggled in the straps, his crown of white hair disheveled, protruding in every direction.

And in the adjoining room lay Mary, passed out, face limp, her black hair falling over one shoulder, knees bent and legs spread, ankles cuffed high. A stream of drool ran down the side of the headrest.

"Oh my God, oh my God," I said, tears of rage welling in my eyes.

"Yes, Joe, we've all got to make sacrifices," Betty said. Her steps neared me, and when she got close enough, I swung at her with my free fist. But she ducked back with a giggle, grabbed my arm, and stuck in the syringe. I tried to swing with the other hand, but the cuffs tugged back, staggering me. Swooning, I collapsed back against the examination table.

"Now just relax, this is painless..." Betty said, patting my head.

But then everything went black again.

Awaking to a bright light, I found my limbs restrained on the table. Thick straps held my wrists, thighs and ankles fast. One even ran across my forehead. But I was upright, and a blurry form came into focus under the lights. Betty was staring down at me. Her eyebrows bounced when she saw I was awake.

"Wakey-wakey," she said, scolding me like she had thousands of patients in the past. "You really should get more sleep, Joe. Patients don't normally conk out like that, even with the double dosage."

She came over and tugged on my straps, making sure they were still dug into my limbs. I struggled against them, but she grabbed my face with a viselike hand and squeezed.

"Now, listen," she said, through gritted teeth. "We've all got to make sacrifices. When I lost my husband, I was strapped in this very chair, Joe. There was no divorce. That was a lie. The Project took him away."

She picked at the corner of her eye with a gloved finger, like she was about to cry. She almost looked human in that moment.

"He was one of the Maruta, you see. A log to be chopped up. I was angry, as angry as you are right now. But I realized there was no use fighting any of it. This thing is bigger than you and me, or Mary, or Wetherspoon. We might as well accept it, take it for what it is. Hell, you might even get lucky—Mary might survive. You should be thankful for that chance."

"You have to be kidding about all this, Betty. Just loosen these straps and let me out."

She stood, straightening her scrubs.

"I'm deadly serious, Joe. You can deny what happened that time in the past. But a hand has been dealt here. We're about to flip the final card, to determine our future."

Her eyes were blank. She moved around to the other side of the chair, so that she was behind me. Her hand crept over my shoulder and down onto my chest, feeling the wild beat of my heart. I stared ahead at the two panels with the two-way mirrors. It was a nightmare vision—Wetherspoon struggling every few moments against his bonds in the left window, Mary drugged and unconscious on the right, the stream of her drool oozing down the side of the chair, glimmering in the fluorescent light.

But now I noticed two screens on the wall over the patients' heads. Both had EKG and vitals readings, like scoreboards for a big game. Mary's was calm and still, a steady heartbeat and breathing rate. The Old Man's fluctuated wildly every time he flailed in a vain attempt to free himself.

Betty leaned in close to my ear and spoke in a voice that mimicked Saxas as she patted my chest.

"What we're going to see now," she said, "is the final experiment in this round of testing. Both of these Maruta have been part of the Project for a few months. The 105-year-old male on the left had an early exposure to a particular nerve agent some time ago during his time with the Bureau. We've been monitoring the ambient toxicity in the bloodstream for years. He's been put into contact with trace levels of the chemical hidden in his drinks over the last few weeks. We're going to test whether the feedback is enough to kill him with a dose just a—teensy-weensy—bit bigger."

A small haze wafting from a darkened vent in the far corner. Gas started to fill the room. Wetherspoon strained harder against his bonds.

"Neal!" I shouted.

But Betty covered my mouth with her latexed hand, the nauseating rubber odor making me gag.

"Joe, this is not the time for hysterics—you might ruin the data," she said. "He can't hear you anyway. But he knows what's coming. I mean, he led the experiments for so many years, he has to know the smell of the gas. He knows he's only got a minute at most before his heart stops."

The white fog drifted in, curled once around the ceiling, and fell to the floor. Wetherspoon cringed as it blanketed him. His heart rate spiked—the cosine wave whipped across the display at 200 beats a minute. The Old Man held his breath for a minute or more, his chest still and unmoving even as his head whipped from side to side, as his body cried out for oxygen. But he was losing the fight against his own burning lungs, I could see. My mentor's mouth moved—and though I could not hear him, I understood his words clearly.

Joe, he said. Stop. Them.

Wetherspoon exhaled, then reflexively sucked in the fog of death around him. A second's pause, then he shook. His limbs flailed against the restraints, his head jerked against the skull strap, his eyes bulged in their sockets. His skin went red, then purple, and the veins in his neck swelled. Blood gushed out his nose. His head fell back, his body collapsed, deflated.

The EKG on the monitor plummeted, then evened out.

Zero heartbeats.

"No!" I screamed.

Betty stood, went around to the front of the examination room table toward the window panel. She pushed a button on her Atman.

"Maruta Number 2087-11203 has flatlined," she said. "Activate ventilation in test room one, and ready forensic team to retrieve the body for further tests," she said. "Prepare room two for further readings—and inform Doctor Abbud that Marutas M616754 and M616755 are prepped and waiting."

I stared at the corpse of the Old Man through the observation window. I strained against my bonds. Betty shook her head at me and clucked her tongue disapprovingly.

"Joe, haven't we talked about this?" she said, lowering the Atman. "The experiment is nearly done. Mary might pull through. After all, it's not like we're pumping toxic gas into a closed room with her." She laughed, a twinkle to her eyes.

"What are you doing to her?" I said, teeth clenched.

"I really don't know, Joe. Abbud is very secretive—he only shares his data with Dr. Fujimi."

She leaned in close, a whiff of her perfume stinging my nostrils.

"Now don't quote me but… He's been trying different inputs for the Atmans, seeing what would happen with birth rates with different frequencies."

"Oh my God—Mary—the morning sickness…"

"Yes, that's probably a symptom," the nurse said, nodding. "But by and large, it's not fatal. This is the final appointment with her for the second trimester—though obviously trimesters don't really mean anything at this point."

"Don't really mean anything? What does that mean? What are you doing to her?"

The nurse shook her head.

"I told you, Joe—we all need to make sacrifices. Sometimes the most painful ones are the most necessary. After all, Mary is my friend, too. We'll just have to wait and see what the experts have planned."

She patted me on the cheek with her latex palm, then turned back to her Atman.

The white fog had completely cleared from the left room. A team in NBC suits streamed in from a side door and took readings throughout the small space, checks of the ambient air near the corpse. It was a silent flurry of activity. Some felt for a pulse at the jugular vein of the corpse, others removed some wires from his wrist and chest, peered inside his throat with a speculum, prodded the tongue, lifted the eyelids, inspected the unblinking stare. A half-dozen needles were stuck in the arms, blood was drawn. The largest member of the group walked up with a large cranial saw and positioned himself at Wetherspoon's head, lining up for the first stroke of the razor-sharp teeth into the skull. But another member of the team held up a hand, wagging a gloved finger in the face of the sawman, whose shoulders slumped as he lowered the cranium cutter in evident disappointment. They continued collecting data on the cadaver. It was an orgy of violence, of precision brutality in the name of science.

"And to think," Betty mused, "That Old Man lived over a century, for millions of heartbeats—and all it took was a single breath of his own gas to stop it forever. Truly, I think there's some kind of lesson right there. Probably something more poetic than scientific."

"You bitch," I said.

"Save the commentary, Joe," she said, pointing to the other panel in the wall.

Abbud, maskless, walked in from the right side of Mary's room. An elfin figure in a mask and cap followed him. Abbud checked his Atman, then said something. A tall male nurse came in behind them, pushing a cart with gleaming steel implements. The three split up. Abbud did a circle around Mary, looking her over, talking into his Atman. The small person with him tapped into their own Atman—a stance I recognized but couldn't quite place. The male nurse arranged the implements, holding them up for inspection. Forceps, a turkey baster, a scalpel, another speculum. I tugged again at my bonds.

"Well, this is no fun," Betty said. "We can't hear anything going on. Let me get some sound here."

She tapped at her Atman. Seconds later, Abbud's voice came through the tiny speaker embedded at the base of her thumb.

"Can you hear me now?" he said, glancing through the two-way mirror.

"Loud and clear," Betty said. "Doctor, we have an audience today. A neutral third party to peer review your data."

Everyone laughed—except for me.

"Dr. Barnes, I presume," Abbud said, holding up a latex-gloved hand. "Hello, Joe. I'm glad you could finally be let in on the Project. Some of the progress we've made."

"If you hurt my wife, I will kill you, Abbud. You hear me?"

On the other side of the mirror, Abbud giggled, and waved his hand dismissively.

"Joe, Joe, Joe. No reason to be hostile," he said, a split second's delay between his gestures behind the window and his voice coming through Betty's Atman. "There's very little chance at all that Mary will suffer any permanent effects. She's been extremely resilient to the toxins over the last three months, you know."

Taking a turn around the unconscious form on the examination chair, Abbud made some notes on the device on his wrist. His hand drifted to the table, and he picked up a scalpel. He held the blade high, and it spliced a ray of light. He smiled.

"But I'd say there's a distinct chance—maybe thirty percent, maybe more—of severe blood loss, and there just isn't that much plasma on hand at the hospital today. So really, Joe—we should all brace ourselves for anything."

Setting the scalpel back on the table, he glanced through the two-way glass. This time he stared directly at me.

"Because after all—there's nothing definite in medicine." He smiled. "As I have told you many times over our years working together."

A door swung open on the other side, and Abbud snapped to attention. In walked Dr. Yoshiro Fujimi, also maskless. Swinging around his neck was my own stethoscope, which he promptly flung aside. The speaker cut out on Betty 's wrist Atman. Fujimi was enraged. He looked like a madman in a manic episode, hands swinging up toward the ceiling, spit flying out of his mouth, his normally-sculpted hair exploding at its part like a baseball ripped at its seams. Abbud cowered, backing away a few steps toward the corner. The tiny masked person sidestepped and exited out through the door, still tapping into their Atman, not even looking up. The male nurse just stood at attention. Betty left my side and darted out through the door.

Something was amiss, amid their chaotic plan. There would never be a better time to free myself. As Fujimi continued his silent ravings, I yanked and tore against the straps. The prong on the strap around the left wrist was protruding the slightest bit. If I rotated my arm, the leather would come farther up the metal pin, almost to the hole. I tried twice, but it wouldn't go. It just wouldn't go, no matter how much I cursed at it. All that separated me from freedom and saving Mary was a tiny goddamned prong. I tried again. Again, nothing. A noise coming, a sound of footsteps. I leaned back. Betty Bathory came back through the door. Her hair was awry, tendrils of it snaking up off her shoulders.

"A hell of a day, Joe," she said. "You know those days when you'd swear the world was spinning slower? Well, this is one of those days."

I was just waiting for her to turn away so I could keep working at the strap. I glared at her, unable to contain the hatred coursing hot in my eyes. But she stared right back, her wrist raised to her face, one edge of her mouth curling up in amusement. For a second our gaze was locked in a magnetic hold. She turned, and I worked again frantically at the strap.

But she spun back around quickly, and I froze.

"Don't get too excited, Joe. Even if you undo that strap, I'll still have this," she said, holding up a taser that she zapped in the air. "I'll knock you flat on your ass. So be good—and pay attention. They're about to begin."

On the other side of the mirrors the scene was orderly again, three men ready for the big procedure. Abbud assumed a position at the base of the chair, his Atman raised to record. Fujimi had calmed, and he was drawing the mask slowly over his face. He was now the model of concentration, brow creased, eyes narrowed, spectacles tilted on his sweaty nose. Approaching the unconscious form of Mary, he rolled the sleeves of his lab coat up his arms.

"Goddamnit! I'll kill you, motherfucker!" I screamed.

But it was no use. Betty had turned the microphone off, and the wall was soundproof. Fujimi didn't even flinch, and his voice was steady as he spoke.

"Maruta number M616754, of the P-137 Almachius sample group, prepped for procedure," he said. "Female is 37 years old, fertile. The Maruta has been given regular regimen of the Q-36 Ovulation Modulator to simulate pregnancy. The Maruta has been dosed with indexed toxin for four months through drinking water supply. Latest observations to be recorded at the moment of conception with control-group sperm."

The words came out in a torrent, and I was focused mostly on freeing myself from the cuffs. But the words echoed in my ears, and one by one they fell into place into my brain—their meaning, their import.

Drinking water.

To. Simulate. Pregnancy.

Moment. Of. Conception.

Control group.

Sperm.

Abbud had drifted to the space between Mary's spread legs. His back was to the mirror. The Atman was still raised. But he pushed out his elbows, and the ends of his lab coat billowed out to either side. Then he was fiddling with something around his midsection. Then he stooped ever so slightly. I angled my head to get a better look, even though, in my utter horror, I already understood what they intended to do.

Abbud was unfastening his pants. Turning, he showed himself to be naked from the waist down—the pale fleshiness of the spindly legs, the black hairy mass surrounding a tiny stiffening member. A profane smile spread across his face. Fujimi stepped forward, held up a finger.

"One second, doctor," Fujimi said. "Before you begin the operation, we may yet appeal to the scientific curiosity of Dr. Barnes."

He tapped on the glass.

"Dr. Barnes—can you hear me? Let me explain one thing. We're working on a toxin used as a kind of prophylactic we've been giving your wife. The entire time she believed herself pregnant, it was really this pregnancy simulator. Her doctor, Abbud here, has been taking an antitoxin for about the same four-month period in preparation."

"Why?" I screamed.

"Why, you may ask," Fujimi continued, unhearing on the other side of the soundproof wall. "Simply, doctor, we're testing population-level birth control. The world's growth hasn't slowed down like it's supposed to. It has accelerated. We'll be at twenty billion people by the year 2100. We believe we can fix that. We believe we can make a better living through a bit of chemistry. But we also need to make sure we can reverse it when necessary. Hence, the coupling you're about to see—the test of whether the right toxin and antitoxin can cancel each other out, and whether the Maruta can conceive."

"That's my wife, you motherfucker," I said. "Not a goddamned log."

"Now the Maruta," Fujimi said, continuing on, still unable to hear me, "is in a sedated state, so she won't remember a thing. And lowered doses of this birth control toxin actually accelerate the maturation of the fetus. Essentially, Mary will have a child at the expected time. She will have the baby, and she will love the baby. Only you—and the Project—will be the wiser."

The doctor glanced over at Abbud, who still stroked his weedy genitals, as he stared up at the ceiling with a blissful look on his disgusting face. Fujimi patted him on the shoulder.

"All this, of course, if the good doctor is successful in his injection," he said.

The three men in the room laughed, as Abbud's hand kept working his penis.

Betty hit a button. A light came up on her Atman, and she held it to my face. The microphone light glowed. I roared.

"If you touch her..." I growled.

"I want you to know this is a harmless procedure," Fujimi said, still laughing. "We've done it at least five hundred times in this very room. It's an age-old procedure; it's been going on as long as there's been a human race. Birds do it, bees do it. Just here there's a bit more biochemistry to it."

More general laughter. I roared.

"So the procedure is rape. Rape in the name of Science, right?"

Fujimi shook his head, pacing the floor at the back wall, behind Mary's head.

"You have such an ugly way of putting things, Doctor," he said, stroking a lock of Mary's hair from her brow. "Don't be so dramatic. We usually use a syringe. But Dr. Abbud said he was eager to administer the X-factor himself."

Abbud waggled his cock at the mirror. Everyone on the other side laughed again. Pointing at me, Fujimi approached the two-way glass.

"In a few hours, you'll have your own choice," Fujimi said, wagging his finger. "It's up to you which side of the scalpel you'll end up on, Dr. Barnes."

His voice lingered slowly on the last word. No one moved. A silence hung—the doctors and the nurse on one side, and Betty Bathory and myself on the other. Abbud continued masturbating with a stupid grin on his face.

A crash broke through the Atman. The three on the other side jumped, then scampered to the left. My heart leapt. I tried to sit up, but the straps held me fast.

A gun loomed in from the right side of the window. Two uniformed arms leveled it at the three. And then the shoulders and face of the gunman came into view.

It was Lanza. I whooped.

The encounter played out silently. Lanza shook the gun, yelled something. His face was set hard, like stone. The three men retreated toward the back-left corner, Abbud shuffling foot to foot, trying to drag his pants up from the floor. Mary's head rolled on her shoulders. Everything moved in silence.

Mary, wake up, Lanza's lips said, grabbing her knee, shaking her.

What... she said, head stirring, eyes still closed.

"Zo, get her out!" I yelled.

Lanza's head picked up, like he had heard. He looked around and squinted at the two-way mirror for a moment. But he turned back to Mary.

Mary, get up, Lanza's lips said. He undid the straps carefully on her legs, averting his eyes from seeing underneath her gown. Lowering her legs to the ground, he loosened the straps on her wrists, still pointing the gun at the three men in the corner.

"Zo!" I hollered.

Lanza turned to the mirror, shielding his eyes from the overhead lights as he tried to peer through the two-way glass.

Joe? said Lanza's lips.

"Zo, get Mary out!"

Betty, who hadn't moved at all since the unexpected arrival of the cop, rushed through the door on the left side of our room, the entryway the orderlies had carried me through. Lanza approached the glass, shielding his eyes with his hands.

In the background, the male nurse had removed his mask. It was Culling. His lip curled to a sneer. He took a step forward, then another. His hand felt along the tray of instruments and grasped a scalpel. I watched in horror as the nurse crept up behind Lanza, the blade raised.

"Behind you!" I screamed, my screech reaching an unholy register.

Lanza stepped to his left—revealing the reflection of the nurse behind him. He spun around just as Culling lunged at him with the scalpel, bringing it down in an arc at Lanza's neck. Three flashes burst from the gun, as they both fell out of sight beneath the window.

Another flash of the pistol. Then—nothing.

That moment was an agonizing eternity. A wave of nausea rushed up my throat. I only vaguely saw Mary stir, weakly trying to raise herself from the chair. The two doctors rushed at the spot where the two combatants had fallen. Two more pistol flashes and Abbud dropped his pants and fell, face frozen in an instant, blasted once through the chest. The other shot, however, missed Fujimi. It splintered a hole in the wall over his head just as he retreated to the other room and into the crowd of NBC-suited men.

The gunfire had roused Mary. She was on her feet, her hands raised to her face in horror. She stepped forward twice in a druggy shuffle and stooped down below the windowframe. Seconds passed, the medical experiments room on the right was like a still-life painting—the tiny bullet holes, the wispy blood spatter on the far wall from Abbud's exploded heart. I waited—and prayed.

How could all this insanity, this senseless carnage, be happening a few floors below the rooms where I had saved lives for years? How could all the horrors of death have been secreted just yards beneath all the miracles of modern science?

I hollered with a hoarse throat as Mary emerged with Lanza, one of his arms around her shoulder. The hand still holding the gun was coated in blood, clutching at his trapezius muscle. He said something to her, she nodded and said something back, and they headed toward the exit on the right side of the room. They opened the door and limped out, drugged and wounded. They disappeared outside.

"Oh, thank God. Thank. God," I said.

I resumed working my way at the left wrist strap. Twice the pin held fast, sliding back into place just as I thought it was about to give. But on the third attempt, it poked up and out of the hole. One hand was now free. I reached over and undid the other, then worked at my legs. I rubbed my wrists and stood—wobbly on my feet, and groggy from the drugs. A pair of nurse's scrubs lay on the floor. I took off the flimsy gown and got dressed.

Looking up, my eye caught a dramatic turn unfolding in the left room. Fujimi was in midst of the swarm of NBC suits. The white figures encircled their unprotected boss, who had just appeared in the contaminated room. He was barking orders at them, pointing toward the door on the left. But they didn't move. They just looked at him with curious, tilted heads. He tried to make a step in that direction, but two stepped forward to block his way. Fujimi raved and shouted, his hair flopping side to side. But before he could work himself into another fury, he doubled over in a coughing fit. Clutching at his throat, hacking, he collapsed atop the body of Old Man Wetherspoon.

The biohazard specialists surrounded their latest subject. At first a few gestured at one another, apparently in deliberation. With a few shrugs and a few nods, they closed in. Two pulled Wetherspoon's body down from the chair. Three more pulled their struggling boss up in its place. As Fujimi was held down, four others strapped down his outstretched limbs. The ring of suited researchers held up their instruments, pointed them at their new Maruta, and another brought over the tray of surgical implements, a few grabbing swabs and syringes. The hulking cranium cutter slapped the blade of the bonesaw in his palm, waiting impatiently. Another reprogrammed the vital-signs scoreboard up on the wall.

"Karma's a bitch," I said.

On my side, the door flew open. Mary appeared, limping in, Lanza's bloody arm clinging to her neck. Her free hand carried the gun. Lanza slid to the floor.

"Oh my God," I said, rushing forward, catching the bulk of the dead weight. Lanza smiled up at me through dreamy, glassy eyes.

"My hero," Lanza said.

I tore the edge off my discarded gown and pressed it down on Lanza's wound. I glanced at Mary. She wiped some of the blood off on the thigh of her own gown, then kissed me. A joy of relief surged through me at her touch. Her jaw clenched.

"We need to get out of here—now," she said, sliding the magazine out of the gun, counting the rounds. "We don't have enough ammunition to shoot our way through any hospital security."

"Too risky," Lanza added, grimacing. "Who knows what kind of guards the Bureau has down here."

Mary slapped the clip back up in the gun. I trudged toward the opposite door, half-dragging Lanza with me.

"Where are you going?" Mary asked.

"Back the way I came in," I said. "There's a chute where they dump the Maruta."

"Meruda?" Mary said.

"Ma-Ru-Ta. I'll tell you later," I said. "Let's go."

I shoved at the door. It wouldn't budge. I pounded at it. Lanza gasped in pain and started sliding to the floor. I caught him, and Mary came up and put herself on Lanza's other side. Together we propped him up on his unsteady feet.

"Here, take this," Lanza said, out of breath.

Something was in his hand. I took it and saw it was Culling's handheld Atman, smeared in blood.

"Took it off that bastard while he was choking on his own blood," Lanza said, grimacing. "Might give us access."

I swiped it at the reader next to the door, and there was a soft click. I pushed it open.

"Alright—ready?" I asked the two of them.

Both nodded. But I was distracted by movement in the left room. Something strange was happening. The men in the biohazard suits were still struggling with Fujimi. His one hand was free, and he was hitting himself in the face. Mary turned to look. She chuckled.

"That man's completely lost his mind," she said, shaking her head.

"I don't think so," I said. "Quick, Mary. Turn off your Atman. Do it now."

"Why?" she said.

"Just do it. Do it now. Please."

"Fine." She tilted Lanza's weight onto me and raised her wrist.

She shrieked. The space where her Atman had been was raw and pink, a long row of angry stitches holding her flesh together in its place.

"What happened to my Atman?" she hollered.

"Thank God it's gone. Watch."

I nodded over at the window, because I knew what was coming next. Mary and Lanza turned to look. Fujimi was struggling against the white figures. But he wasn't struggling for freedom—instead he smashed his Atman against his nose again and again and again, blood smearing his face. He collapsed back in the chair, exhausted by his efforts.

But the NBC suits did not move to pin him down. They had frozen in place. They stood stunned as he shifted over and unfastened the strap on his other wrist. The suited figures began to convulse—some falling to the floor, others banging on their helmets, others running at the door and slamming into one another. A few scratched at the flesh within their protective gear like wild, mangy animals. As they all hit the floor, a coughing-but-calm Fujimi loosened his ankle restraints. He freed himself and stood, glancing briefly at the two-way mirror. He walked out of the room.

"We should go kill him," Lanza said, a rumble in his throat.

"Not now," I said. "Not while we can still make a clean escape out of here."

We went through the door. The long hallway window on our left showed a panorama of abomination: women and children in that waiting room struggled in the same death throes, same as the suited workers back in the laboratory. Bodies mid-seizure fell out of their chairs, women dropped infants, who tumbled hard on the carpet. Three young boys were slumped against the wall, blood dripping out their mouths, eyes staring at nothing. A roomful of healthy people died in front of our eyes.

"My God, Joe—what the hell is happening?" Mary said.

"Their secret project—the Tojo Virus," I said. "A deadly germ disseminated through their Atmans. The Bureau of Wellness wasn't waiting to deploy it after they got their land war in Asia. But I guess Fujimi had other plans, when he was about to become a guinea pig."

Lanza coughed.

"Unbelievable," the cop said, wincing as Mary let go of him to open the door. "Guess I owe you an apology."

"Stop talking," I said, grabbing him. "Keep walking."

Mary swiped the Atman, a little light next to the handle turned green, and she pushed through, holding the door for us. But she stopped short, grunting as the door slammed on Lanza's shoulder, making him groan in agony.

"Mary, can't you hold the damned..." I started to say.

But my voice broke off. Up against the wall, just a few feet into the next hallway, sat the trembling form of Betty Bathory. Her eyes were open, she was breathing, but her face was blank, frozen.

"My God, Joe—is she..." Mary said.

"Well, she has an implant," I said. "My guess is she'll die."

Mary started to cry, her face in her one free hand, gun hanging limp in the other one. I reached out and squeezed her shoulder.

"I wouldn't cry for her too much. She's part of it. She set you up with Abbud, helped fake the pregnancy, everything."

She turned slowly toward him. All the color drained from her face.

"'Fake the pregnancy?'" she said.

I stared at her. At that crucial moment, my voice failed me. And at that crucial moment, from far off somewhere, an alarm blared—loud, soft, loud, persistent. Lanza shifted his weight, grunting in pain.

"We have to get out of here," he said. "Can you guys talk about this after we get out of here?"

"Fake the pregnancy?" Mary repeated, not moving.

"I was going to tell you once we were…" I started to say.

Mary shrieked and stooped. Betty's hand was wrestling with the barrel of the gun, pulling the muzzle toward her mouth.

"Kill me," the nurse hissed, black bile bubbling off her lips. "Just kill me."

Mary jerked the gun free. She sobbed, shoulders heaving, a heavy wheezing from deep within. I touched her face, and she drew away.

"Kill me," gasped Betty, face turning purple. "I killed…your baby… I…murdered it… So, the Project…could do…its test…"

Mary stood tall, towering above the traitor. She pointed the gun at the nurse's face. Her finger quivered on the trigger.

"It was…a boy," said the nurse, wheezing.

The gun went still. Mary flicked the safety off. She breathed hard.

"Yes…it was…a boy," the nurse said. "I aborted it so we…could run…the experiment…use your body…"

The silence hung. Mary was completely still. I shuffled forward with Lanza.

"Mary," I said softly. "She doesn't deserve this."

I glanced down. My free hand gently touched her trembling wrist. I nodded.

"She doesn't deserve quick. She deserves to drown in her own fluids. Her organs liquefied. Slow. Painful. With agony."

Trembling, Mary lowered the gun. Her head gave the slightest of nods. She clicked the safety back on. She got on the other side of Lanza. Betty's eyes bulged, her death throes complete and utter torture. At least another few minutes of suffering left for her. I knew how the evil and conscienceless must feel as I smiled down at her.

"And good luck to you, Betty," I said, stepping away. "Because you'll need it in hell."

"No," she said, gasping. "Have mercy…"

We turned and walked all the way to the next door without looking back. We could hear the nurse's death rattles, the anguished spasms. But we ignored it. Mary reached for the doorknob.

"Wait," I said. "There were two big orderlies in there. You'll have to shoot them."

"Okay—stand behind me," Mary said. "I got this."

Counting to three, she slammed through the door, swinging the gun wildly from wall to wall. But the orderlies lay on their backs, eyes open, fresh blood smeared on their jaws, their large limbs twisted in impossible agonized contortions. The Atmans on their wrists flashed.

"Guess…most got…the big whammy," Lanza said. "I wonder…how far it reached."

"I wonder how many idiots have those things implanted in their bodies," I said. Mary scowled at me, and I shrugged. "At least none of us has one anymore."

Stepping past the corpses, the three of us made it to the soft landing pad where I had been dumped just an hour before, as far as I could tell. Propping Lanza against Mary, I pulled myself up toward the opening of the chute. I reached and felt along the sheer surface for any kind of handhold for climbing. But the surface was smooth and slick. I tried to claw my way up, but I slid back down into the soft padding. I stepped back and folded my arms.

"Any way to get up there?" Mary said.

"No chance," I said. "They made it escape-proof."

"And the rest of the hospital could be a war zone," Lanza said, shaking his head.

"Maybe not," I said. I pointed toward the orderlies' contorted forms. "If Fujimi's transmission went everywhere, then there are a lot of bodies up there. Probably a lot of the bad guys, along with the good. Only Fujimi was prepared for it."

We went back the way we came, Mary with the gun drawn, checking corners, her steps military-precise. Lanza and I slouched after her. We passed Betty Bathory, whose eyes were crimson, filled with blood. Her breathing had stopped. Mary kicked at her leg, and the body slumped down to the floor. Mary spat on her old friend and kept going.

But we came to the first door in the hallway—and it would not open. It had a numeric key pad, and a biometric reader with a red laser light in a black oval. I tried the passcode 137. I tried 731. I tried my hand, my thumb, my iris—but nothing worked. Lanza tried it, too—but to no avail. I howled in frustration for minutes. Then I had an idea. I went back to Betty's body and I dragged it back toward the reader, and smugly scanned her fingerprints, her limp hand, her lifeless eyes. Nothing worked. Minutes more passed. I realized I would try everyone in those rooms of death. Going around, I dragged the individual bodies around the corner to the reader. None worked. Then I went through each and every finger on each and every body. And when I reached Cullen's pinky finger, it clicked.

"Leave it to the Project to make some murderous nurse's little finger the skeleton key," I said.

"So we go up and through the hospital—and just walk out the front door?" Mary said.

"That's the plan," I said, shouldering Lanza's weight again. "But we need to go quick—keep us covered."

We went down the hallway, where the children and their mothers were all dead, like a horrific still-life. We went through the room where I had been held prisoner. Culling and Abbud's messy bodies lay in the right room. Everyone had died in the left, with the remains of the NBC-suited workers scattered around the corpse of Wetherspoon. But no Fujimi. We moved forward. Mary swiped Culling's Atman, and after a second, the light turned green, and she pushed the door gently open. We stepped through.

Three bodies lay in the white hallway, red smears on the walls around them: a nurse, an orderly, another figure in an NBC suit. Mary looked back and shrugged. I was baffled. I had never seen any of this wing of the hospital. But Wetherspoon's office would be at the far western part of the basement, probably somewhere dead-ahead, as far as I could tell. We just had to push through the chaos. I pointed forward. Mary checked around each doorway. Most of the doors were closed, but the few in the row which were open showed cadavers on gurneys, in various stages of dissection, wet organs bloated on hanging scales. Staff members lay dead all around.

It was an abattoir. Nothing more. No medical science to speak of—just death and depravity. I took a deep breath, swallowing the panic and fear and hatred coursing through me.

"What in the name of all hell…" Lanza said.

"Let's just push through as fast as possible," I said.

But one room stopped me. No body lay on the table, but there was a strange shape at the far edge. It was covered with a white shroud. I stopped, took a step, stopped again. Curiosity won out. I called out for Mary to stop too, and I propped Lanza up against the wall. The office was one in a straight row of autopsy rooms. Dread overcame me as I stepped closer to the draped cloth. But I crept forward. It looked like a jar underneath. As I neared within a step or two I noticed wires running out from underneath the shape to a tiny Atman that lay on a table next to it. I walked over and touched it, but recoiled as it burned my hand. I picked up a scalpel and tapped at the touch screen with its handle. Brainwave monitoring on a horizontal, like an EKG, waved across the screen. But no heart rate—no breathing rate. I tapped the screen once more, and with a quiet ping, a name appeared.

Esmeralda Foyle. The name of the girl glowed on the screen, with the mugshot I had come to know in my daydreams and nightmares, the green eyes and the tattoo of the yellow rose on her arched neck. How could she be here—was this entry old, some kind of error? I paused. I steeled myself. Reaching out with a shaking hand, I yanked the sheet off.

And there she was—at least a part of her. Esmeralda's pretty head was frozen in a roiling cauldron of fluids, with the wires running through the jar and into the base of her neck. It had been perfectly, surgically severed just below that beautiful flower.

I stared. My hands balled into fists. Leaning forward, I stared into those young eyes. Those eyes I had sought for weeks. I felt the impotence of having lost another patient through this whole sordid ordeal—the cataclysm which had consumed my life and my dreams. I had failed this patient, too. I had never even had a chance, but I had failed. And this girl had never had a chance once she fell into the evil machine of the Bureau of Wellness and their experiments. Tears of rage fell down my cheeks.

The head blinked. I leapt back. The eyes flicked in my direction, and the mouth inside the fluid moved, but emitted no bubbles in that churning fluid. The severed head was forming words, but not in any human language. Horror twisted the face, in a way that was no longer human. It tilted toward me, the cloudy eyes boring right through me. I lunged forward, pulled the plug connecting the Atman to the jar, and tossed the sheet back over it. I staggered backward, back toward the hallway where Lanza and Mary were waiting. They had seen nothing.

"What?" Mary said, gun raised, scanning in both directions. "What did you see?"

"Nothing," I said, wiping my face. "Nevermind. Just keep going."

We reached the last door. Mary swiped the card and pushed through.

We found ourselves in the main hallway just outside Wetherspoon's office. We had come through an unmarked door I had never noticed before. I must have walked past it a thousand times, but never taken notice. I turned us left and to the stairwell, where we pushed through another exit. Two more bodies—doctors this time—were splayed out on the stairs, limbs discolored and contorted. The three of us stepped around them, careful not to slip on the blood spatter. Mary led the way to the first-floor door. She pushed through quietly. She stopped suddenly, hands limp at her sides.

"Holy shit," she said.

"What? What is it?" I said.

But she didn't need to answer. A vision of hell opened before us. A line of bodies strewn along the hallway led to the front lobby of the hospital. At the far end, underneath the bright lights, was a lumpy mountain of...something. Two men in black were moving around it. It looked like they were dancing. The pile stretched at least halfway up to the forty-foot ceiling.

"Jesus, we have to go through there," Lanza said. "Every other exit is locked."

"If we have to go through, let's try not to shoot anybody we don't have to," I said.

Mary flicked the safety off the gun, chambered a round. She nodded.

"Let's break it down, Barney-style," she said. "Keep it real simple."

We stepped forward.

Corpses lay every few feet in the hallway—the same twisted and bloody faces, and the same contorted limbs. A few lights flickered overhead—perhaps the electronic virus had also infected the power grid. We proceeded forward, slowly, waiting for an ambush. I glanced into the faces of the corpses we passed every few feet. Two nurses, a janitor I'd known for my entire career, a half-dozen patients. Even Paddy McDermott, the trauma surgeon, lay motionless next to a vending machine, his sneer as contrarian in inglorious death as it had been in life.

"Goddamn, Paddy," I whispered. "Not you too."

"At least it was fairly quick," Lanza said, grimacing, squeezing his shoulder tight. "I can tell you from personal experience: bleeding to death ain't fun."

Lanza's foot slipped in a puddle of urine on the tiles. I caught his weight just before he could tip over. Using all my strength, I straightened us both.

"You're not bleeding to death," I said. "A real hospital will patch you up. Just hold on."

Mary had reached the entryway to the lobby. She froze. My eyes couldn't immediately focus on what the mountain was. But then, after some moments, I saw a small hand and an upturned face…within the mound. And I understood.

It was a pile of bodies. Limbs tossed, discolored, piled on like so many bundles of sticks. Mary lunged at some waiting-area chairs and retched, like her morning sickness sounds. I stared at the unmoving heap. It was an image that belonged in Wetherspoon's book on the 20th century: those horrifying pictures of a girl crying, bodies being bulldozed into ditches. I saw heads and hands and feet and naked shoulders and ankles. The two black-clad forms came from around the sides of the pile, splashing liquid in huge arcs from metal cans they held in two hands. Their movements were rhythmic, almost jolly. They were completely engrossed in their work, headphones jammed in their ears.

I deposited Lanza over on the chairs near Mary. The waterfall next to the entryway wasn't gushing water—it trickled a pinkish sanguinary ooze. Lanza groaned, and he slumped toward the floor. I went over to Mary, who was still retching. Blood was in the puddle beneath her. I rubbed her back and spoke into her ear.

"Just hold on for a minute, Mary," I said, sliding the gun from her hand. "I've got to get us through that door. I'll be right back."

"You remember how to use that?" she said, between blood-stained teeth, between heaves.

"You taught me. Our dates at the gun range," I said.

"Shoot to kill. There's no backup, and the police ain't coming," Lanza mumbled, leaning his head to indicate his shoulder camera. "And remember to take the safety off."

But the safety was already off. I nodded and stepped toward the pile of bodies.

As I neared within twenty feet, the shock of recognition struck me. The two moving figures were Stash and Stanislaw. A pungent aroma I remembered from childhood struck me. After a few steps I placed it.

Old-time gasoline. The flammable fuel. The mound was about to become a pyre.

Why on Earth would they burn down the hospital? But then I realized: they would also be getting rid of the evidence. I moved closer, the gun trained on them. At ten feet I lowered it. The two guards actually were dancing—Stash was doing a little stutter-step shuffle, and Stanislaw was bouncing in time with his great heaving douses of accelerant on the pile of the dead. They worked around the edges, splashing it up high toward a bloody naked fat man at the peak, bloated and stained red like a cherry, with a tiny stemlike prick dangling between his legs. I watched as gasoline splashed up on the fat man's face. I recoiled, seeing a ghastly greenish glow from within the mountain of the dead. The two guards were about to destroy evidence for the Bureau. But they looked unarmed—I had the drop on them.

"Hey guys," I said, both hands on the gun.

No response. Stanislaw sang the off-key bars of the feel-good hit of '87:

"Now, now, baby, baby / Now, now, now…"

I glanced at the door. It was already locked down. I would have to get the key from the two bozos.

"Hey guys!" I hollered.

"Now, now, baby, yeah…" Stash crooned, answering his partner in song.

I pointed the pistol up and pulled the trigger once. Reverb of the shot echoed through the huge high lobby, and a little plaster tumbled down from the ceiling at Stanislaw's feet. He looked up, then all around him. When he saw me, his eyes widened with surprise. Flicking his earphones off his head, he stammered.

"Doc!" he said. "D—didn't expect to see you here!"

Stanislaw stepped over and tapped his partner on the shoulder, who looked up and stumbled back in shock. They held up their hands and stared fearfully at the gun.

"Doc! We thought you were dead," Stash shouted, his headphones still in his ears.

"Glad to be among the living, Stash," I said. "What exactly are you two doing?"

"We're security guards," said Stash, as Stanislaw pulled out his earphones. "We secure and guard the hospital."

"Sure—I know why you're here most of the time," I said slowly. "But that doesn't explain why you're throwing gasoline on a pile of corpses in the hospital lobby."

"Sure it does," said Stash.

"It's all part of the emergency lockdown plan," added Stanislaw.

"You're supposed to start a bonfire of corpses in case of emergency," I said.

"Sure. Look up there," Stash said, pointing behind me.

I glared at them, stony faced. I did not want to turn my back for even a second on anyone within the hospital at that point. But their stares looked so simple, Polish eyes so blue and pale, souls so pure. I whipped my head around and caught a glimpse of a pulsing red light before spinning back. The two guards hadn't moved. I stepped back, turned fully around, and really looked. It was some kind of alarm, apparently.

"The Kraken gave us an employee handbook when she hired us," Stash said. "But she told us only one thing really mattered. And it wasn't in the book."

"The only important thing is, when that red light comes on, we start the Bureau of Wellness decontamination plan," Stanislaw said.

"Decontamination plan?"

"Yes," said Stanislaw, clearing his throat purposefully. He began to recite, like a child memorizing words learned for a school test: "In the event of a catastrophic breakdown in Bureau safeguards, employees are to burn all the bodies and equipment in the hospital." He blinked those vapid eyes, smiling at me. "It is our responsibility to lock down all the doors, burn the remains, and start the sprinklers."

"Acid sprinklers," Stash added, nodding. "Mixed in monsoon tanks on the roof. We're supposed to prevent the disease from spreading. At all costs."

"You thought I was dead," I said, changing the subject, "Why is that?"

Stash and Stanislaw exchanged a glance. They nodded.

"Dr. Fujimi told us you were dead," Stash said.

"Fujimi?" I said. "You've seen him?"

"He went to the elevator a few minutes ago," said Stanislaw. "He was sick or something. His face was all messed up. He kept shouting at us to start the fire. He pointed up at the warning light, gestured toward the morgue, and limped away. So we started throwing all the bodies in a pile and got out the gasoline, as the orders say."

"The dude left some trail of weird goo," Stash added, pointing to black streaks on the ground. "It was coming out of his ears, and he kept wiping it off on his sleeve. It was running down his leg, too."

Not taking my eyes off them, I crouched and poked at the goo with the gunbarrel. It was gelatinous, a black tinged with green—a jelling pus that wouldn't come off the pistol.

"Guess the doctor is pretty sick?" Stanislaw said.

"He's a very sick man, but I think I have just the cure," I said, squeezing the grip of the gun. "Do you know where he is, exactly?"

"He took the elevator to your—I mean his—office on the third floor," Stash said. "But the elevator stopped working, with the automatic lockdown. You'll have to take the stairs."

"Thanks. And guys," I said, "is there any way I can get my wife and my friend outside? They really need to get some medical attention themselves, at some other hospital. As soon as possible."

"The hospital's in lockdown—no one gets in or out now," said Stanislaw, reciting again, like a boy repeating a nursery rhyme he'd learned by heart.

"All the decontamination has to be completed, so no germs can escape," Stash added, in his own robotic voice.

"So what happens to you, when all this decontamination is going on, with the acid and the fire and all that?"

Stash and Stanislaw glanced at one another. Their eyes grew wide. They shook their heads.

"They never told us that," Stash said, a finger scratching at his temple.

"We never got that far in the handbook," Stanislaw said, biting his lip.

"Does Fujimi just expect you to die?" I said. "Is the Bureau ordering you to kill yourselves?"

The two security guards exchanged another look. Stanislaw raised his eyebrows. Stash coughed.

"You know, Doc," Stanislaw said, "just between us, there's a door underneath the staircase we leave open to get outside to smoke cigarettes. That one is never locked."

"Thanks, guys," I said. I took a step back toward Mary and Lanza, but remembered something and turned around. "You know—I would watch out for the Atmans on those bodies. If one of them sparks, with all that gasoline—"

An eruption ripped the room apart. The scalding flash and searing blast knocked me backward off my feet. There was screaming somewhere—from within the pile. The security guards ran in circles and slapped at each other, trying to put out the flames on their heads and their uniforms. They ran back toward the security desk, where they grabbed a fire extinguisher. But it fell to the ground.

I sprinted around the massive heat of the bonfire, keeping a wide berth from the raging flames. Sliding on the slippery tiles, I stuffed the gun in my waistband, and picked up another fire extinguisher from the wall. I unattached the hose, aimed it, and squeezed the trigger at the form of Stash, who vanished within the cloud of white. Three bursts, and his flames were snuffed. I chased after the flailing form of Stanislaw, spraying and chasing him back toward the burning pile. I extinguished him at the edge of the fire pile. I threw aside the extinguisher and dragged the burned guard back behind the security desk. Stash was stirring, but Stanislaw lay there, blackened and barely breathing.

"Go…take the staircase," Stash said.

"I'll get help for you," I said.

Footsteps approached behind me. I pulled out the gun and swung around, pointing it. Mary flinched backward. I tucked the gun back at my waist.

"What's the plan?" she said.

"I found a door out. Let's get Zo."

We walked back to Lanza, who was slumped into the chair. From across the lobby he looked asleep, or dead.

"You need to get out of here with Zo, and I need to stop Fujimi," I told her.

"Just call the cops, call the Bureau of Wellness," she said. "Let's just get out of here."

"You still don't get it, Mary," I said. "Fujimi is the Bureau of Wellness. The police are helping him. Our only hope is that I shoot the bastard before he starts some global outbreak."

We reached Lanza. My stomach bottomed out as I stooped to check for a pulse on my old friend, expecting the worst. But Lanza recoiled, smacking away my hand. It looked like the blood had clotted around his neck.

"I'm okay," he said, eyes opening, squirming up in the seat. "Let's roll."

We helped him up, and together we limped toward the raging fire. But as we neared the burning bodies, Lanza slowed.

"That can't be what I think it is…" he said.

"They're already dead," I said.

We walked past the security guards, Stash slumped forward on Stanislaw's body, trying to smack him awake with a blackened sooty hand. He looked up and waved weakly at us.

"Don't worry about us, Doc," he said. "We'll manage. We've had worse."

"Thanks, Stash."

"But do me a favor," the security guard said, holding up a finger.

"What's that, Stash?"

Stash pulled out a pistol and held the grip out to me.

"Let's hit happy hour next week."

"Deal," I said, taking the gun. "How long before those acid sprinklers start?"

"Twenty minutes, maybe. Maybe more. Maybe less," the guard said.

"I'll get help," I said.

Stash nodded, as he rocked his partner like he would have soothed a baby.

We moved on, past the security desk and into the narrow passage to the stairs. The emergency lighting was on, but the corridor was dark. We came to the door, and I opened it to the stairwell. A crack of light from the door to the outside shone, half a flight below. Four bodies with bloody mouths agape were splayed out on the stairs.

The three of us trudged down the few steps to the door, me leading the way around the mess. I opened the door into the cool rainy dusk. We grabbed ponchos from the dispenser by the door to cover our heads from the acrid raindrops. We limped out to a nearby bench, where Lanza fell with a relieved groan. I pulled out my Atman and turned it on. After a few seconds, it had a signal—and it didn't heat up.

"I guess it's just the newer implanted models," I said, handing the device over to Lanza. "Now call someone over at Clara Maass and wait for an ambulance. I'll be back in ten minutes."

I kissed Mary on her sweaty cheek, pulling the second gun from my waistband. She scoffed at me, shaking her head.

"This isn't a damned movie, Joe. You can't be that stupid."

"The guy's infected with one of his own supergerms, he's limping, he's unarmed. I've got two guns. I like my chances."

She stared at me. I squeezed her arm, gave her my most reassuring doctor's face.

"Somebody has to stop this guy," I said. "If he can zap an entire hospital full of people, who knows what else he can do?"

She looked at me. Her frown made her chin dimple. She shook her head.

"Maybe you're right," she said. "But I'm a better shot. I'm coming with you."

I gazed at my wife. Her eyes were cold, hard, steely—like in the pictures I'd seen of her from her tour of duty in the Middle East, before I'd known her. This was a woman who knew how to handle herself. I nodded and handed her one of the guns.

"Okay," I said. "Let's go get him."

"This is for Cornelius," she said, checking the magazine, then smacking it back up into the gun.

I stared at her.

"That was the name I picked," she said. "If it was a boy."

I smiled. I held the door open for her. She walked inside, gun aimed ahead. I started after her.

"Hey Joe," Lanza said.

"Yeah?" I said, pausing at the threshold.

"Follow Mary's lead. She's a Leatherneck. We always save the day."

"Got it. See you in a few."

Lanza gave me a thumb's up.

The stairwell looked darker than before. The emergency lighting cast shadows but didn't actually illuminate anything. There was just enough to see objects in the way, the corpses underfoot. I could make out the jagged outlines of bodies. As my eyes adjusted, I saw Mary. She stood, alert and tense, a few steps above. I came up close behind her.

"Spread out, but keep each other in view at all times," she said. "He could be anywhere, waiting in the shadows. Or just bleeding out somewhere."

"Should we be so lucky" I said, nodding.

She climbed. I grabbed a flashlight off the ground and followed.

MORE THAN THE WORLD DESERVED

U.S.A., 2087

Two dozen bodies covered the stairs on our short climb. Grotesque death on every step, slicks of blood and pus. But we were numb to them already. Mary picked her way around the corpses, and I was two steps behind her. A ceiling camera swiveled, tracking our slow progress.

We came to the third floor, and Mary hesitated. I realized she was the warrior, and I was just the doctor. She sensed something. But there was no time to lose. So I edged around her, and slowly pushed through the door and into the hallway, waving the flashlight to and fro.

Chaos. Blood smeared on walls, bodies on the floor, gurneys upended. Wires zapped, swinging from fixtures. A low hum, the growl of machinery and electronics on the fritz, buzzed from the erratic shadowplay. I moved out, on the right side of the hallway, as Mary fanned out on the left, sweeping in every direction with her gun drawn. We stepped forward.

"Do you know where he is?" she whispered.

"He's in my office," I said. "He has to be."

We walked slowly, scanning ahead and behind, stepping over and around bodies, the destruction, the blood. The stink of piss and shit was everywhere. The chaos of filth and infection had completely overthrown the order of the hospital, in mere minutes. Halfway down the hallway, a bright light shone from underneath a small door.

"Stop," I said. "Wait a second."

"What?" she said.

"Just wait. Cover me."

I jammed the gun in my waistband again. I opened the door. And there, in a brightly-lit closet, were a row of white NBC suits. I grabbed two, thrusting one at her.

"Put this on. We should have some protection before we approach a madman armed with biological weapons," I said.

"Alright—keep watch for a second," she said, setting the gun down on a gurney.

She unracked the protective suit, and slid it over her shoes, up her lithe legs, around her thin waist, and over the swell of her chest. I scoured the hallways, looking for any threat. But as she slowly wormed her way into the suit, an urge coursed through my limbs. An irrational urge for her. I was lost in the moment. For a few moments, I wasn't watching the hallways. Distracted right when I needed focus, right at the moment of danger. I knew it was foolish, but I couldn't help myself. Because we weren't parents-in-waiting any more. Years of trying, months of planning, and a reproductive miracle ultimately denied. None of that mattered any more. Instead, there was the void—the biological imperative nullified.

We would have a child someday, I was sure of that. No matter what, I would see to it. We would be parents someday. If we made it home, we'd try again that very night. If it didn't work for the hundredth time yet again—at least we would be loving one another. So as she zipped up that hood, disappearing inside that rubberized layer of protection, I felt the most acute need for her I could ever remember. I had to have her. I reached out.

A quick footstep behind. I started to turn. But a sharp pain stabbed into my outstretched arm, and I dropped the gun, which clattered to the ground. I howled and spun around. Suzanne Kranklein stood there, a demonic elf with gritted teeth, pressing the plunger of a syringe deep in my shoulder with all her might. I pulled back, and I cracked her across the face with my hand. She went stumbling to the wall. The syringe was still in my arm. I yanked it out. I lunged forward, thrusting it into her own arm. She yelped in terror as I dug it down deep into her bicep, pushing as hard as it would go, scraping at the humerus. I pressed the plunger all the way down to the hilt.

"No, stop—we've got to ask her…" Mary's voice came from far away.

"I don't give a good goddamn what she has to say," I said, tugging at the syringe, then shoving it hard forward, deeper, a different angle into the flesh. The Kraken screamed. Mary pulled me back, but I stayed fast, my forearm jammed hard up under my former boss' chin, choking her the way Lanza had choked me just hours before.

"What's in the syringe, Suzanne?" I growled at her, pressing harder into her windpipe. "Tell me, or I'll kill you."

"I'm a…dead woman…anyway," she croaked.

And she did look like she was dead. Her usually-pale skin was even paler, to a blanched white, broken only by the dark sunken circles underneath her eyes.

Those eyes had a wild, crazed look. Feeling for the Atman in her arm, I burned the tip of my finger on the simmering metal.

The Kraken was doomed, my doctor's intuition told me immediately.

I released my grip on her and backed away. Her hand went to her throat as she wheezed, sucking air desperately.

"Was she part of it, Joe?" Mary said, the gun aimed at the Kraken's head.

"She was," I said. "But this test was above her paygrade. The Kraken never got full immunity."

Anger twisted the Kraken's face, pride overcoming the anguish and the germs coursing through her system. Her Atman flashed erratically and seemed to send up a slight puff of ozone from her wrist.

"What did you call me?" she said, her pale face suddenly turning crimson. Grimacing, she doubled over, and vomited on the floor. I slapped her back instinctively as powerful heaves of blood thrust up out of her throat, splashing everywhere.

"Pretty nasty, Suzanne," I said. I turned to Mary, who was fully suited. "Let's bring her with us. I'm sure we can use her as leverage with Fujimi."

"But Joe," Mary said within her rubber bubble, reaching out and grabbing my arm. "Don't you want to put on one of the suits?"

I stopped to look at her.

"I'm already infected, Mary. What's the point?"

I picked my gun up off the floor, checking the safety was off.

"My only hope is to get a cure," I added.

"No cure," the Kraken said, her head shaking, bile slopping from her lips. "I was promised immunity. No vaccine, no antibody, no inoculation. No cure."

I yanked her by the ear toward my office. The pain in my shoulder powered the rage coursing through me.

"Then we won't have to worry how messy this gets."

Her feet slid on the ground, smearing streaks of red and black fluids. She fell twice, and I dragged her limp body along the floor. After the second time, I kicked her in the ribs, whispered some horrible quiet threats in her ear that shocked even me. We were getting close to the end of the hallway—another fifty feet, twenty feet. A new, astringent smell closed in around us as we came to the darkened threshold of my old office. I herded the Kraken in front of us.

Mary nodded. Taking a deep breath, I shoved our new hostage through the doorway, and we followed her, guns drawn. The Kraken stumbled and fell to the floor. We traced the darkness with our fingers on the triggers.

"Step into my office, Dr. Barnes," said a voice from the area of the desk. The tiny green glow of an Atman popped in the darkness, and over it loomed the vague shadowy face of Fujimi, lit strangely from underneath.

We aimed our guns. He only smiled. It had to be a trap. I looked around but saw nothing in the darkness.

"Come in, Doctor. You too, Mrs. Barnes," Fujimi said. "Have a seat. I haven't set any traps. We have some things to talk about."

Silence—no movement. The Kraken groaned and gurgled softly on the floor. I stooped to haul her up again.

"Don't bother," Fujimi said loudly. "She's not much use as a hostage, since she can die, for all I care."

Fujimi set the Atman down on the desk, which threw a pale green light across the room.

"Now please lower the guns and have a seat."

"Why would we do that?" Mary said, squinting down the pistol sight.

"Well," Fujimi said, his finger hovering over the glowing screen. "If you were to do something rash, then I would have to do something equally rash."

His finger circled over the pulsing Atman.

"What is that?" I said, the hair on my neck prickling even as the question left my lips.

"That's what I want to talk about," Fujimi said. "And you must admit—you're curious about why I don't feel I need a conventional weapon right now. So you may as well sit down and talk this over with me. I might have just what the doctor ordered, you might say. Something to counteract what you're injected with, Dr. Barnes."

Mary and I exchanged glances. We edged slowly around the Kraken toward the chairs, our eyes now accustomed to the dark. We sat. Nothing happened—no traps or ambushes sprung at us. I stared at Fujimi's shadow-crossed face. In the soft green luminescence, I saw little striations along the ridge of his skull line. They were like sores, but they looked darker, and deeper.

"You don't look well yourself, Doctor," I said, gun on my knee, finger still on the trigger guard.

"Oh—this," Fujimi said, scratching at the biggest divot of all, above his right eyebrow. It scraped off like a massive zit, oozing some dark fluids. He wiped it on my old desk blotter. "It's nothing. Just a side effect from one of the vaccines.

"You see, I was ready for an eventual security breach. I always told the Bureau administrators down in Washington that a no-name hospital in New Jersey wasn't the best place to conduct vital Project weapons tests, but they never listened to me. So I took my own precautions."

He winked, jostling loose a flap of flesh from the hole in his brow. He reached to the desk, and Mary pointed the gun at him. Fujimi's hand paused. He smiled and pointed toward a half-full tumbler on the desk. Slowly, he took it in his hand and lifted it to his lips. He drank deeply. His other hand was still poised over the Atman's touch screen, his fingers cool as a gunslinger's, and still as a surgeon's. Something hung in the balance. We had a stand-off. Fujimi set the glass back down.

"What's with the Atman?" I asked, trying to keep my voice level.

"Getting a bit ahead of ourselves, aren't we, Doctor?" Fujimi said, twirling his fingers in the emerald glow. "As doctors, don't we start at the beginning, when it comes to a prognosis?"

Silence.

"Go on," I said.

"First off, most of what dear, departed Cornelius Wetherspoon probably told you about the Bureau is true," Fujimi said. "But he's also been out of the loop for quite some time, so he doesn't know any of the latest developments."

"Latest developments," Mary repeated.

"As in, the coming war," Fujimi said. "All the armies of the globe are converging, as we speak, on a tiny peninsula in Asia. They're going to play out their little war games to determine who controls the world's prosperity for the next century. I'm sure you heard Saxas blathering on and on over the last few days. Tensions have never been higher."

"The Bureau is deploying to Korea," I said.

"Dr. Barnes, you're an intelligent man," Fujimi said, reaching again for the glass. "You already see where this is going."

"Where is this going?" Mary said.

The glass shook, rattling ice cubes, in Fujimi's hand.

"Where this is going, Mrs. Barnes, is that this country has been preparing for the next big conflagration since the last big conflagration. There's been a hundred years of research and development all leading to this. We will ensure American and Japanese interests are safe."

"They're going to release an electronic virus against our enemies in Korea," I said. "Hell, it's not the first time the bastards have used germs in a war there."

Fujimi laughed. It was a harsh, grating sound.

"That's part of it, Doctor," he said. "You've learned quite a bit about Project 137, haven't you? But you still don't know everything."

He chuckled, reached again for the tumbler. With a free finger he pointed at me. But he coughed, a deep cough that rumbled something loose in his chest. He hacked violently. The cubes rattled hard in the glass, some falling out and onto the floor.

Mary and I glanced at each other. Mary's latexed finger quivered near her trigger. Fujimi's hand was still steady, just inches over the glowing Atman. If one of us shot him, that hand would fall right onto the touch screen. I waved her off. She untensed, and I breathed deeply. Fujimi stopped coughing, gargled the liquor, then spat down between his legs onto the floor. A metallic clang reverberated.

"Spittoon," Fujimi said, wiping his mouth with the back of his sleeve, tipping the last of the drink down his throat. "When I moved in, I thought it would be a nice American touch to a bland office, with your kitschy religious sculptures, these pictures of your Maruta."

"Patients, Fujimi. Patients whose lives I saved."

Fujimi smiled. He set the glass down.

"Yes—that's nice. But we're off track, aren't we?" he said. "We were talking about the totality of Project 137. And you were curious about what's on this screen. With a little tap of my finger here, a virus gets uploaded to every fourth-generation Atman on Earth." He laughed.

"The same virus you released before?" I said.

"The same, but different," Fujimi said, picking up a pen and scratching his scalp. When he set it down, a clump of desiccated flesh was stuck to the end, and a foul odor wafted through the room. "More widespread, and virulent. More effective."

"So anyone with a new Atman is going to die," Mary said.

"Almost one-hundred percent of them. But each of the earlier three generations processes the same virus in different ways. The first generation produces a flu-like germ with a mortality rate of ten to twenty percent. The second generation produces a more-extreme kind of fever, violent psychosis, a death rate of one in three. The third acts like a flesh-eating virus in only a small minority of the Maruta. Really, it's only the fourth that causes wholesale death. Like a fast-acting Ebola. Within minutes, in most cases."

"Don't different countries have different versions of the Atman—" I stared to say.

"You catch on quickly, Dr. Barnes," Fujimi said. "Yes, the upload I have right now at my fingertips will only kill some hundreds of thousands in, say, the United States and Japan. That'll be the collateral damage."

He smiled. But then his face turned down in a grimace.

"Europe won't fare as well—some millions will die. Africa will probably have the biggest die-off since colonialism, too. But it's mainland Asia, from China and Mongolia down into Indochina, over to Afghanistan and India, which has the most fourth-generation devices. Heady days of famine and death are coming soon. It should soften the continent up nicely for the next phase of this war."

My mouth hung open, flabbergasted, as these perverse words tumbled out of the madman's mouth. Such sweeping scale, just offhanded indifference to the coming Armageddon. At first, I could think of nothing to say. But after some seconds, I mustered a question.

"What's the death toll?"

"At the Bureau, we prefer the term 'cull count,'" Fujimi said, smile twitching at his lips. "I wouldn't hazard a guess. More of the enemy than of us. Many more. And that's what counts."

Fujimi coughed again.

"No matter how you look at it, the next ten years will be fascinating days for the historians—if there are any left," he said. "We've been overdue for a world conflict for quite some time, especially since the Blackout wiped out accurate accounts of the 20th century. The time is now, the moment is ripe."

"The end," I mumbled. A metallic taste filled my mouth.

"It's going to be the culmination of long years of research and diplomacy," Fujimi said, wagging his finger. "The work my former self started more than a hundred years ago. America is the only reason the world flourished over the last hundred years. It gave me a chance to continue my legacy. The only place that would allow cloning, and the research to proceed."

"Cloning?" I said. "Former self?"

Fujimi grinned, shook his head.

"Perhaps I said too much," Fujimi said. He grabbed at the corner of his lip, twisting a moustache that wasn't there. "You should be feeling rather ill, Dr. Barnes. Would you like something to ease the pain?"

I turned my head, and the room wheeled all around me. My eyes burned. The gun in Mary's hand twitched, but I waved her off. I just had to get Fujimi to pull his hand away, to let down his guard for a moment. I needed that one moment of opportunity.

"I don't have an Atman," I said, stalling him. "I can't have the Tojo Virus."

"Yes, that's true, you don't have an Atman," Fujimi said. "But the electric virus had to have a biological precursor. About fifteen years ago, we perfected the organic strain of the Tojo agent. It was engineered to act like Ebola—but it was too unpredictable for weapons purposes. Our dearly departed colleague on the floor there injected you with that early version. Not elegant, but I would say it will do the trick."

The room spun harder as I glanced over at the lifeless form of the Kraken. Mary's rubber hand slipped into mine. The room seemed brighter, somehow. I could feel my eyes searing in my skull, the room swimming in delirious waves. I could feel my flesh burning from the inside. I knew for the first time the hand of death. Fujimi's voice made my brain wobble. I focused again on Suzanne Kranklein's corpse on the floor. She had contracted the electronic virus maybe an hour before. How long would it take? I could have mere moments, or maybe days. Or perhaps Fujimi was lying again, a madman playing a poker hand with the chips down. I felt unconsciousness closing slowly over me.

"The plan is all ready to go into effect," Fujimi said, still talking. "The war begins, and we start with a magnificent advantage. We've got cures and vaccines up our sleeves. Cures for cancers, genetic fountains of youth. The answers to a billion DNA riddles. The Bureau of Wellness has only been waiting for the bloodletting to unveil all sorts of medical miracles.

"The second Pax Americana will be a true paradise—a culled population, plenty of food, plenty of medicine, enlightenment," he added, his voice becoming a harsh rasp. "It will be a place on earth for the true believers. The best people, selected for their value to the country. The Bureau will make sure of that."

My ears rang—perhaps another symptom of the pathogen surging in my veins. Fujimi's words echoed in his head. Plenty of medicine, true believers, the ones who survive.

My eyes flamed. Sight and sound blurred—the world was closing shut. But the tremors wracking my body were as much from rage as they were from the virus. I could barely see the scab who sat in my chair, the murderer who had caused untold suffering, who had beheaded a young girl in the name of science. The killer who had orphaned an awkward teenager twenty years before.

In one motion, without aim, I swung the gun up and squeezed the trigger.

It was a perfect shot. The bullet punched through Fujimi's trachea. A panicked look crossed his face as his eyes bulged in disbelief, and his hand fell onto the Atman touch-screen. The blood spurted from the hold in his throat as he gurgled. He reached for his glass, then crumpled sideways to the floor. I had dropped the gun after the recoil, but I stumbled up, leaning heavily on the desk, and grabbed for the Atman. I couldn't see the screen, but I picked it up. It was so heavy. Finally, I could read the words.

"Upload beginning," it said.

The superbug was being injected out into cyberspace, then pumped to the hearts and brains of billions, I knew. The meter clicked up—first at ten, then twenty-five, then thirty-five percent.

I tapped at the screen, frantically fumbling, trying to kill the program. At my feet, Fujimi choked and drowned in his own blood. I kicked him once with the last of my rage but focused on the screen in front of me.

The machine asked for a password. I knew it had to be the forbidden code word.

MERUDA, I typed in.

Wrong password.

I smacked my face with my palm.

Fifty-five percent.

MARUTA, I corrected myself, cursing.

Wrong password.

The meter crept up to sixty, seventy, then eighty percent. The green bar neared its end.

Upload nearly complete, it said.

I stumbled, knocking the Atman a bit to the one side. But something had stopped it from sliding across the blotter. Blindly I ran my hand over the edges of the machine—and my fingers closed around a cord. A wire running from the flashing uploading Atman, off into the darkness of the office somewhere. My brain was whirling, but I yanked it.

The screen went black—completely dead. Perhaps the virus had killed the machine, I thought dreamily. I felt unsteady on my feet, like I was about to fall. We had failed, and an apocalypse was nigh. I shut my eyes.

But then something tapped me on the forehead. I looked up drunkenly. It was a plug. Mary's hand held the end of a power cord in front of my face. Despite my weakening eyes, I saw her wide grin.

"For being a genius, the guy was pretty stupid, running on auxiliary power," she said. "You stopped him, Joe."

I smiled. I was so sleepy. I tried to smile, but I felt a tickle at the sides of my mouth, and I saw my wife's eyes open in horror, her mouth shouting something. My eyes rolled back in my head, and I collapsed face down on my old desk.

THE DREAM OF THE DEEP

Water compressed my face. My lungs burned. The darkness was total, once again. I waited for the cavernous deep, the bowels of the fish, to rise from the depths and swallow me whole. The fight in me was gone, my limbs formless, my form amorphous. I was sick and dying. So I went limp, surrendering to the all-consuming void.

But then—air. The water parted from my eyes and cheeks and mouth, and I gasped, drawing in huge sucking breaths.

A great shaking, a trembling reverberated through me.

Then there was light. Brighter and brighter, totally blinding. It flickered.

My eyes opened. I awakened.

I was in a car. The backseat of a car. The sun in the upside-down window overhead burning my cheeks. The shadows of trees whipped past, rippling the rays of light. Warm and fuzzy, a bit numb, and soundless. The car hit something, bouncing me hard in the seat. Suddenly I heard tinkling, the clatter of a million pieces of metal. My head ached, throbbed.

"What—the—hell," I said.

"Awake—finally. Thank God, thank God," Mary's voice said from somewhere.

I turned my head, and Mary was in the driver's seat, steering the car, reaching up and angling down the rearview mirror to get a better look at me. Her eyes were raw, red. and wet in the reflection.

"Mary," I said, my voice dry and cracked.

"You were sick, and you got better," she said. "Just close your eyes and rest. We'll stop for the night soon. I'll tell you then."

She kept checking the sideview mirrors, checking the traffic behind them.

"But Mary—"

"Shush and get some rest," she said. "I'll tell you everything once we get somewhere safe."

She fixed the mirror and kept driving. I groaned, but it was lost in the blare from the radio—it was that damned song, the feel-good hit of the summer of '87.

Now, now, baby, baby / Now, now, now…

Now, now, baby, yeah…

She hummed the tune, off-key. The music and the fatigue overcame me. As I faded into limbo, the radio played on. A series of ads for the new Atman release, a rerun of *How Low Can You Go*—and then the song again, cycling the electronic choruses, repeating and repeating and repeating. I hummed along as I drifted away, not realizing I knew the song by heart.

When I opened my eyes, it was cool and dark. The car had stopped. At my feet, the door opened. I lifted my head, and Mary stood there.

"We're here, hon," she said, grabbing my ankles, gently tugging me out.

I slid out of the car to the ground with her help, my knees cracking and my muscles throbbing. The dusk was fading to black. The car was parked in front of a long two-story building with many doors. A sign overhead said "OLUMBUS OTEL" in pink neon, the first letters short-circuited. The place had to be a hundred years old—maybe two hundred.

"Where are we?" I asked.

She took a deep breath, hands on her hips.

"Nebraska," she said.

"Nebraska?" I asked.

She nodded and walked away, lugging a big suitcase in each hand. I grabbed a light satchel and followed. I looked up, and all around, but I saw no cameras following my movements. She stopped in front of room 217, put down one suitcase, and unlocked the door with a brass key.

The motel room was clean and spare, beige and brown, with a TV and a fridge with tiny bottles of liquor. It smelled like chemicals, and the plastic sheets on the bed had a certain sheen. Mary set down the luggage and locked herself in the small bathroom. The shower gushed. I sat on the edge of the bed, staring at a fly which crashed into the window again and again. My mind was blank, my body fairly pulverized. I felt at my jugular for a pulse, and pinched my limbs for any symptoms, any vestige at all, of the Tojo virus. I felt like I had a hangover—but nothing worse than that. When the door opened again, Mary's middle third was wrapped in a towel, as she twisted her hair into two braids. She went into the fridge and poured herself something from an amber-colored nip. She sat next to me on the edge of the bed.

"Mary, why are we in Nebraska? What happened at the hospital?"

She took a long pull of the drink, then handed me the glass. It was whiskey.

She smiled, then reclined on the bed. The back of her hand went onto her forehead. It was very dramatic. She spoke in a weary voice.

"You were unconscious for three days since you died," she told me.

"Died?" I said, panic rising.

"Yes—died," she said.

So she told me a story.

The virus had stopped my heart after I had shut down the Atman—and the upload of the Tojo Virus to the rest of the world, she said. She had scrambled, panicking, not knowing what to do around my dying body. But then she thought of the Old Man's words.

Before the experiments began, Mary and Wetherspoon had been restrained on pallets in an antechamber while the rooms were prepped, the equipment calibrated, and the supplies restocked. The Bureau staff thought their two guinea pigs were unconscious from the drugs, but the doses had not been mixed strong enough. They were groggy, but they still had enough sense to commiserate like drunk friends.

The Old Man told her about his decades observing human experiments. The voiceless souls who died in secret basements of hospitals, or wasted away at home, poisoned for the greater good of the nation. He told her about some colleague who had blown his head off from the guilt of what he had done, Bill Something or Other. The Old Man explained how he had resolved to bring justice to the people who he had not saved, his victims-by-proxy. He spoke in an unwavering voice, but as Mary watched, a procession of tears trickled down his ragged cheek, falling on the shoulder of his blue hospital gown.

Wetherspoon explained his plans for Joe Barnes, her husband the wunderkind who would take over his work. The younger doctor had been groomed for the part: to stop the Bureau of Wellness' operation before it infected the rest of America, he said.

"He spoke in grandiloquent terms like that," Mary said. "He was something, that Old Man."

"What else did he say?" I asked, rubbing at my eyes, trying not to cry.

"He told me about your parents, Joe. And about the test tube," she said.

I reached for the necklace I'd worn my entire adult life. But it was gone.

"Where is my necklace?" I said, the tears then starting to tumble down my face.

"'The most important thing,' Wetherspoon said, 'was to realize the Tojo Virus was going to get released, one way or another. And we would have to protect ourselves. There is no known cure—officially.

"But a single test tube contained a dead sample of the prototype virus taken from one of the first victims, Neal had said. A vaccination which held the crucial antibodies to destroy the germ. That sample was thought to be lost. But it had been thrown in the lap of a teenaged orphan nearly twenty years ago, Wetherspoon told me."

"You mean—"

"I injected you with the fluid in the test tube," said Mary. "It was Wetherspoon's crazy idea. And you lived, Joe. That dinky little trinket you wore around your neck for as long as I've known you actually saved your life."

Upon hitting my veins, Mary did chest compressions, then zapped me with a defibrillator paddle she'd found in the hallway. My heart again began to beat, and my breathing returned—first fitful, then stable. Then she hauled me out on a gurney and pushed me down the hallway and carefully down the stairs. When we were outside, Lanza still sat there on a bench, clutching his bloody trapezius with one hand, the other pointing a few fellow cops toward the front entrance of the hospital. The officers rushed in that direction, not noticing two more haggard survivors emerging from the back stairwell. Lanza whistled as we approached, winced, and tossed Mary the keys to his patrol car.

"They won't notice it's gone for a few hours," Lanza said. "By that time, I'll be so high on painkillers I won't remember who stole the keys". He winked. "But drive fast," he added.

Mary dumped me into the passenger seat, and she got behind the wheel. Then she drove to the house. She packed a few things, pictures and soap, water. She ditched the patrol car, loaded up our own car. And then she drove west, without stopping, until dark fell. Parking at a scenic overlook off the ultrahighway in western Pennsylvania, she slept alongside my comatose body on the backseat, listening to my heartbeat.

They'll be looking for you, Lanza had instructed her before she fled west. Stay off the ultrahighway. Take the local roads. Stay at the dirtiest motels. You're not the Bureau's top priority, and as long as you're off the main circuits of the grid, they won't find you. They're going to be too busy covering their own tracks, after the Sick Saint Almachius Atrocity. That's what they're calling this on the news—an isolated outbreak of disease which wiped out an entire hospital in New Jersey. The TV reporters might actually have to ask the tough questions this time. The Bureau will be too busy with that to hunt you."

So after that first high-speed burn down the ultrahighway and the first fitful night of sleep on a darkened hillside, she pulled onto the rambling one-lane roads, the reedy capillaries of America. And she kept heading west, stopping at the red lights in small towns, turning off every few hundred miles to fuel up and pick up a cheeseburger, paying for all of it with the emergency cash she'd taken from the cookie jar in the kitchen. The slack-jawed merchants at the roadside dives looked at her with wide yellowed eyes; they hadn't seen cash since the Blackout. But they took it.

No swiveling cameras or pilotless planes tracked our movement toward the setting sun on the horizon.

She turned onto the shoulder of the road and injected me with fluids and nutrients every couple hundred miles, tying off the tourniquet and finding a vein like we were vagabond junkies of old. I started murmuring in my sleep, alive, but still catatonic.

Mary talked to me. I had to be somewhere in there, just mustering up the strength again to wake up, she figured. So she discussed things with me—about what the clouds looked like in the blue sky, whether rain was coming, asking what I thought about discovering my parents were murdered all those years ago, and could you believe what a fucking traitor Betty Bathory was. How we had stopped the Tojo Virus from being uploaded and saved billions of lives. Things like that. She didn't mind the silence.

She drove during the day. She had no compass, no map—but she had an old analog clock. She didn't go fast—just the speed limit the entire way. She fled the sun in the morning and chased it west in the afternoon. When it disappeared for the night, she turned off and tucked in by the side of desolate country roads where American progress had never touched.

Suddenly, out of the flatness of the Great Plains, a washed-out sign announced, *Nebraska…the Good Life*. It had to be at least a hundred years old. That was the third night. The following day, just as she thought she could not go on driving, stopping, fueling, talking herself hoarse in the rearview, I awoke to the jarring car. And here we were, in a fleabag motel in the Heartland of America. On the run, in the vast empty miles at the center of a continent.

I scratched at my beard, full and thick now along my jaw. She hadn't moved. I finished the glass of whiskey, stood, and walked toward the fridge.

"So we're fugitives," I said.

"Not exactly," she said. "It's just better if we lay low for a while."

"Where can we go? A million security cameras will see us. We can't hide forever."

She turned on her side, drawing up her knees, raising her elbow, propping her head on her hand.

"They won't see us if we're careful," she said. "As long as we stay off the ultrahighways, we're off the grid, Lanza told me. They never reconnected most of the locals in Middle America after the Blackout, he told me. The Heartland is still in the dark. It's like we've gone back in time, to a simpler place."

She smiled at me.

"*Nebraska is the Good Life*," she said. "The sign said so. My sister says so. It must be true."

I poured a short glass, tipped it back, and drained it. My head swam. I could almost believe it—the Good Life. I was already drunk. Or maybe I was just released from my worries.

"The money was…" I started to say.

"I know, Joe," she said. "It doesn't matter anymore. We're doing the best we can with what we have now. That's all we need."

"So—where are we headed?" I asked, wiping my eyes free of the few tears welling there.

She leaned back, arms spread wide. She closed her eyes.

"Just come here and kiss me," she said, a blind smile spread across her face.

With a tired stoop, I lay down next to her, the plastic sheets crinkling beneath us.

THE END

Acknowledgments

This book could not have happened without the helping hands of many, both the dead and the living.

Chief among these is Arafat Kazi, a man who saw the value in some depraved history. Susan Breen noticed ways to improve everything. Meg LaTorre was a person whose enthusiasm is catching, and whose eyes are keen. Greg Watry provided more astute insight. Dick Paterson's red pen gave this book added merits I may not have added on my own. Leonard Cole's authoritative works on biological weapons were not only inspirational, they were crucial to understanding some concepts that would have otherwise eluded me.

A bit about people I never met: the historian Sheldon Harris was a man who I would have loved to interview, and this book benefited wholly from his crucial work on Unit 731, Factories of Death. Hal Gold and Daniel Barenblatt followed in his considerable footsteps, and also illuminated some all-consuming darkness in their respective works. The tragic figure of Iris Chang (and her inability to shake the ghosts) was somewhere in the background here, too.

Pandamoon Publishing is a great garden in which to plant these roots. Zara Kramer saw the value from the outset. Heather Stewart and Rachel Schoenbauer have laser-like precision with words and story. Christine Gabriel and Elgon Williams and Laura Kemp have been as encouraging as colleagues can be. Any shortcomings are my own.

And of course, this story would never have happened without my resident ladies, wife (and secret editing weapon) Amy, and my little girl Izzy. My mom Trish is pretty great, too.

About the Author

Seth Augenstein is a writer of fiction and non-fiction. His short stories have appeared in more than a dozen magazines and fiction podcasts. He spent a decade writing for New Jersey newspapers, most recently at *The Star-Ledger*. He picked up some state journalism awards. Currently he writes about true-life horror and crime solving for *Forensic Magazine*. In college he studied under Nobel Laureates Saul Bellow and Elie Wiesel, graduating with a degree in English and History, and a concentration in British Romanticism. For a stint of several months, he was also a tour guide at the James Joyce Centre in Dublin. Now back in the Garden State, he lives on a wooded ridge overlooking a New Jersey highway with a wife, daughter, cats, a dog named Mishima, and the occasional interloping mouse.

Thank you for purchasing this copy of **Project 137**. If you enjoyed this book, please let the author know by posting a review.

Growing good ideas into great reads…one book at a time.

Visit www.pandamoonpublishing.com to learn about other works by our talented authors.

Mystery/Thriller/Suspense

- *A Flash of Red* by Sarah K. Stephens
- *Evening in the Yellow Wood* by Laura Kemp
- *Fate's Past* by Jason Huebinger
- *Graffiti Creek* by Matt Coleman
- *Juggling Kittens* by Matt Coleman
- *Killer Secrets* by Sherrie Orvik
- *Knights of the Shield* by Jeff Messick
- *Kricket* by Penni Jones
- *Looking into the Sun* by Todd Tavolazzi
- *On the Bricks Series Book 1: On the Bricks* by Penni Jones
- *Project 137* by Seth Augenstein
- *Rogue Saga Series Book 1: Rogue Alliance* by Michelle Bellon
- *Southbound* by Jason Beem
- *The Juliet* by Laura Ellen Scott
- *The Last Detective* by Brian Cohn
- *The Moses Winter Mysteries Book 1: Made Safe* by Francis Sparks
- *The New Royal Mysteries Book 1: The Mean Bone in Her Body* by Laura Ellen Scott
- *The New Royal Mysteries Book 2: Crybaby Lane* by Laura Ellen Scott
- *The Ramadan Drummer* by Randolph Splitter
- *The Teratologist* by Ward Parker
- *The Unraveling of Brendan Meeks* by Brian Cohn
- *The Zeke Adams Series Book 1: Pariah* by Ward Parker
- *This Darkness Got to Give* by Dave Housley

Science Fiction/Fantasy

- *Becoming Thuperman* by Elgon Williams
- *Children of Colonodona Book 1: The Wizard's Apprentice* by Alisse Lee Goldenberg
- *Children of Colonodona Book 2: The Island of Mystics* by Alisse Lee Goldenberg
- *Chimera Catalyst* by Susan Kuchinskas
- *Dybbuk Scrolls Trilogy Book 1: The Song of Hadariah* by Alisse Lee Goldenberg
- *Dybbuk Scrolls Trilogy Book 2: The Song of Vengeance* by Alisse Lee Goldenberg
- *Dybbuk Scrolls Trilogy Book 3: The Song of War* by Alisse Lee Goldenberg
- *Everly Series Book 1: Everly* by Meg Bonney
- *.EXE Chronicles Book 1: Hello World* by Alexandra Tauber and Tiffany Rose
- *Fried Windows (In a Light White Sauce)* by Elgon Williams
- *Magehunter Saga Book 1: Magehunter* by Jeff Messick
- *Revengers Series Book 1: Revengers* by David Valdes Greenwood
- *The Bath Salts Journals: Volume One* by Alisse Lee Goldenberg and An Tran
- *The Crimson Chronicles Book 1: Crimson Forest* by Christine Gabriel
- *The Crimson Chronicles Book 2: Crimson Moon* by Christine Gabriel
- *The Phaethon Series Book 1: Phaethon* by Rachel Sharp
- *The Sitnalta Series Book 1: Sitnalta* by Alisse Lee Goldenberg
- *The Sitnalta Series Book 2: The Kingdom Thief* by Alisse Lee Goldenberg
- *The Sitnalta Series Book 3: The City of Arches* by Alisse Lee Goldenberg
- *The Sitnalta Series Book 4: The Hedgewitch's Charm* by Alisse Lee Goldenberg
- *The Sitnalta Series Book 5: The False Princess* by Alisse Lee Goldenberg
- *The Wolfcat Chronicles Book 1: Wolfcat* by Elgon Williams

Women's Fiction

- *Beautiful Secret* by Dana Faletti
- *The Long Way Home* by Regina West
- *The Mason Siblings Series Book 1: Love's Misadventure* by Cheri Champagne
- *The Mason Siblings Series Book 2: The Trouble with Love* by Cheri Champagne
- *The Mason Siblings Series Book 3: Love and Deceit* by Cheri Champagne
- *The Mason Siblings Series Book 4: Final Battle for Love* by Cheri Champagne
- *The Seductive Spies Series Book 1: The Thespian Spy* by Cheri Champagne
- *The Seductive Spy Series Book 2: The Seamstress and the Spy* by Cheri Champagne
- *The Shape of the Atmosphere* by Jessica Dainty
- *The To-Hell-And-Back Club Book 1: The To-Hell-And-Back Club* by Jill Hannah Anderson
- *The To-Hell-And-Back Club Book 2: Crazy Little Town Called Love* by Jill Hannah Anderson